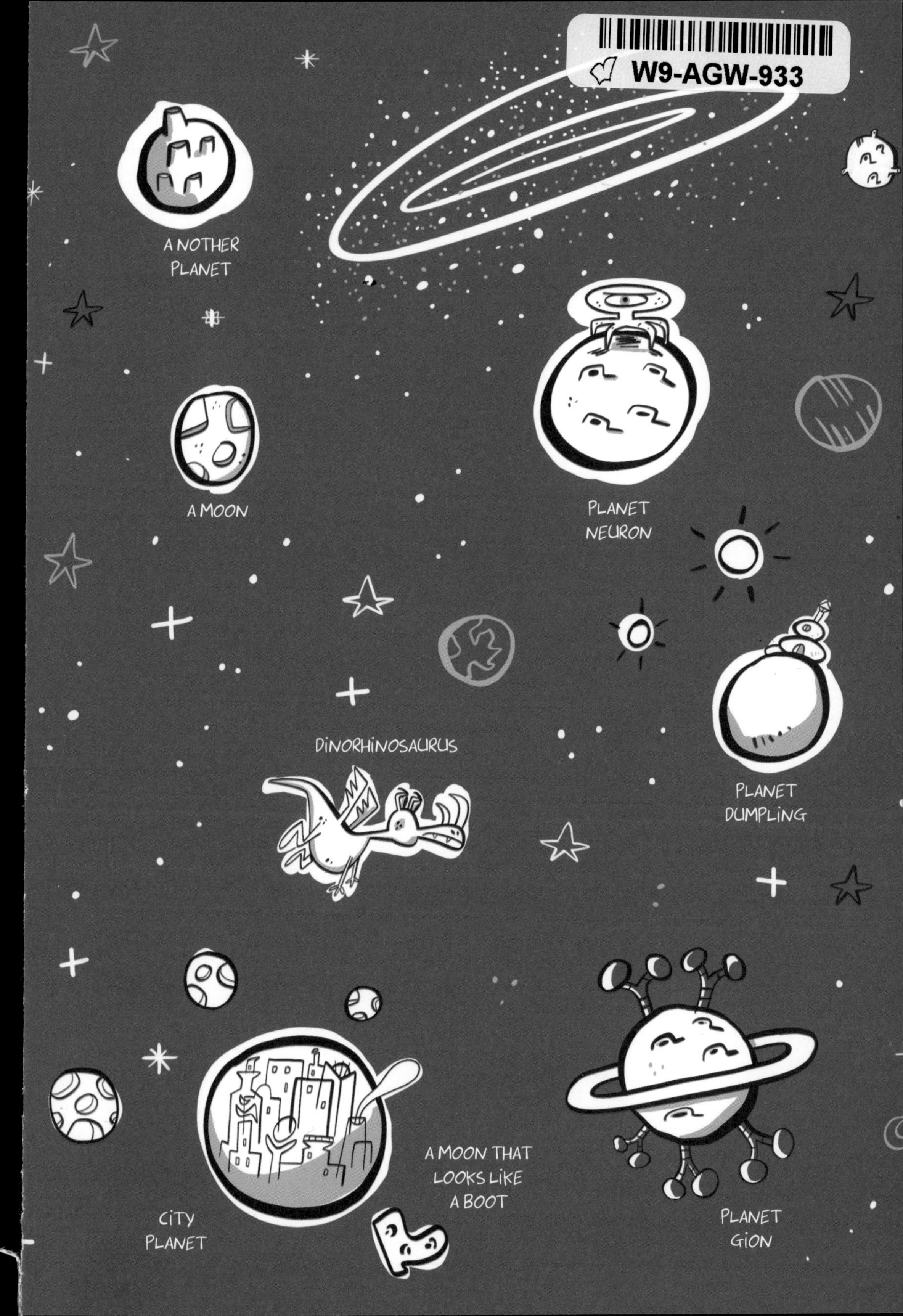
A NOTHER PLANET
A MOON
PLANET NEURON
DINORHINOSAURUS
PLANET DUMPLING
CITY PLANET
A MOON THAT LOOKS LIKE A BOOT
PLANET GION

FERMÍN SOLÍS

ASTRO MOUSE
AND LIGHT BULB

NEW YORK

FERMÍN SOLÍS

ASTRO MOUSE
AND LIGHT BULB

#2 "Astro Mouse vs. the Troublesome Four"

FERMÍN SOLÍS
Script and Art

© Fermín Solís
© Bang. Ediciones, 2015-2021
contacto@bangediciones.com
All rights reserved.
Originally published as
Astro-Ratón y Bombillita #3: Patatator Cocido, 2015
and *Astro-Ratón y Bombillita #4: El Planeta Peladilla*, 2018
English translation and all other Editorial Material
© 2021 Papercutz
www.papercutz.com

Paperback ISBN: 978-1-5458-0726-2
Hardcover ISBN: 978-1-5458-0725-5

Special thanks to Stephanie Barrouillet, Agnés Phillippart,
Immaculada Bordell, Léa Jaillard, Maxi Luchini + Ed

Jeff Whitman – Translator, Letterer, Production, Editor
Jordan Hillman – Editorial Assistant
Jim Salicrup
Editor-in-Chief

Printed in China
December 2021

Papercutz books may be purchased for business or
promotional use. For information on bulk purchases
please contact Macmillan Corporate and Premium Sales
Department at (800) 221-7945 x5442.

Distributed by Macmillan
First Papercutz Printing

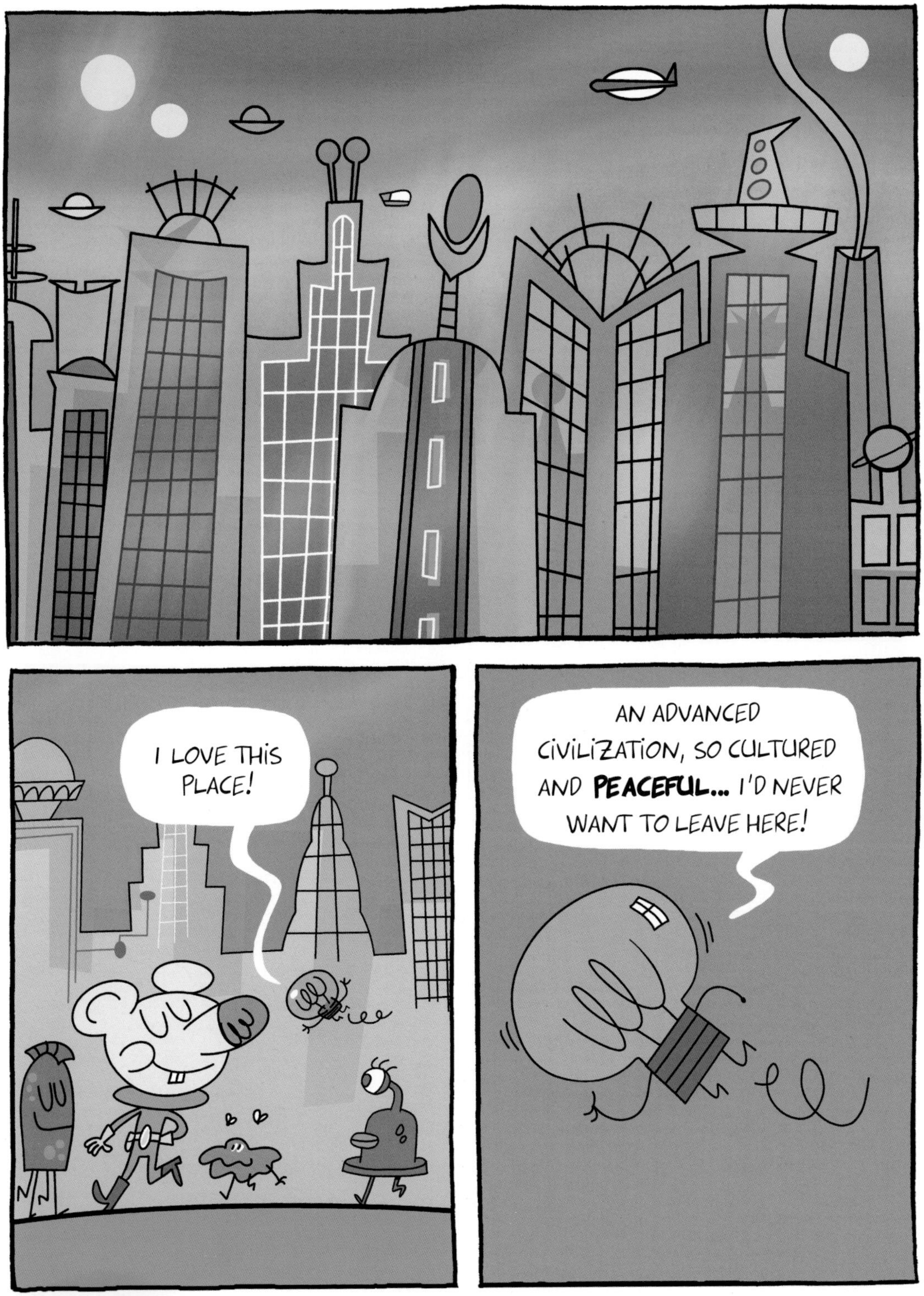
I LOVE THIS PLACE!
AN ADVANCED CIVILIZATION, SO CULTURED AND **PEACEFUL...** I'D NEVER WANT TO LEAVE HERE!

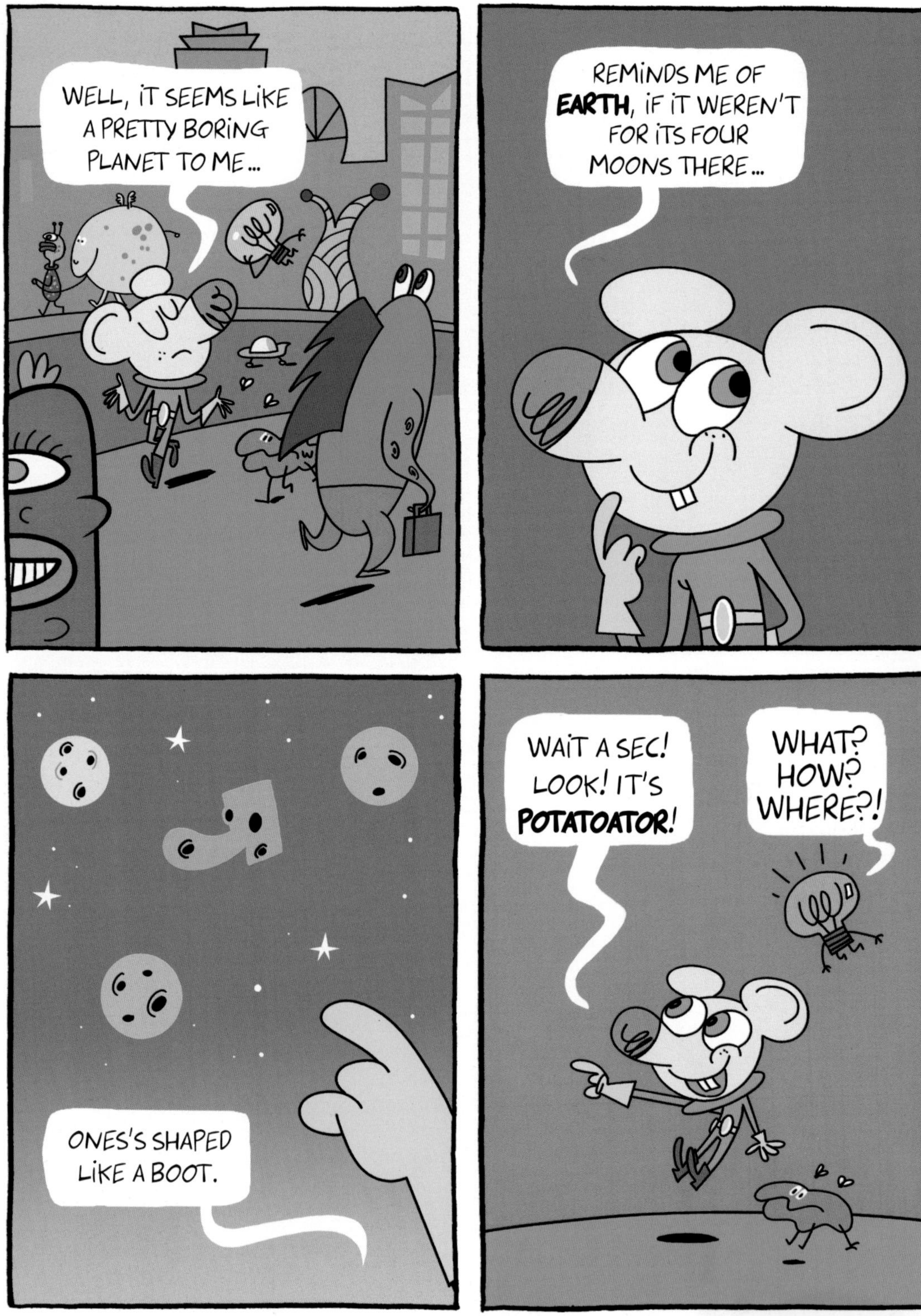
WELL, IT SEEMS LIKE A PRETTY BORING PLANET TO ME...
REMINDS ME OF **EARTH**, IF IT WEREN'T FOR ITS FOUR MOONS THERE...
ONES'S SHAPED LIKE A BOOT.
WAIT A SEC! LOOK! IT'S **POTATOATOR**!
WHAT? HOW? WHERE?!

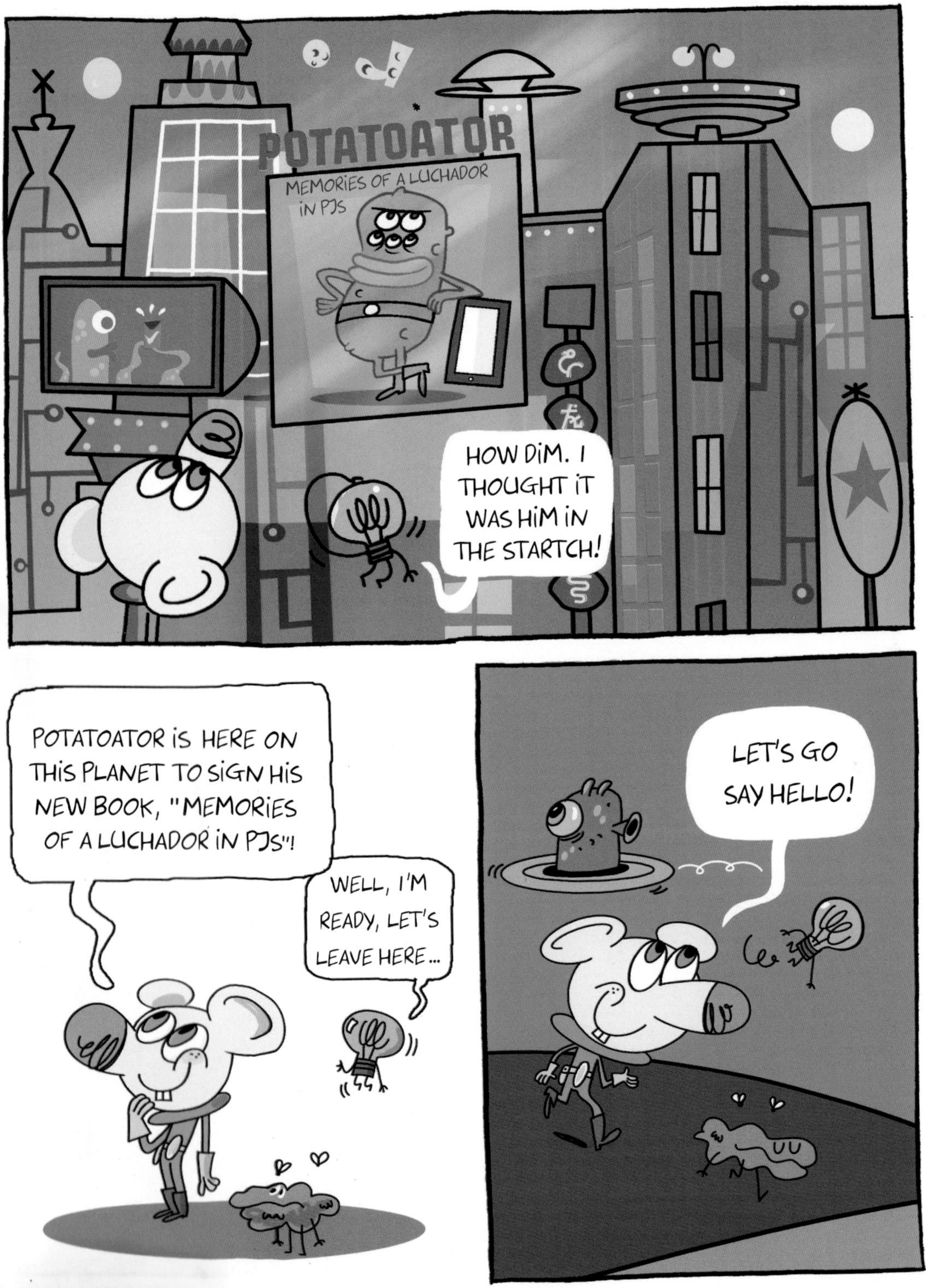
POTATOATOR
MEMORIES OF A LUCHADOR IN PJS
HOW DIM. I THOUGHT IT WAS HIM IN THE STARTCH!
POTATOATOR IS HERE ON THIS PLANET TO SIGN HIS NEW BOOK, "MEMORIES OF A LUCHADOR IN PJS"!
WELL, I'M READY, LET'S LEAVE HERE...
LET'S GO SAY HELLO!

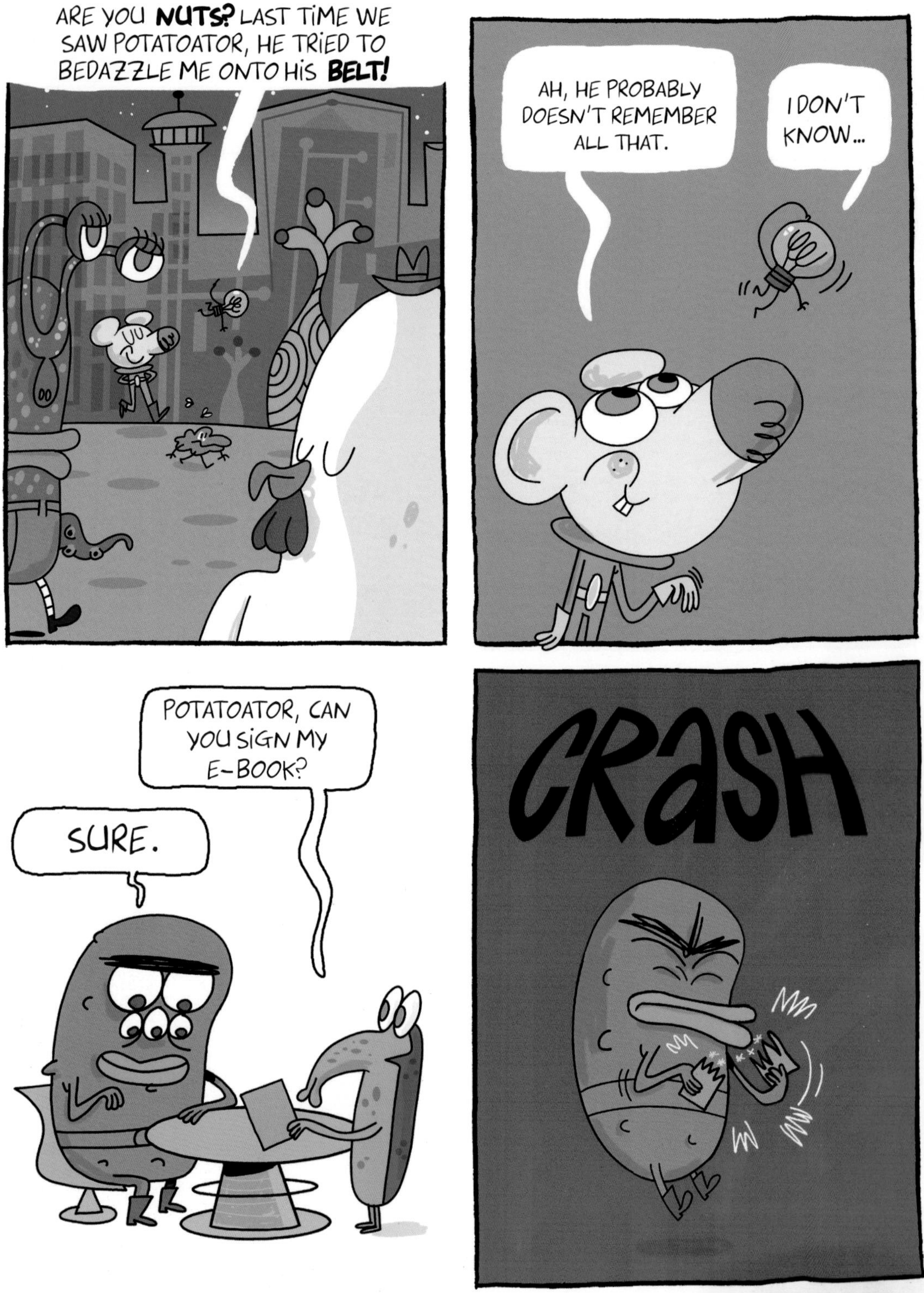
ARE YOU **NUTS?** LAST TIME WE SAW POTATOATOR, HE TRIED TO BEDAZZLE ME ONTO HIS **BELT!**
AH, HE PROBABLY DOESN'T REMEMBER ALL THAT.
I DON'T KNOW...
POTATOATOR, CAN YOU SIGN MY E-BOOK?
SURE.
CRASH

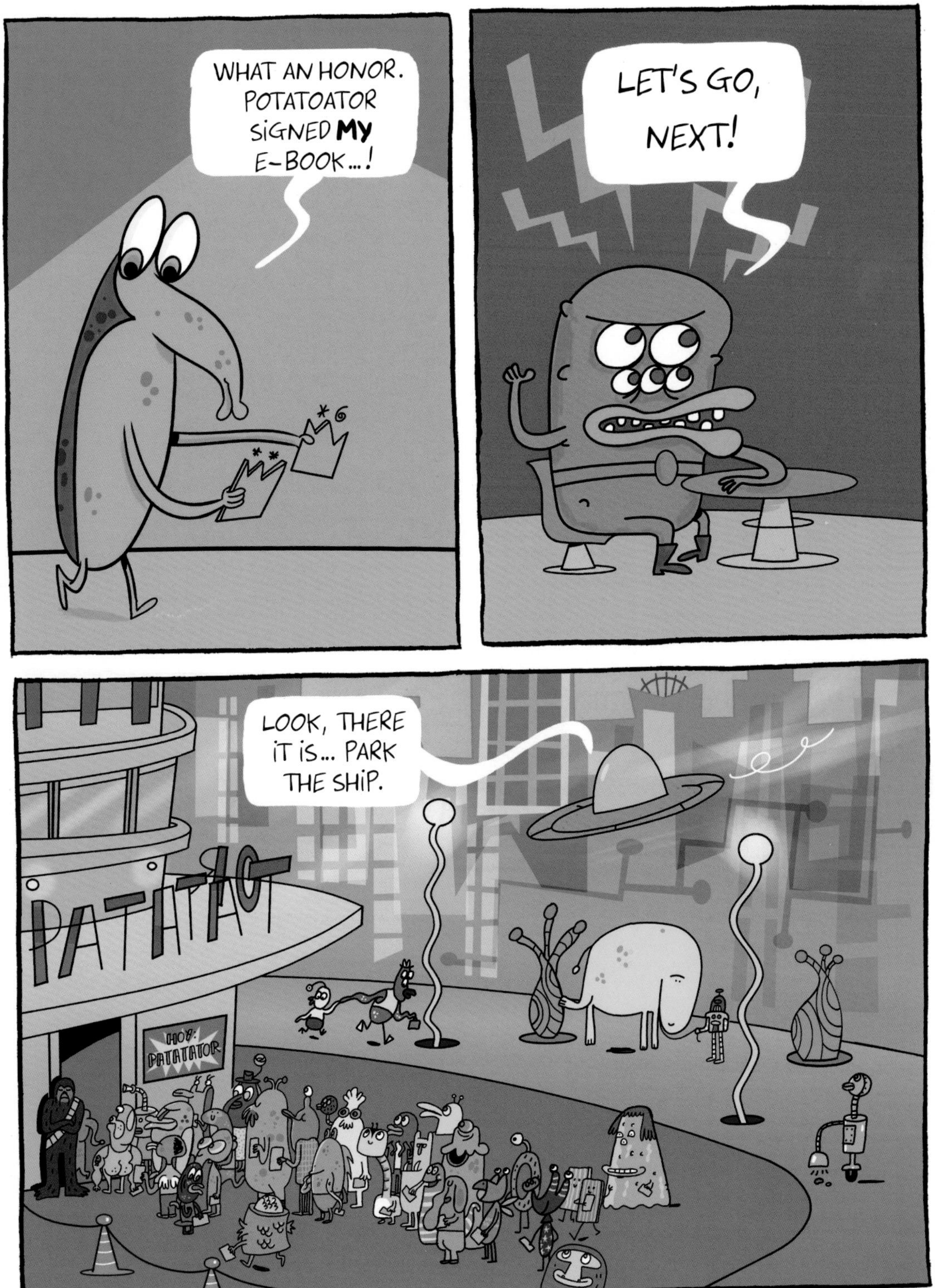
WHAT AN HONOR. POTATOATOR SIGNED **MY** E-BOOK...!
LET'S GO, NEXT!
LOOK, THERE IT IS... PARK THE SHIP.
HOY: PATATATOR

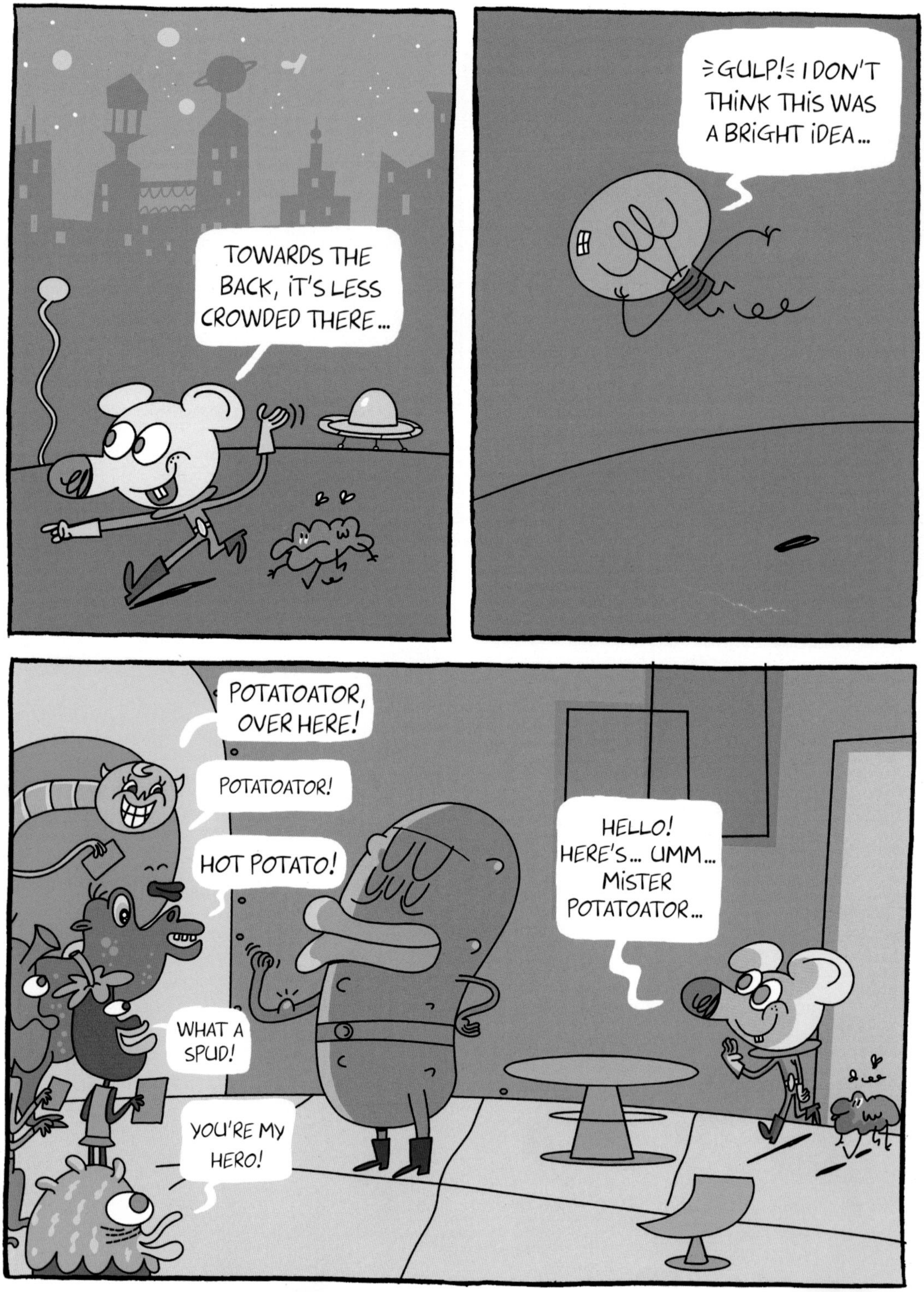
TOWARDS THE BACK, IT'S LESS CROWDED THERE...
≥GULP!≤ I DON'T THINK THIS WAS A BRIGHT IDEA...
POTATOATOR, OVER HERE!
POTATOATOR!
HOT POTATO!
WHAT A SPUD!
YOU'RE MY HERO!
HELLO! HERE'S... UMM... MISTER POTATOATOR...

YES?

MISTER POTATOATOR, SIR! I'M A HUGE FAN OF YOURS, COULD I HAVE AN AUTOGRAPH, PLEASE?

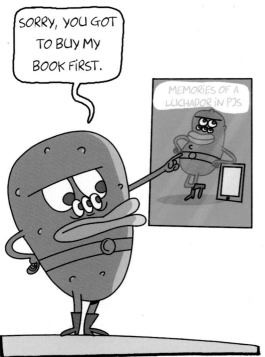

SORRY, YOU GOT TO BUY MY BOOK FIRST.

MEMORIES OF A LUCHADOR IN PJs

OH, RIGHT... I BOUGHT IT ALREADY BUT I FORGOT IT IN THE SHIP. HEH! HEH! HEH...

WHAT A HAM...

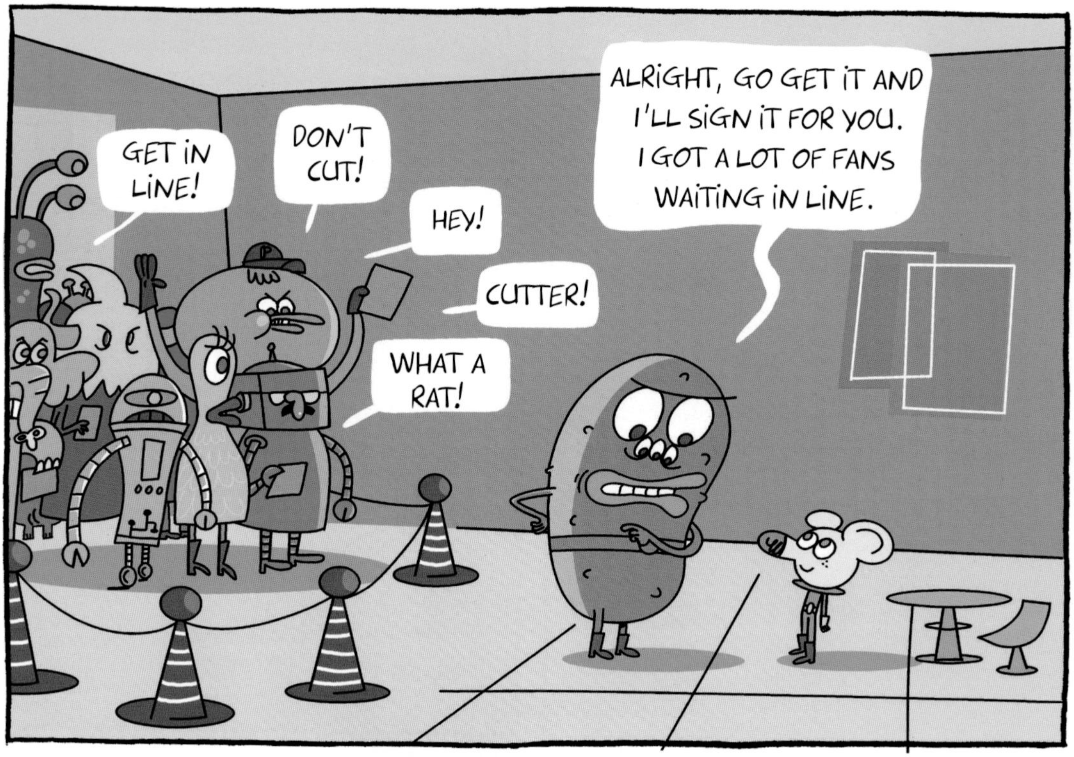
GET IN LINE!
DON'T CUT!
HEY!
CUTTER!
WHAT A RAT!
ALRIGHT, GO GET IT AND I'LL SIGN IT FOR YOU. I GOT A LOT OF FANS WAITING IN LINE.

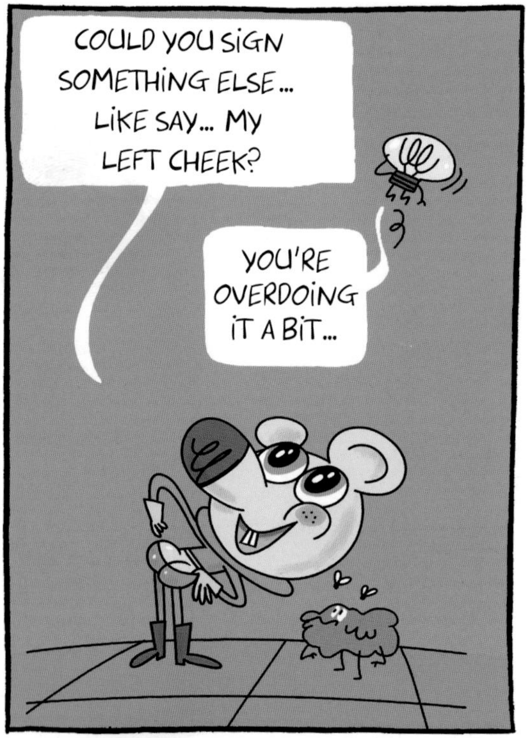
COULD YOU SIGN SOMETHING ELSE... LIKE SAY... MY LEFT CHEEK?
YOU'RE OVERDOING IT A BIT...

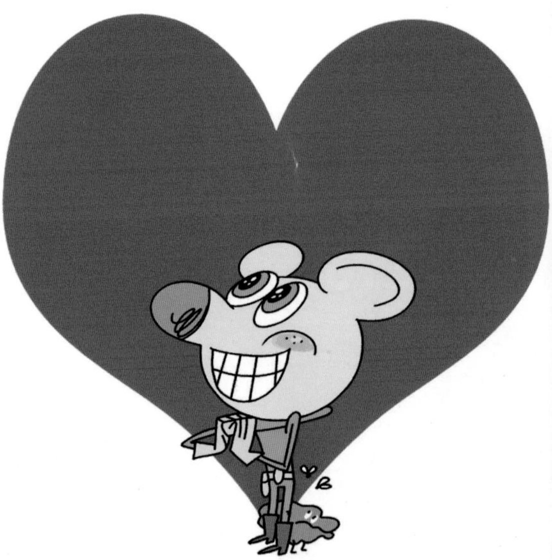

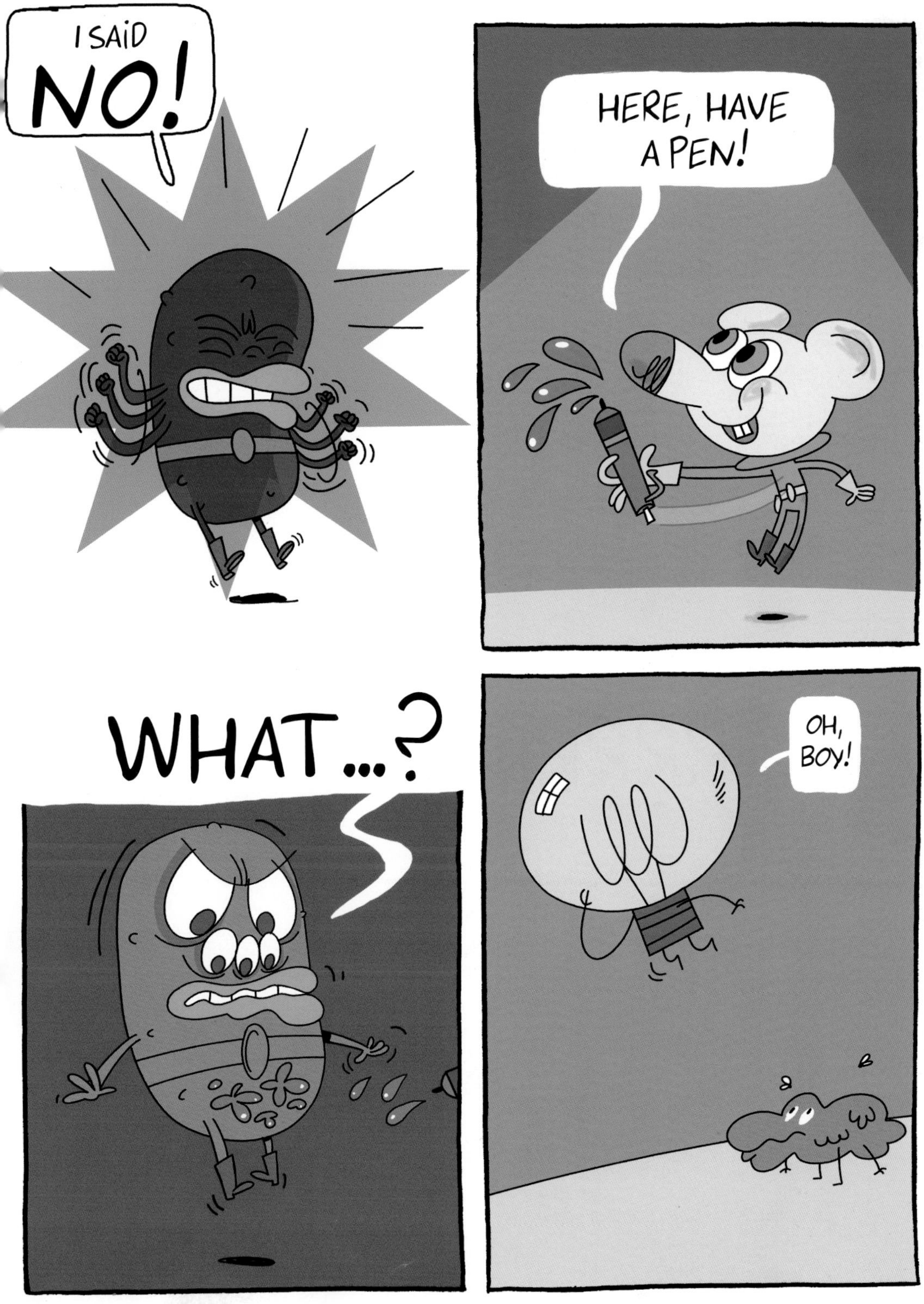
I SAID NO!
HERE, HAVE A PEN!
WHAT...?
OH, BOY!

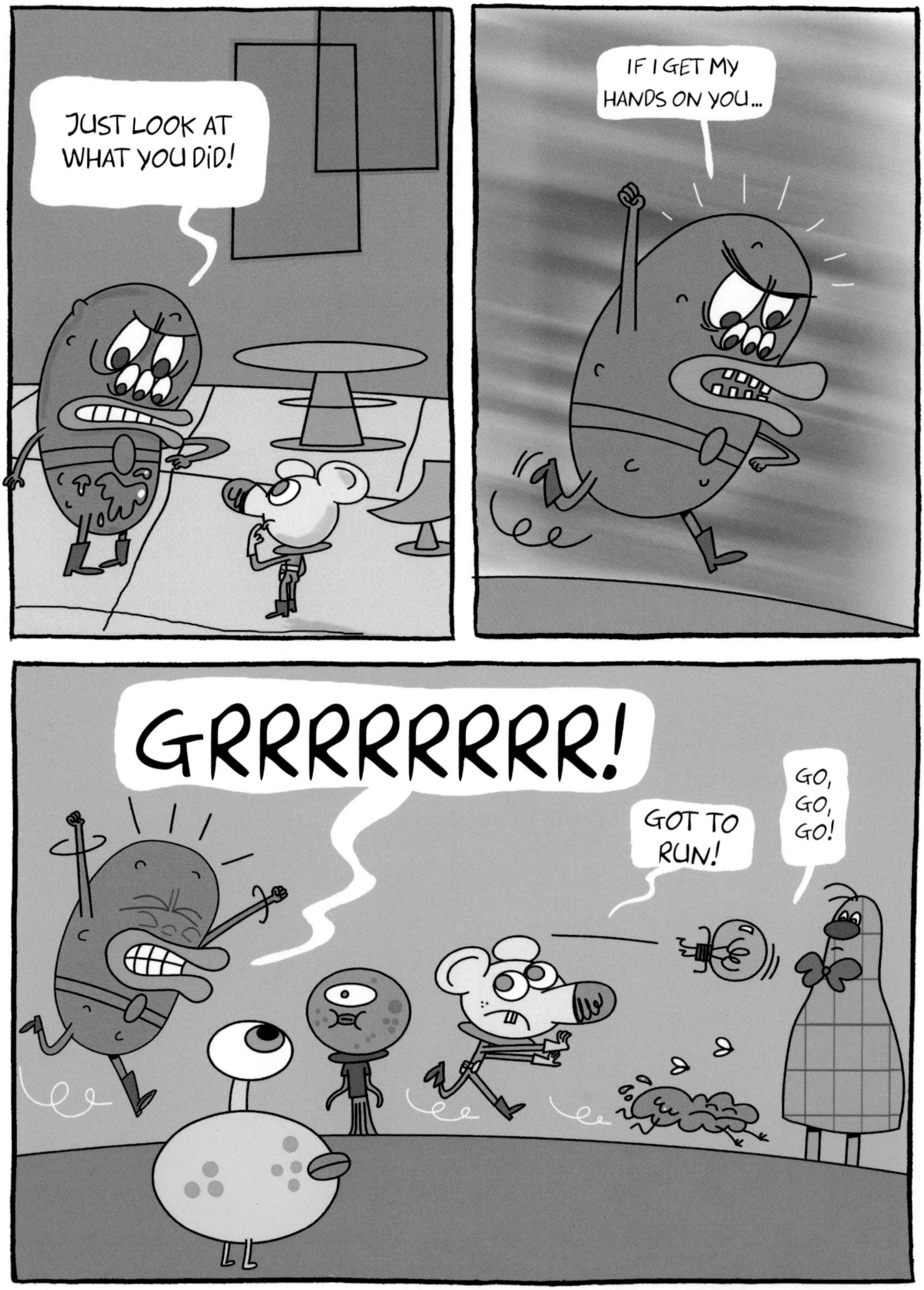
JUST LOOK AT WHAT YOU DID!
IF I GET MY HANDS ON YOU...
GRRRRRRRR!
GOT TO RUN!
GO, GO, GO!

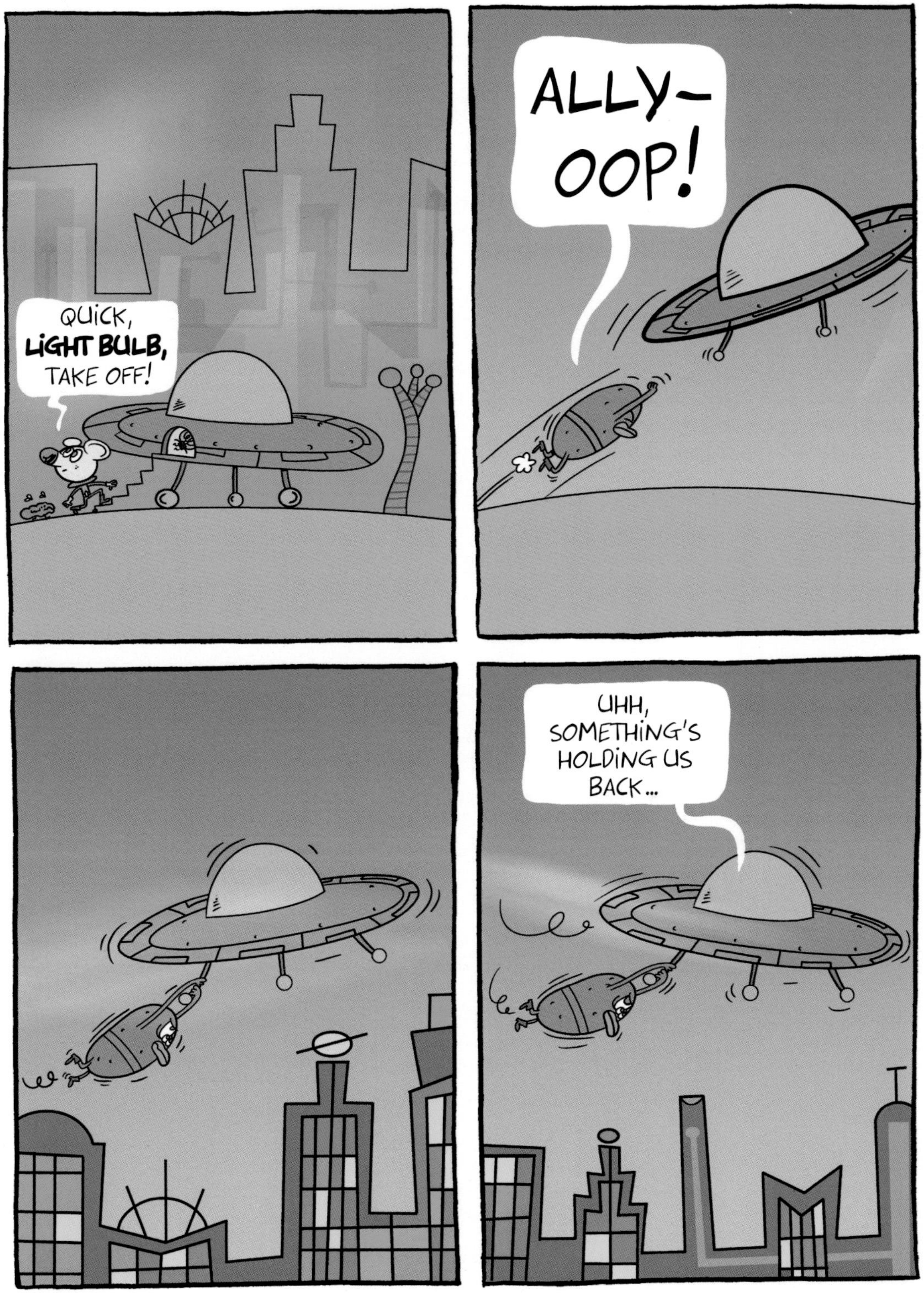
QUICK, **LIGHT BULB,** TAKE OFF!
ALLY-OOP!
UHH, SOMETHING'S HOLDING US BACK...

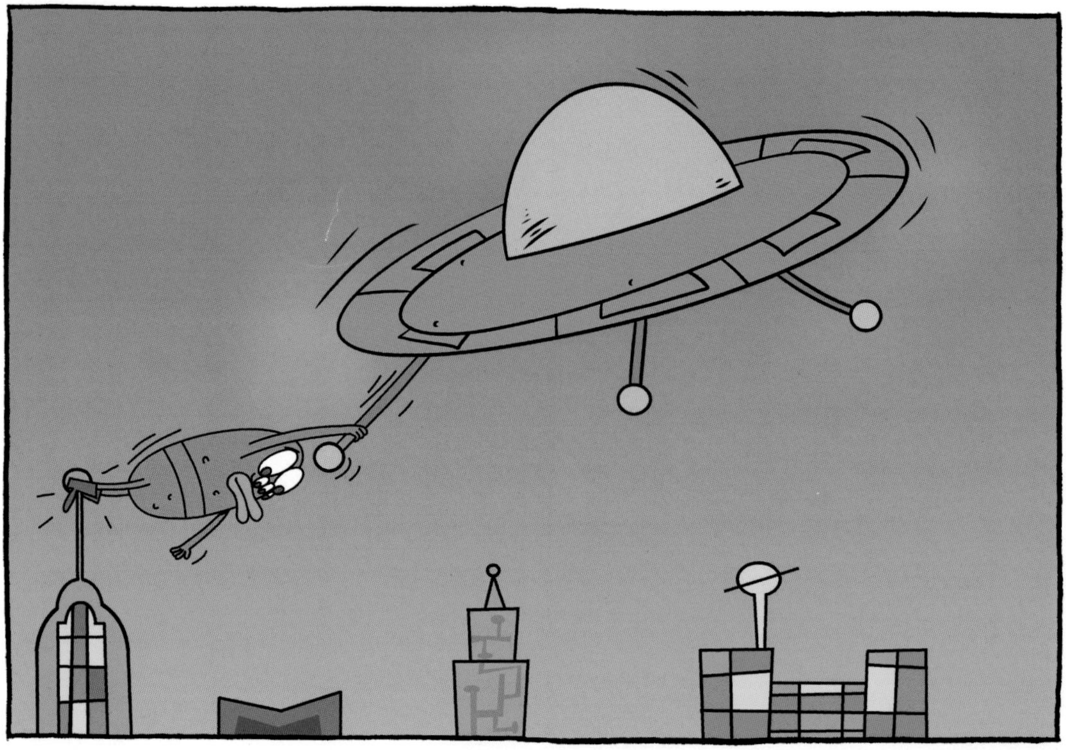

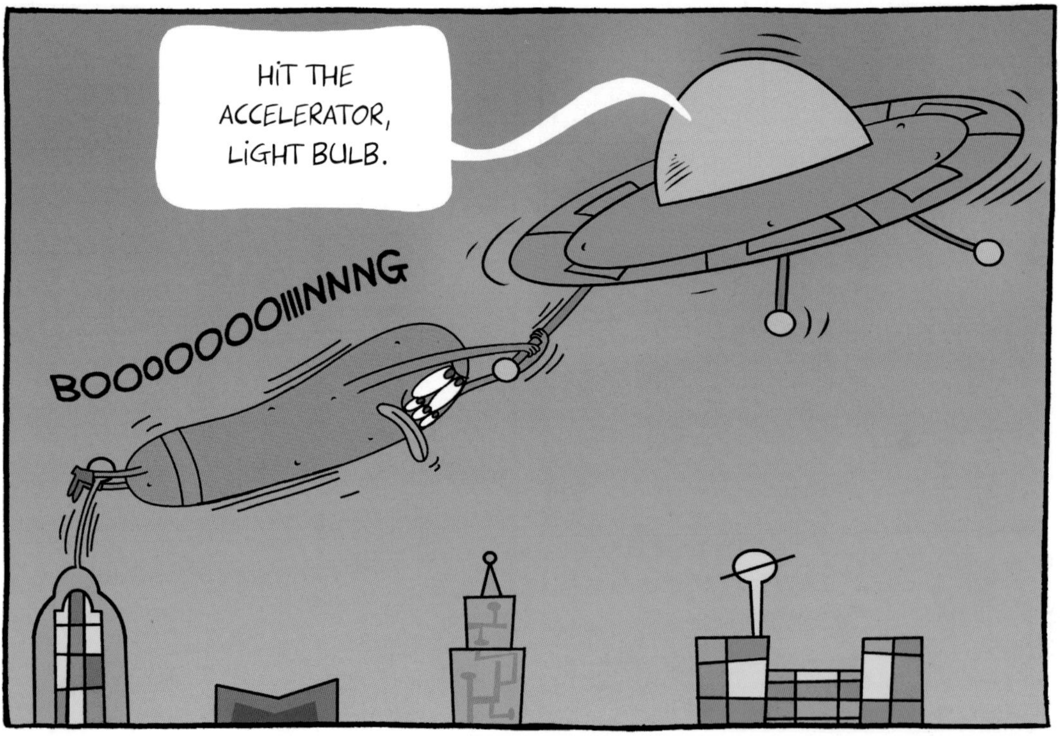
HIT THE ACCELERATOR, LIGHT BULB.
BOOOOOOOOIIIINNNG

CRASH

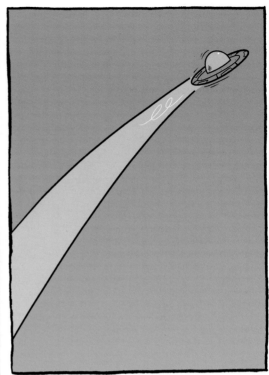

HEY, SEE? I HAVE YOUR BOOK. WILL YOU SIGN IT, MISTER POTATOATOR?

AAARRGG! WAIT TIL I GET YOU AND THEN YOU'LL SEE.

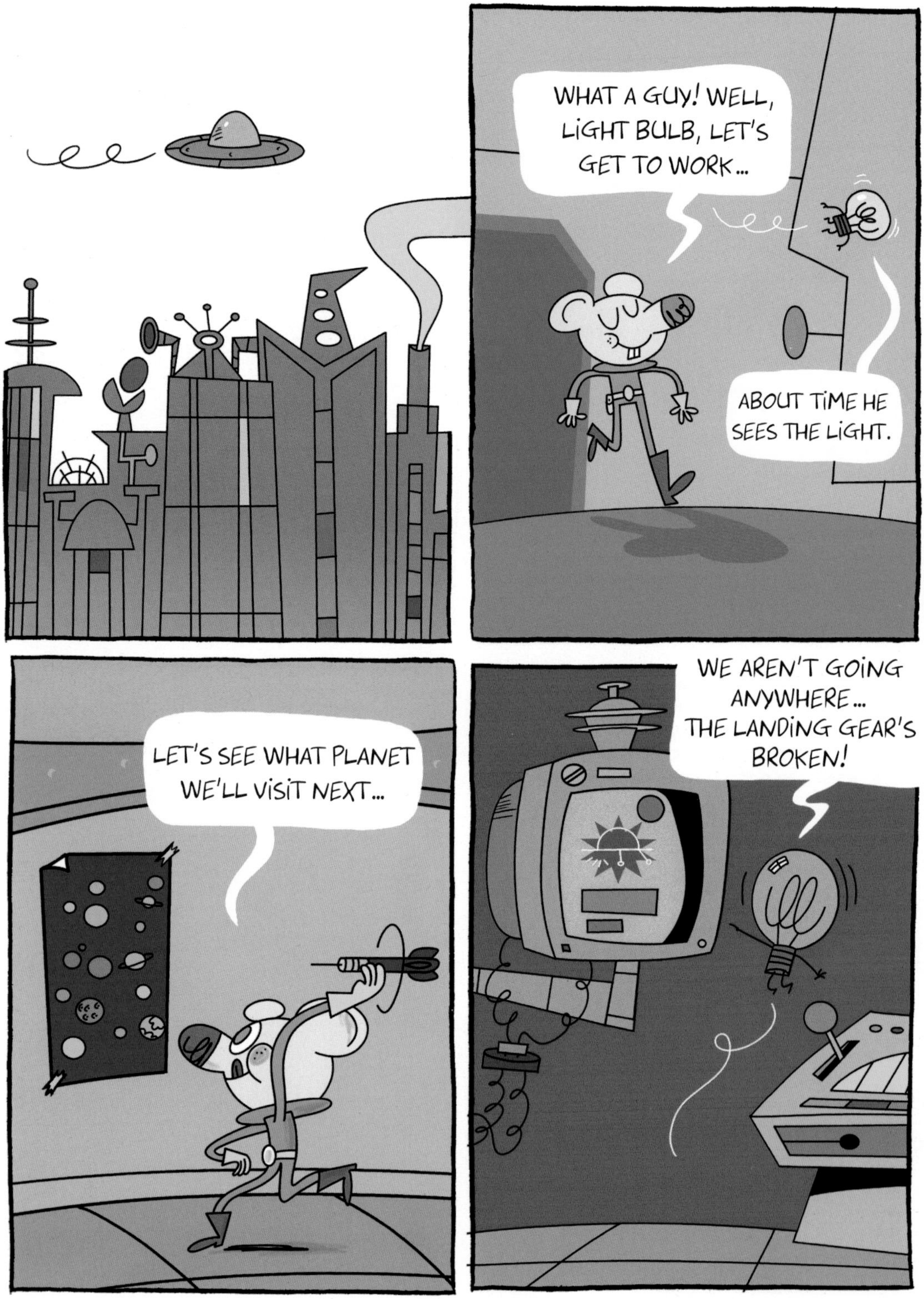
WHAT A GUY! WELL, LIGHT BULB, LET'S GET TO WORK...
ABOUT TIME HE SEES THE LIGHT.
LET'S SEE WHAT PLANET WE'LL VISIT NEXT...
WE AREN'T GOING ANYWHERE... THE LANDING GEAR'S BROKEN!

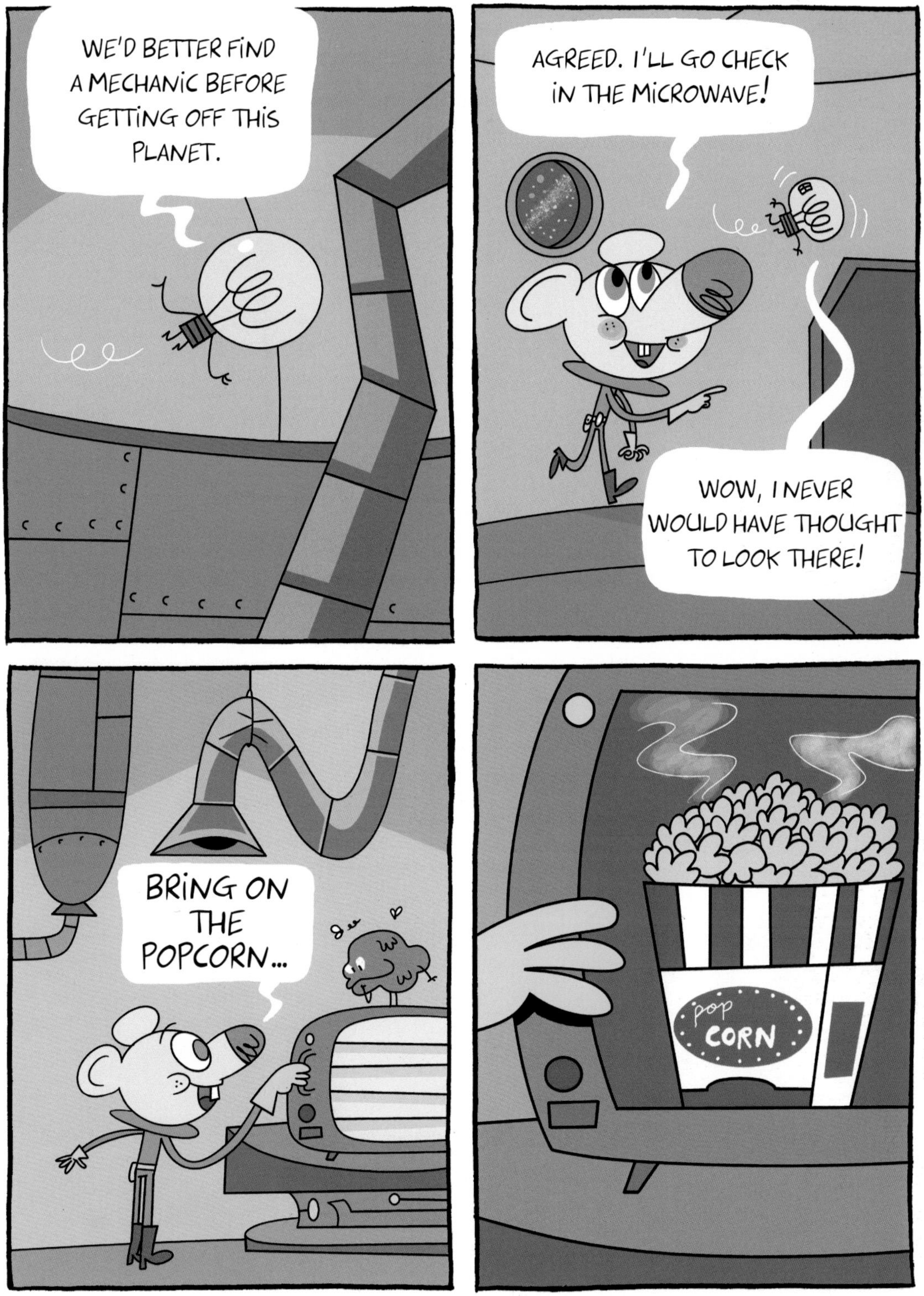
WE'D BETTER FIND A MECHANIC BEFORE GETTING OFF THIS PLANET.
AGREED. I'LL GO CHECK IN THE MICROWAVE!
WOW, I NEVER WOULD HAVE THOUGHT TO LOOK THERE!
BRING ON THE POPCORN...
pop CORN

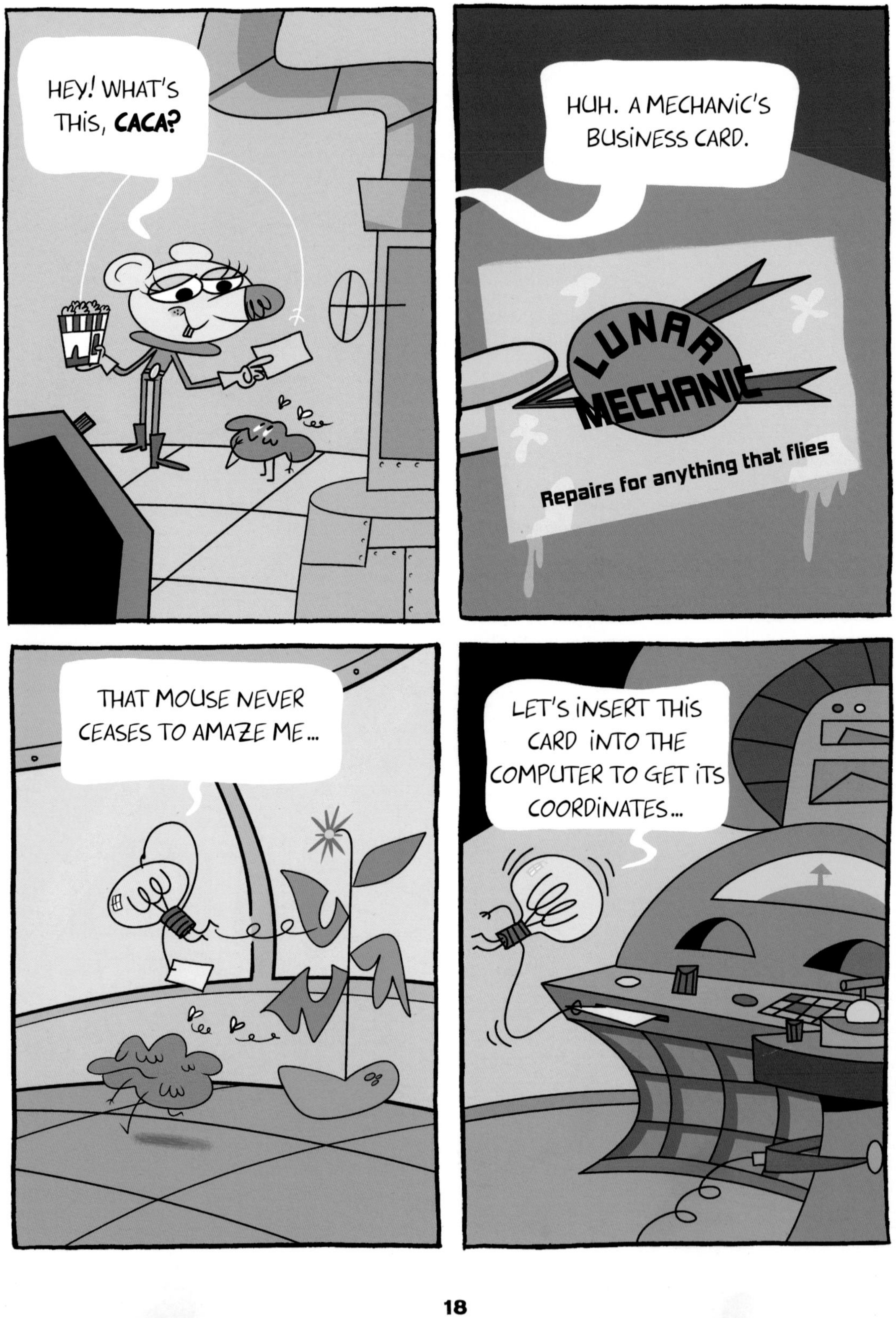
HEY! WHAT'S THIS, **CACA?**
HUH. A MECHANIC'S BUSINESS CARD.
LUNAR MECHANIC
Repairs for anything that flies
THAT MOUSE NEVER CEASES TO AMAZE ME...
LET'S INSERT THIS CARD INTO THE COMPUTER TO GET ITS COORDINATES...

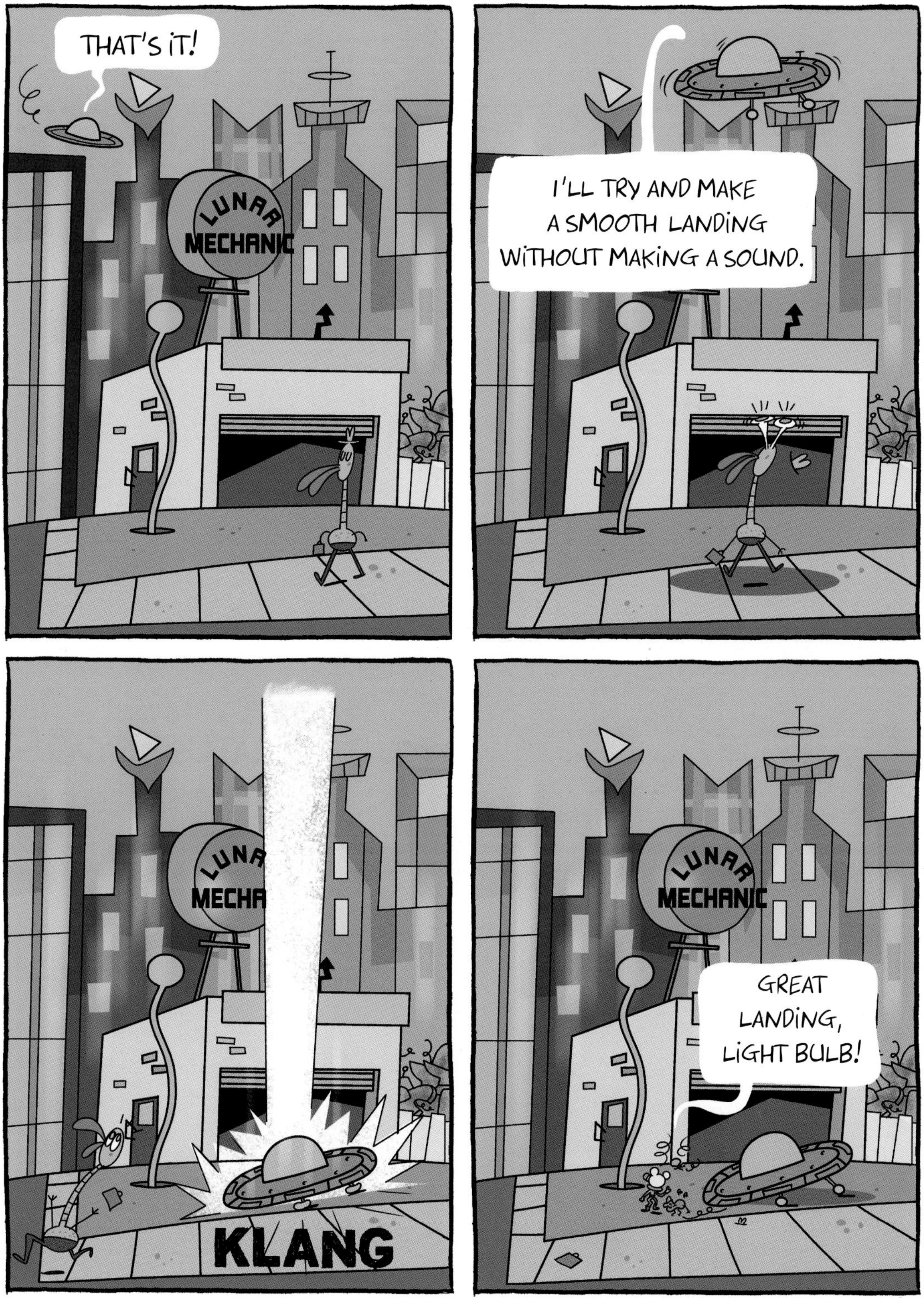
THAT'S IT!
LUNAR MECHANIC
I'LL TRY AND MAKE A SMOOTH LANDING WITHOUT MAKING A SOUND.
KLANG
GREAT LANDING, LIGHT BULB!

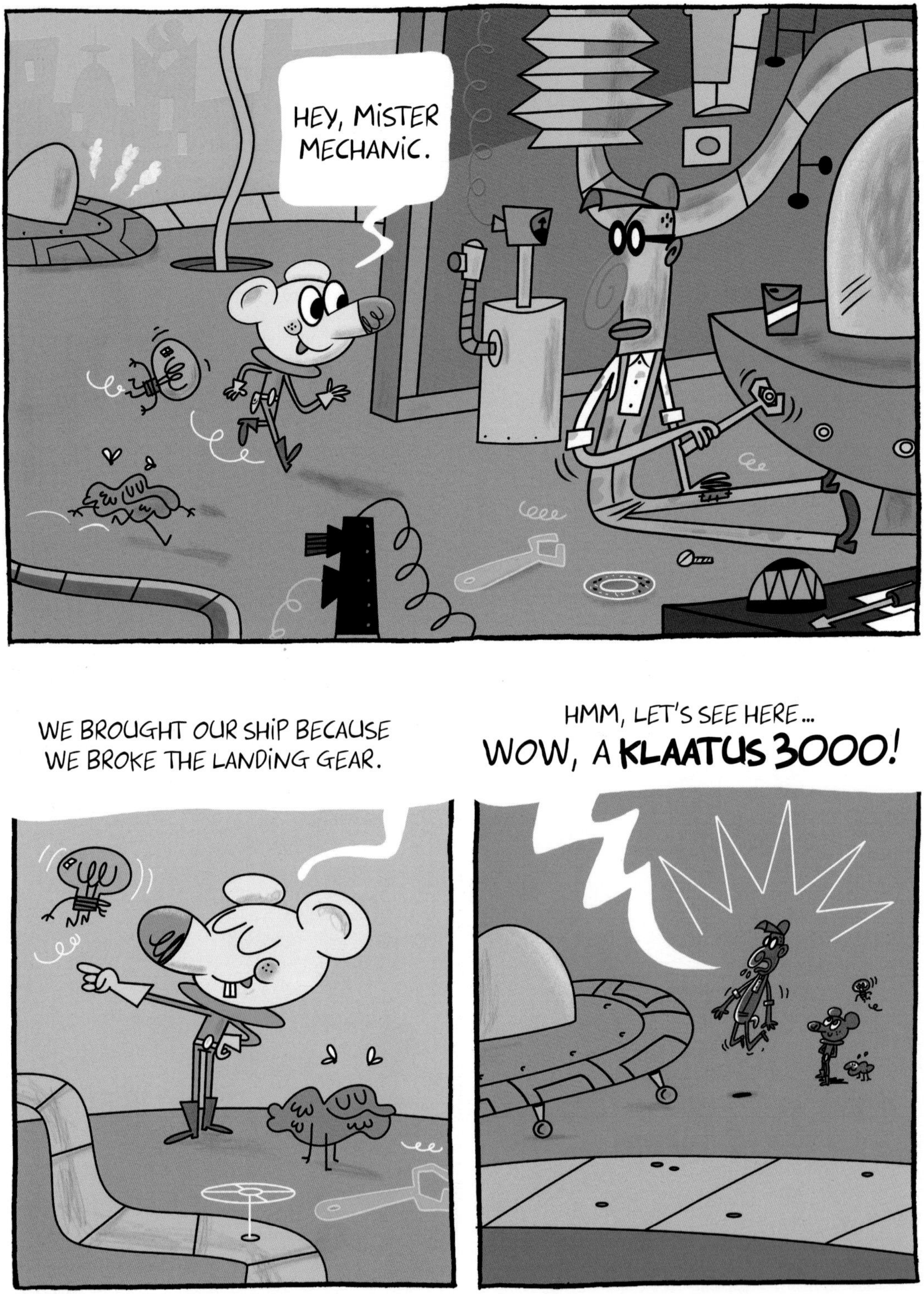
HEY, MISTER MECHANIC.
WE BROUGHT OUR SHIP BECAUSE WE BROKE THE LANDING GEAR.
HMM, LET'S SEE HERE...
WOW, A KLAATUS 3000!

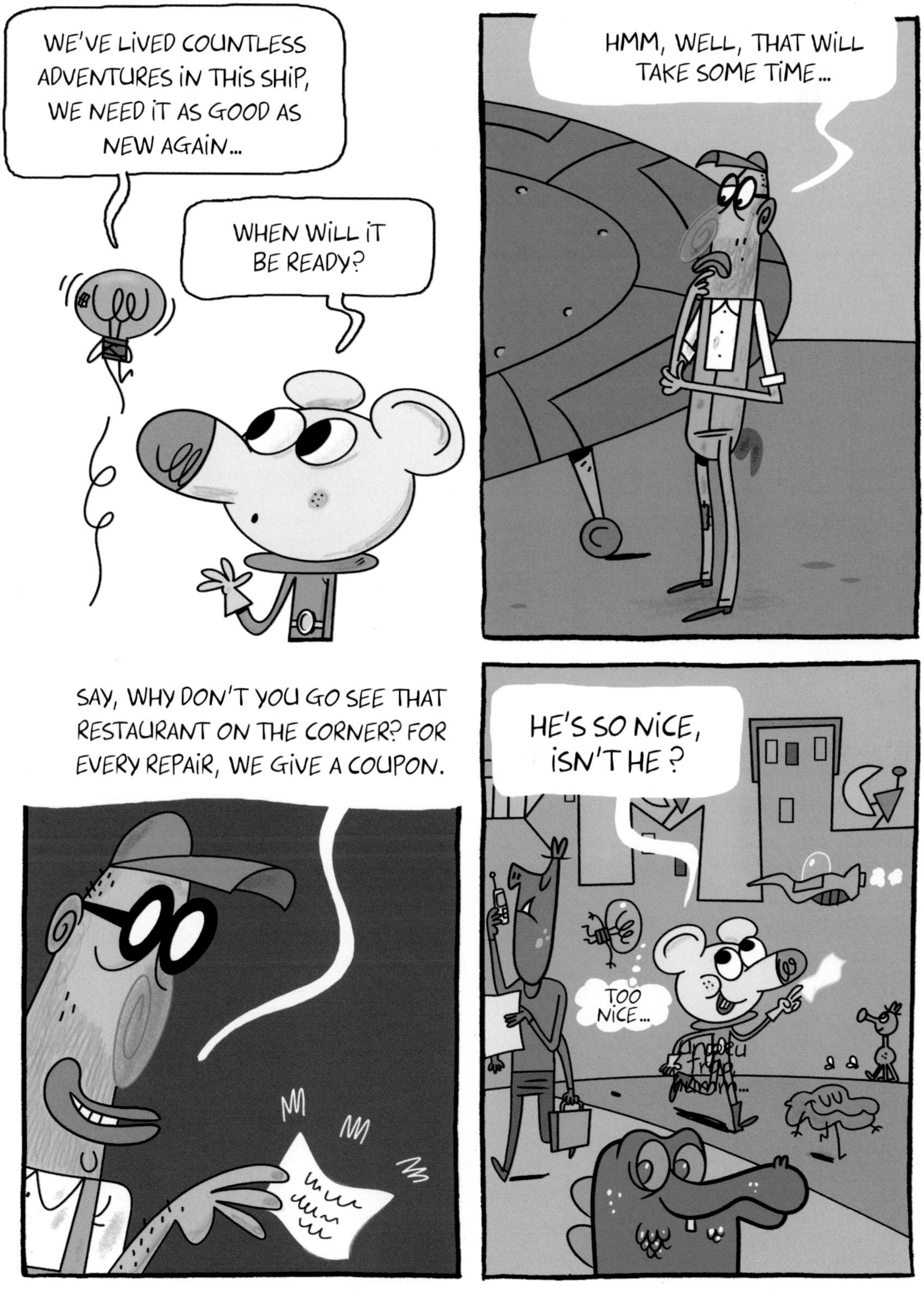
WE'VE LIVED COUNTLESS ADVENTURES IN THIS SHIP, WE NEED IT AS GOOD AS NEW AGAIN...
WHEN WILL IT BE READY?
HMM, WELL, THAT WILL TAKE SOME TIME...
SAY, WHY DON'T YOU GO SEE THAT RESTAURANT ON THE CORNER? FOR EVERY REPAIR, WE GIVE A COUPON.
HE'S SO NICE, ISN'T HE ?
TOO NICE...

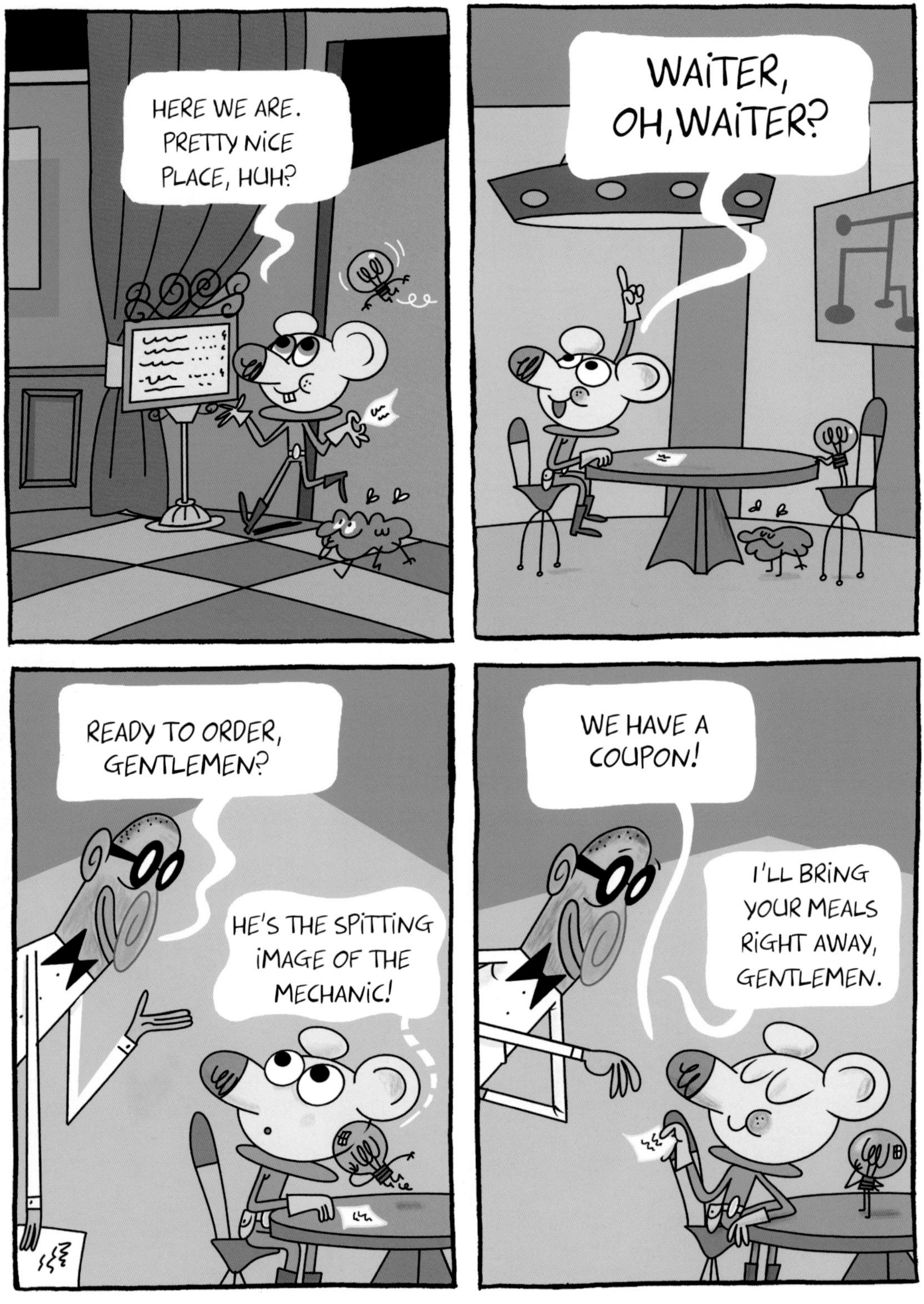
HERE WE ARE. PRETTY NICE PLACE, HUH?
WAITER, OH, WAITER?
READY TO ORDER, GENTLEMEN?
HE'S THE SPITTING IMAGE OF THE MECHANIC!
WE HAVE A COUPON!
I'LL BRING YOUR MEALS RIGHT AWAY, GENTLEMEN.

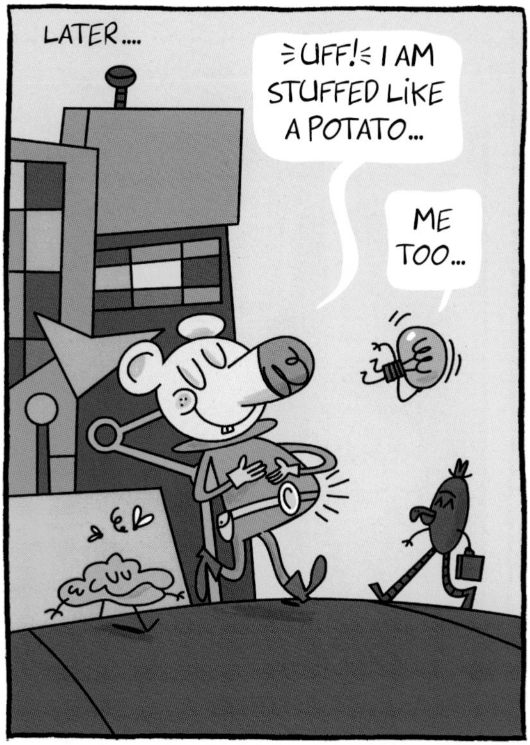
LATER....
UFF! I AM STUFFED LIKE A POTATO...
ME TOO...
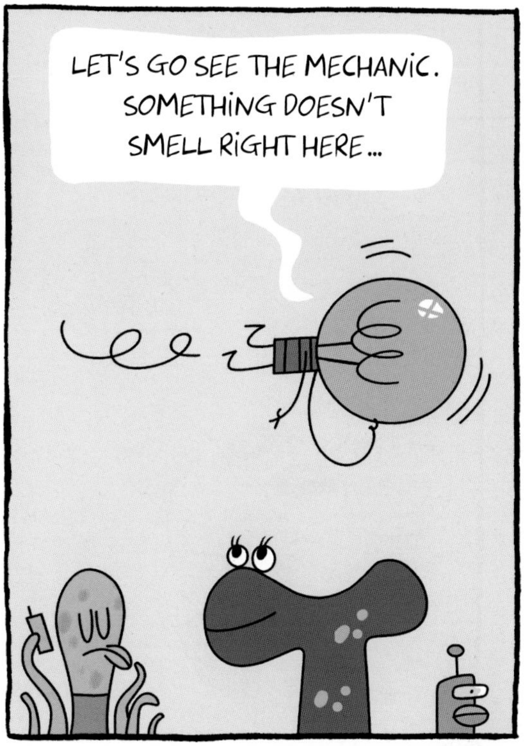
LET'S GO SEE THE MECHANIC. SOMETHING DOESN'T SMELL RIGHT HERE...
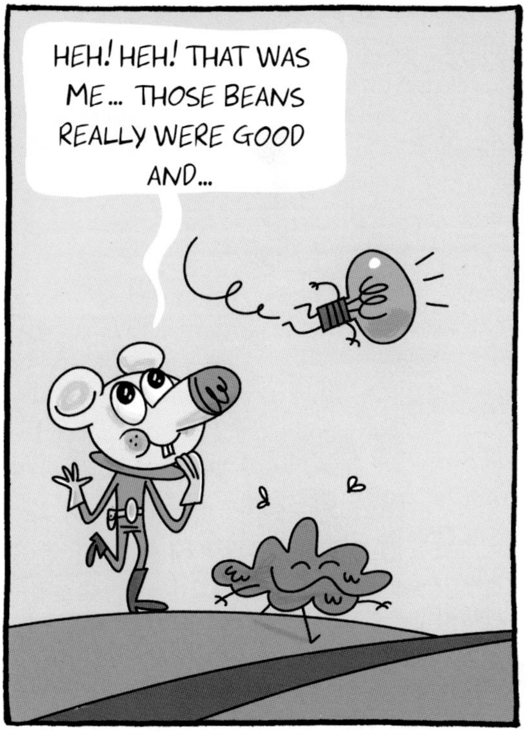
HEH! HEH! THAT WAS ME... THOSE BEANS REALLY WERE GOOD AND...
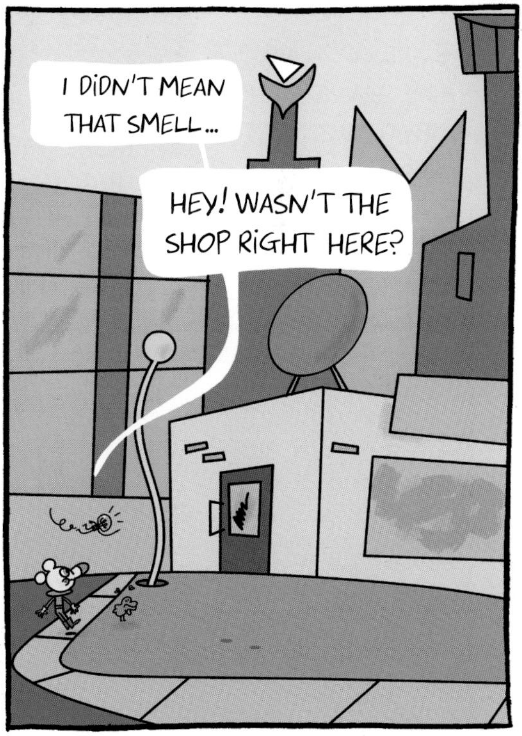
I DIDN'T MEAN THAT SMELL...
HEY! WASN'T THE SHOP RIGHT HERE?

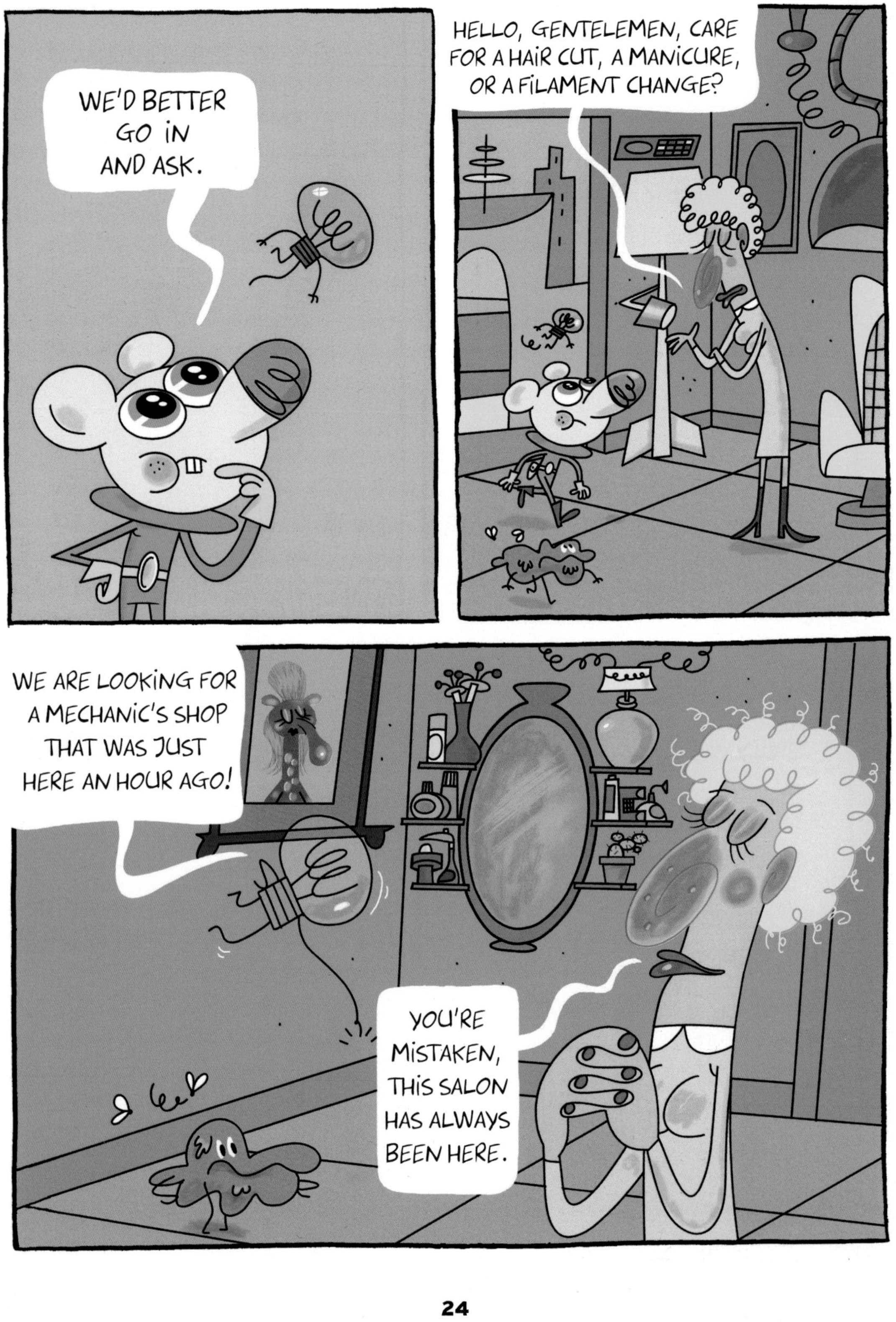
WE'D BETTER GO IN AND ASK.
HELLO, GENTELEMEN, CARE FOR A HAIR CUT, A MANICURE, OR A FILAMENT CHANGE?
WE ARE LOOKING FOR A MECHANIC'S SHOP THAT WAS JUST HERE AN HOUR AGO!
YOU'RE MISTAKEN, THIS SALON HAS ALWAYS BEEN HERE.

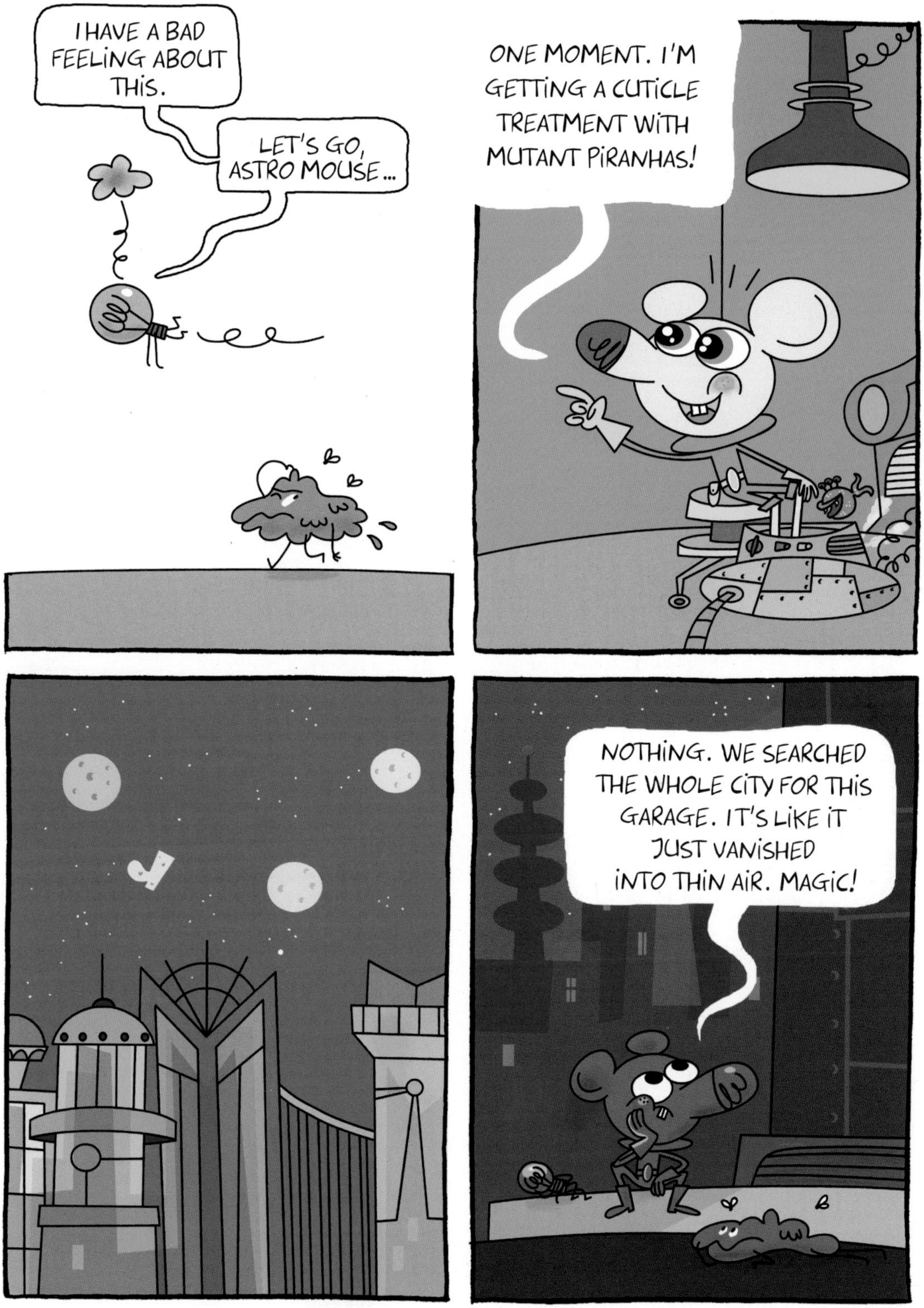
I HAVE A BAD FEELING ABOUT THIS.
LET'S GO, ASTRO MOUSE...
ONE MOMENT. I'M GETTING A CUTICLE TREATMENT WITH MUTANT PIRANHAS!
NOTHING. WE SEARCHED THE WHOLE CITY FOR THIS GARAGE. IT'S LIKE IT JUST VANISHED INTO THIN AIR. MAGIC!

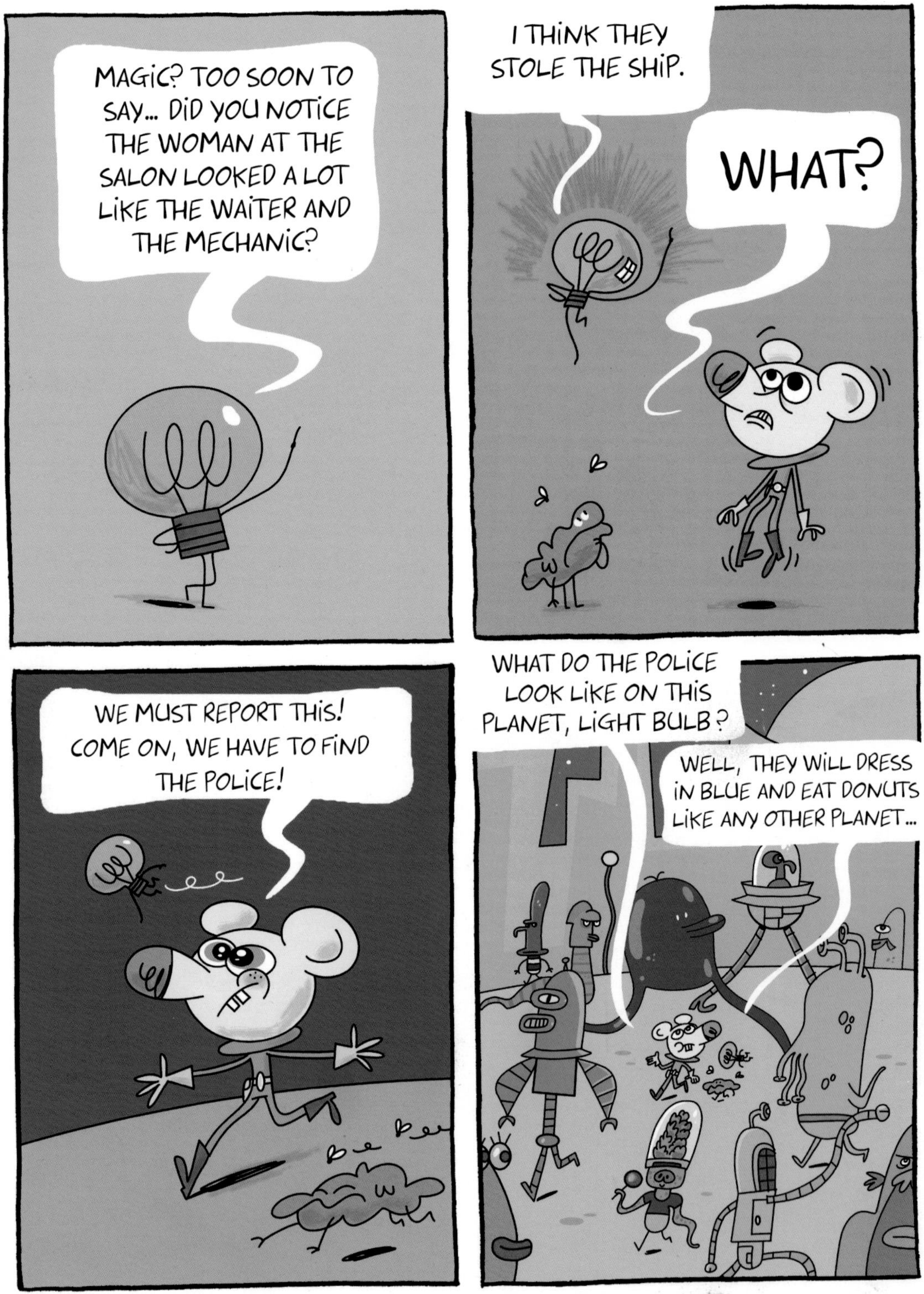
MAGIC? TOO SOON TO SAY... DID YOU NOTICE THE WOMAN AT THE SALON LOOKED A LOT LIKE THE WAITER AND THE MECHANIC?
I THINK THEY STOLE THE SHIP.
WHAT?
WE MUST REPORT THIS! COME ON, WE HAVE TO FIND THE POLICE!
WHAT DO THE POLICE LOOK LIKE ON THIS PLANET, LIGHT BULB?
WELL, THEY WILL DRESS IN BLUE AND EAT DONUTS LIKE ANY OTHER PLANET...

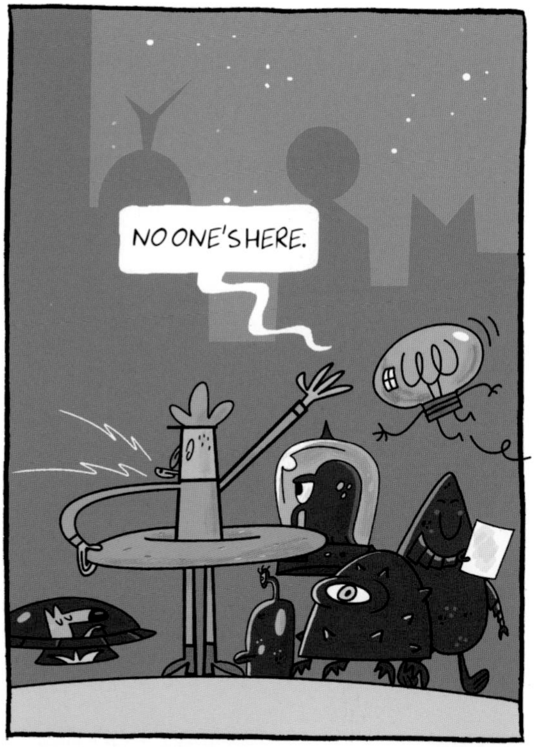
NO ONE'S HERE.

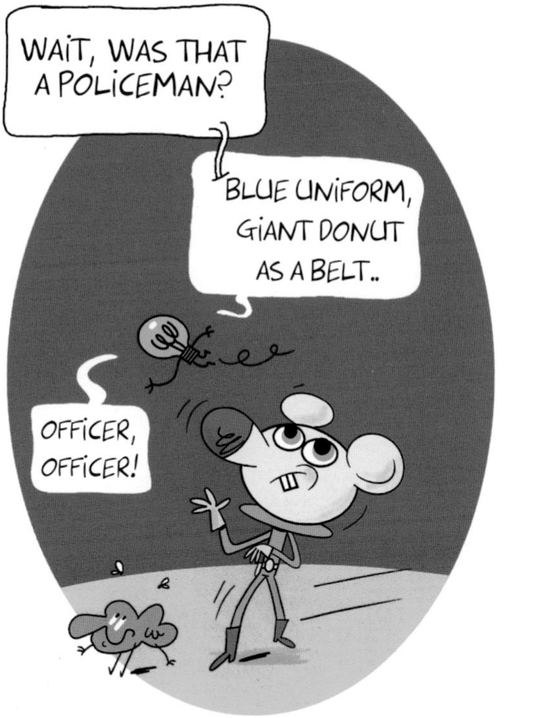
WAIT, WAS THAT A POLICEMAN?
BLUE UNIFORM, GIANT DONUT AS A BELT..
OFFICER, OFFICER!

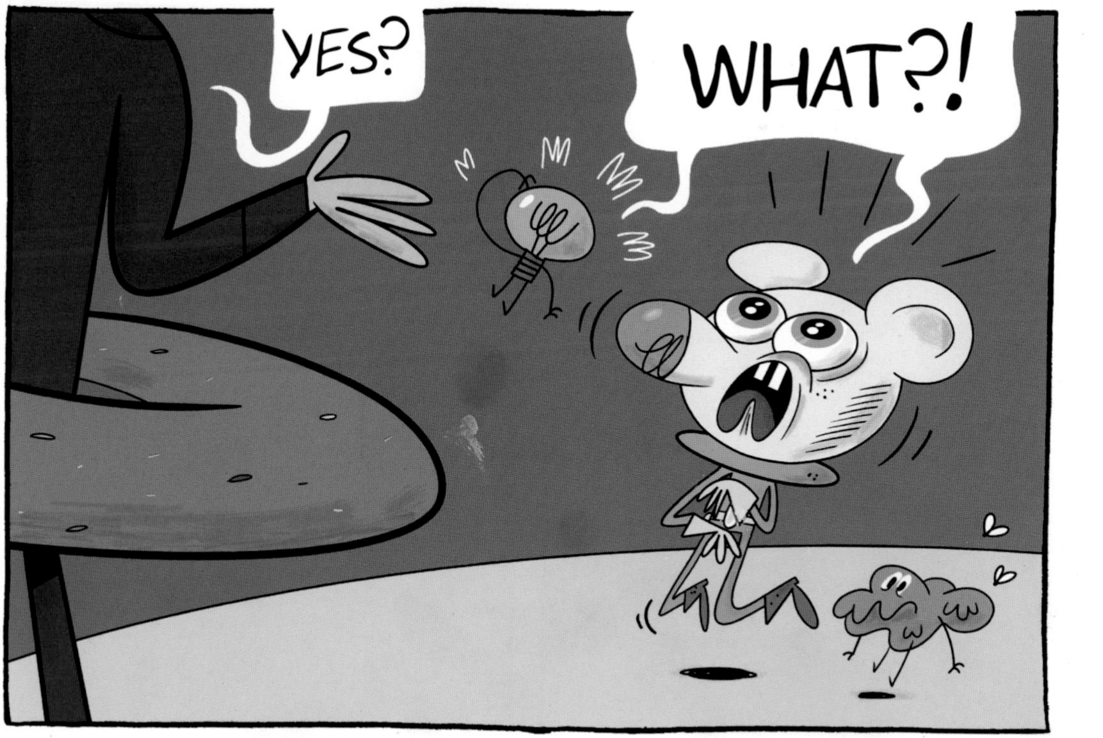
YES?
WHAT?!

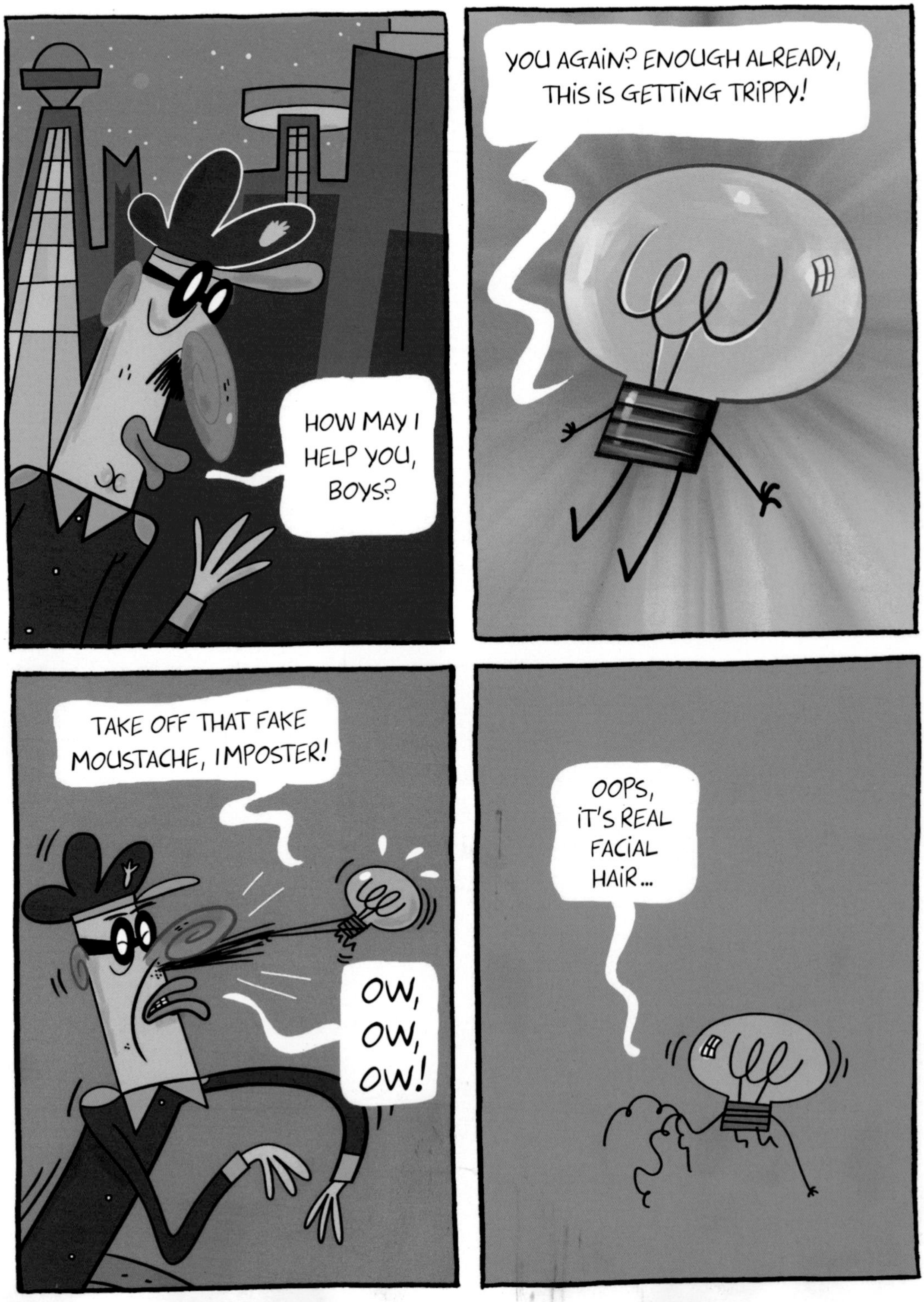
HOW MAY I HELP YOU, BOYS?
YOU AGAIN? ENOUGH ALREADY, THIS IS GETTING TRIPPY!
TAKE OFF THAT FAKE MOUSTACHE, IMPOSTER!
OW, OW, OW!
OOPS, IT'S REAL FACIAL HAIR...

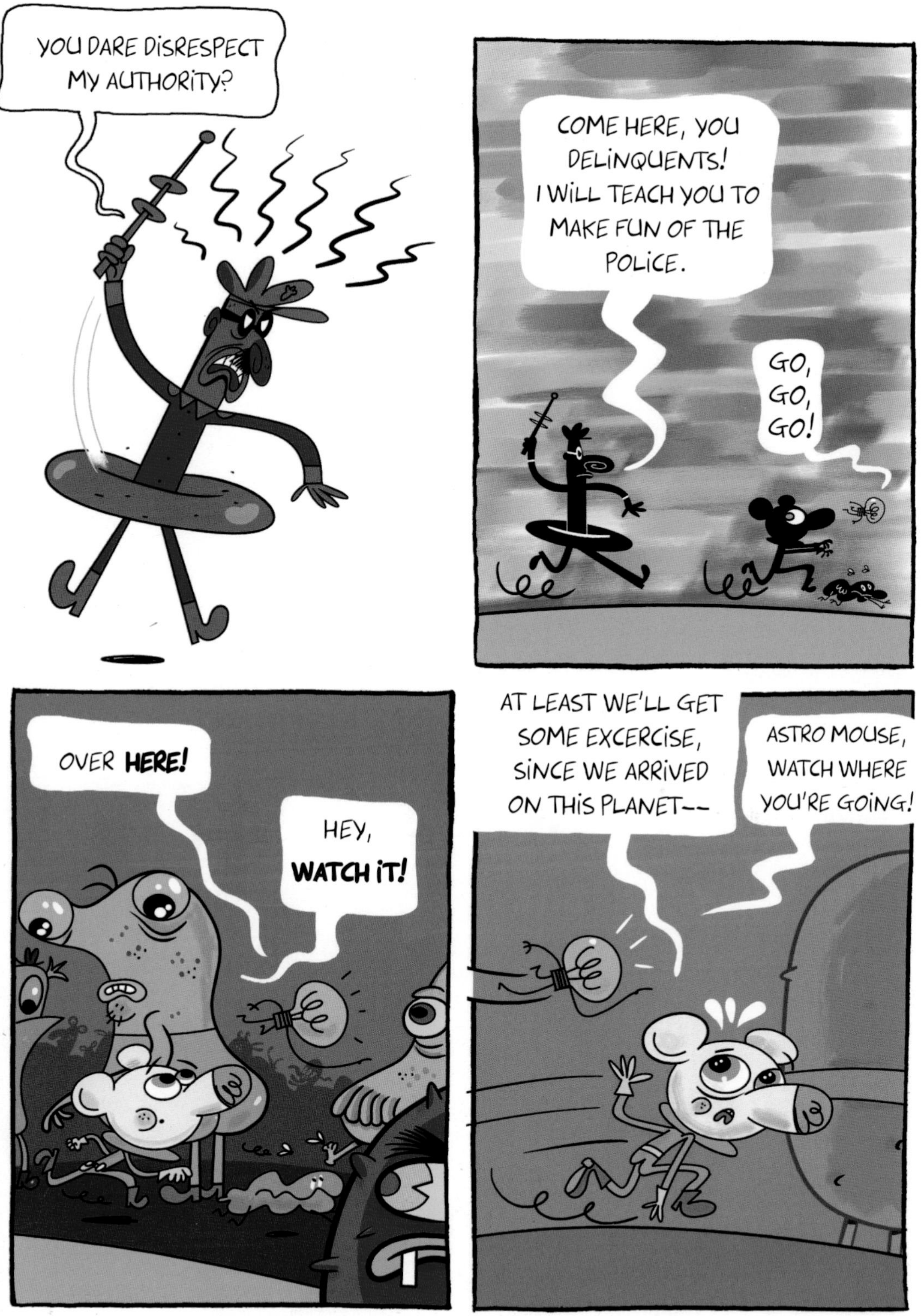
YOU DARE DISRESPECT MY AUTHORITY?
COME HERE, YOU DELINQUENTS! I WILL TEACH YOU TO MAKE FUN OF THE POLICE.
GO, GO, GO!
OVER **HERE!**
HEY, **WATCH IT!**
AT LEAST WE'LL GET SOME EXCERCISE, SINCE WE ARRIVED ON THIS PLANET--
ASTRO MOUSE, WATCH WHERE YOU'RE GOING!

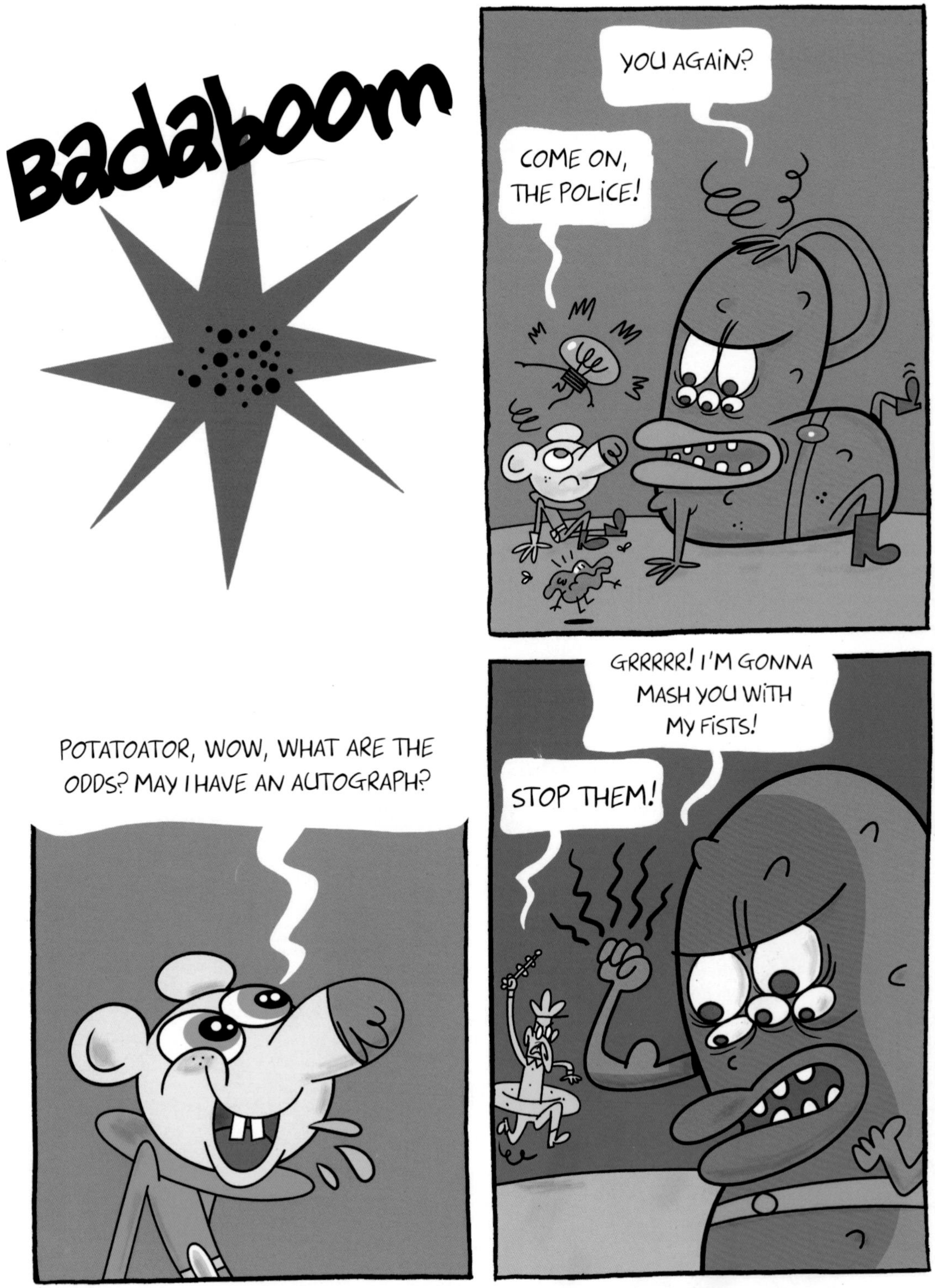
Badaboom
YOU AGAIN?
COME ON, THE POLICE!
POTATOATOR, WOW, WHAT ARE THE ODDS? MAY I HAVE AN AUTOGRAPH?
GRRRRR! I'M GONNA MASH YOU WITH MY FISTS!
STOP THEM!

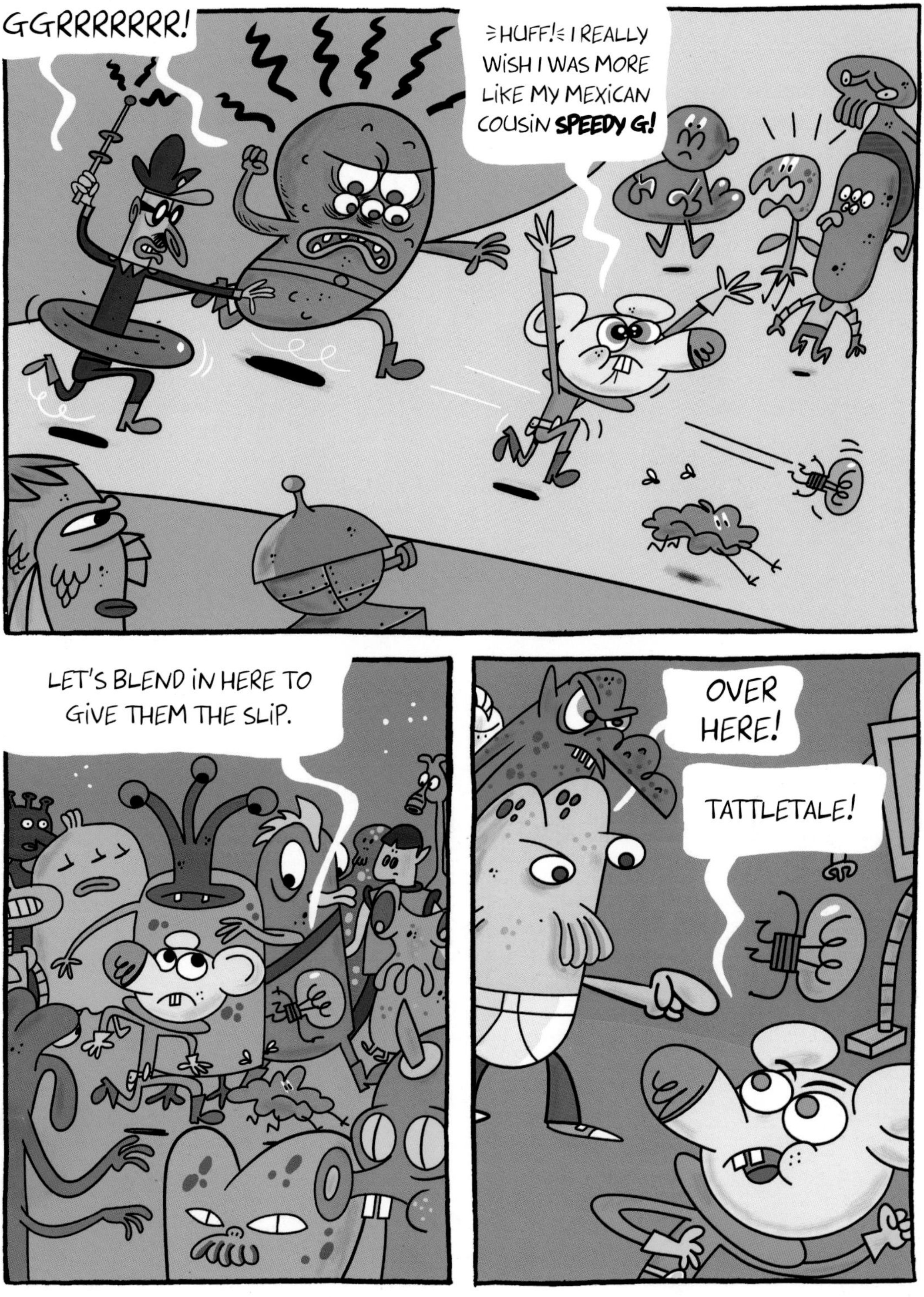
GGRRRRRRR!
HUFF! I REALLY WISH I WAS MORE LIKE MY MEXICAN COUSIN **SPEEDY G!**
LET'S BLEND IN HERE TO GIVE THEM THE SLIP.
OVER HERE!
TATTLETALE!

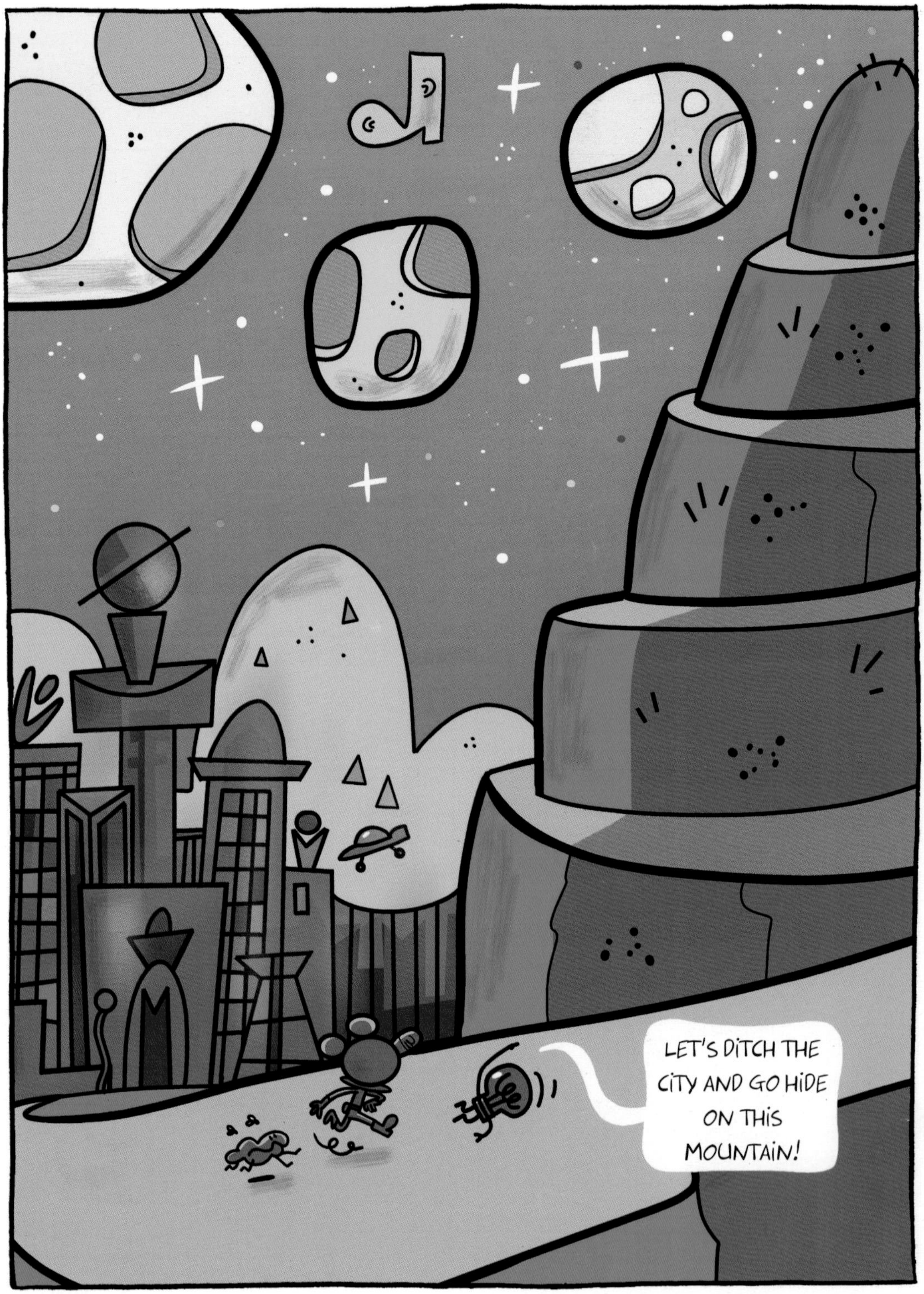
LET'S DITCH THE CITY AND GO HIDE ON THIS MOUNTAIN!

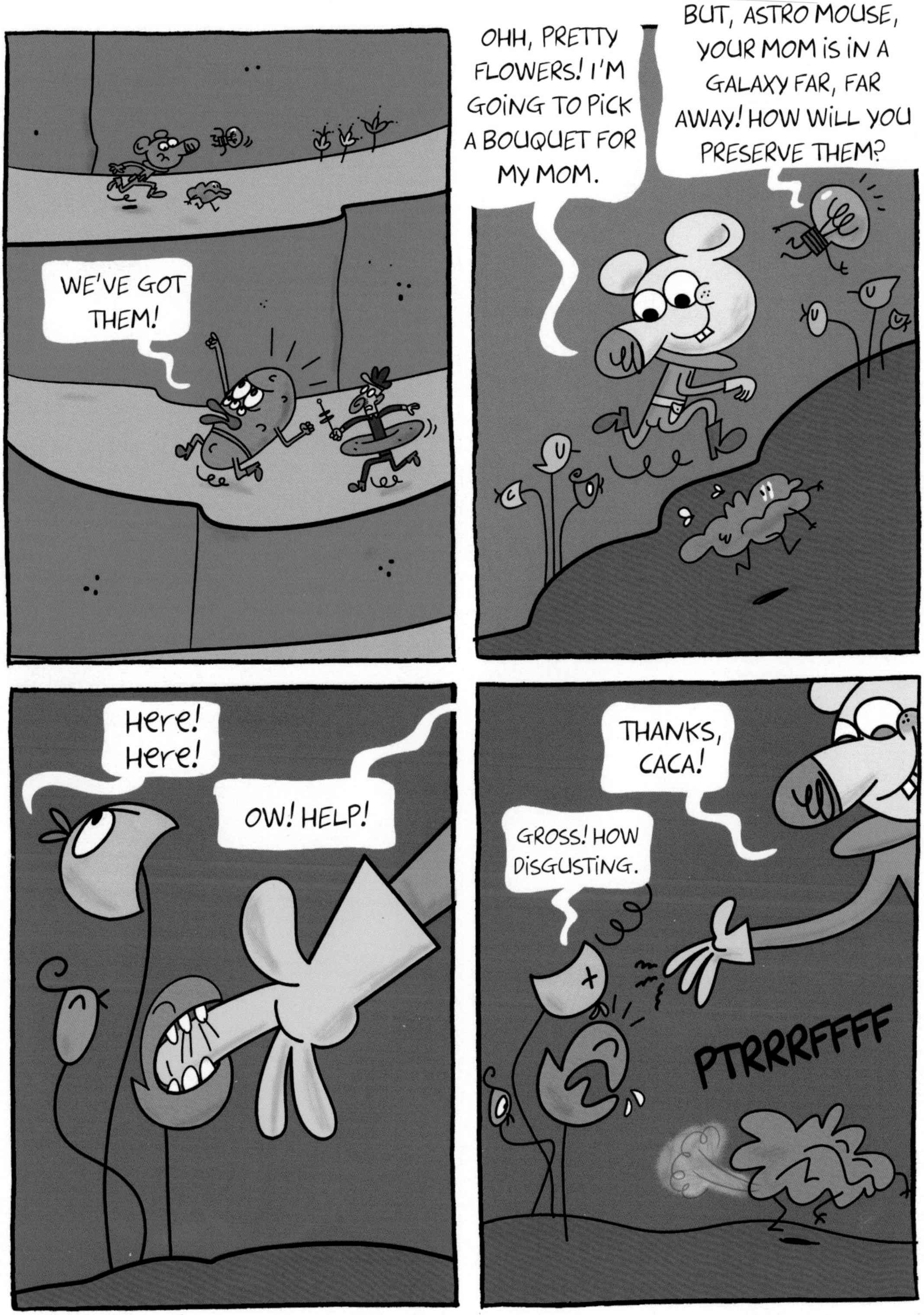
WE'VE GOT THEM!
OHH, PRETTY FLOWERS! I'M GOING TO PICK A BOUQUET FOR MY MOM.
BUT, ASTRO MOUSE, YOUR MOM IS IN A GALAXY FAR, FAR AWAY! HOW WILL YOU PRESERVE THEM?
Here! Here!
OW! HELP!
THANKS, CACA!
GROSS! HOW DISGUSTING.
PTRRRFFFF

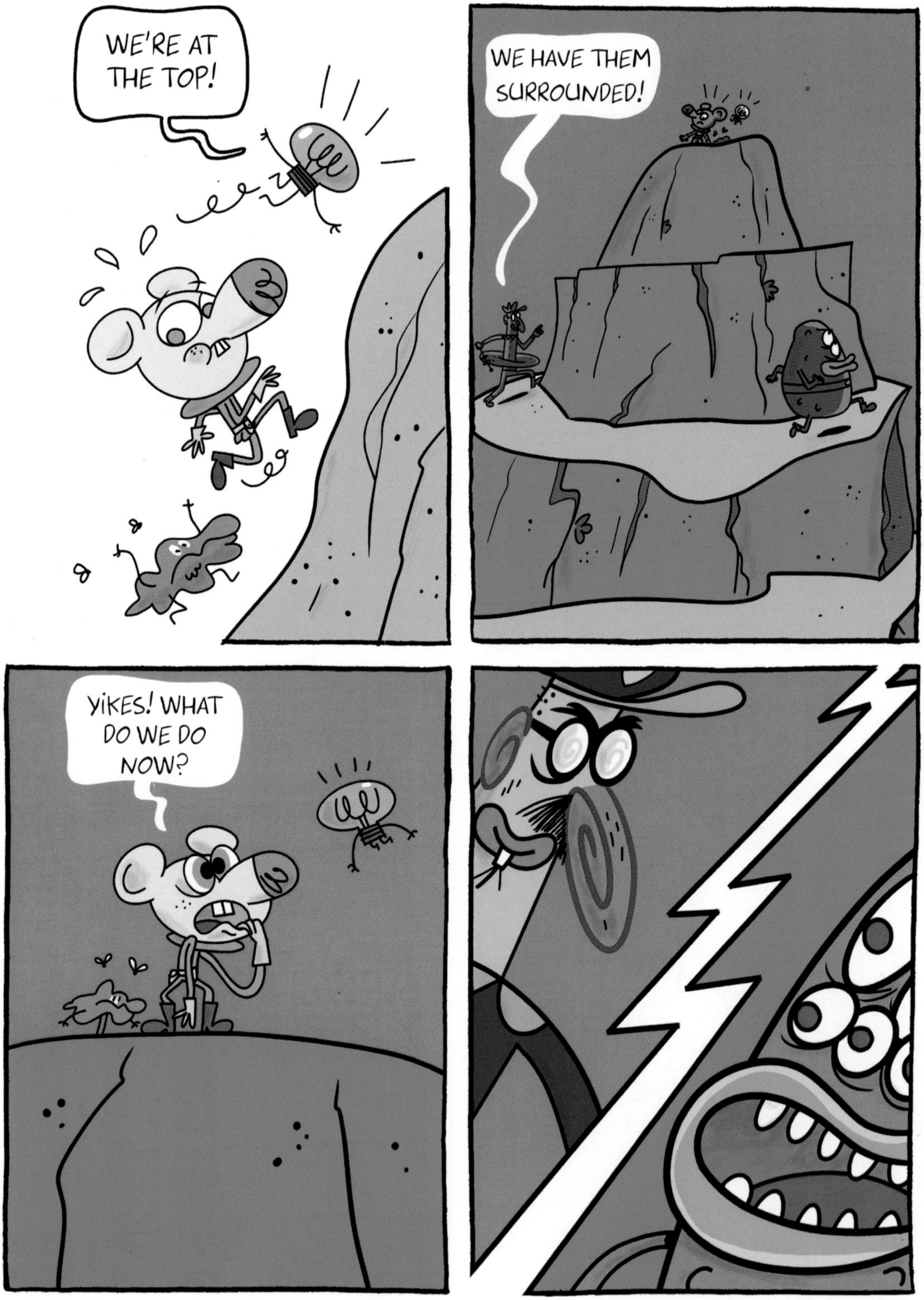
WE'RE AT THE TOP!
WE HAVE THEM SURROUNDED!
YIKES! WHAT DO WE DO NOW?

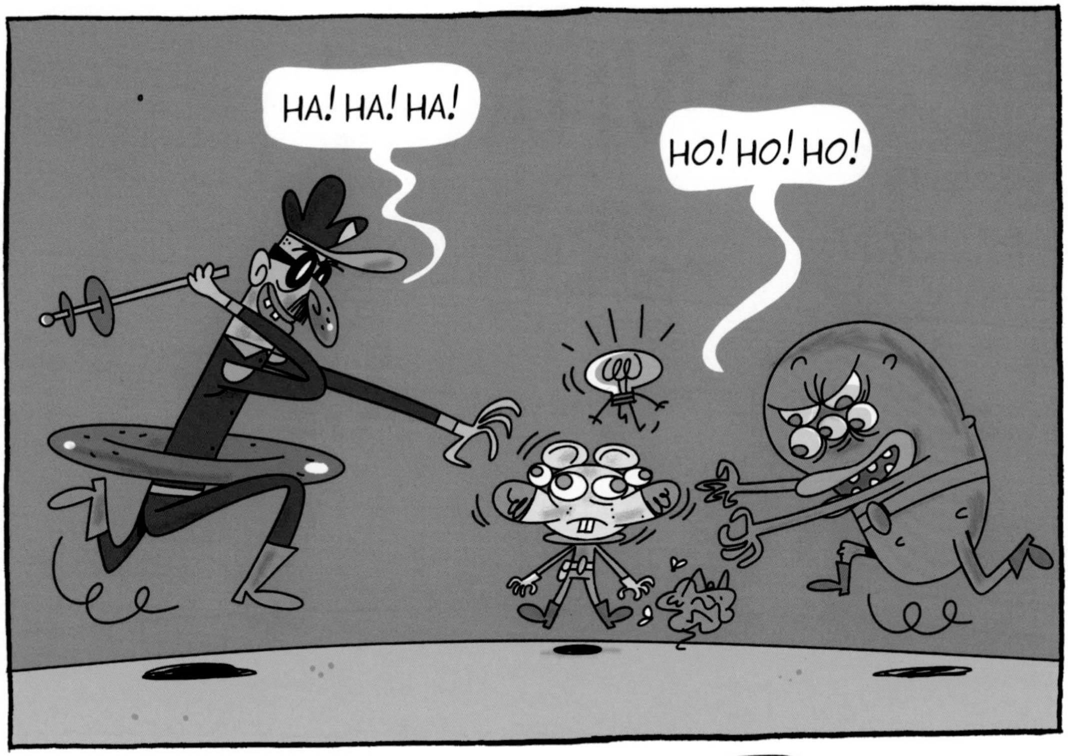
HA! HA! HA!
HO! HO! HO!

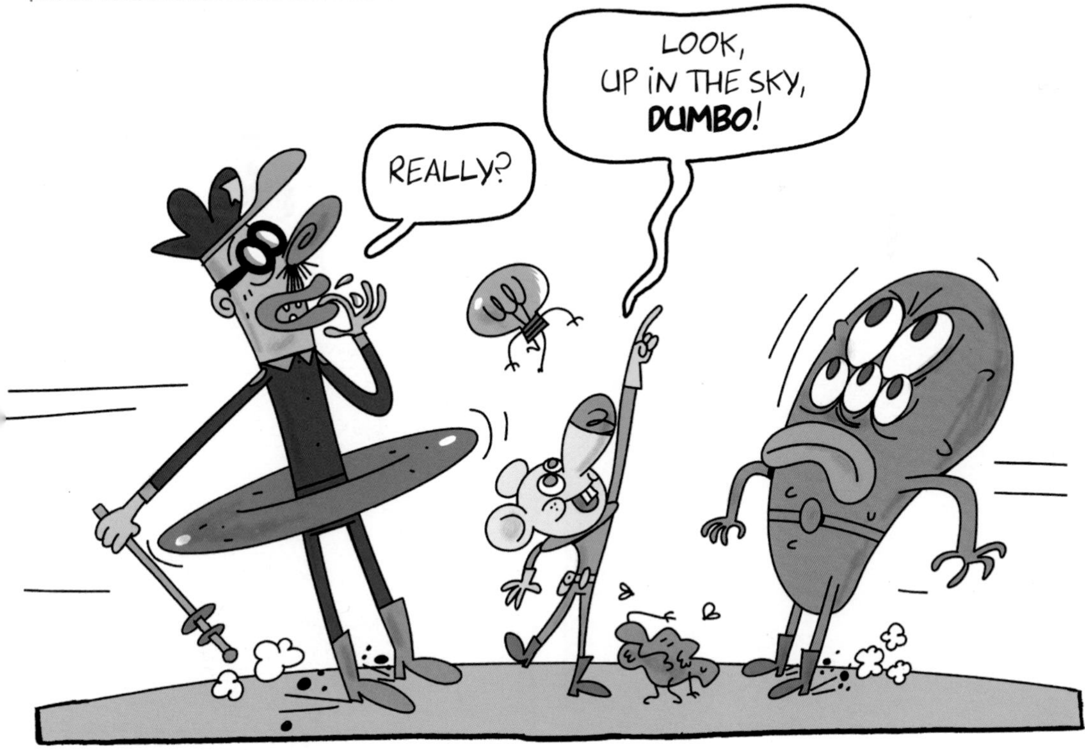
REALLY?
LOOK, UP IN THE SKY, **DUMBO**!

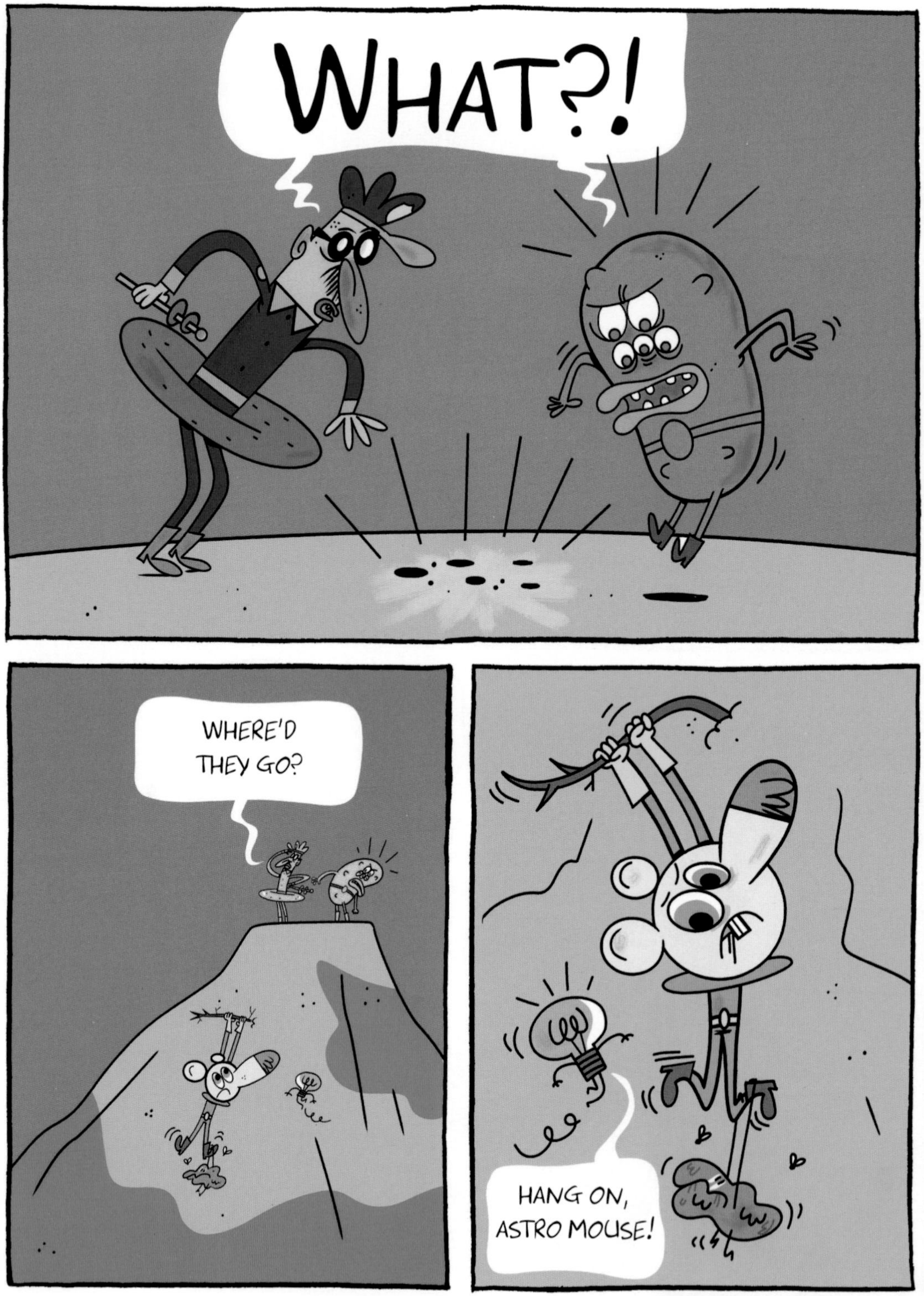
WHAT?!
WHERE'D THEY GO?
HANG ON, ASTRO MOUSE!

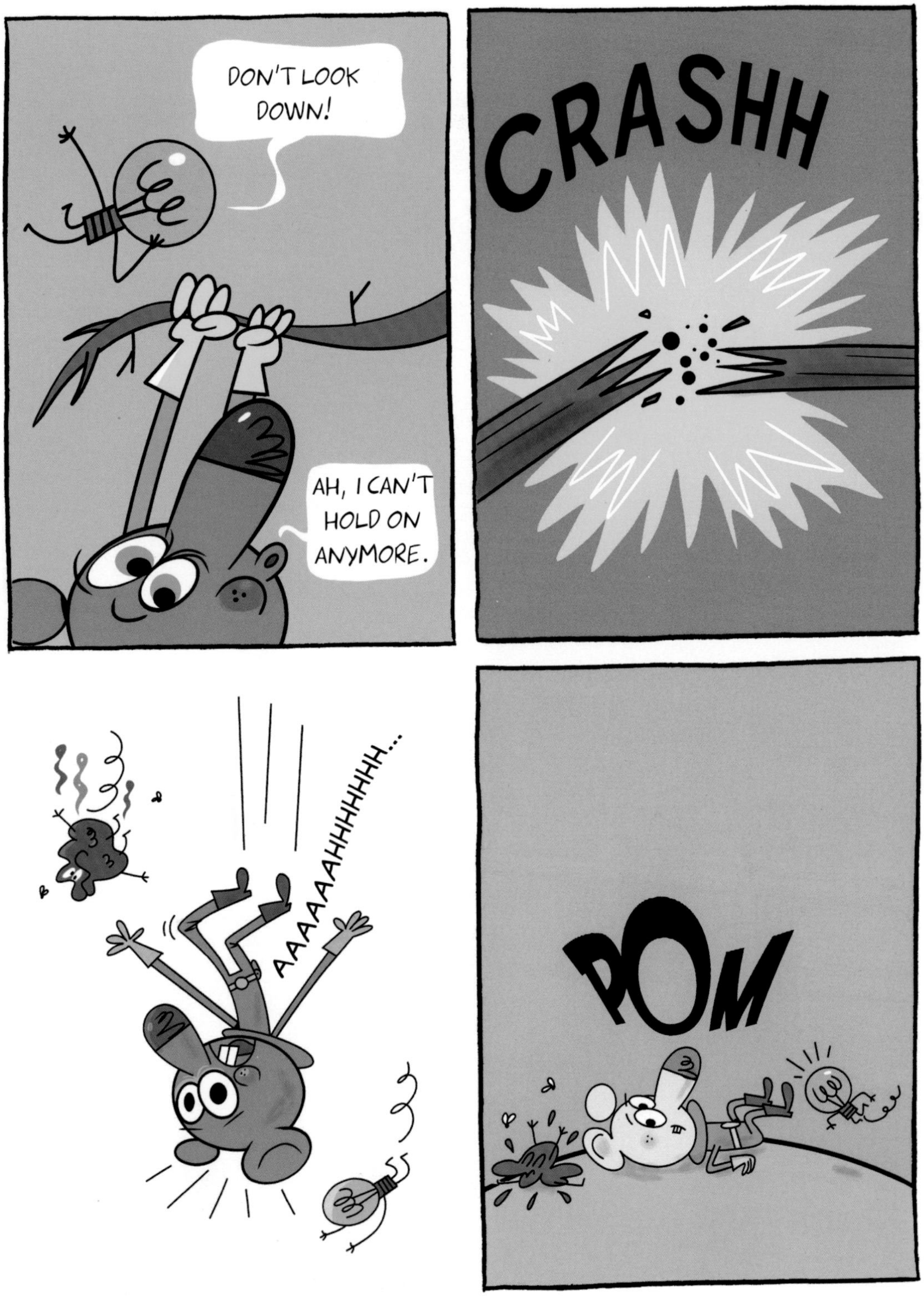
DON'T LOOK DOWN!
AH, I CAN'T HOLD ON ANYMORE.
CRASHH
AAAAAAHHHHHHHH...
POM

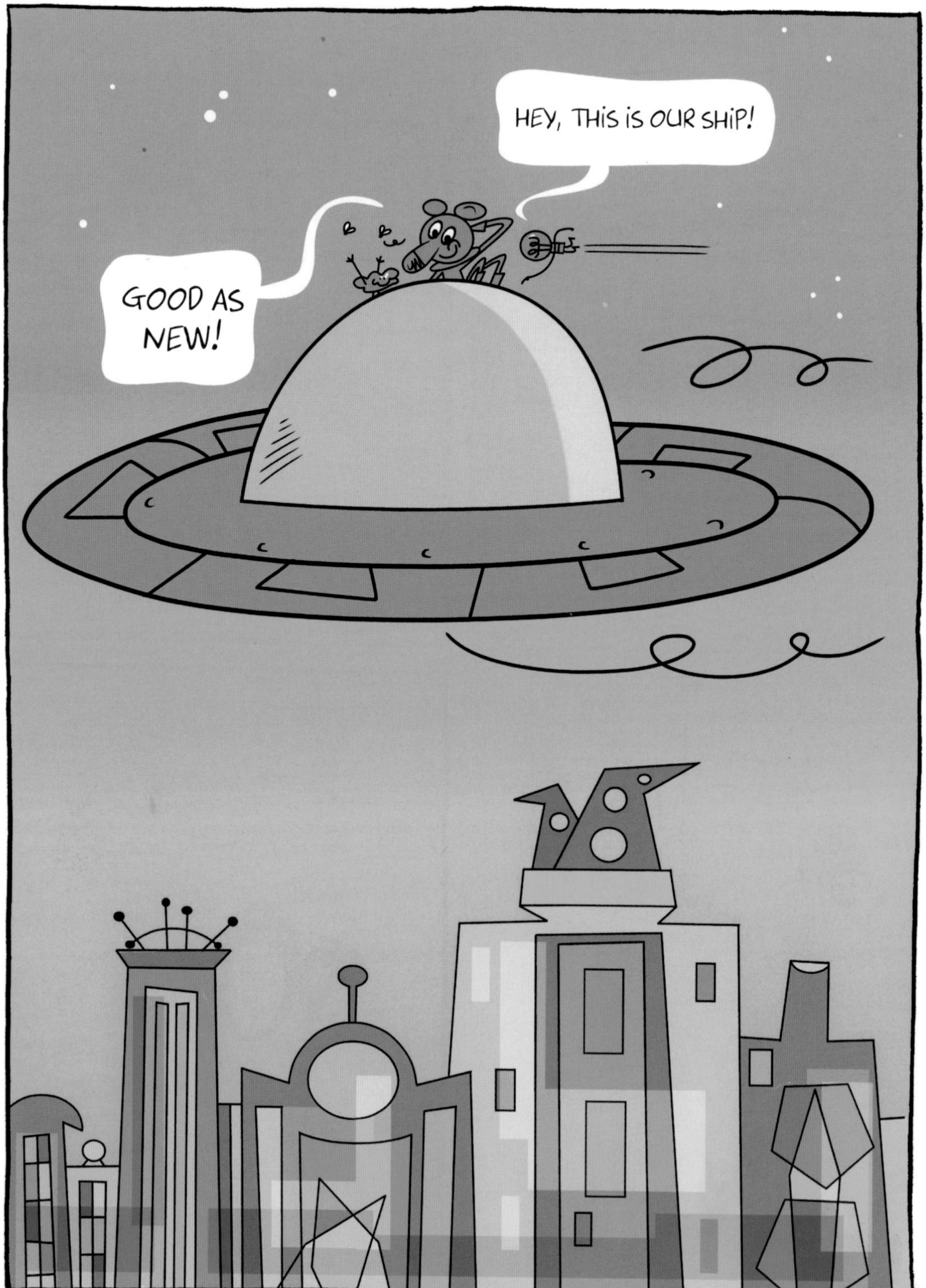
HEY, THIS IS OUR SHIP!
GOOD AS NEW!

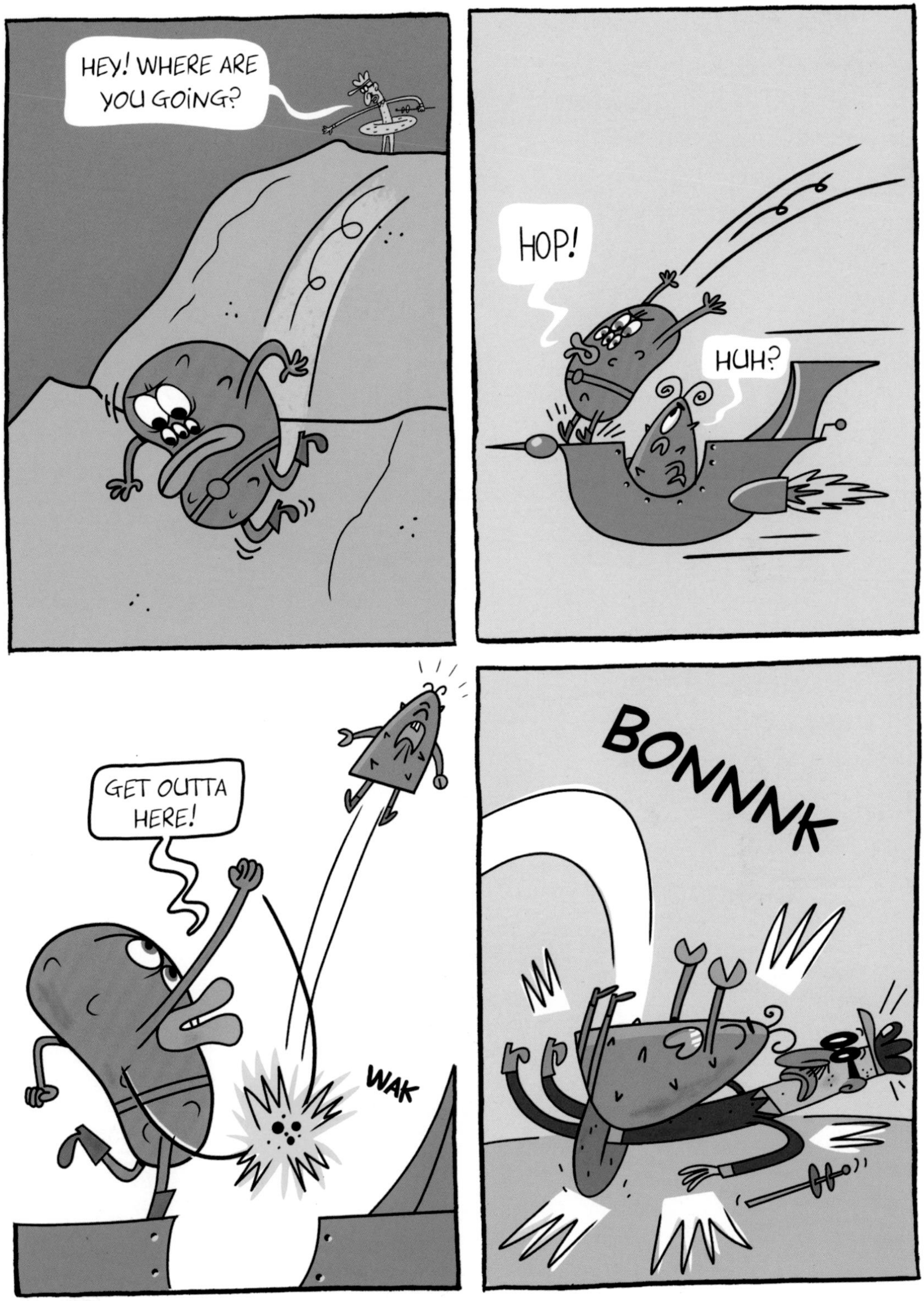
HEY! WHERE ARE YOU GOING?
HOP!
HUH?
GET OUTTA HERE!
WAK
BONNNNK

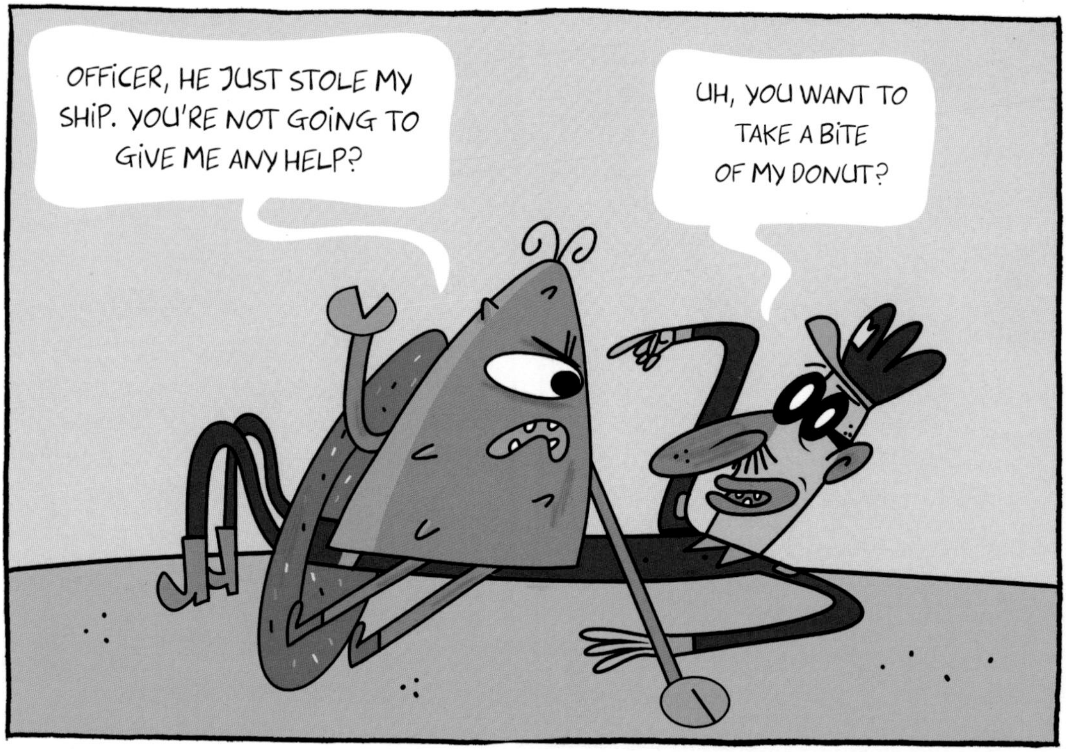
OFFICER, HE JUST STOLE MY SHIP. YOU'RE NOT GOING TO GIVE ME ANY HELP?
UH, YOU WANT TO TAKE A BITE OF MY DONUT?

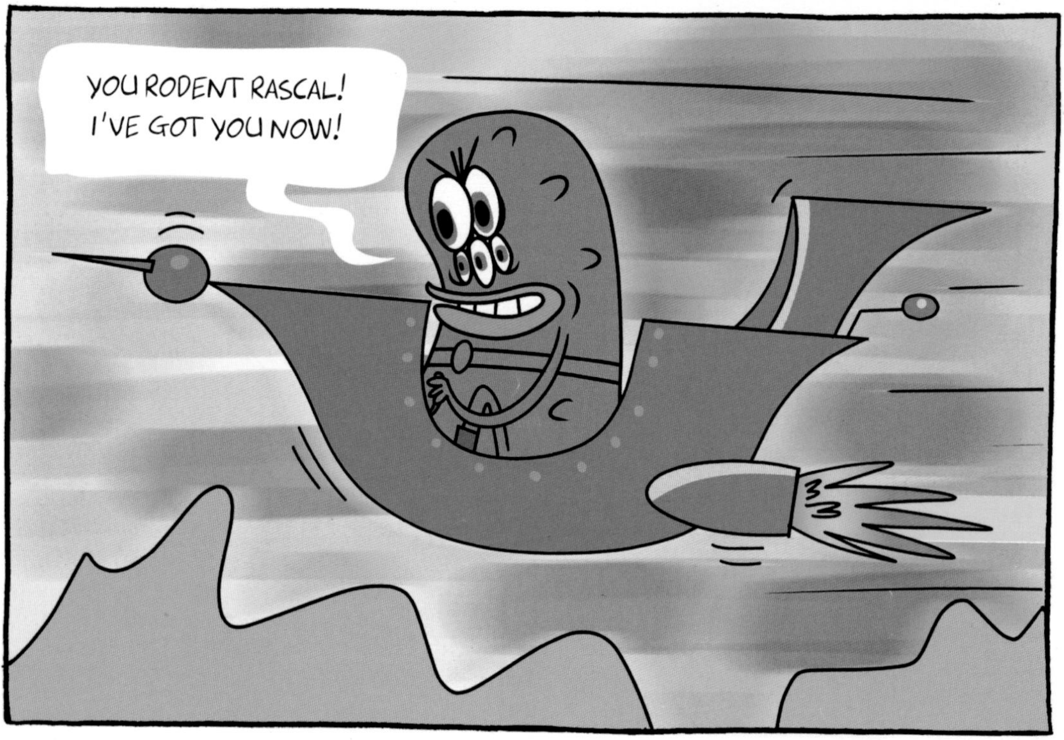
YOU RODENT RASCAL! I'VE GOT YOU NOW!

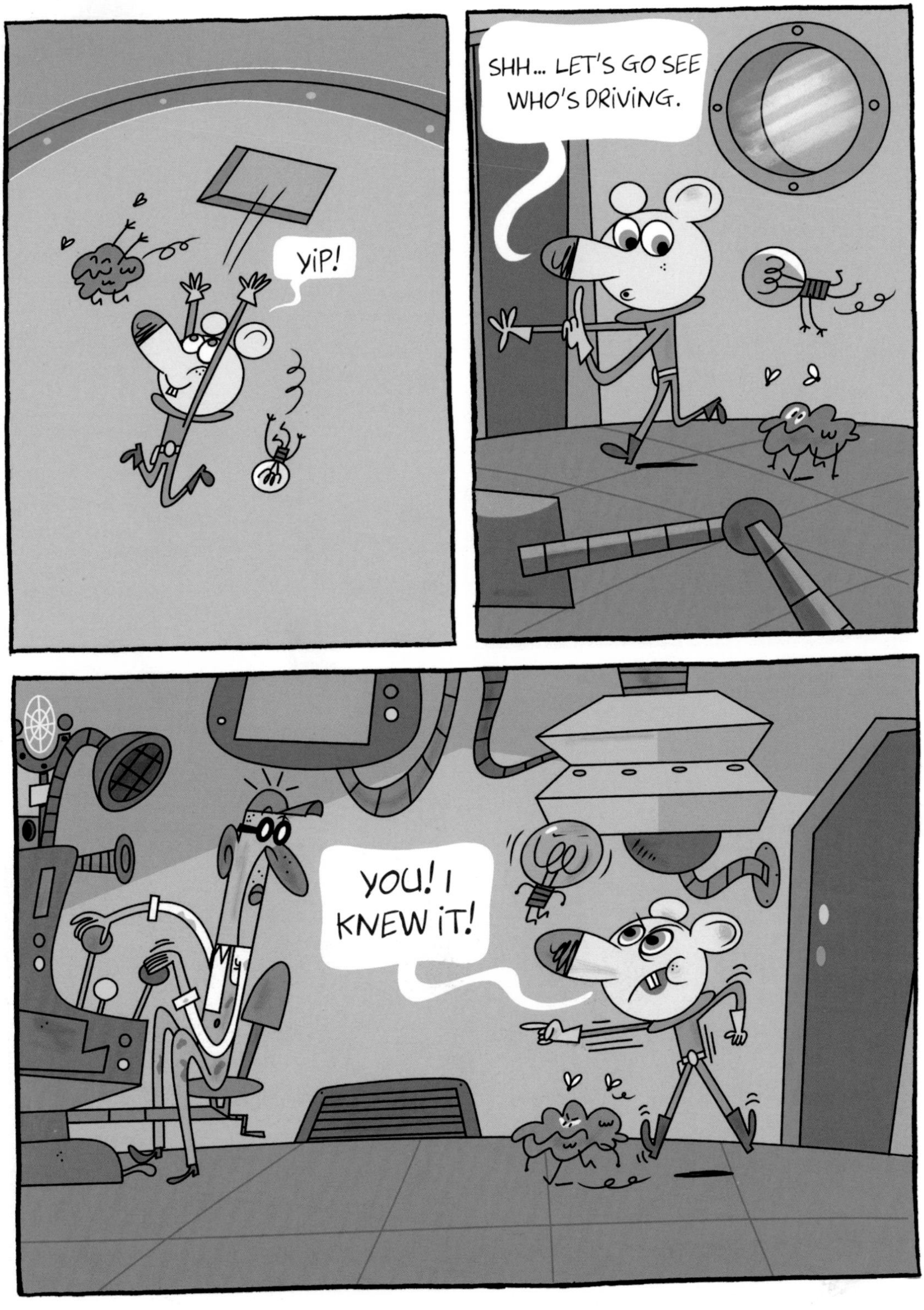
YIP!
SHH... LET'S GO SEE WHO'S DRIVING.
YOU! I KNEW IT!

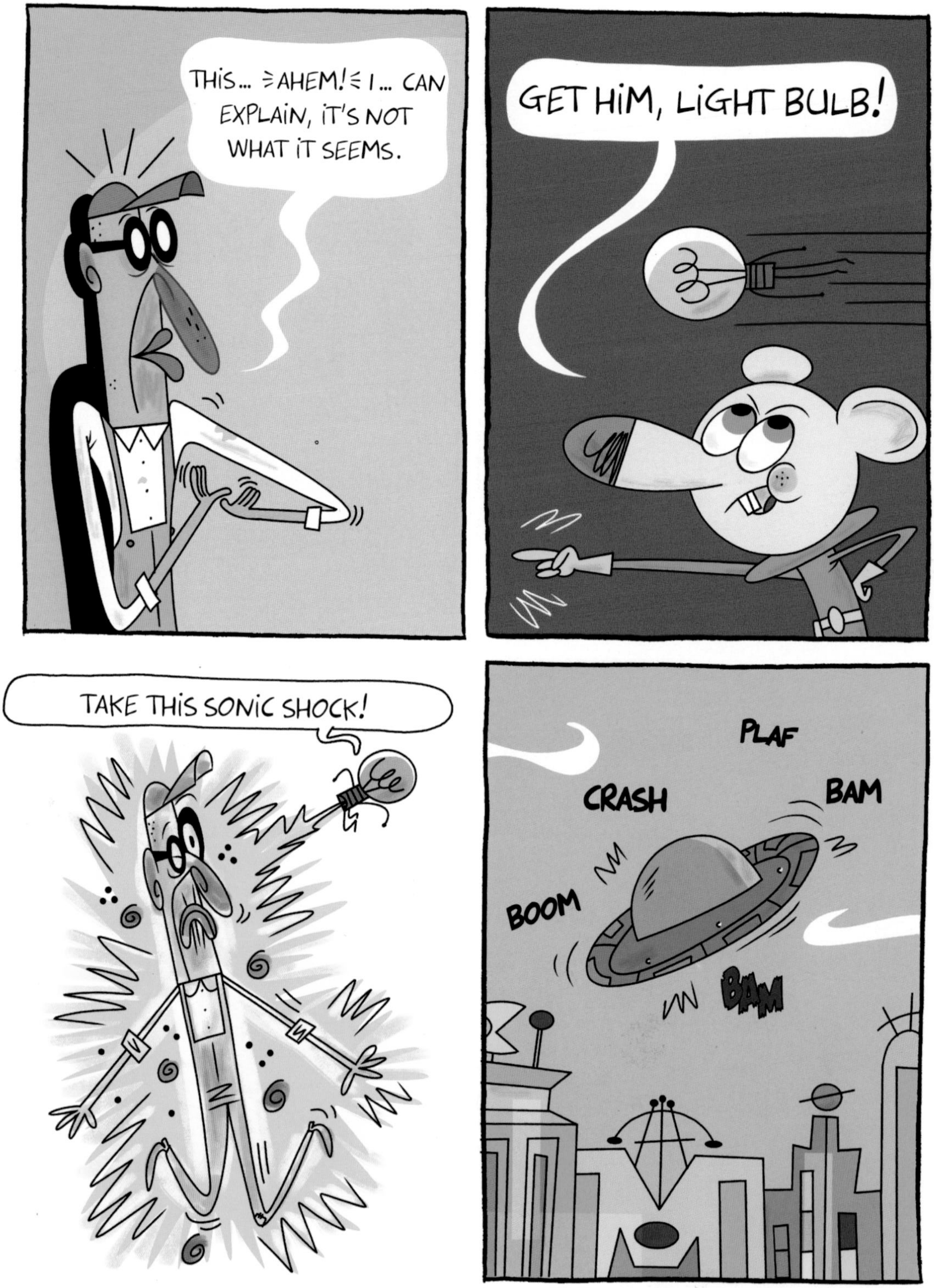

THIS... ≥AHEM!≤ I... CAN EXPLAIN, IT'S NOT WHAT IT SEEMS.
GET HIM, LIGHT BULB!
TAKE THIS SONIC SHOCK!
PLAF
CRASH
BAM
BOOM
BAM

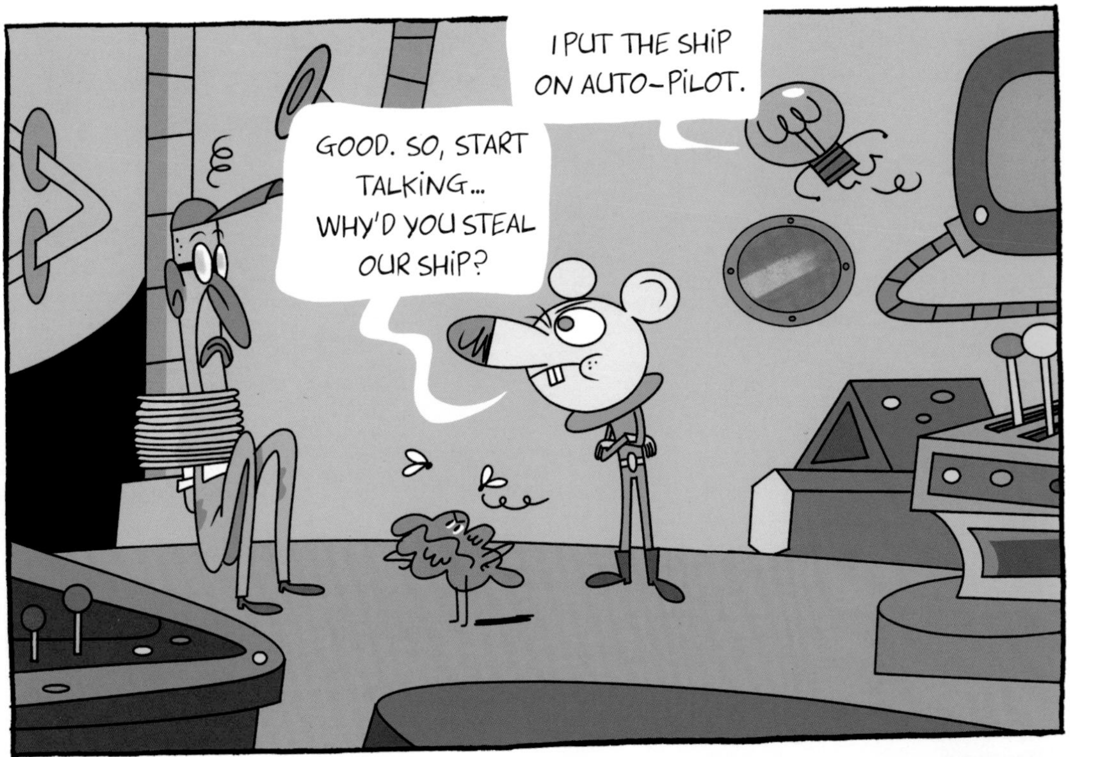
I PUT THE SHIP ON AUTO-PILOT.
GOOD. SO, START TALKING... WHY'D YOU STEAL OUR SHIP?

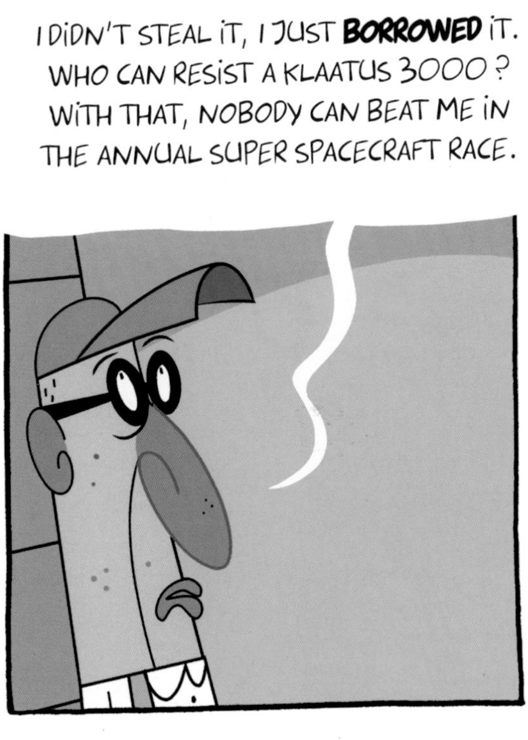
I DIDN'T STEAL IT, I JUST **BORROWED** IT. WHO CAN RESIST A KLAATUS 3000? WITH THAT, NOBODY CAN BEAT ME IN THE ANNUAL SUPER SPACECRAFT RACE.

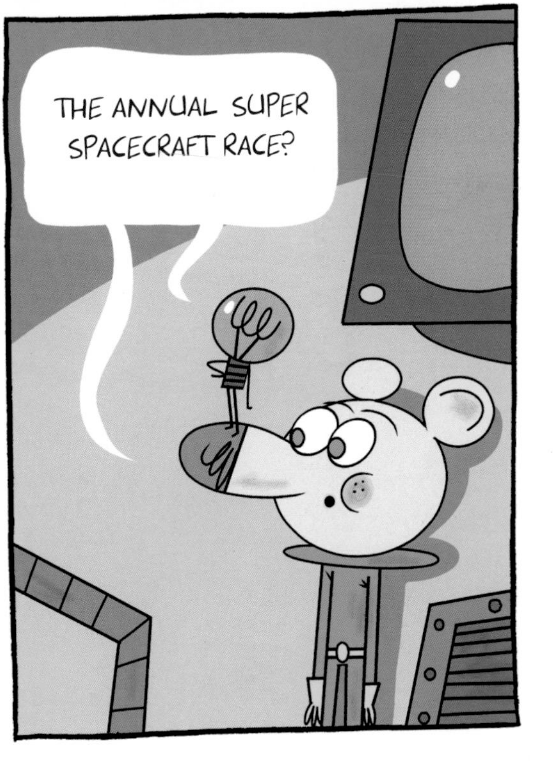
THE ANNUAL SUPER SPACECRAFT RACE?

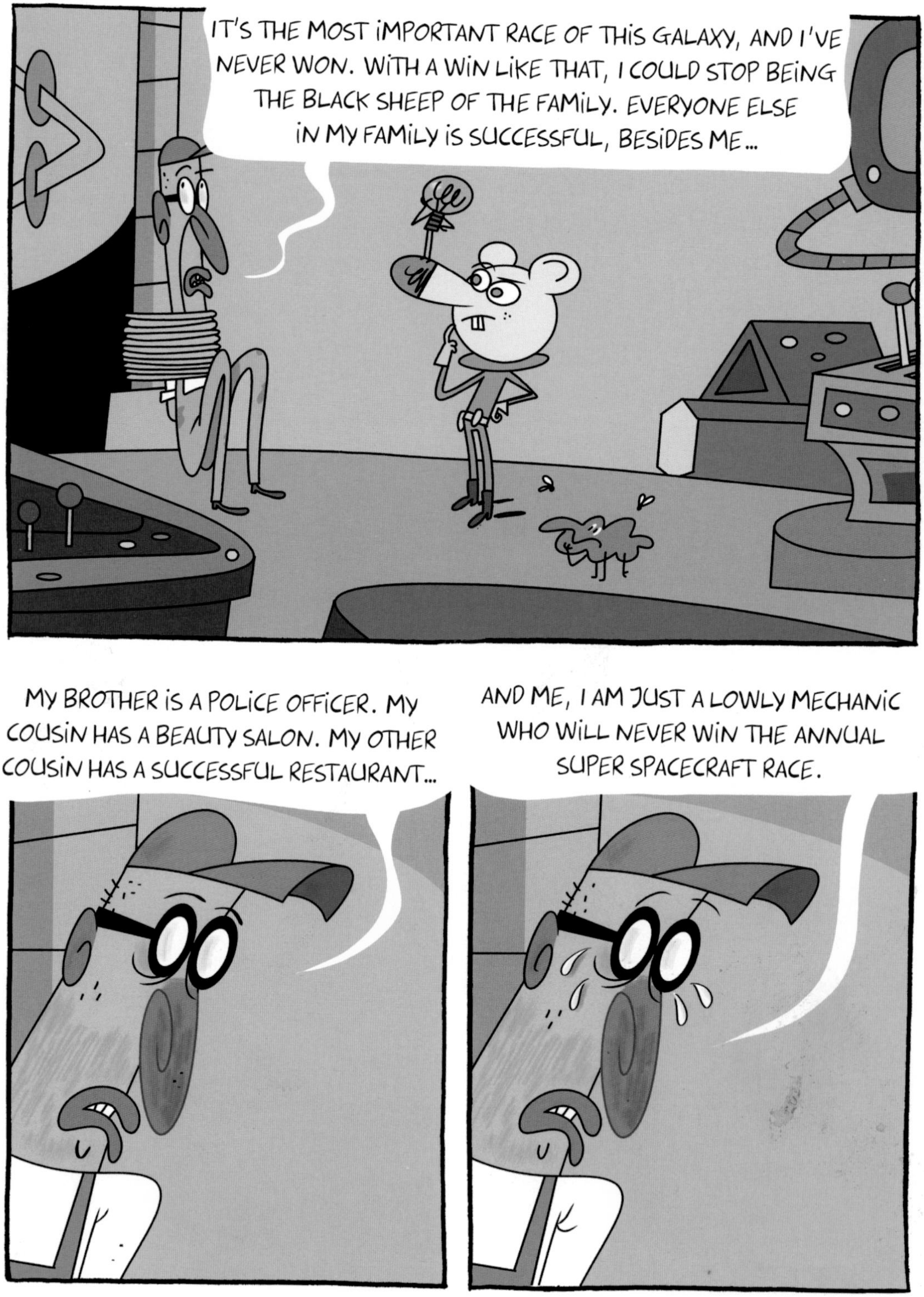
IT'S THE MOST IMPORTANT RACE OF THIS GALAXY, AND I'VE NEVER WON. WITH A WIN LIKE THAT, I COULD STOP BEING THE BLACK SHEEP OF THE FAMILY. EVERYONE ELSE IN MY FAMILY IS SUCCESSFUL, BESIDES ME...
MY BROTHER IS A POLICE OFFICER. MY COUSIN HAS A BEAUTY SALON. MY OTHER COUSIN HAS A SUCCESSFUL RESTAURANT...
AND ME, I AM JUST A LOWLY MECHANIC WHO WILL NEVER WIN THE ANNUAL SUPER SPACECRAFT RACE.

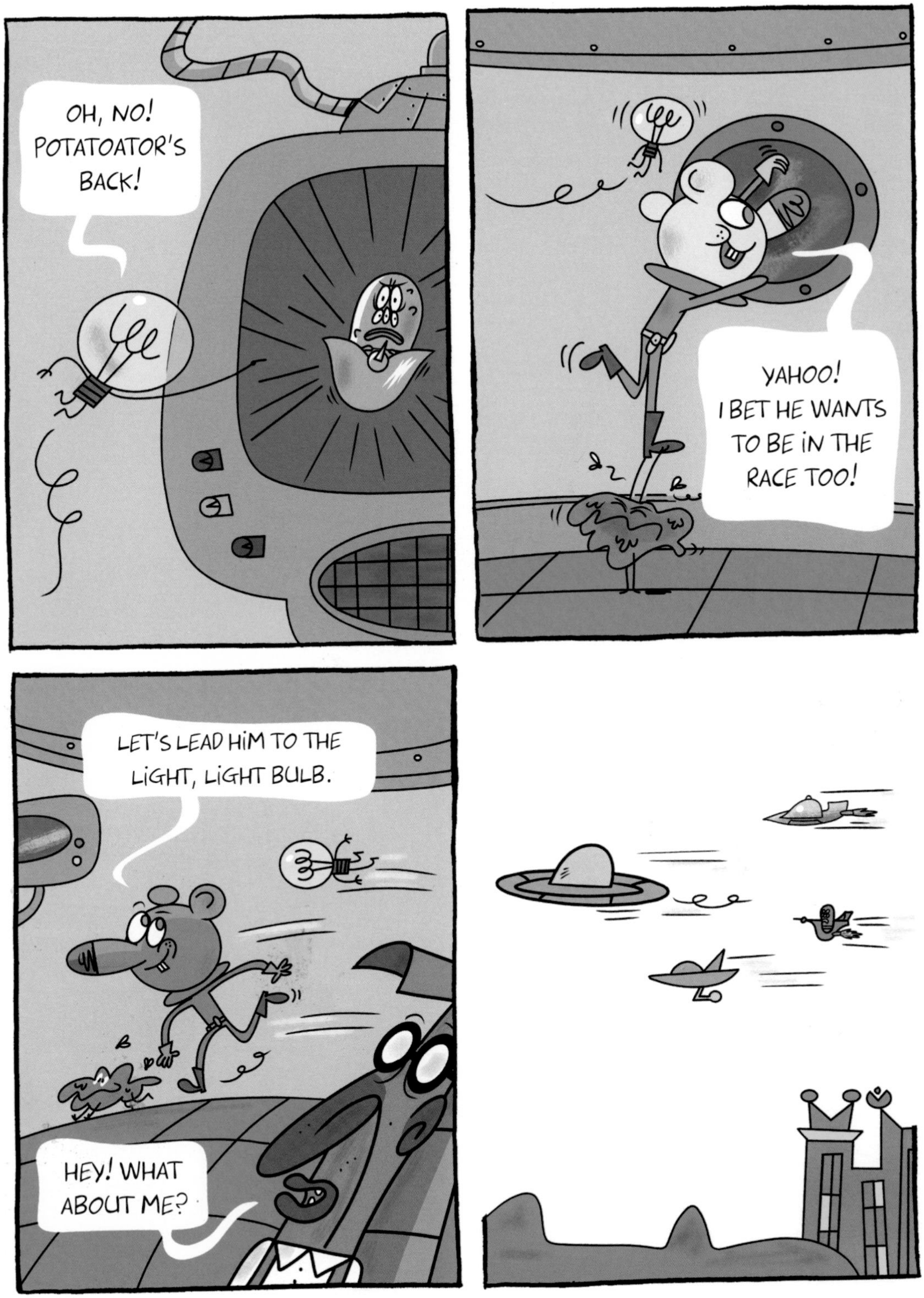
OH, NO! POTATOATOR'S BACK!
YAHOO! I BET HE WANTS TO BE IN THE RACE TOO!
LET'S LEAD HIM TO THE LIGHT, LIGHT BULB.
HEY! WHAT ABOUT ME?

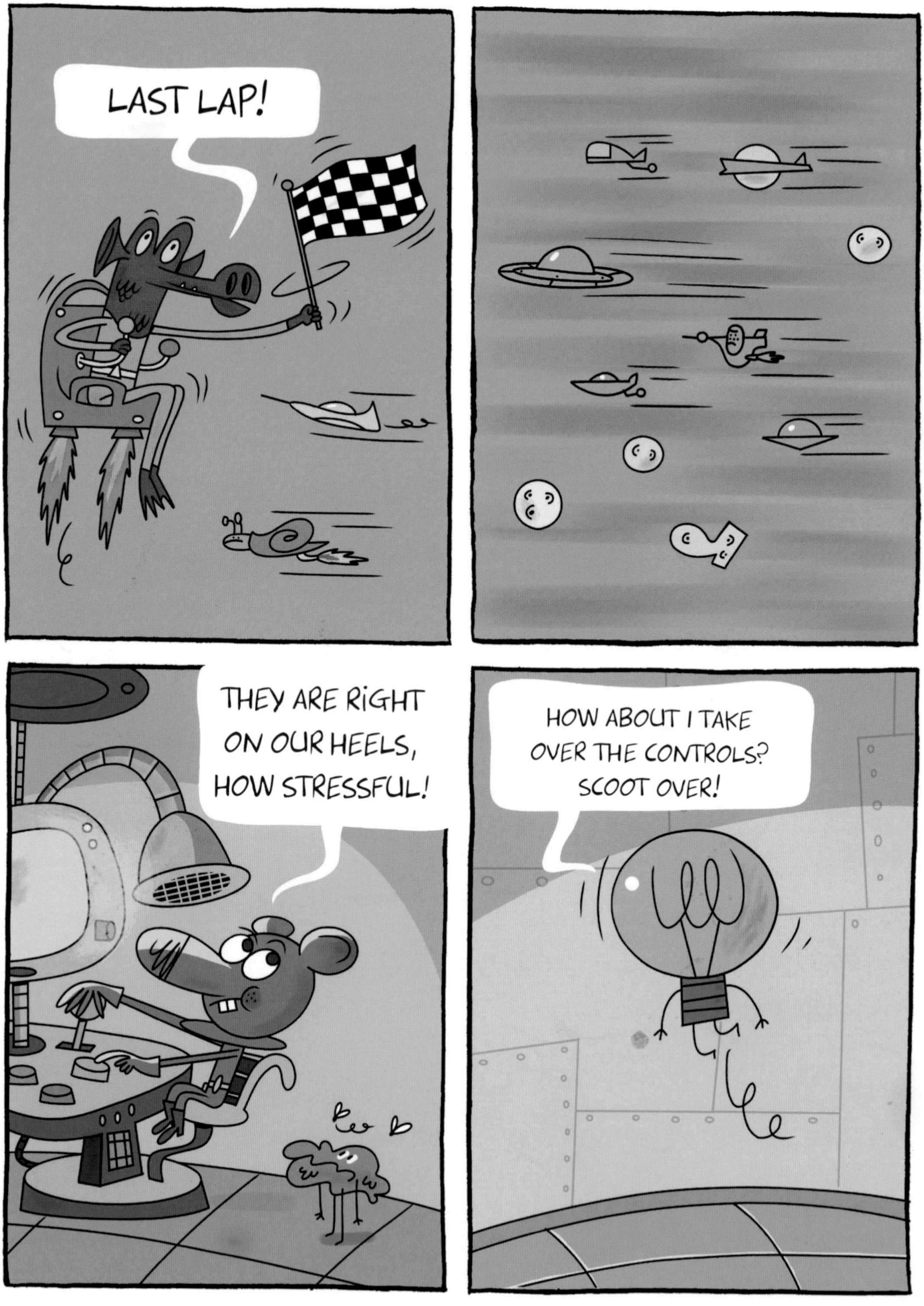
LAST LAP!
THEY ARE RIGHT ON OUR HEELS, HOW STRESSFUL!
HOW ABOUT I TAKE OVER THE CONTROLS? SCOOT OVER!

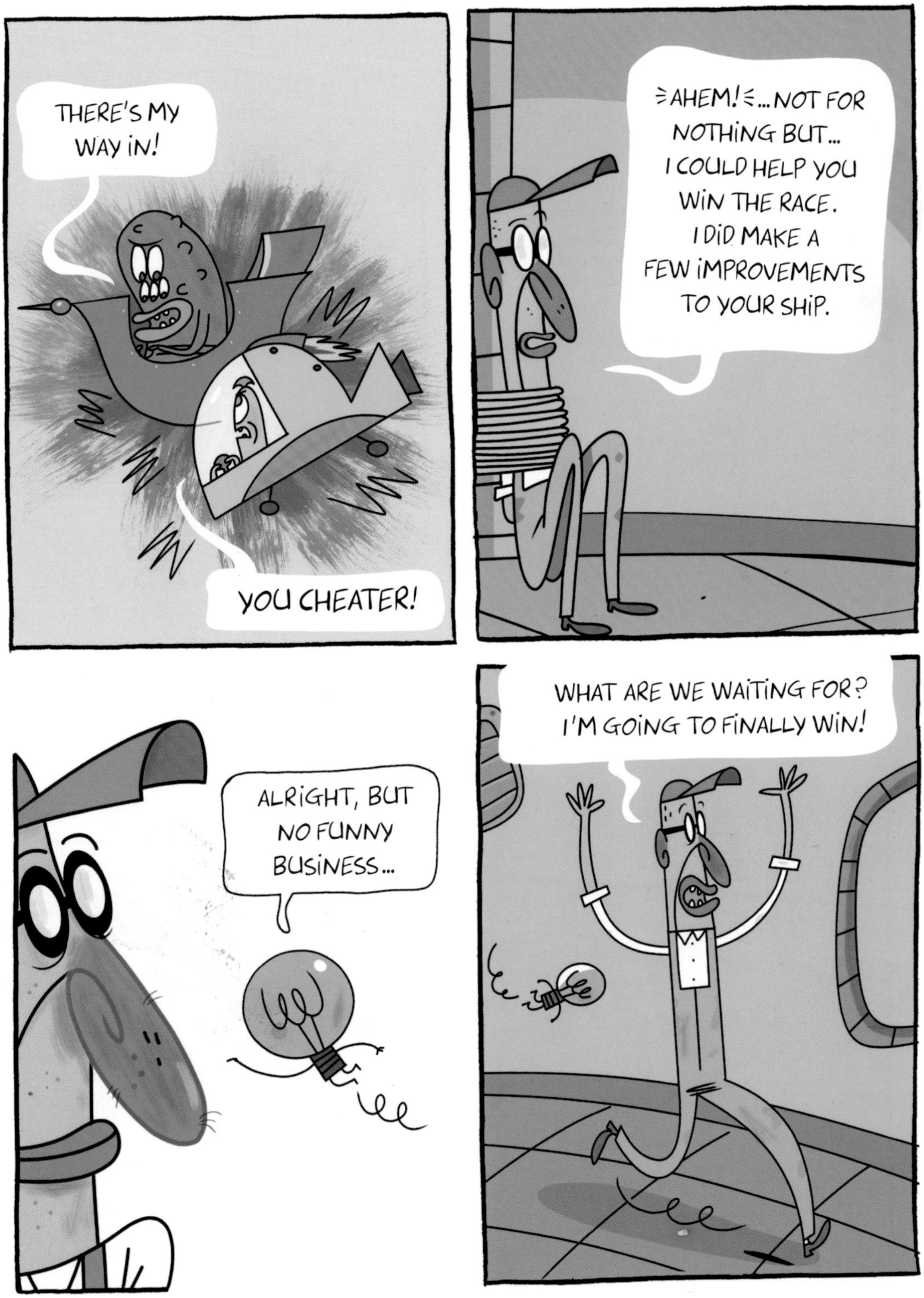
THERE'S MY WAY iN!
YOU CHEATER!
AHEM! ...NOT FOR NOTHiNG BUT... I COULD HELP YOU WiN THE RACE. I DiD MAKE A FEW iMPROVEMENTS TO YOUR SHiP.
ALRiGHT, BUT NO FUNNY BUSiNESS...
WHAT ARE WE WAiTiNG FOR? I'M GOiNG TO FiNALLY WiN!

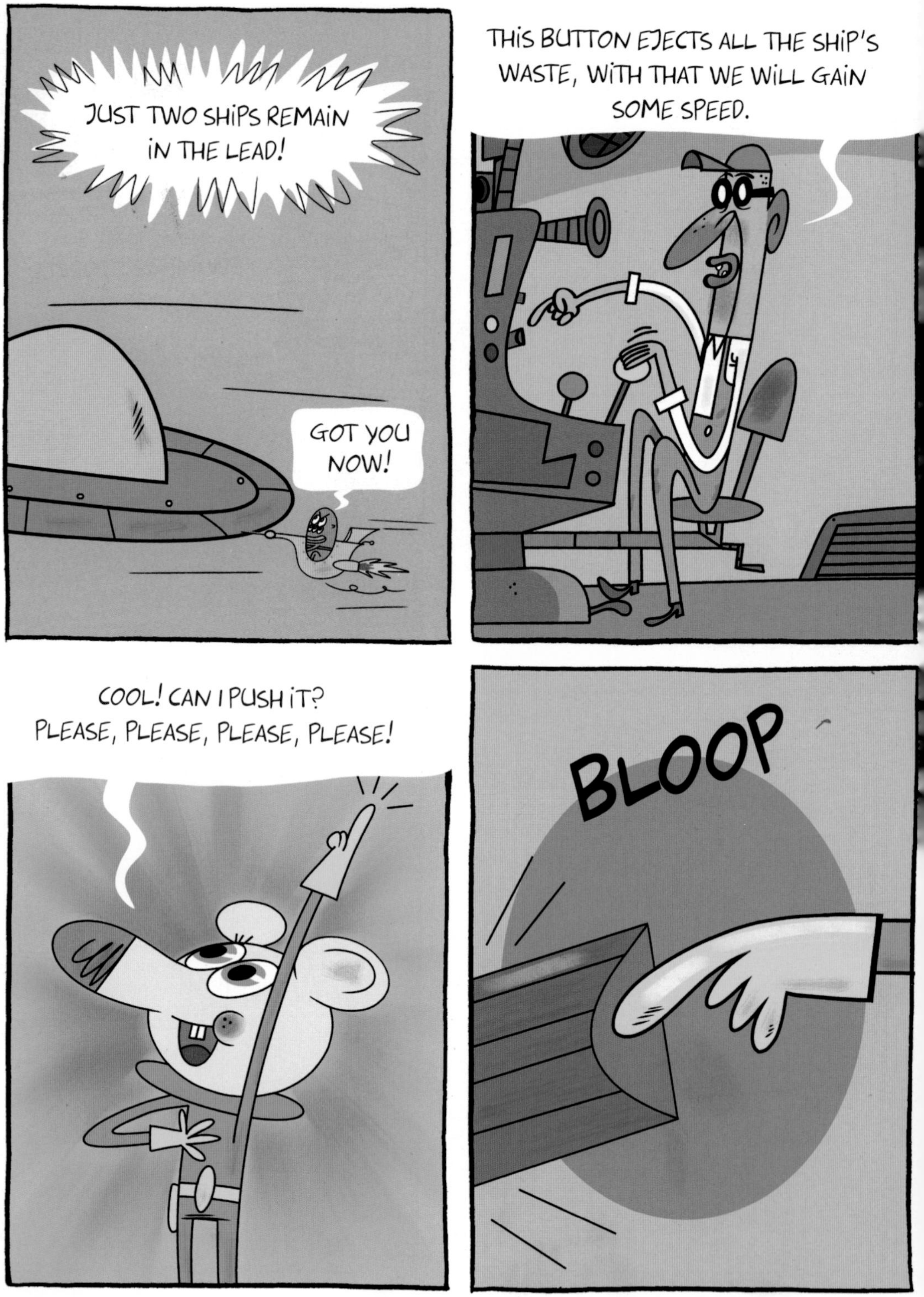
JUST TWO SHIPS REMAIN IN THE LEAD!
GOT YOU NOW!
THIS BUTTON EJECTS ALL THE SHIP'S WASTE, WITH THAT WE WILL GAIN SOME SPEED.
COOL! CAN I PUSH IT? PLEASE, PLEASE, PLEASE, PLEASE!
BLOOP

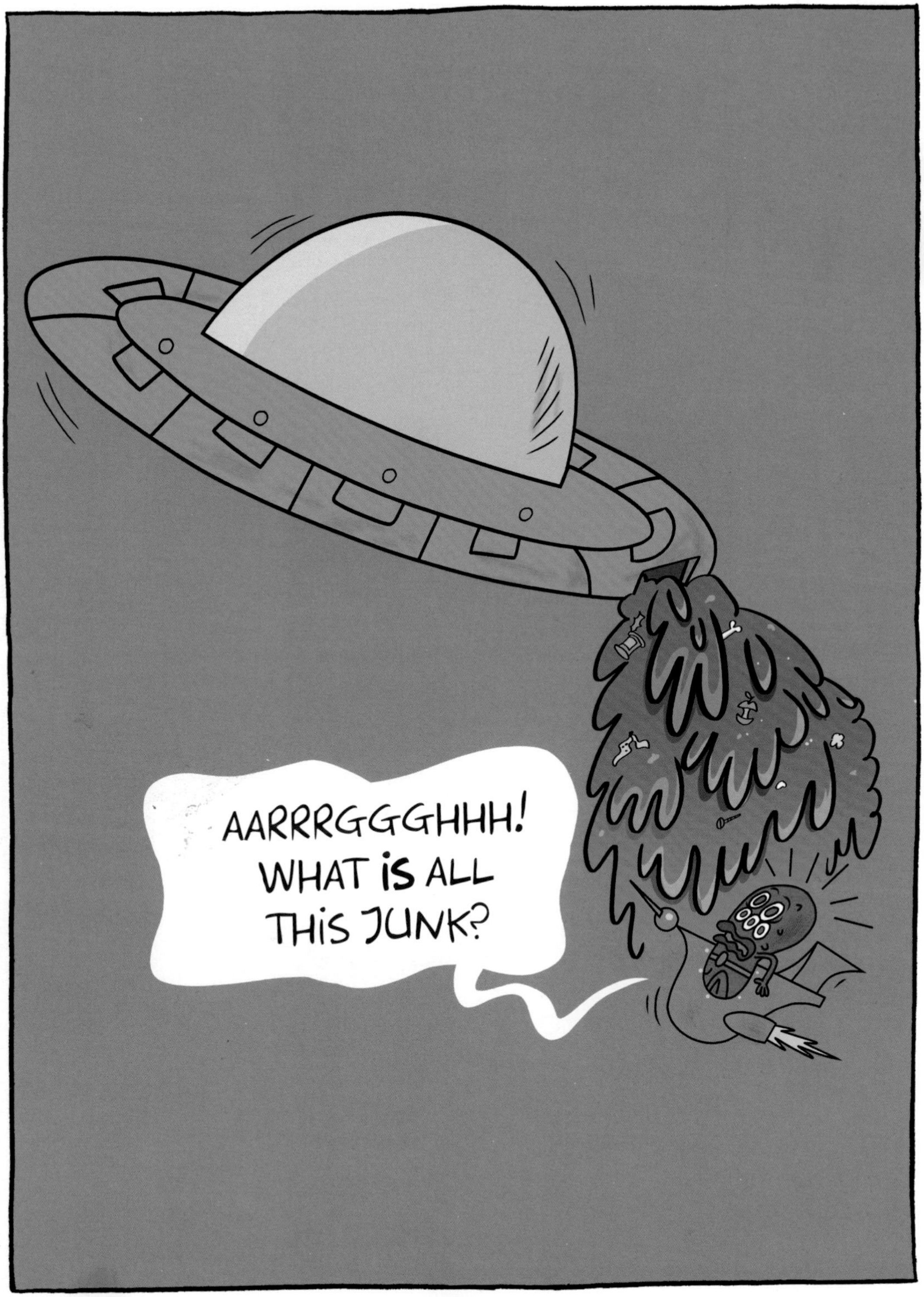
AARRRGGGHHH! WHAT IS ALL THIS JUNK?

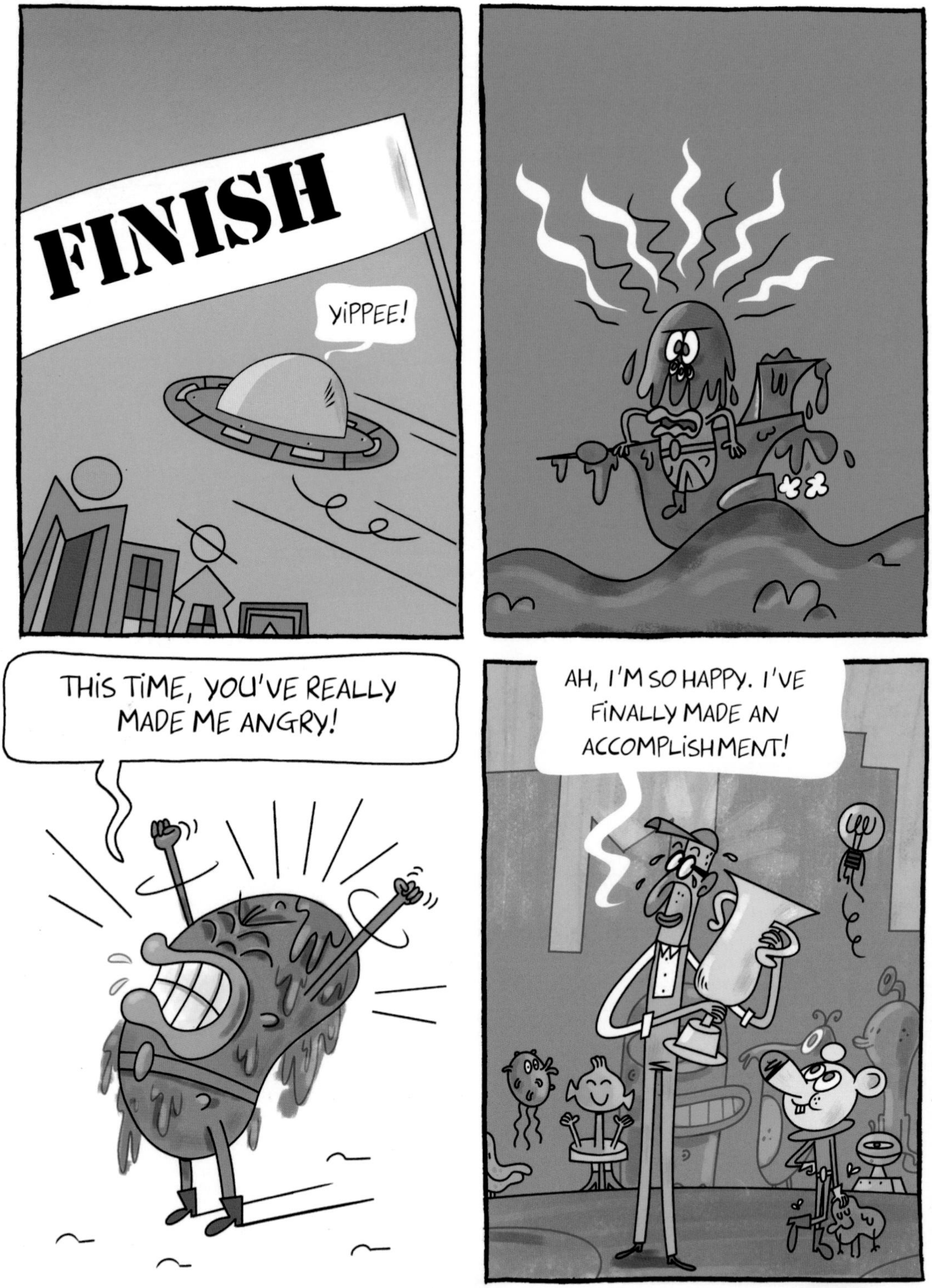
FINISH
YiPPEE!
THiS TiME, YOU'VE REALLY MADE ME ANGRY!
AH, I'M SO HAPPY. I'VE FiNALLY MADE AN ACCOMPLiSHMENT!

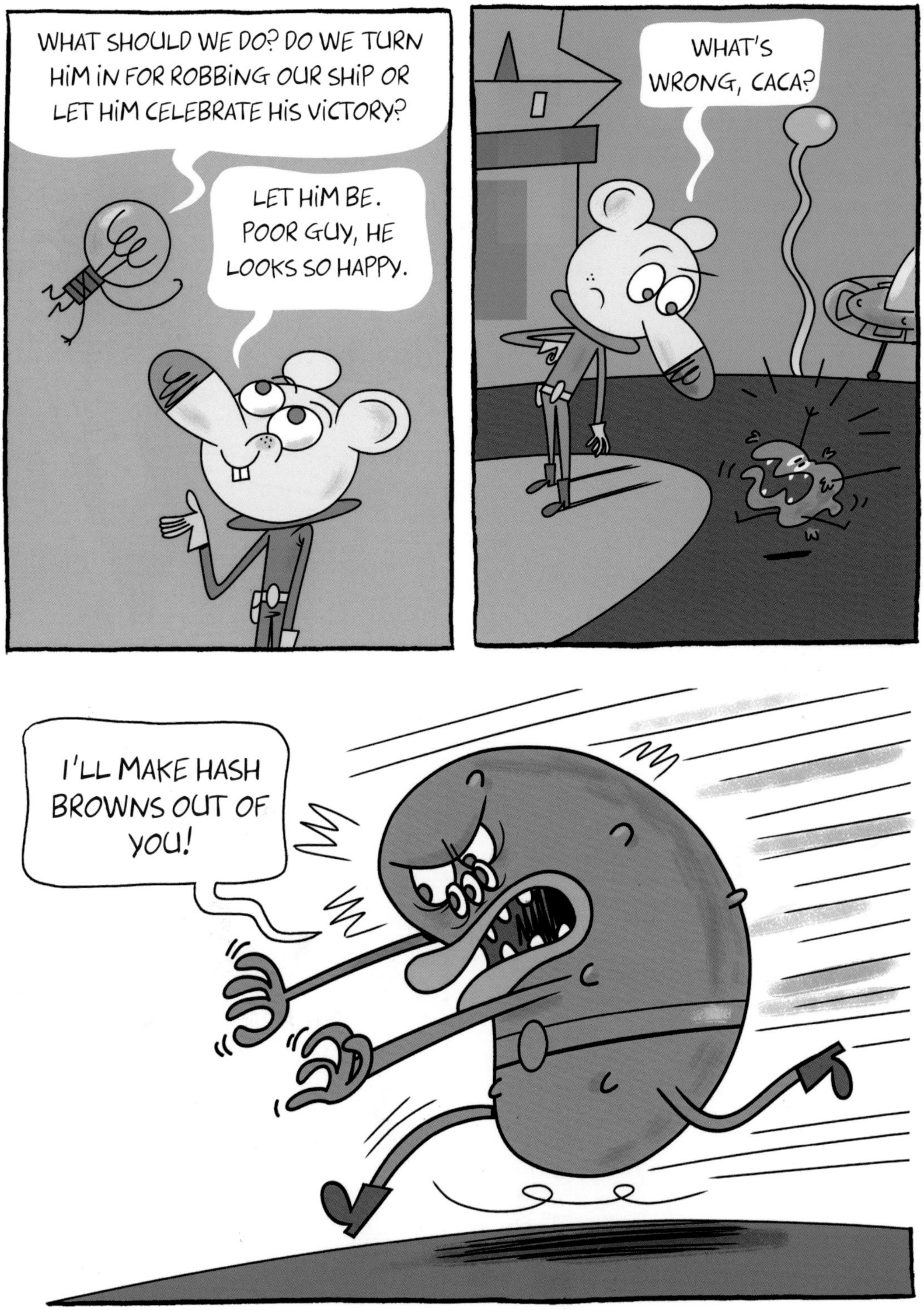
WHAT SHOULD WE DO? DO WE TURN HIM IN FOR ROBBING OUR SHIP OR LET HIM CELEBRATE HIS VICTORY?
LET HIM BE. POOR GUY, HE LOOKS SO HAPPY.
WHAT'S WRONG, CACA?
I'LL MAKE HASH BROWNS OUT OF YOU!

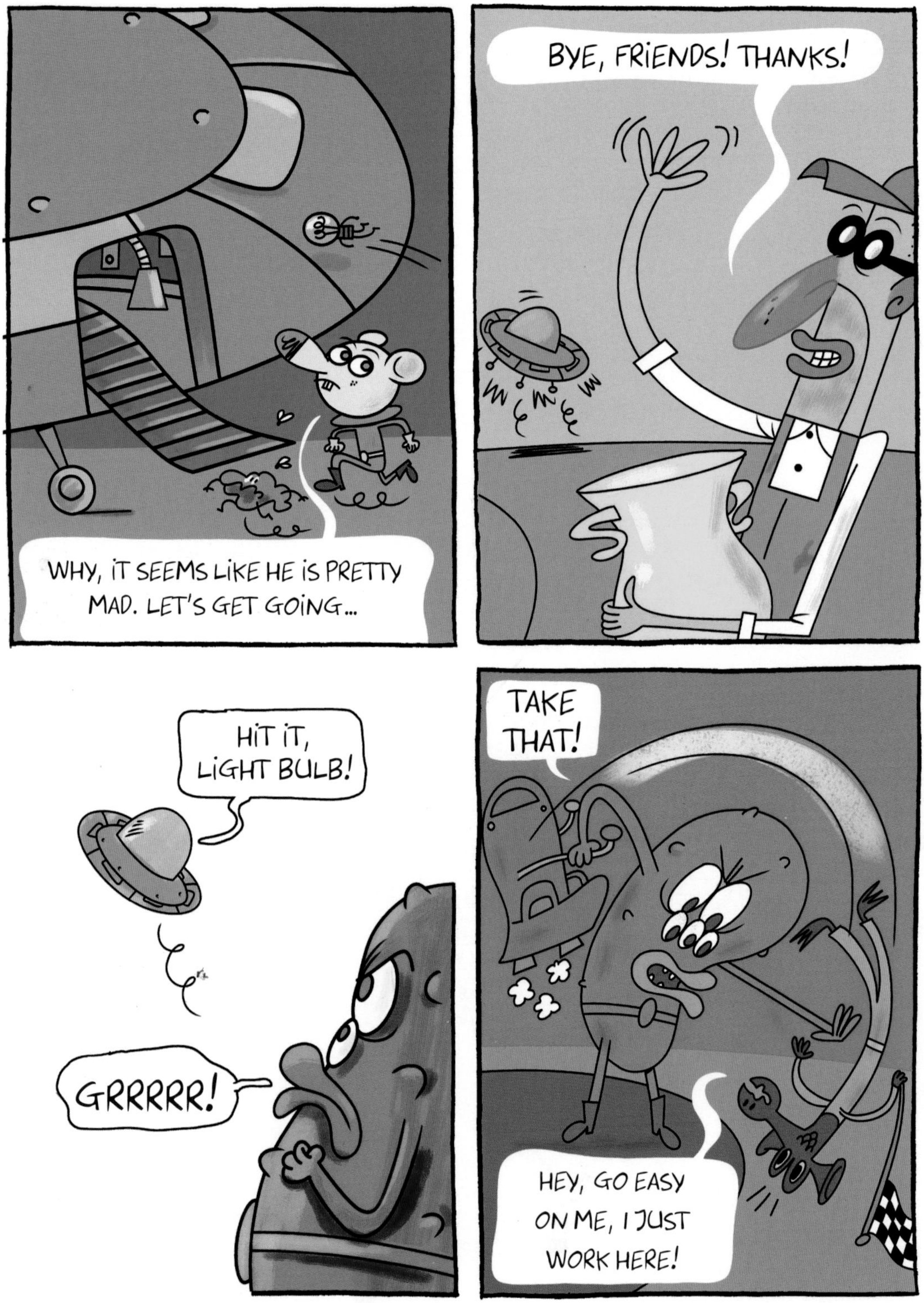
WHY, IT SEEMS LIKE HE IS PRETTY MAD. LET'S GET GOING...
BYE, FRIENDS! THANKS!
HIT IT, LIGHT BULB!
GRRRRR!
TAKE THAT!
HEY, GO EASY ON ME, I JUST WORK HERE!

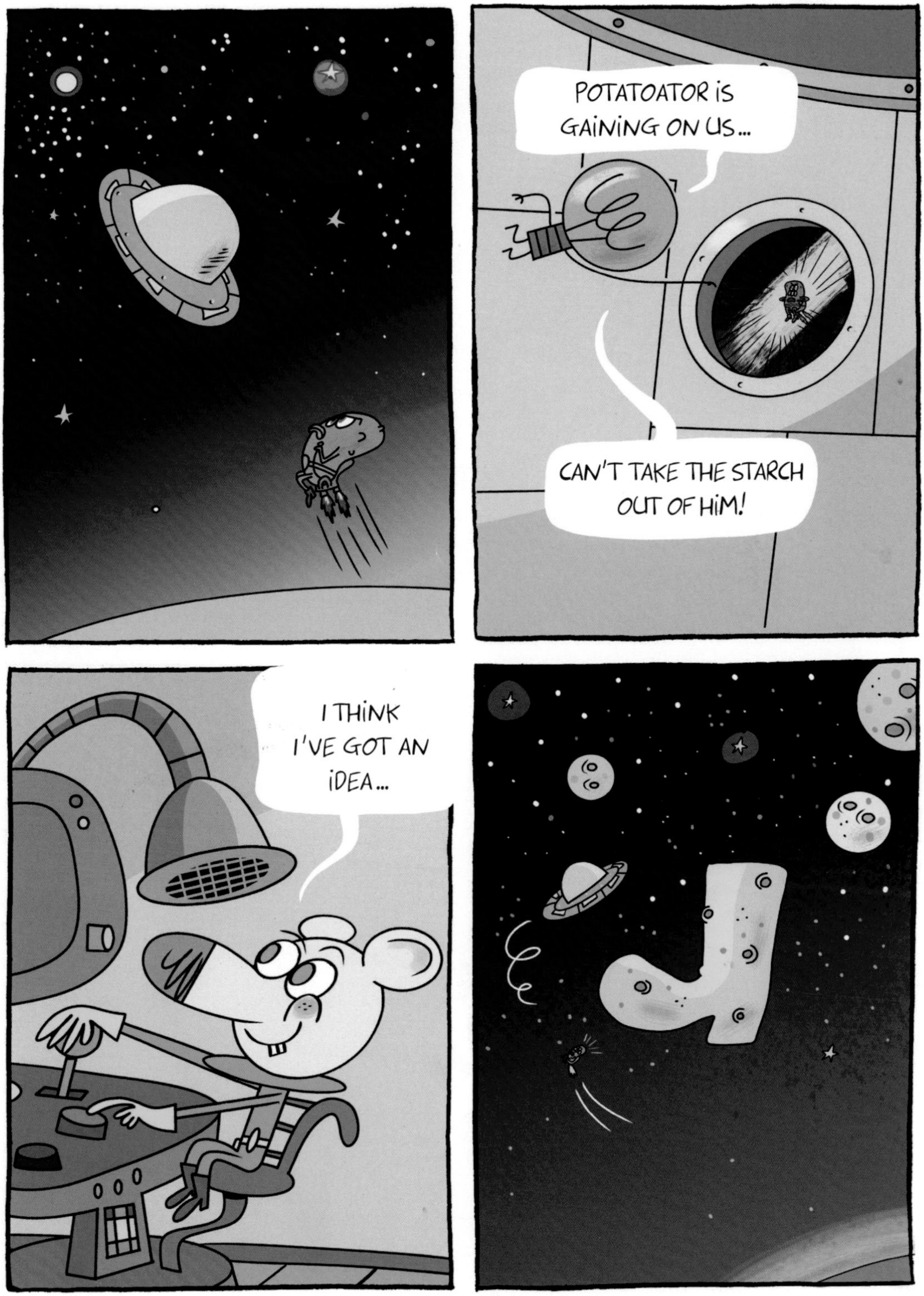
POTATOATOR IS GAINING ON US...
CAN'T TAKE THE STARCH OUT OF HIM!
I THINK I'VE GOT AN IDEA...

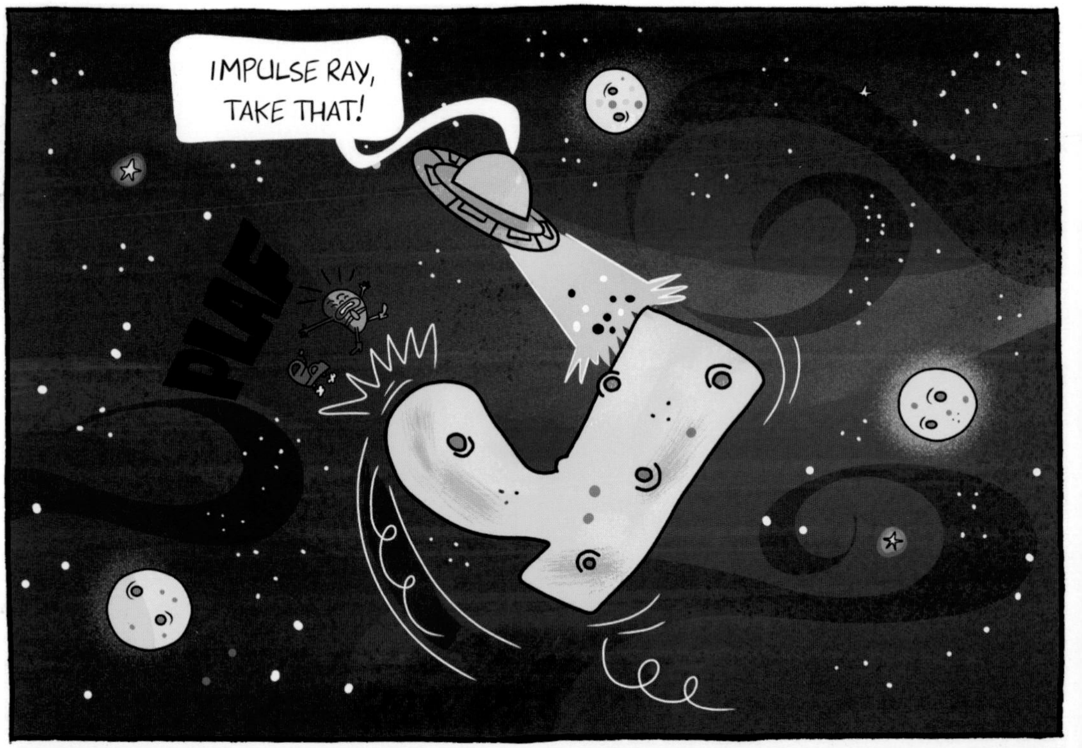
IMPULSE RAY,
TAKE THAT!
PLAF

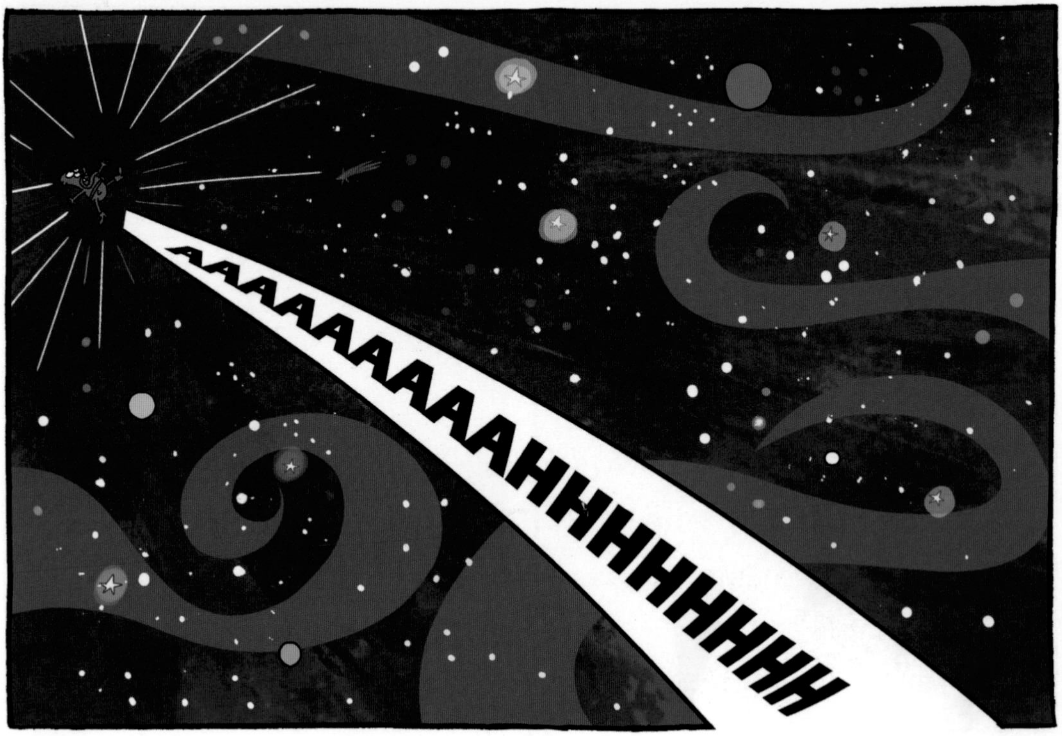
AAAAAAAAAHHHHHHHHHHH

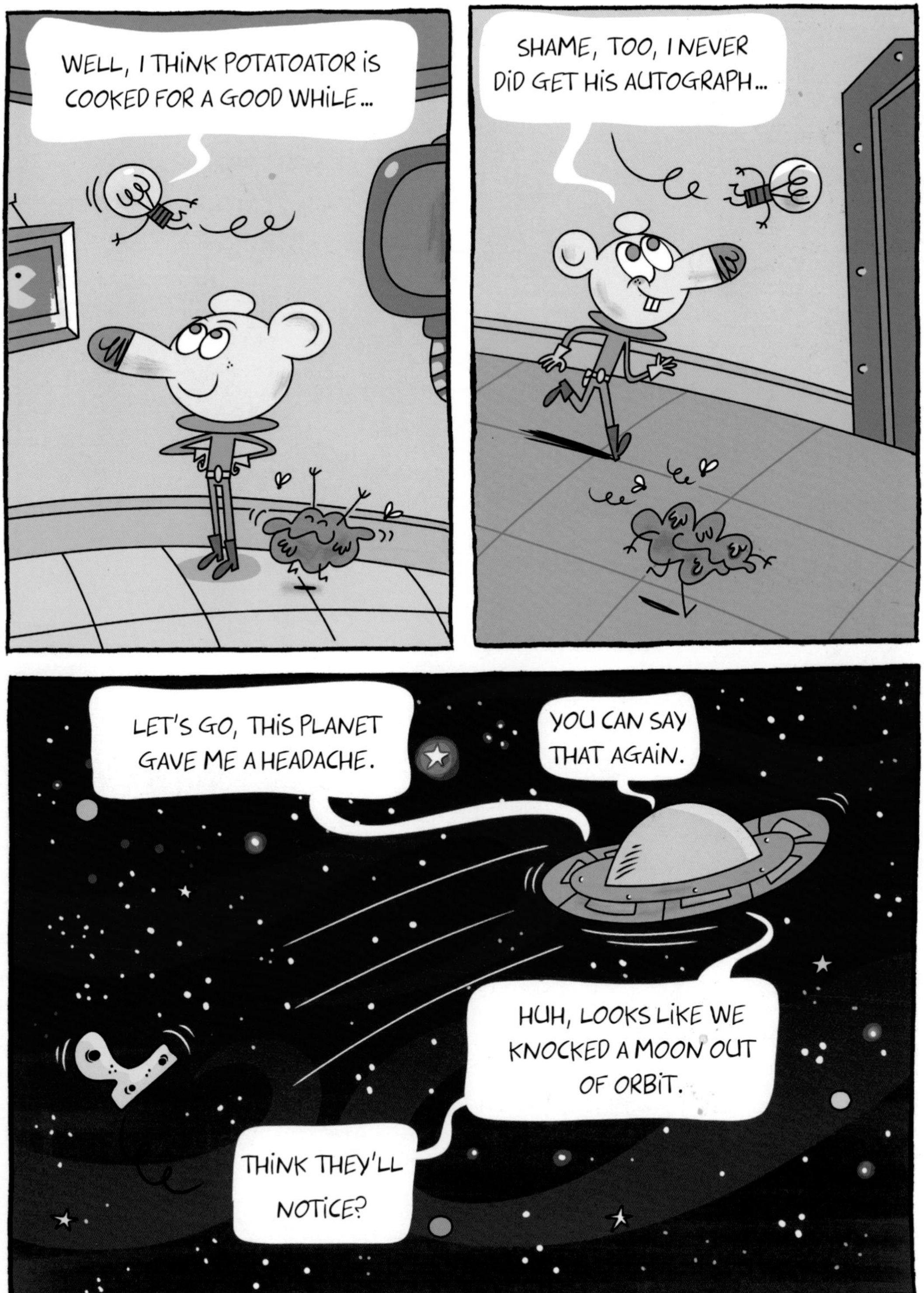
WELL, I THINK POTATOATOR IS COOKED FOR A GOOD WHILE...
SHAME, TOO, I NEVER DID GET HIS AUTOGRAPH...
LET'S GO, THIS PLANET GAVE ME A HEADACHE.
YOU CAN SAY THAT AGAIN.
HUH, LOOKS LIKE WE KNOCKED A MOON OUT OF ORBIT.
THINK THEY'LL NOTICE?

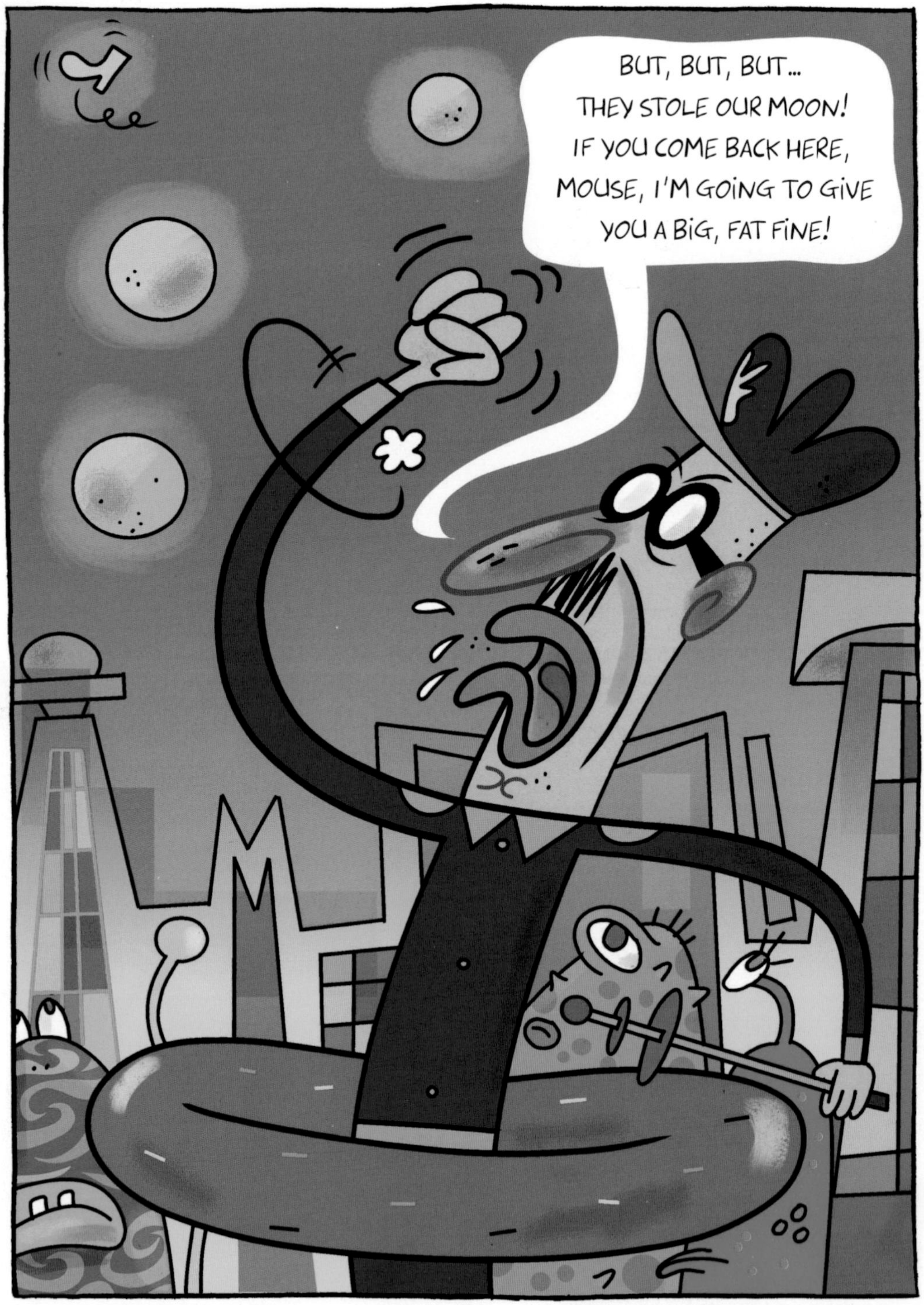
BUT, BUT, BUT...
THEY STOLE OUR MOON!
IF YOU COME BACK HERE,
MOUSE, I'M GOING TO GIVE
YOU A BIG, FAT FINE!

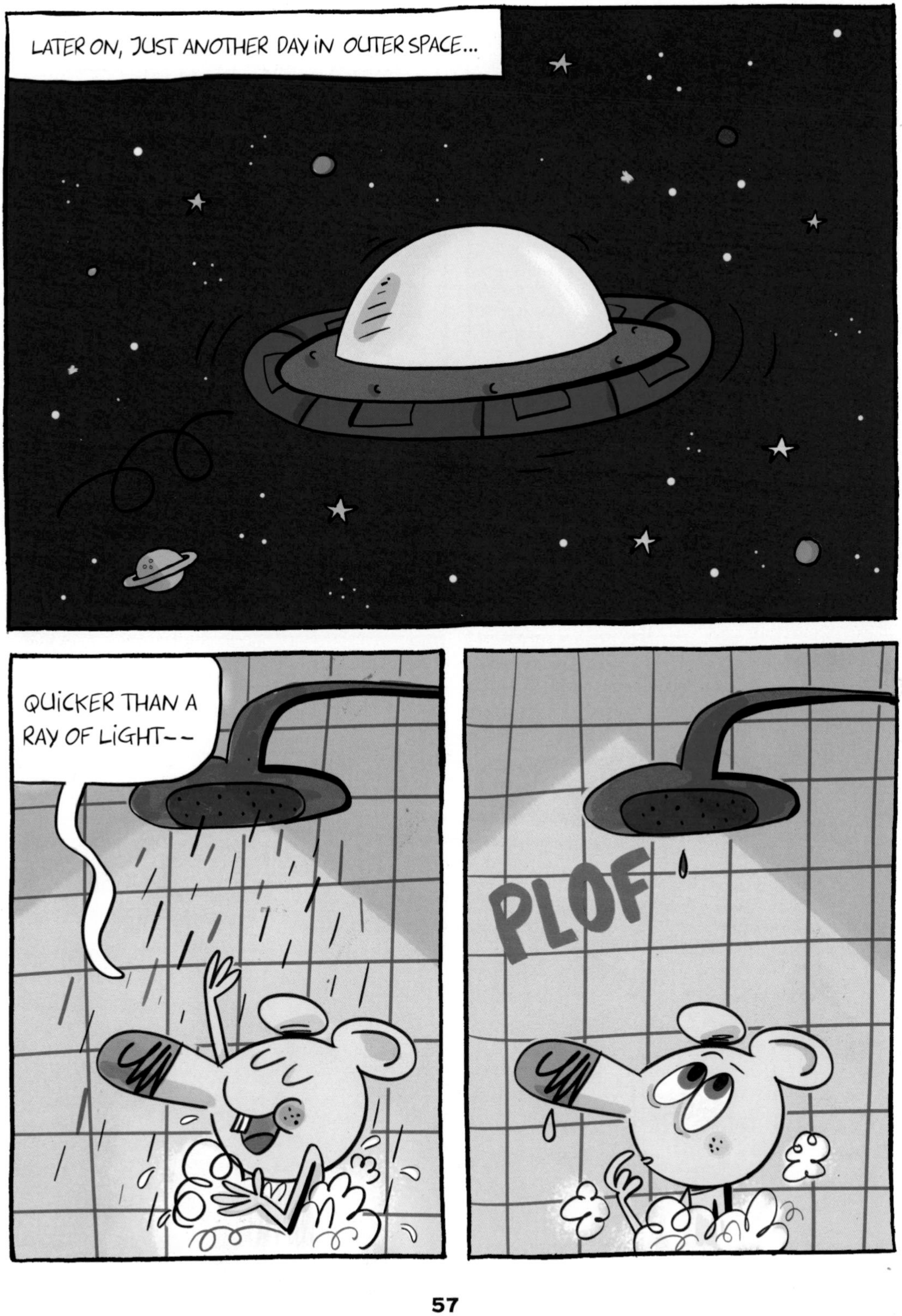
LATER ON, JUST ANOTHER DAY IN OUTER SPACE...
QUICKER THAN A RAY OF LIGHT--
PLOF

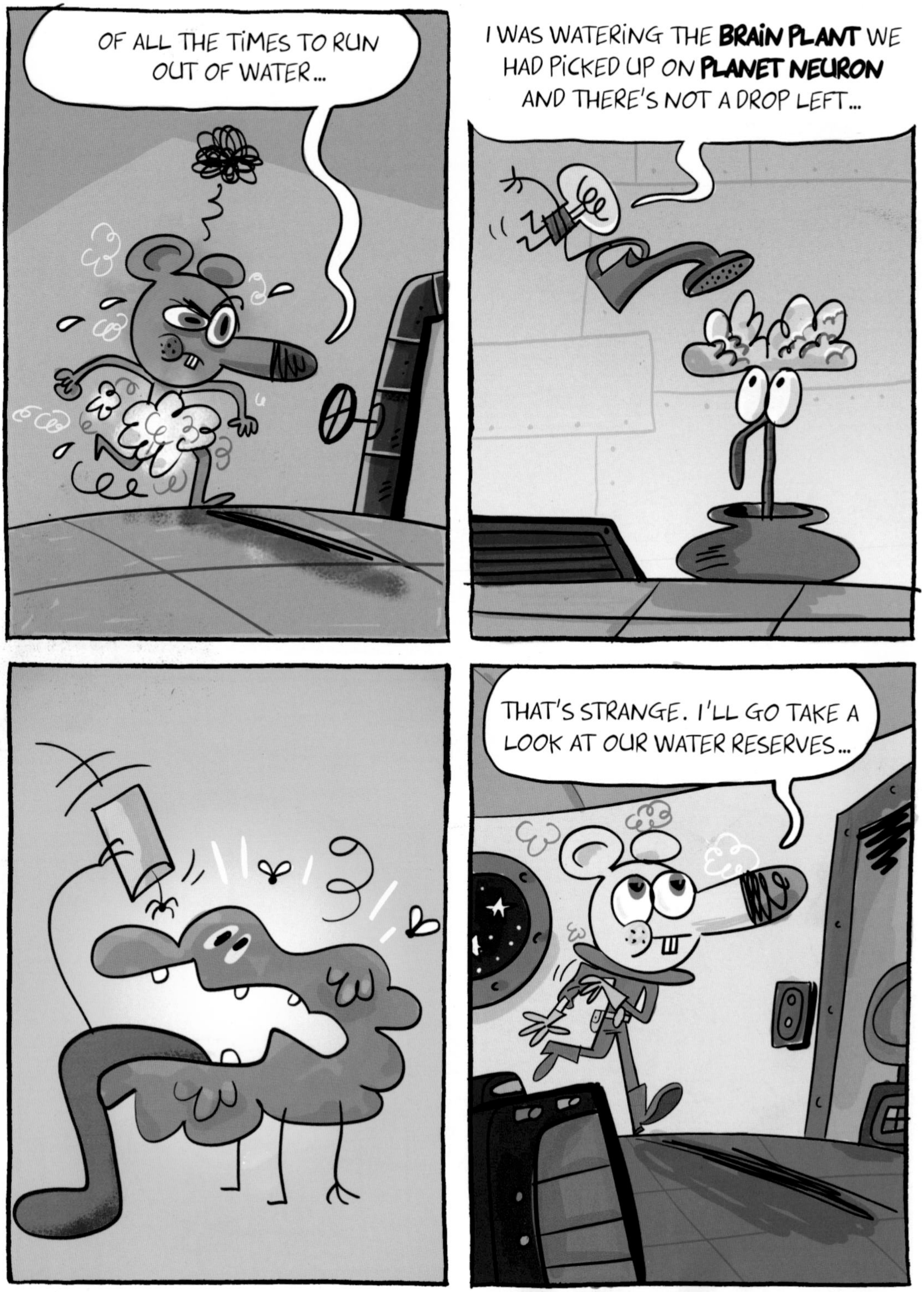
OF ALL THE TIMES TO RUN OUT OF WATER...
I WAS WATERING THE **BRAIN PLANT** WE HAD PICKED UP ON **PLANET NEURON** AND THERE'S NOT A DROP LEFT...
THAT'S STRANGE. I'LL GO TAKE A LOOK AT OUR WATER RESERVES...

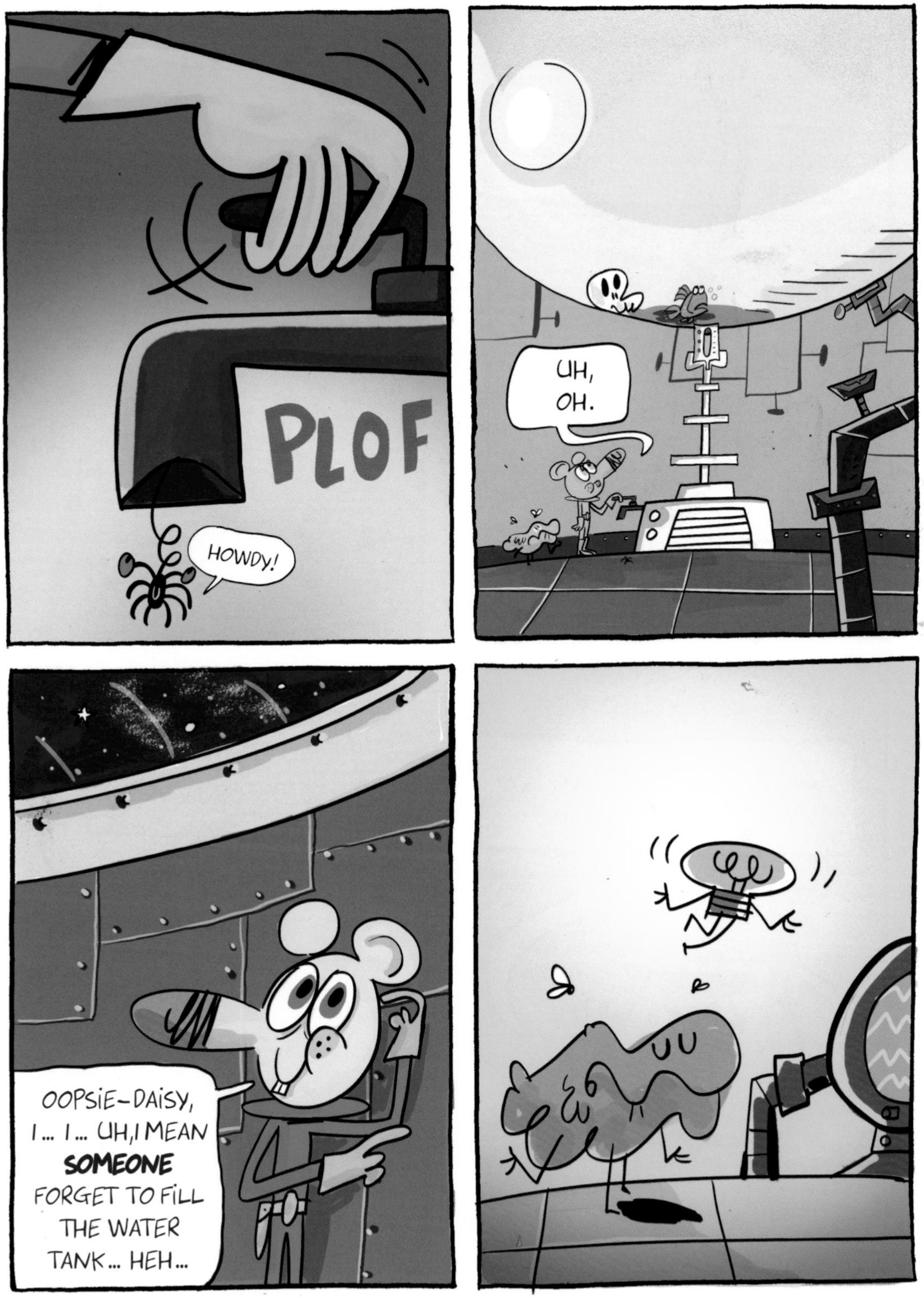
PLOF
HOWDY!
UH, OH.
OOPSIE-DAISY, I... I... UH, I MEAN **SOMEONE** FORGET TO FILL THE WATER TANK... HEH...

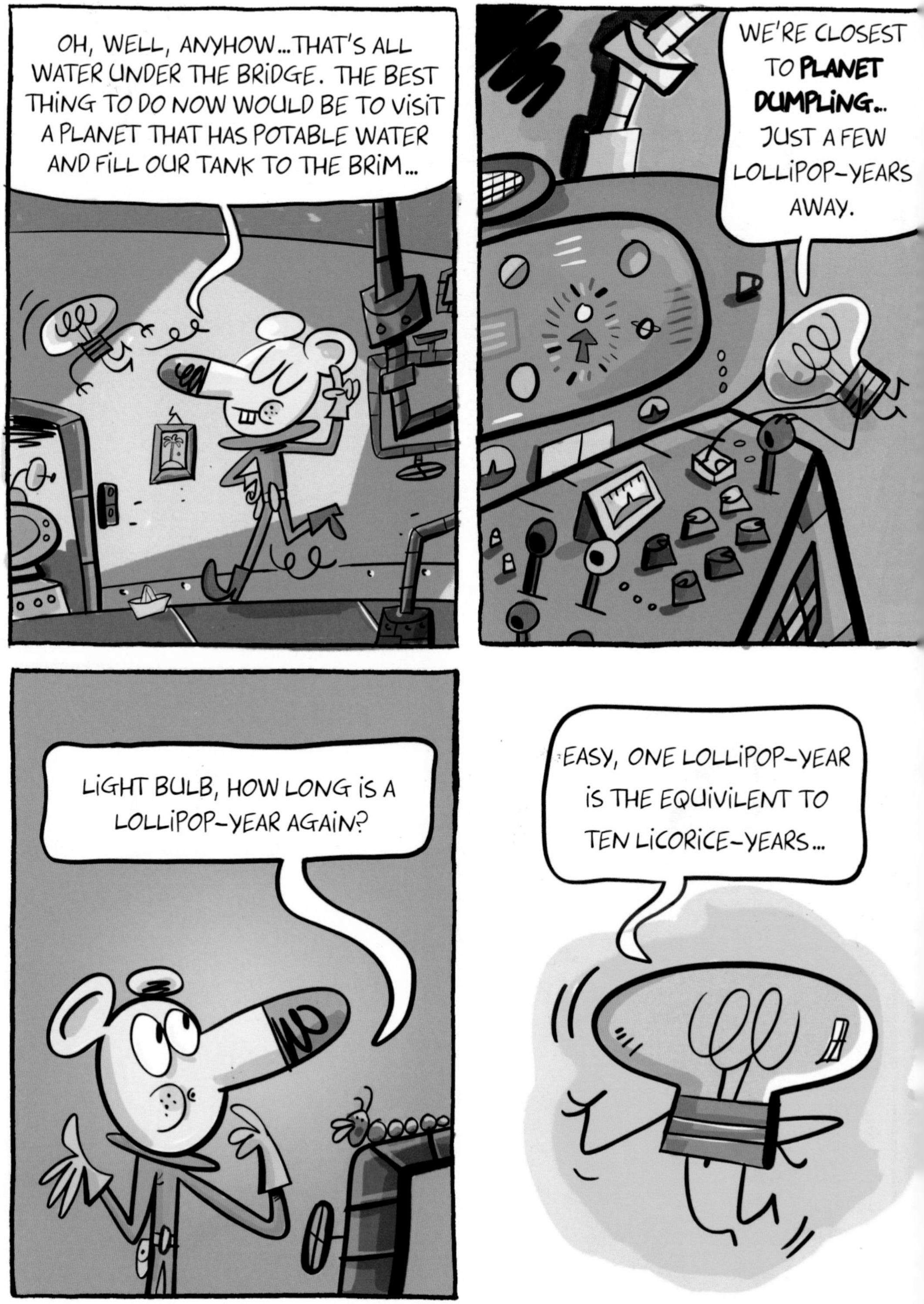
OH, WELL, ANYHOW...THAT'S ALL WATER UNDER THE BRIDGE. THE BEST THING TO DO NOW WOULD BE TO VISIT A PLANET THAT HAS POTABLE WATER AND FILL OUR TANK TO THE BRIM...
WE'RE CLOSEST TO **PLANET DUMPLING**... JUST A FEW LOLLIPOP-YEARS AWAY.
LIGHT BULB, HOW LONG IS A LOLLIPOP-YEAR AGAIN?
EASY, ONE LOLLIPOP-YEAR IS THE EQUIVILENT TO TEN LICORICE-YEARS...

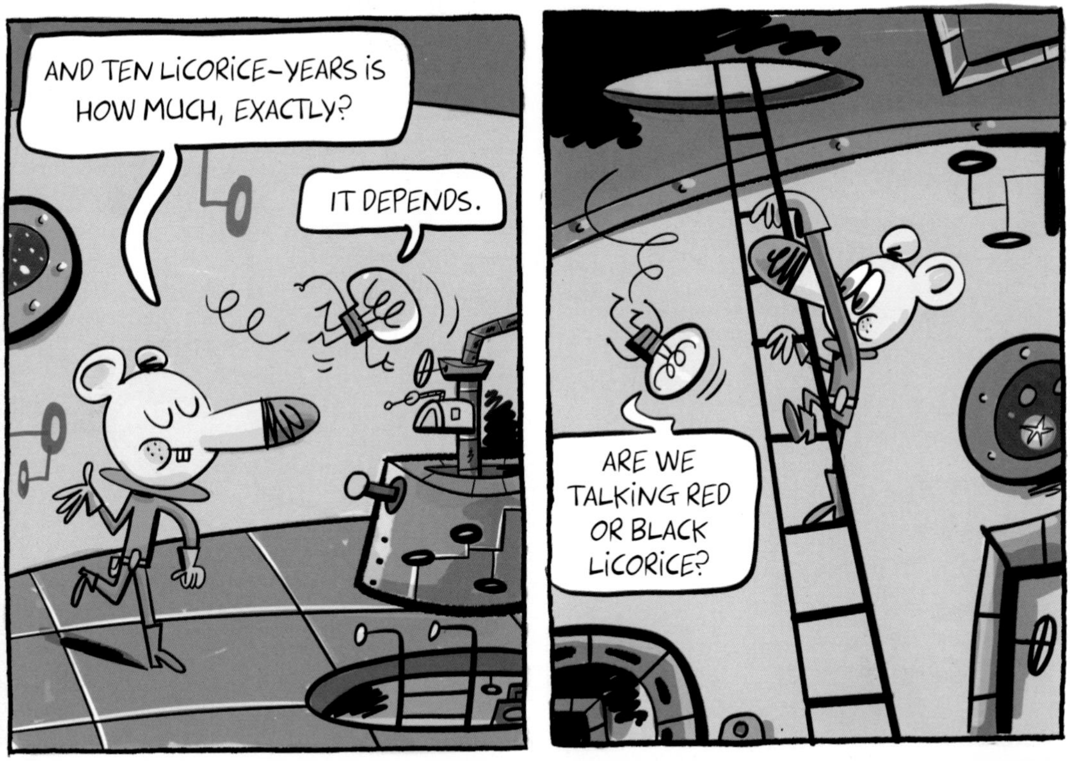
AND TEN LICORICE-YEARS IS HOW MUCH, EXACTLY?
IT DEPENDS.
ARE WE TALKING RED OR BLACK LICORICE?

TWENTY (RED) LICORICE-YEARS LATER...

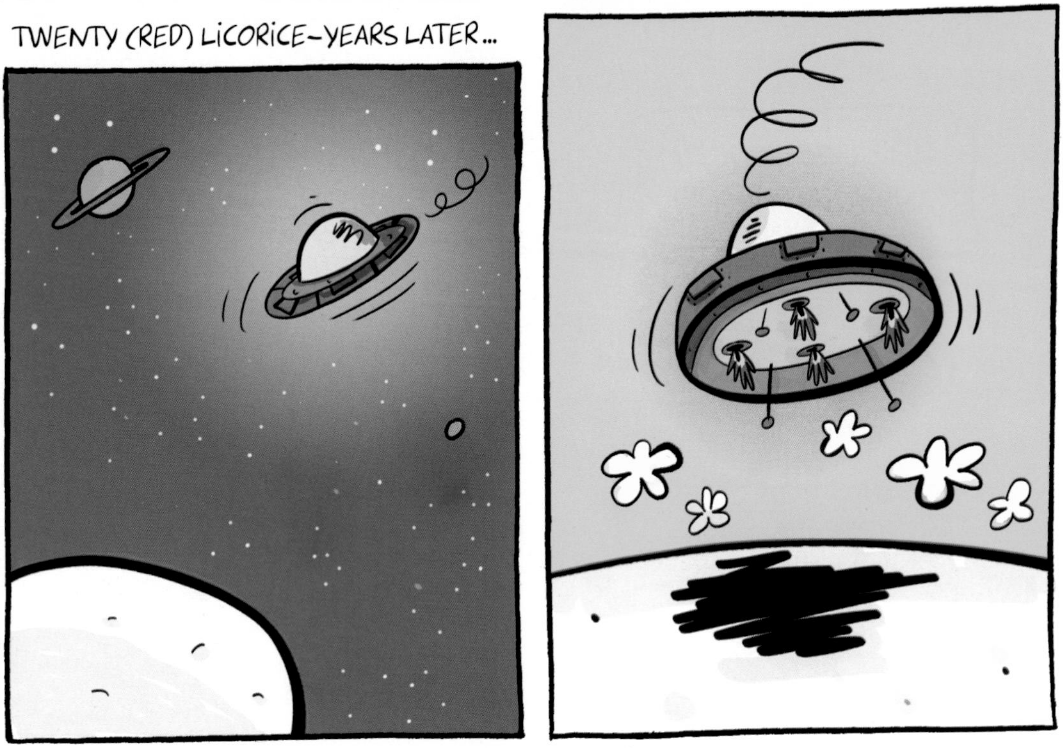

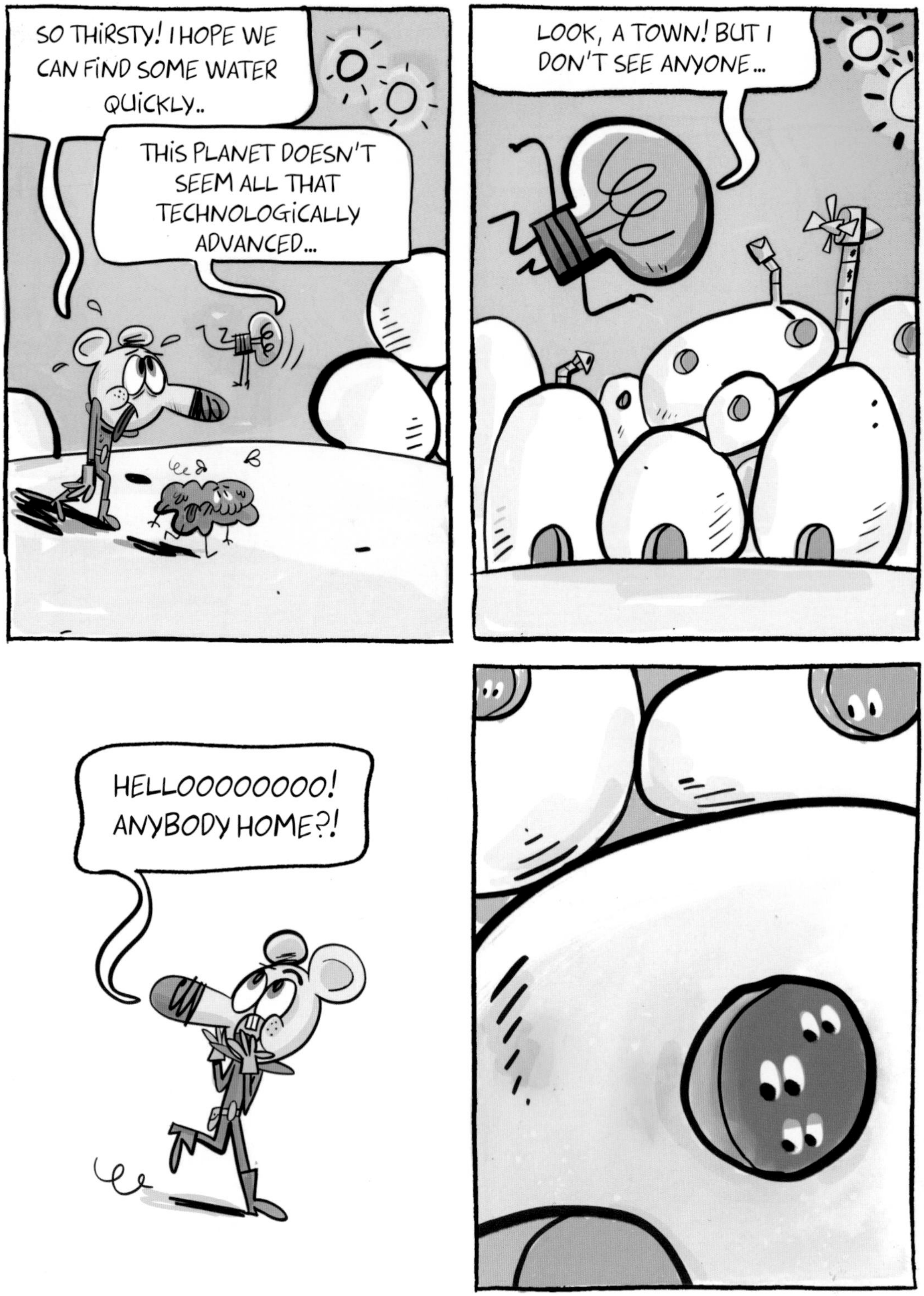
SO THIRSTY! I HOPE WE CAN FIND SOME WATER QUICKLY..
THIS PLANET DOESN'T SEEM ALL THAT TECHNOLOGICALLY ADVANCED...
LOOK, A TOWN! BUT I DON'T SEE ANYONE...
HELLOOOOOOOOO! ANYBODY HOME?!

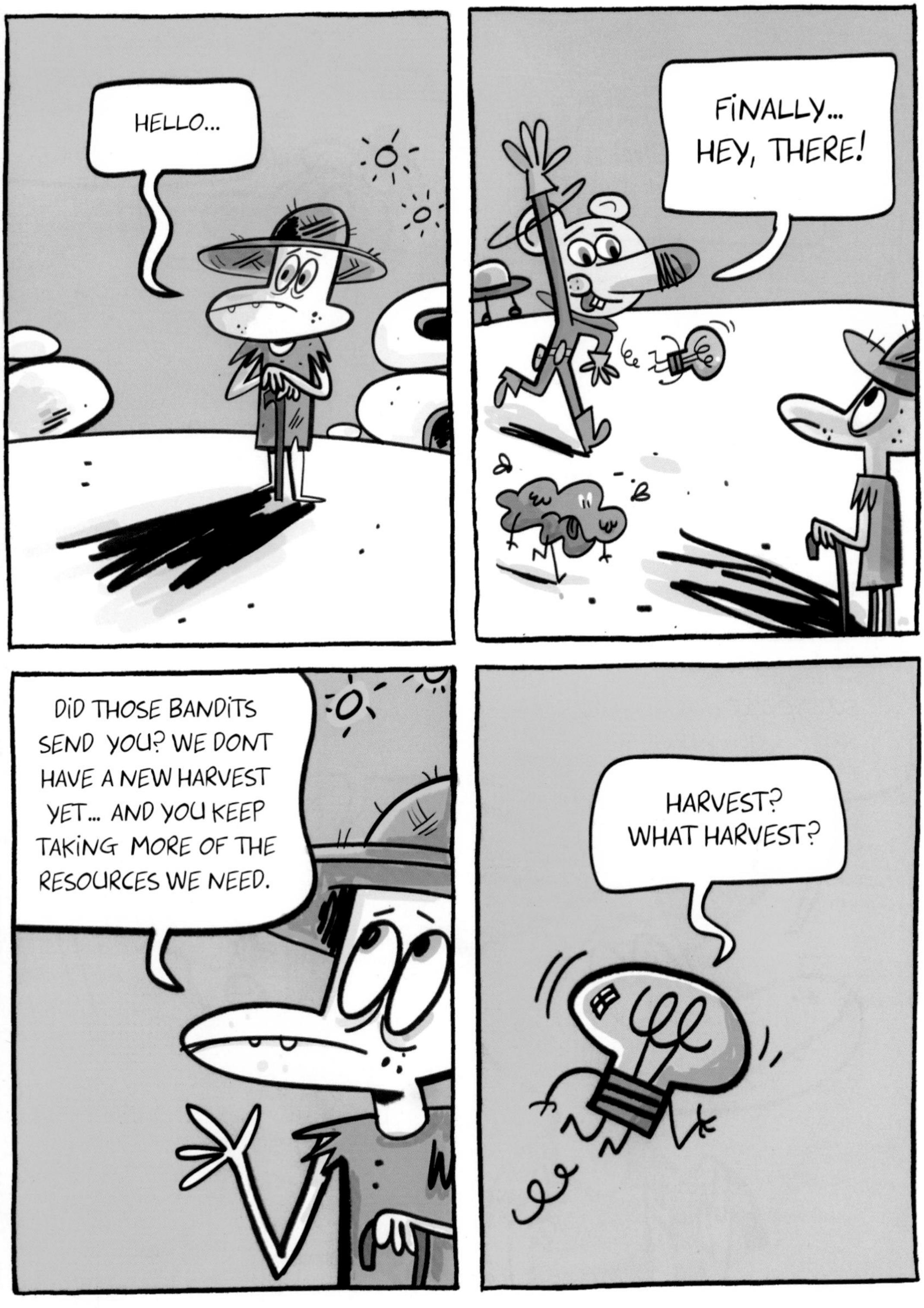
HELLO...
FINALLY... HEY, THERE!
DID THOSE BANDITS SEND YOU? WE DONT HAVE A NEW HARVEST YET... AND YOU KEEP TAKING MORE OF THE RESOURCES WE NEED.
HARVEST? WHAT HARVEST?

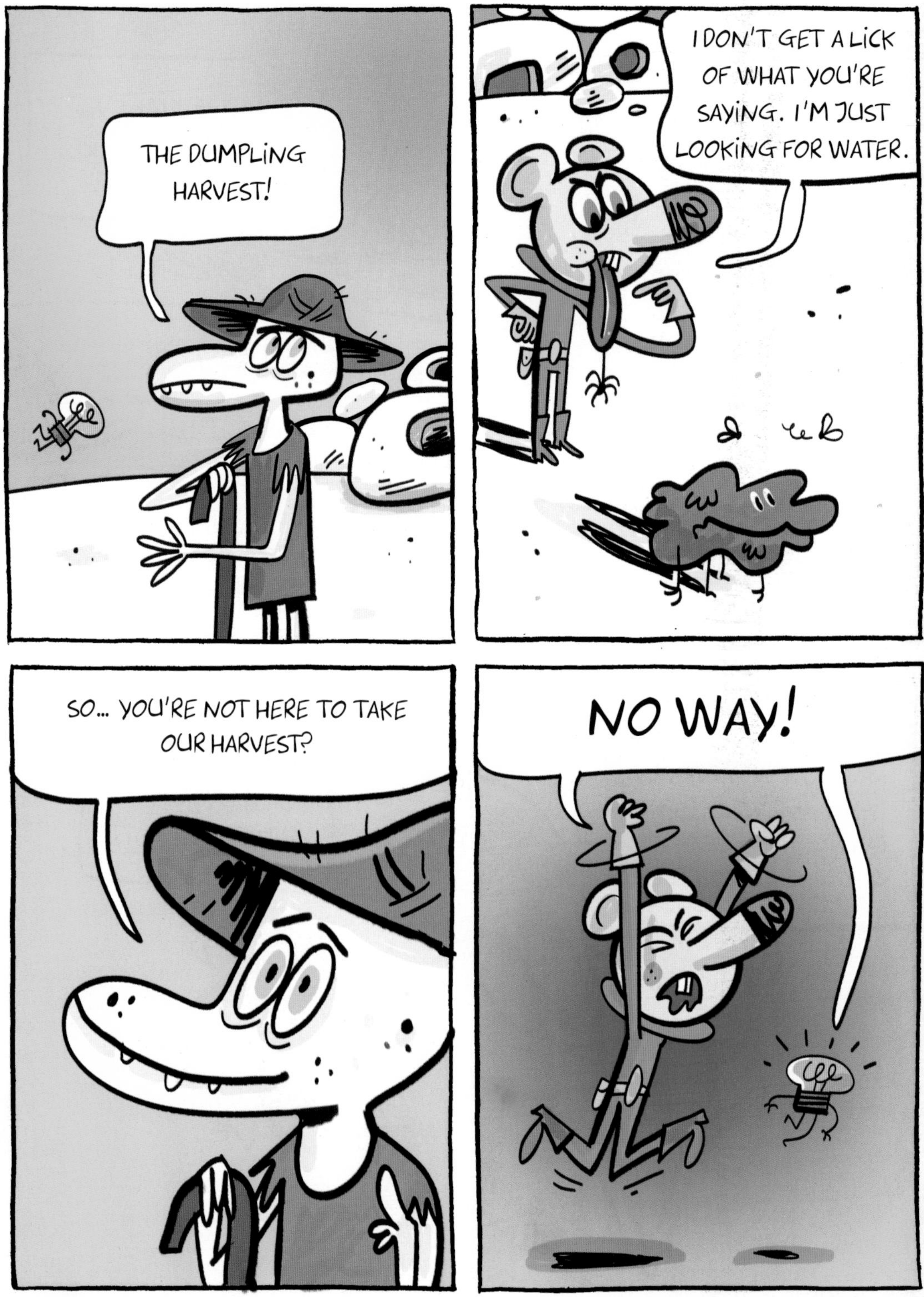
THE DUMPLING HARVEST!
I DON'T GET A LICK OF WHAT YOU'RE SAYING. I'M JUST LOOKING FOR WATER.
SO... YOU'RE NOT HERE TO TAKE OUR HARVEST?
NO WAY!

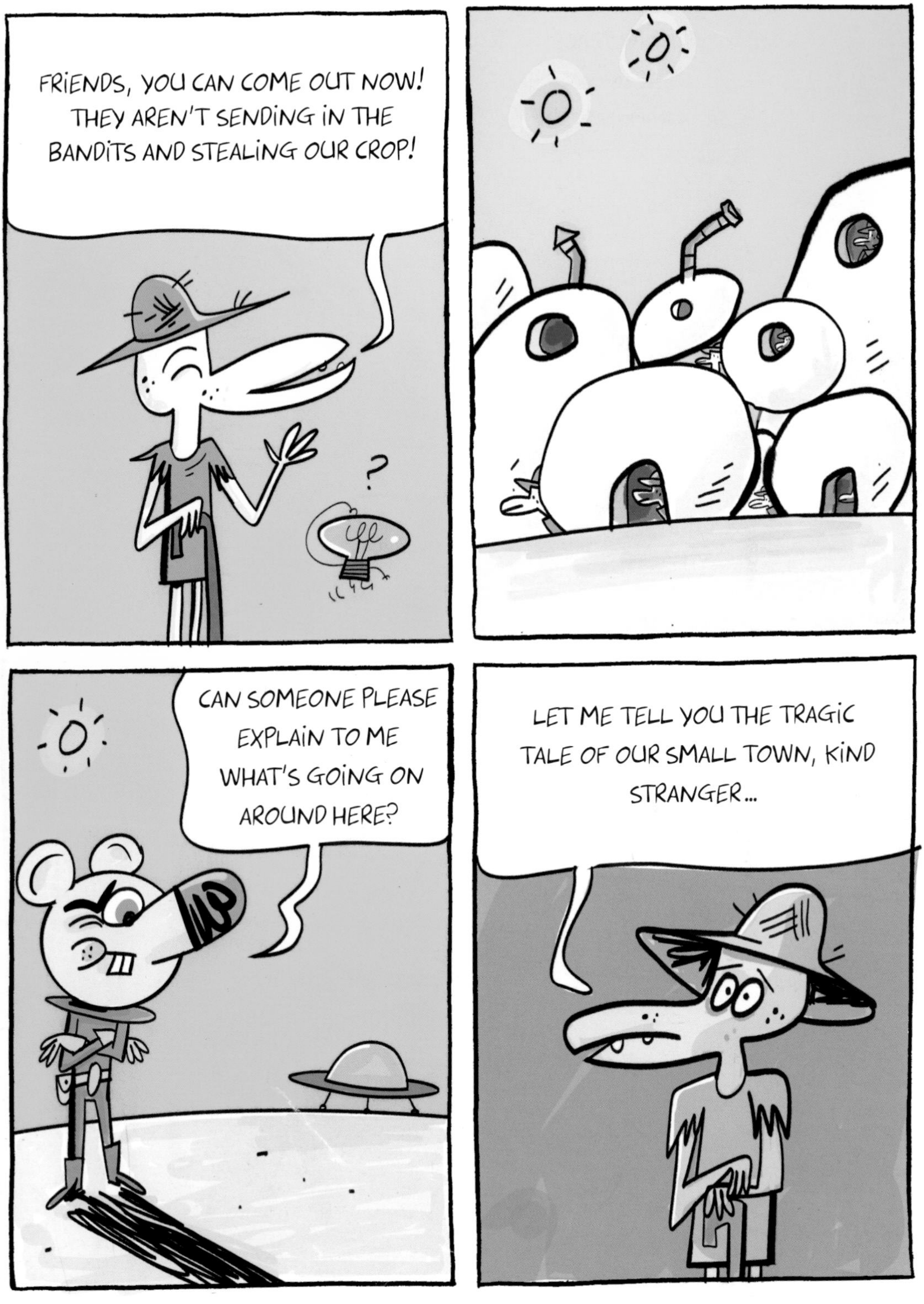
FRIENDS, YOU CAN COME OUT NOW! THEY AREN'T SENDING IN THE BANDITS AND STEALING OUR CROP!
?
CAN SOMEONE PLEASE EXPLAIN TO ME WHAT'S GOING ON AROUND HERE?
LET ME TELL YOU THE TRAGIC TALE OF OUR SMALL TOWN, KIND STRANGER...

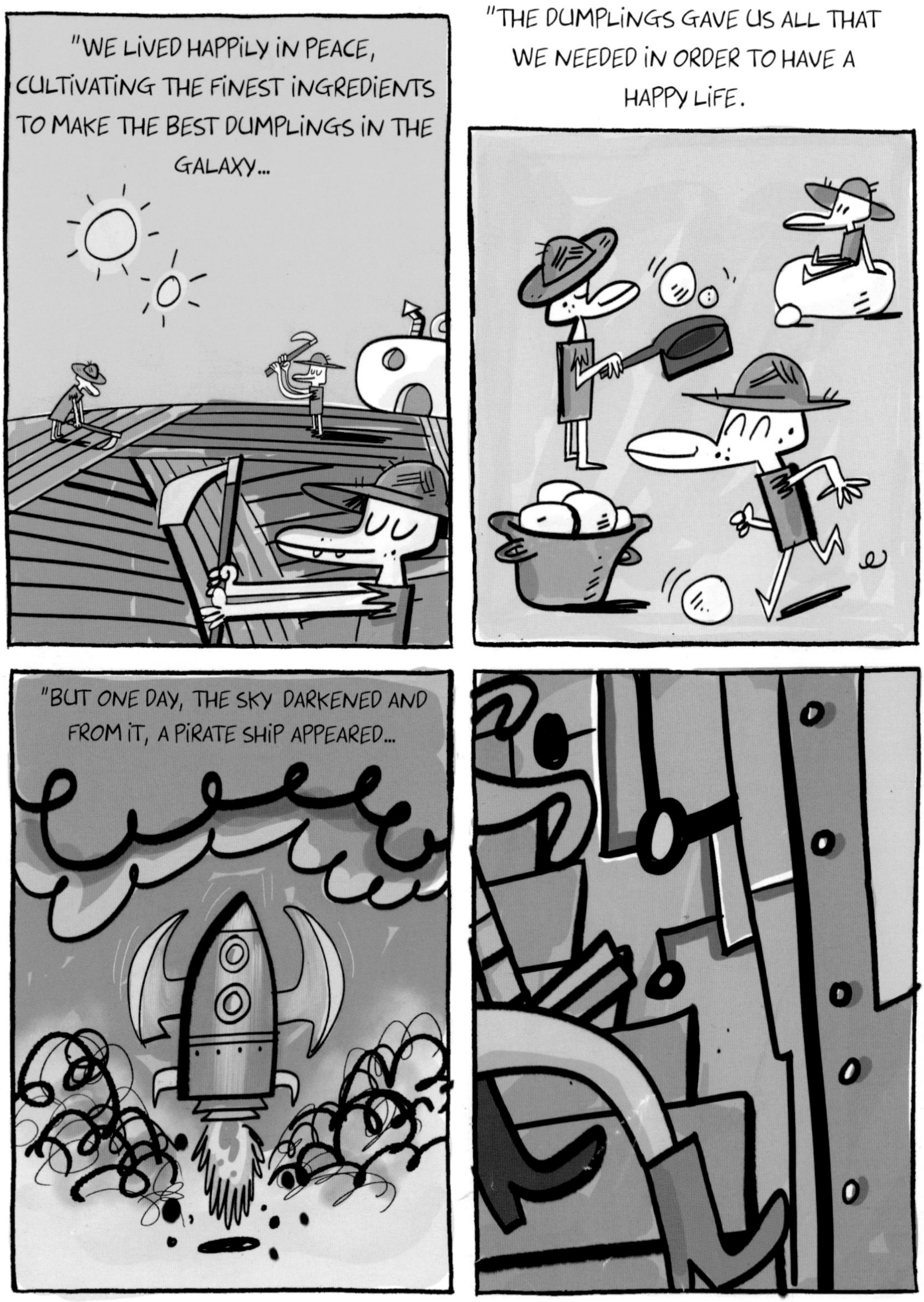
"WE LIVED HAPPILY IN PEACE, CULTIVATING THE FINEST INGREDIENTS TO MAKE THE BEST DUMPLINGS IN THE GALAXY...
"THE DUMPLINGS GAVE US ALL THAT WE NEEDED IN ORDER TO HAVE A HAPPY LIFE.
"BUT ONE DAY, THE SKY DARKENED AND FROM IT, A PIRATE SHIP APPEARED...

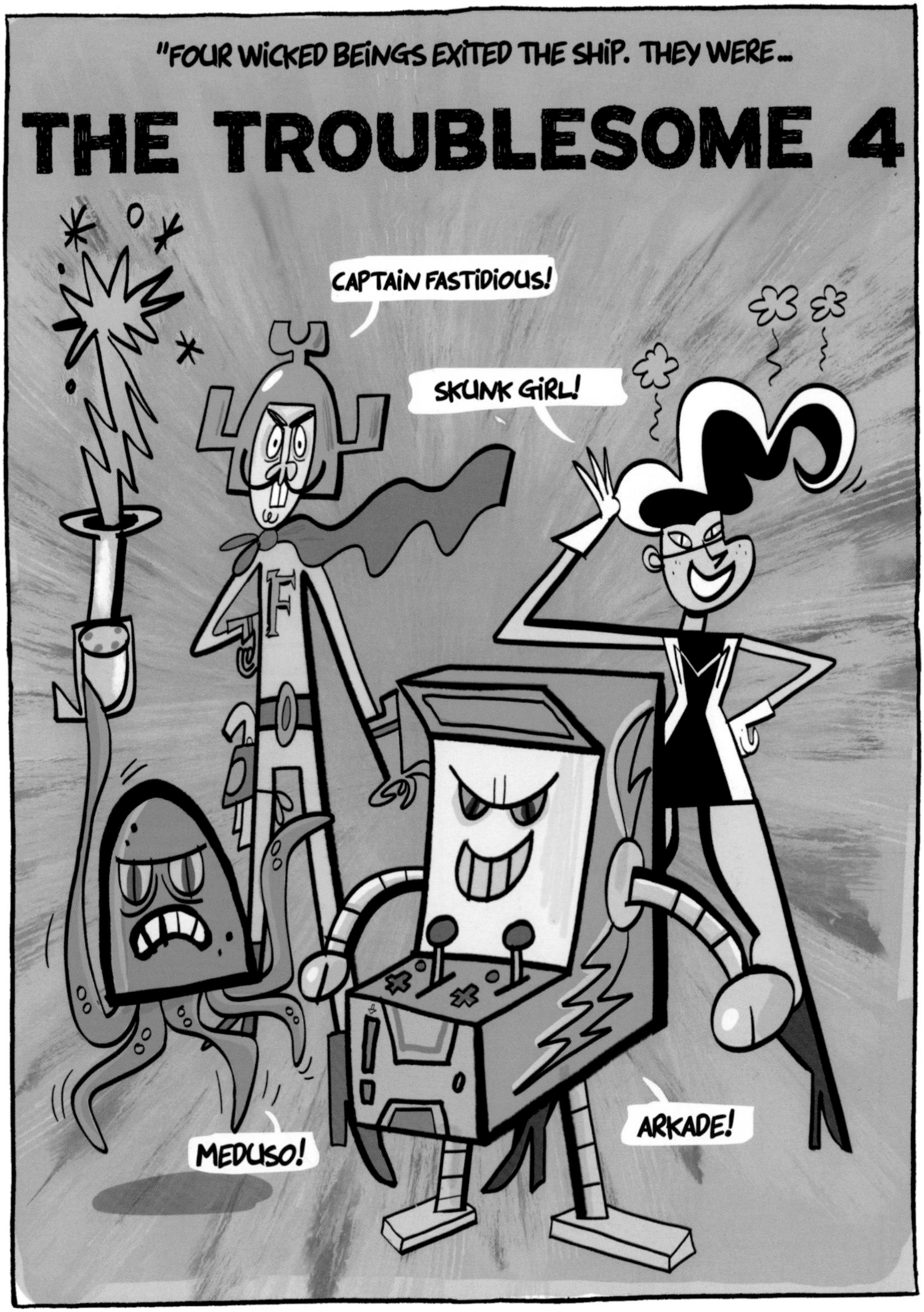
"FOUR WICKED BEINGS EXITED THE SHIP. THEY WERE...
THE TROUBLESOME 4
CAPTAIN FASTIDIOUS!
SKUNK GIRL!
MEDUSO!
ARKADE!

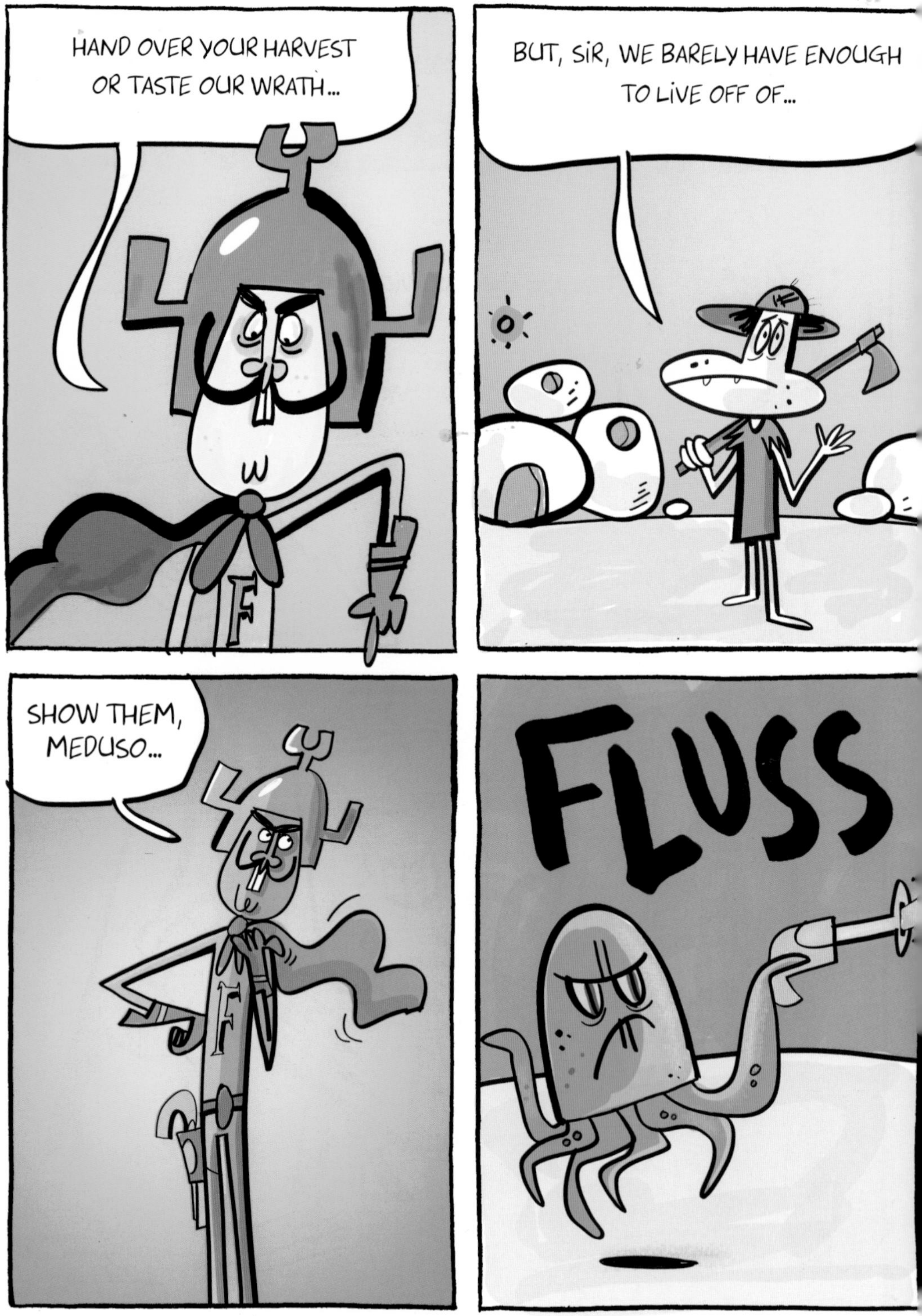
HAND OVER YOUR HARVEST OR TASTE OUR WRATH...
BUT, SIR, WE BARELY HAVE ENOUGH TO LIVE OFF OF...
SHOW THEM, MEDUSO...
FLUSS

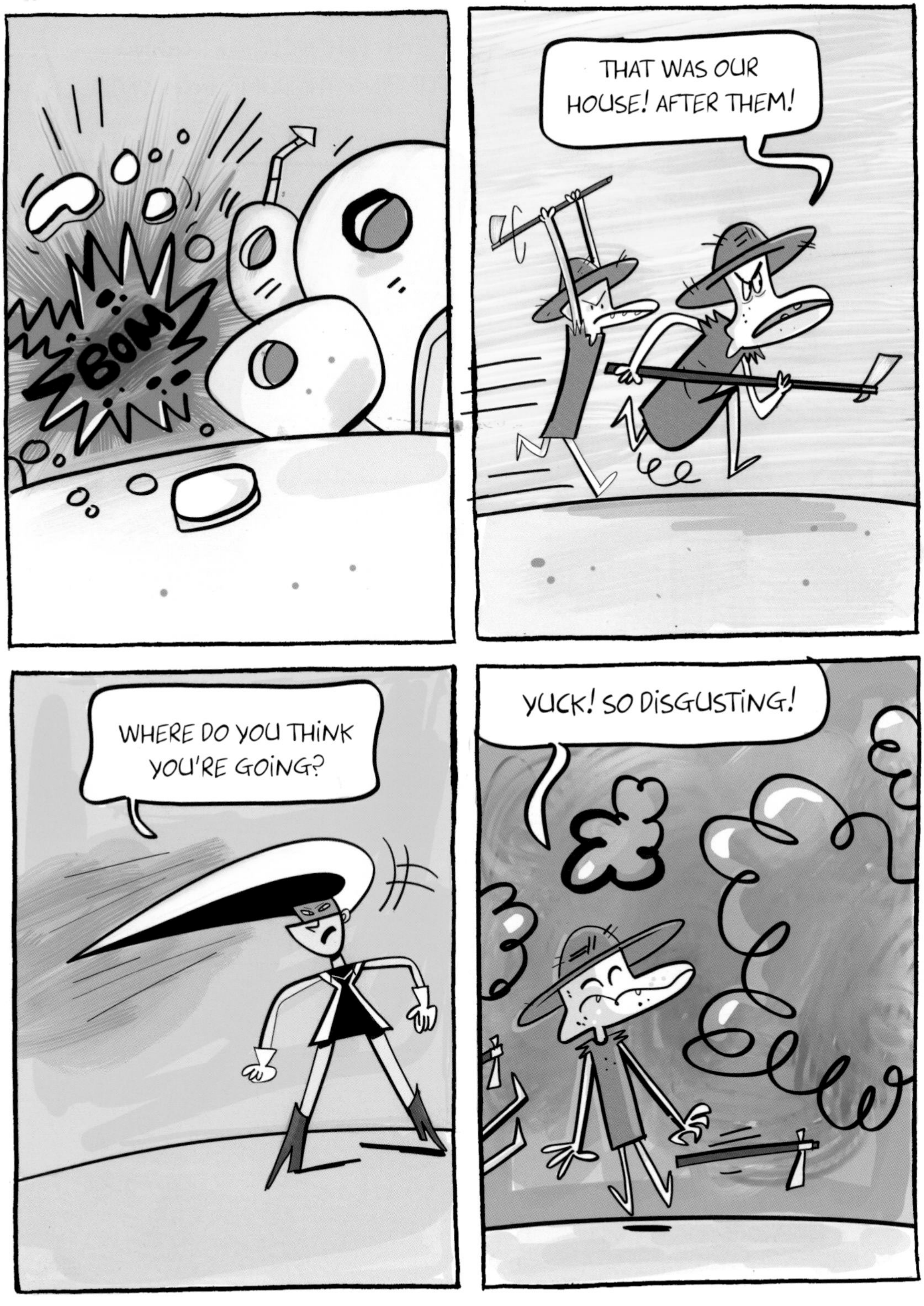
BOM
THAT WAS OUR HOUSE! AFTER THEM!
WHERE DO YOU THINK YOU'RE GOING?
YUCK! SO DISGUSTING!

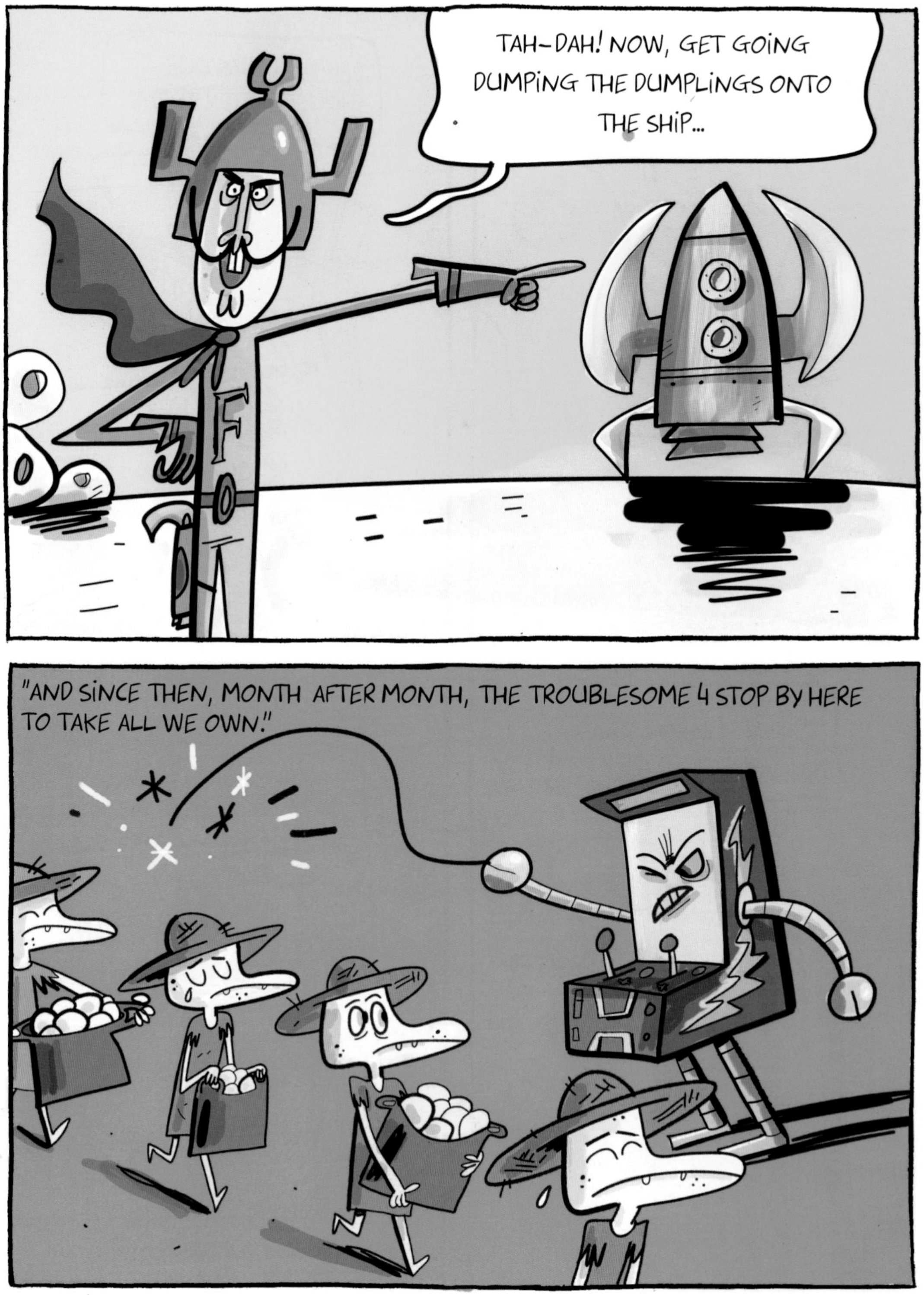
TAH-DAH! NOW, GET GOING DUMPING THE DUMPLINGS ONTO THE SHIP...
"AND SINCE THEN, MONTH AFTER MONTH, THE TROUBLESOME 4 STOP BY HERE TO TAKE ALL WE OWN."

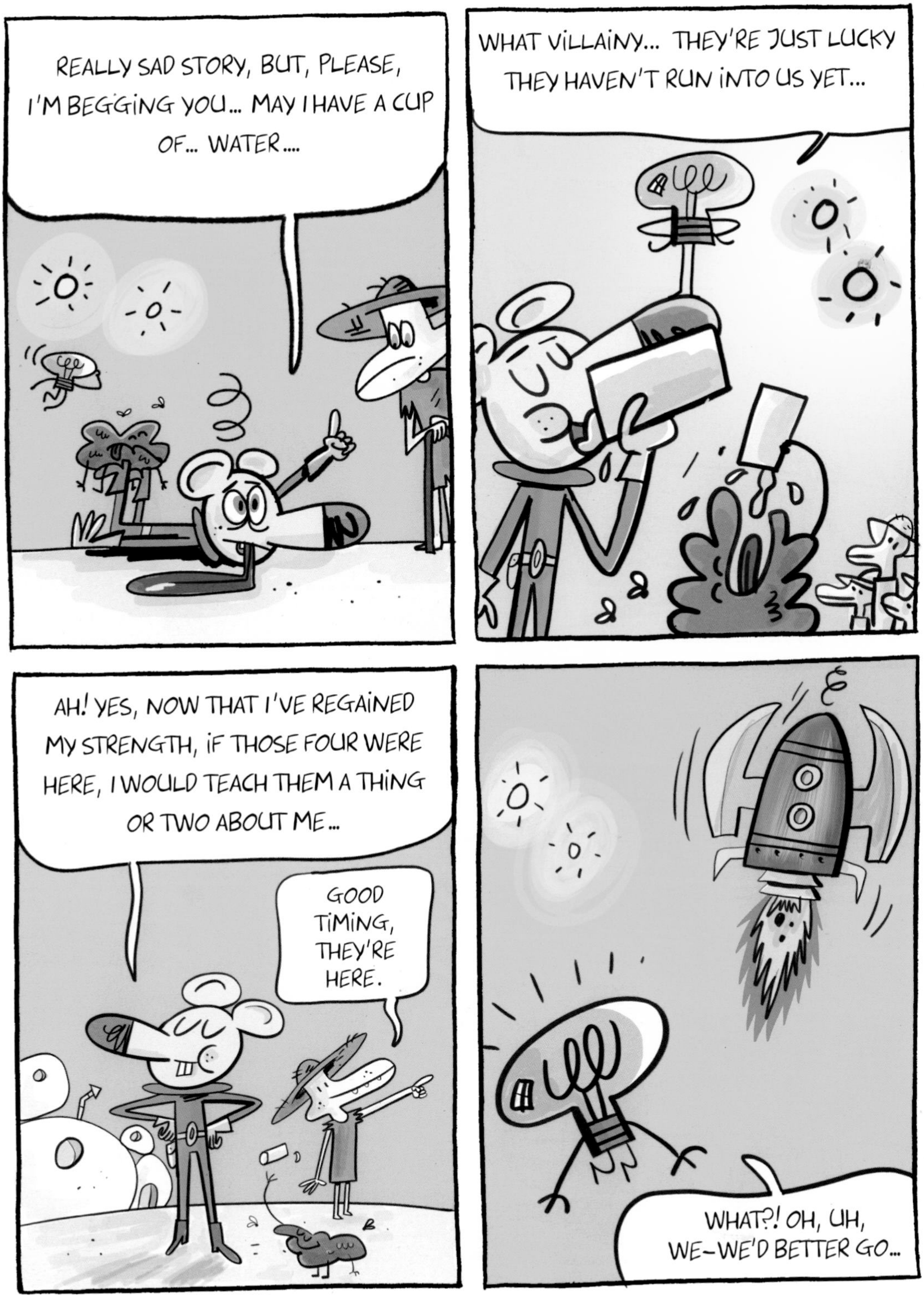
REALLY SAD STORY, BUT, PLEASE, I'M BEGGING YOU... MAY I HAVE A CUP OF... WATER....
WHAT VILLAINY... THEY'RE JUST LUCKY THEY HAVEN'T RUN INTO US YET...
AH! YES, NOW THAT I'VE REGAINED MY STRENGTH, IF THOSE FOUR WERE HERE, I WOULD TEACH THEM A THING OR TWO ABOUT ME...
GOOD TIMING, THEY'RE HERE.
WHAT?! OH, UH, WE-WE'D BETTER GO...

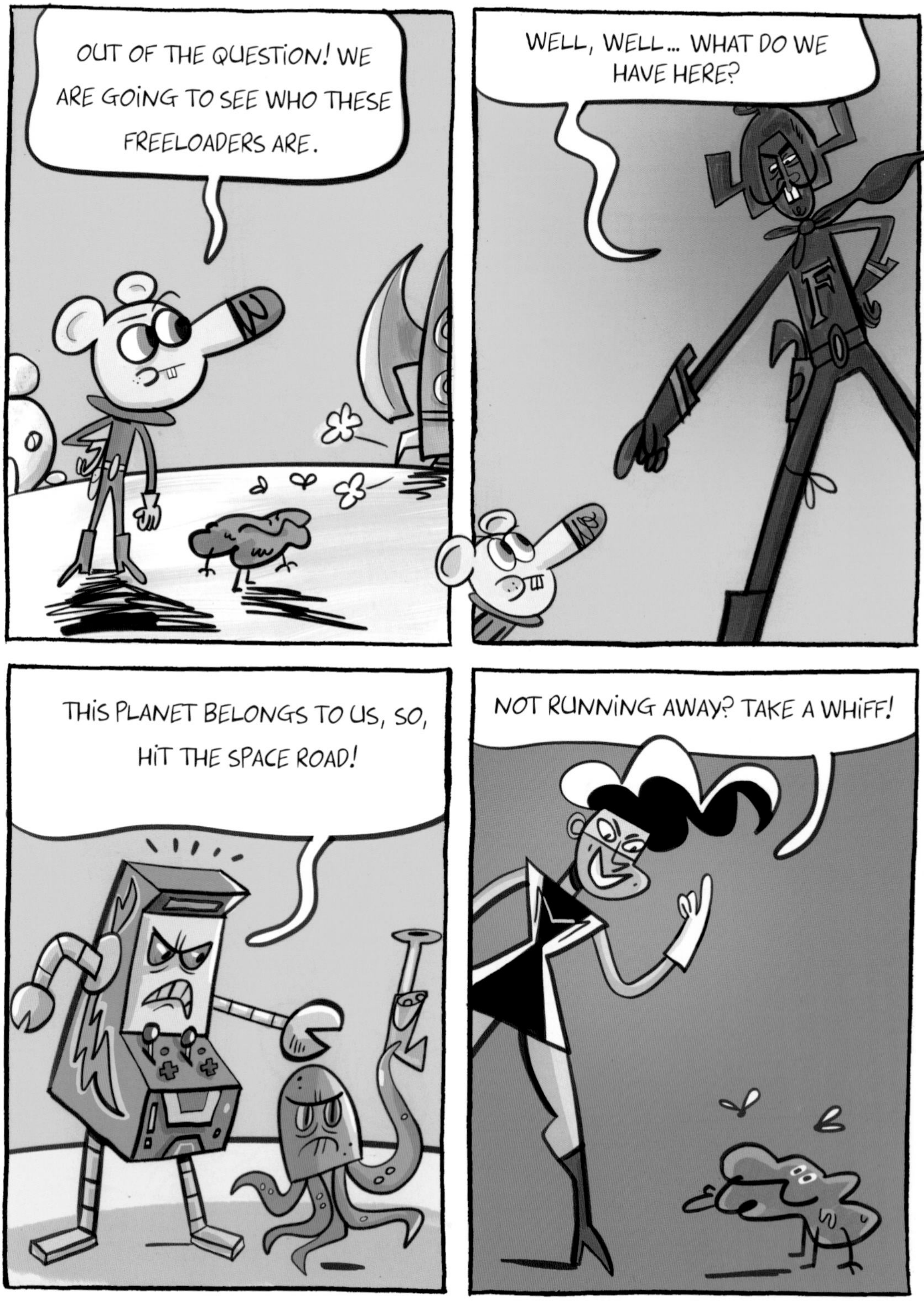
OUT OF THE QUESTION! WE ARE GOING TO SEE WHO THESE FREELOADERS ARE.
WELL, WELL... WHAT DO WE HAVE HERE?
THIS PLANET BELONGS TO US, SO, HIT THE SPACE ROAD!
NOT RUNNING AWAY? TAKE A WHIFF!

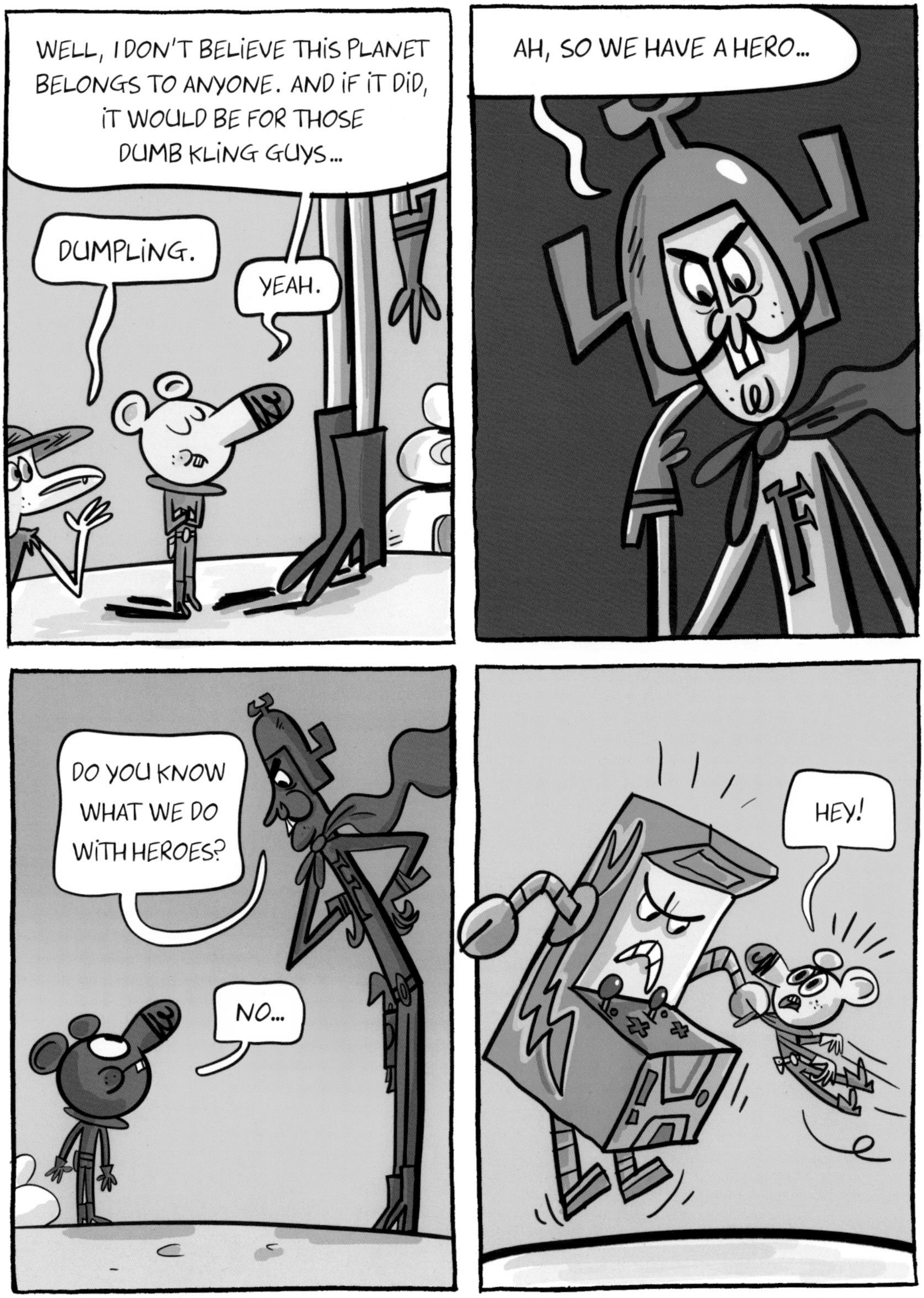
WELL, I DON'T BELIEVE THIS PLANET BELONGS TO ANYONE. AND IF IT DID, IT WOULD BE FOR THOSE DUMB KLING GUYS...
DUMPLING.
YEAH.
AH, SO WE HAVE A HERO...
DO YOU KNOW WHAT WE DO WITH HEROES?
NO...
HEY!

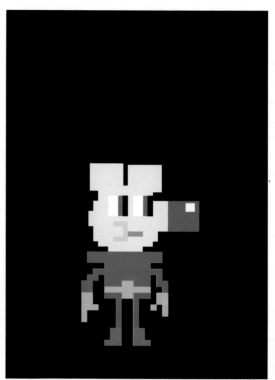

Light Bulb, help!

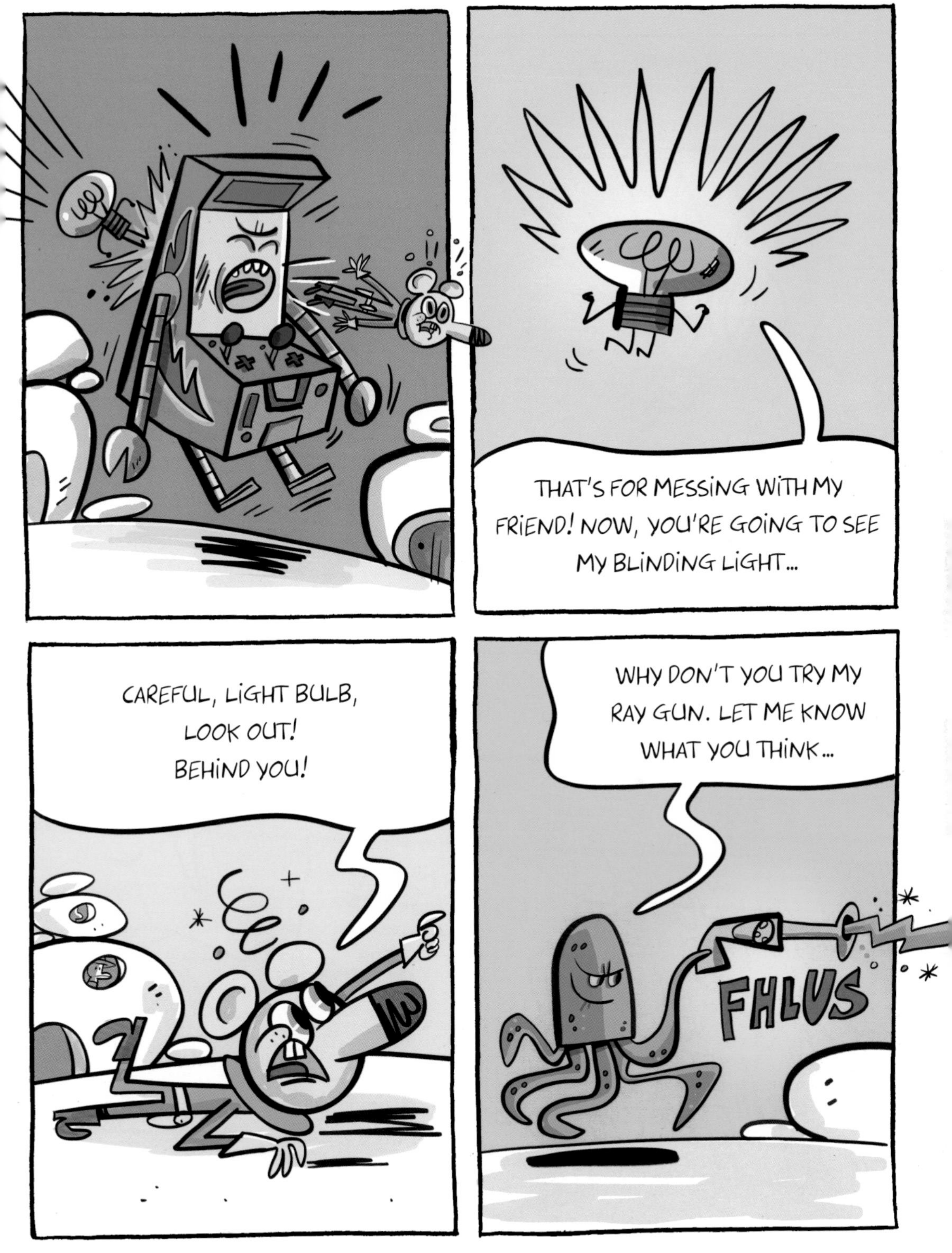
THAT'S FOR MESSING WITH MY FRIEND! NOW, YOU'RE GOING TO SEE MY BLINDING LIGHT...
CAREFUL, LIGHT BULB, LOOK OUT! BEHIND YOU!
WHY DON'T YOU TRY MY RAY GUN. LET ME KNOW WHAT YOU THINK...
FHLUS

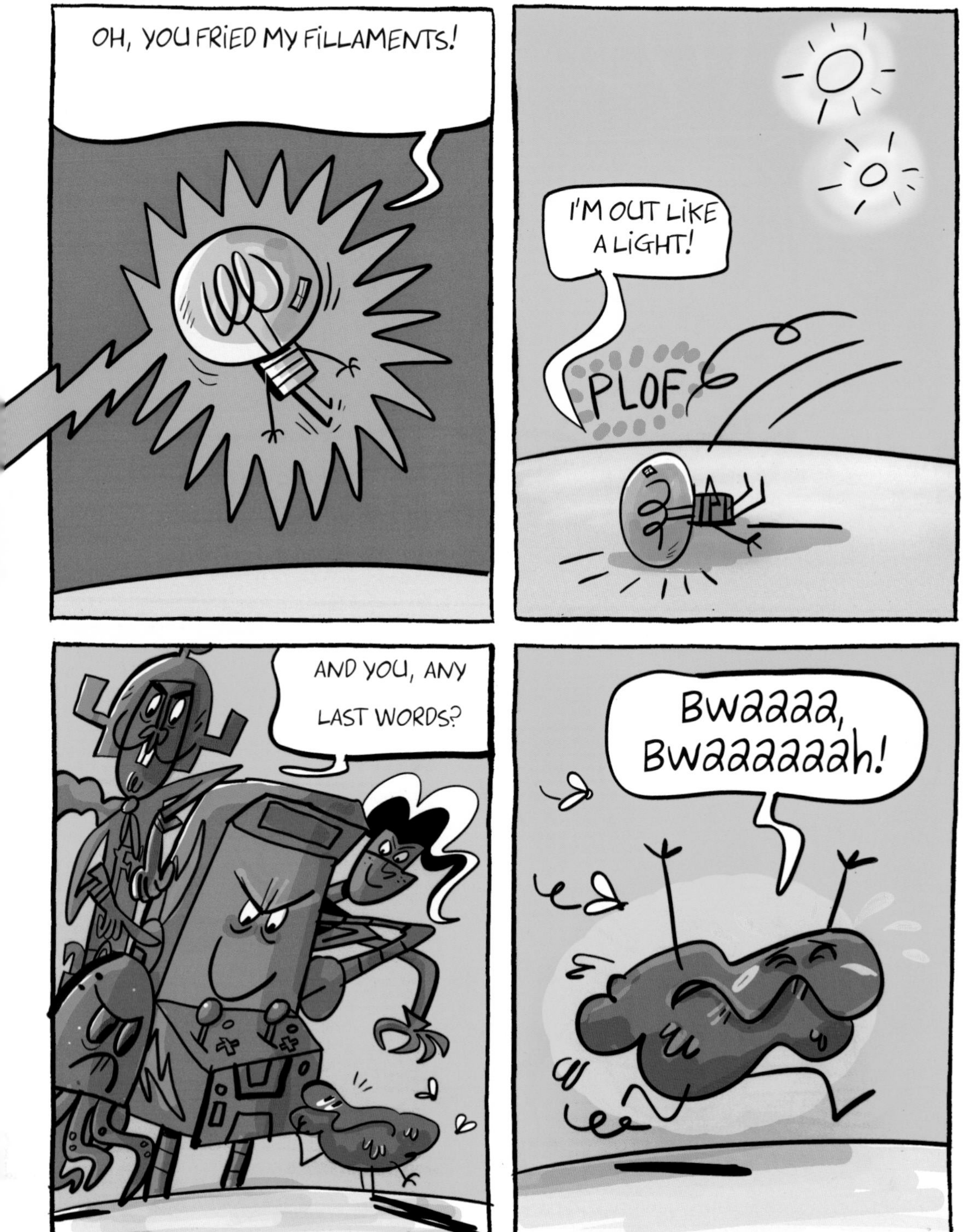
OH, YOU FRIED MY FILLAMENTS!
I'M OUT LIKE A LIGHT!
PLOF
AND YOU, ANY LAST WORDS?
Bwaaaa, Bwaaaaaaah!

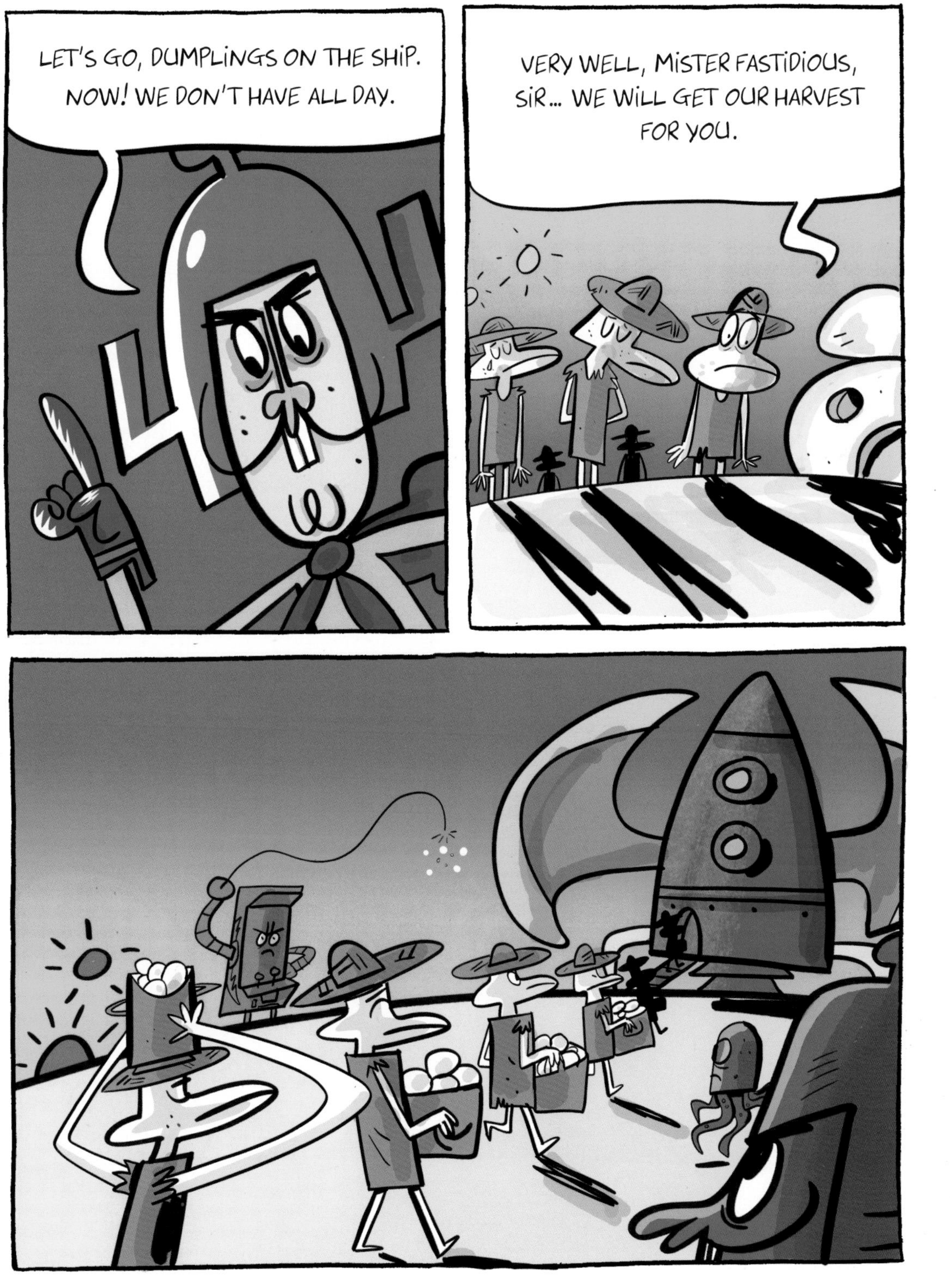
LET'S GO, DUMPLINGS ON THE SHIP. NOW! WE DON'T HAVE ALL DAY.
VERY WELL, MISTER FASTIDIOUS, SIR... WE WILL GET OUR HARVEST FOR YOU.

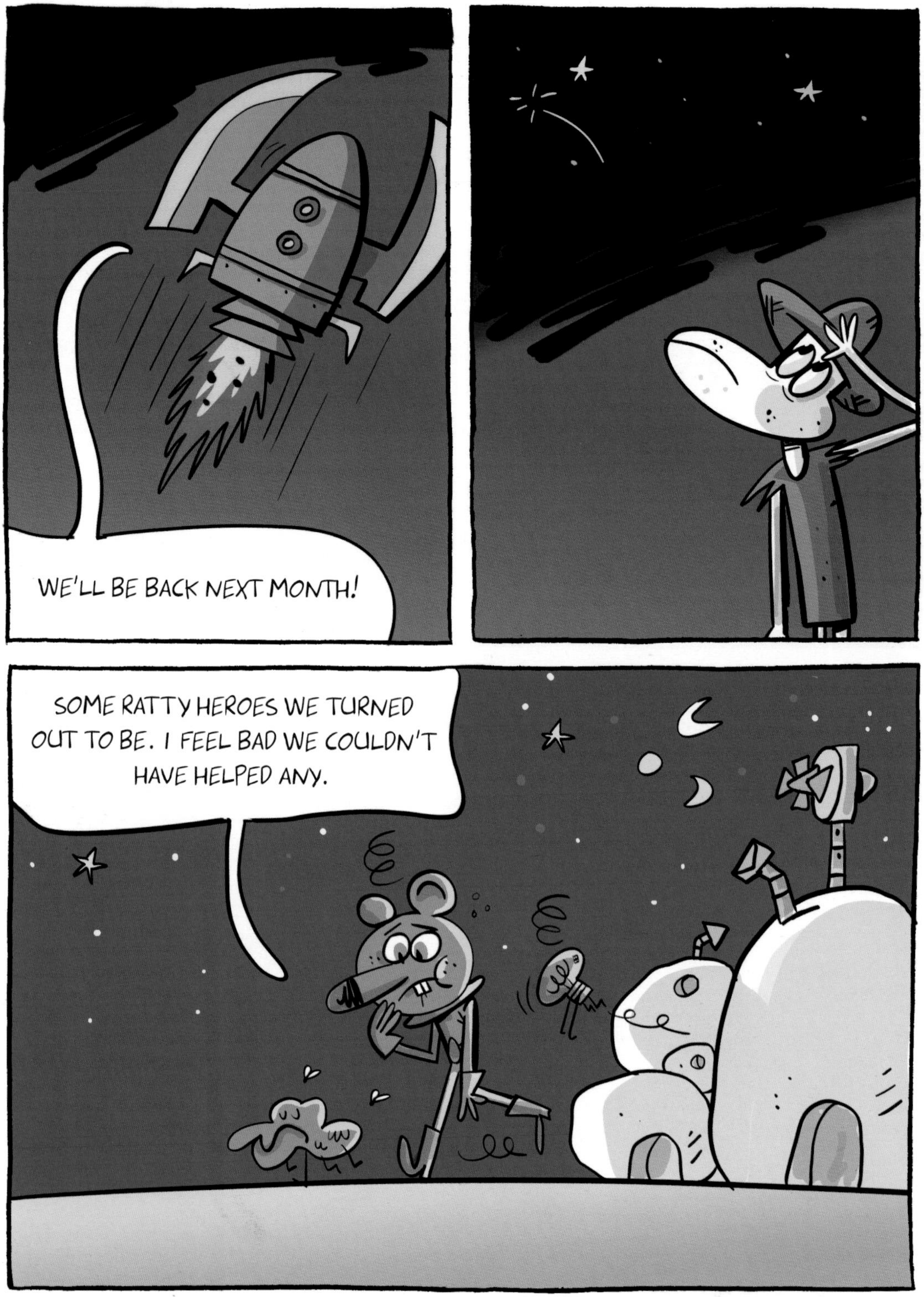
WE'LL BE BACK NEXT MONTH!
SOME RATTY HEROES WE TURNED OUT TO BE. I FEEL BAD WE COULDN'T HAVE HELPED ANY.

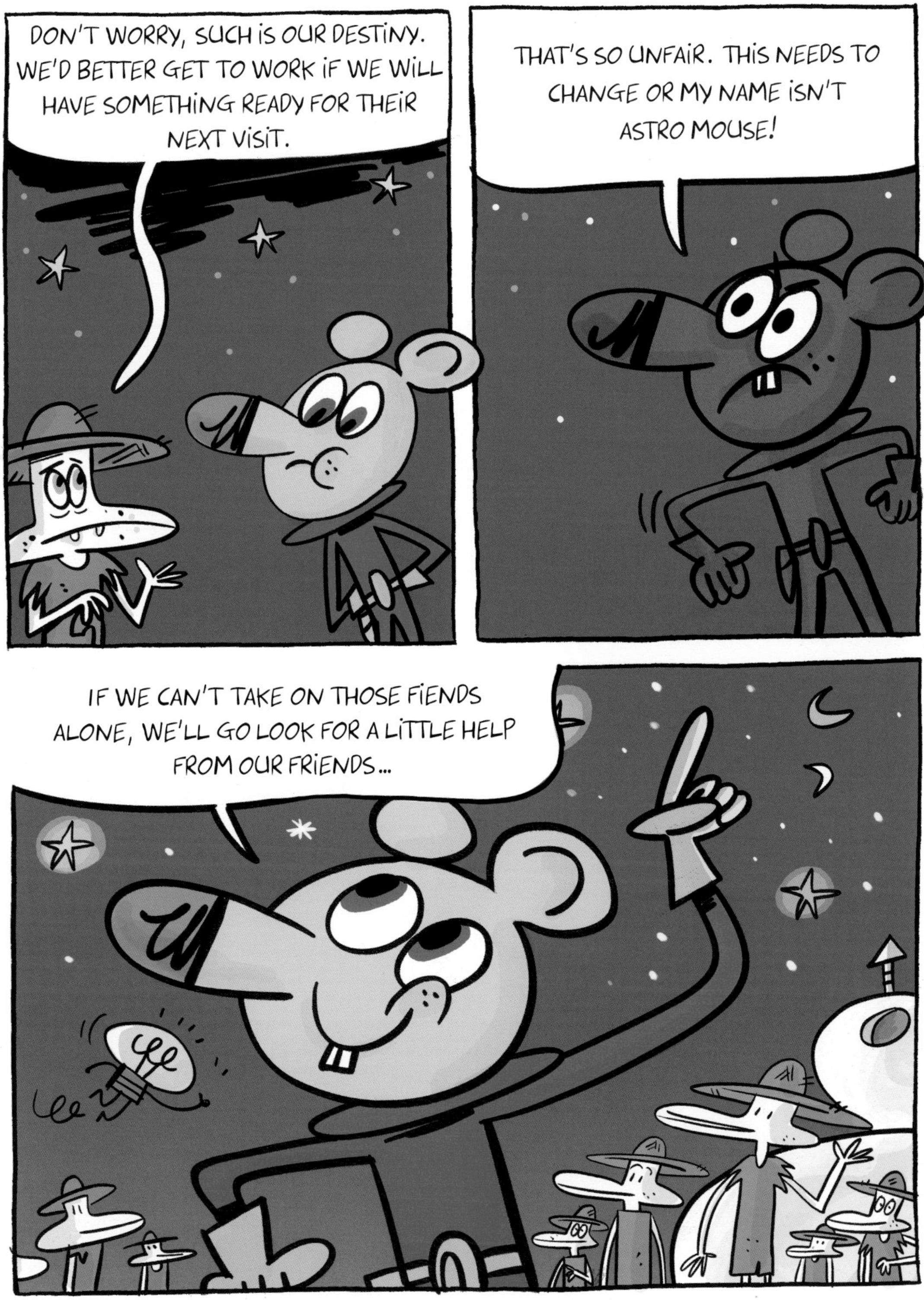
DON'T WORRY, SUCH IS OUR DESTINY. WE'D BETTER GET TO WORK IF WE WILL HAVE SOMETHING READY FOR THEIR NEXT VISIT.
THAT'S SO UNFAIR. THIS NEEDS TO CHANGE OR MY NAME ISN'T ASTRO MOUSE!
IF WE CAN'T TAKE ON THOSE FIENDS ALONE, WE'LL GO LOOK FOR A LITTLE HELP FROM OUR FRIENDS...

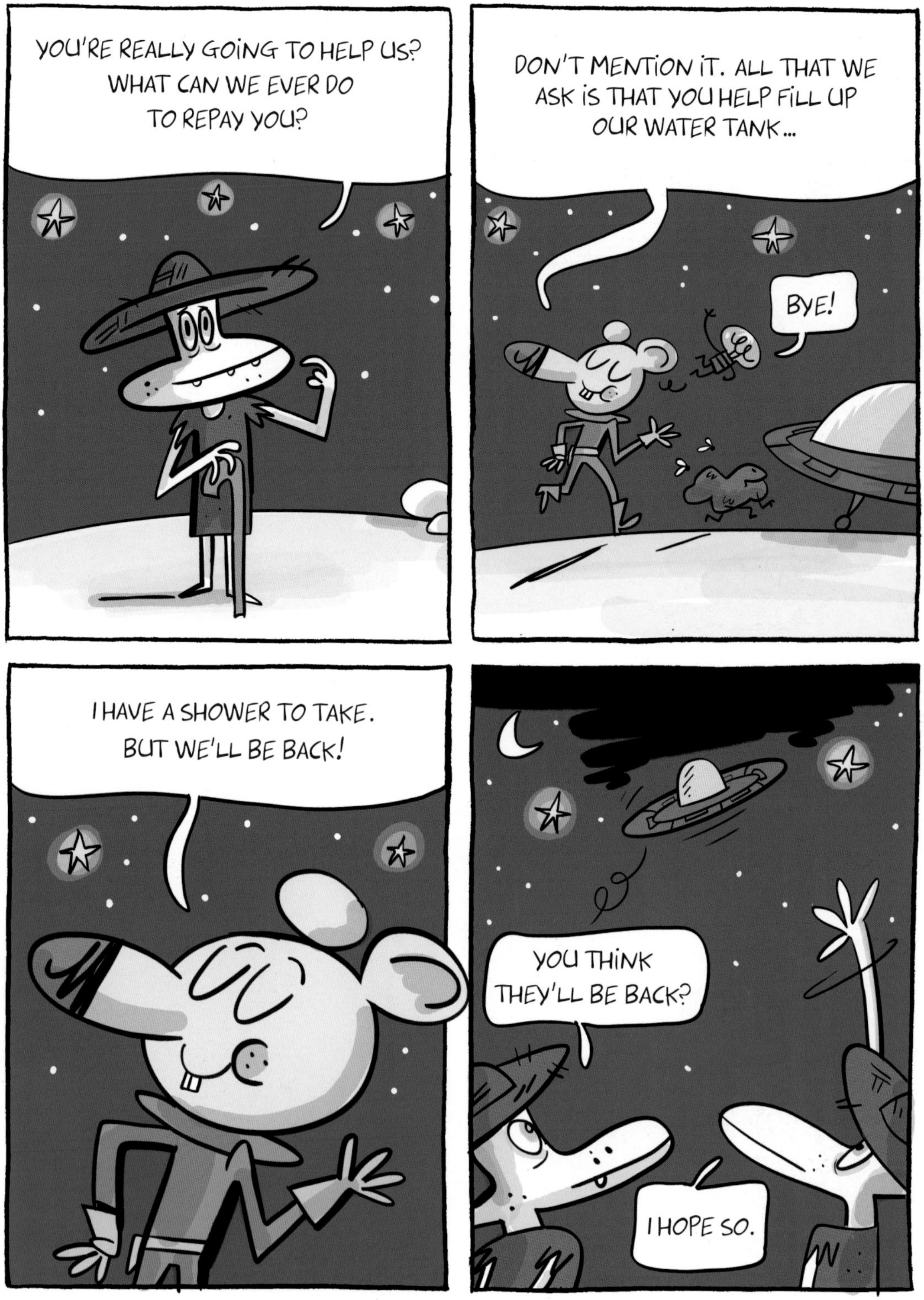
YOU'RE REALLY GOING TO HELP US? WHAT CAN WE EVER DO TO REPAY YOU?
DON'T MENTION IT. ALL THAT WE ASK IS THAT YOU HELP FILL UP OUR WATER TANK...
BYE!
I HAVE A SHOWER TO TAKE. BUT WE'LL BE BACK!
YOU THINK THEY'LL BE BACK?
I HOPE SO.

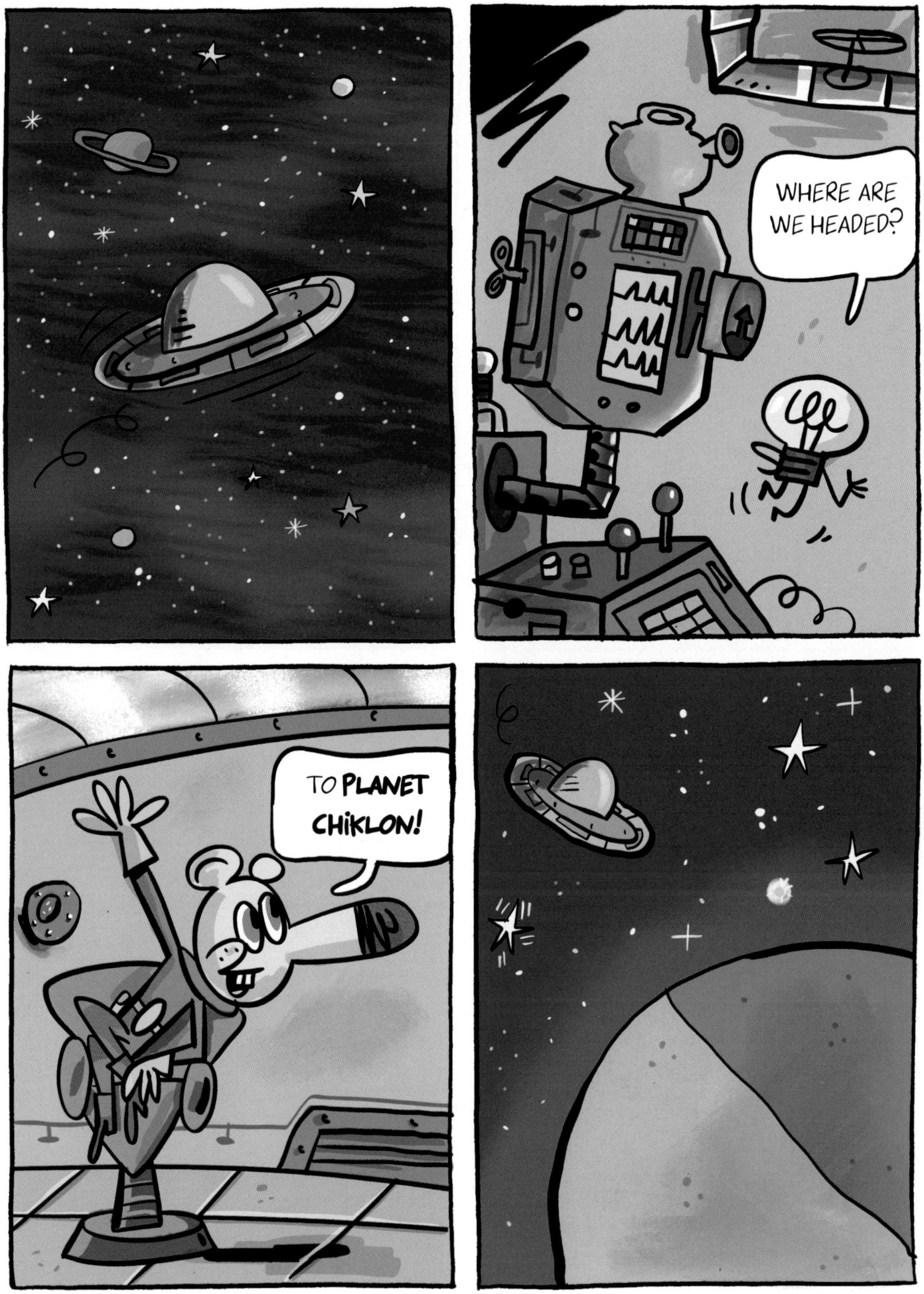
WHERE ARE WE HEADED?
TO PLANET CHIKLON!

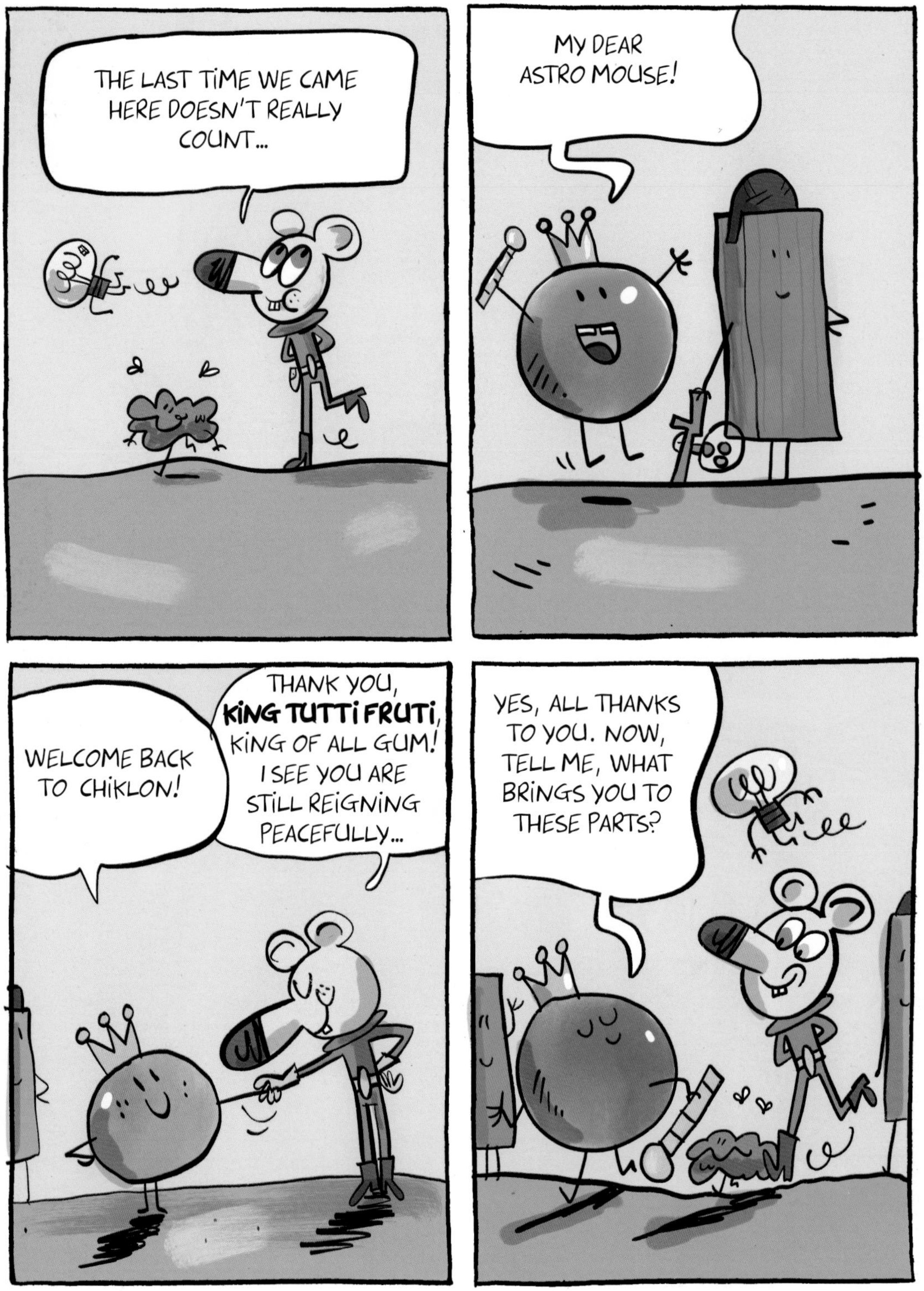
THE LAST TIME WE CAME HERE DOESN'T REALLY COUNT...
MY DEAR ASTRO MOUSE!
WELCOME BACK TO CHIKLON!
THANK YOU, KING TUTTI FRUTI, KING OF ALL GUM! I SEE YOU ARE STILL REIGNING PEACEFULLY...
YES, ALL THANKS TO YOU. NOW, TELL ME, WHAT BRINGS YOU TO THESE PARTS?

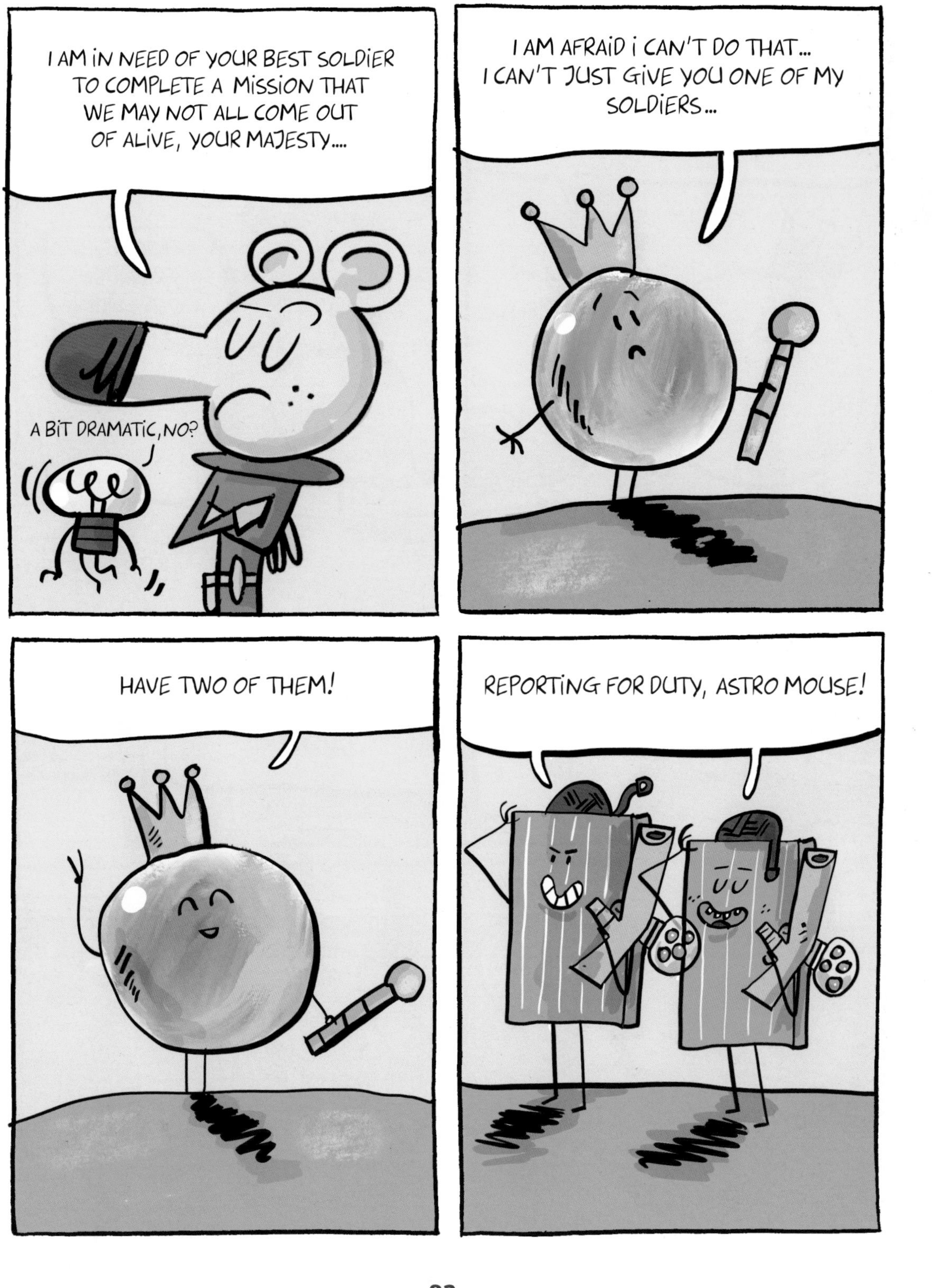
I AM IN NEED OF YOUR BEST SOLDIER TO COMPLETE A MISSION THAT WE MAY NOT ALL COME OUT OF ALIVE, YOUR MAJESTY....
A BIT DRAMATIC, NO?
I AM AFRAID I CAN'T DO THAT... I CAN'T JUST GIVE YOU ONE OF MY SOLDIERS...
HAVE TWO OF THEM!
REPORTING FOR DUTY, ASTRO MOUSE!

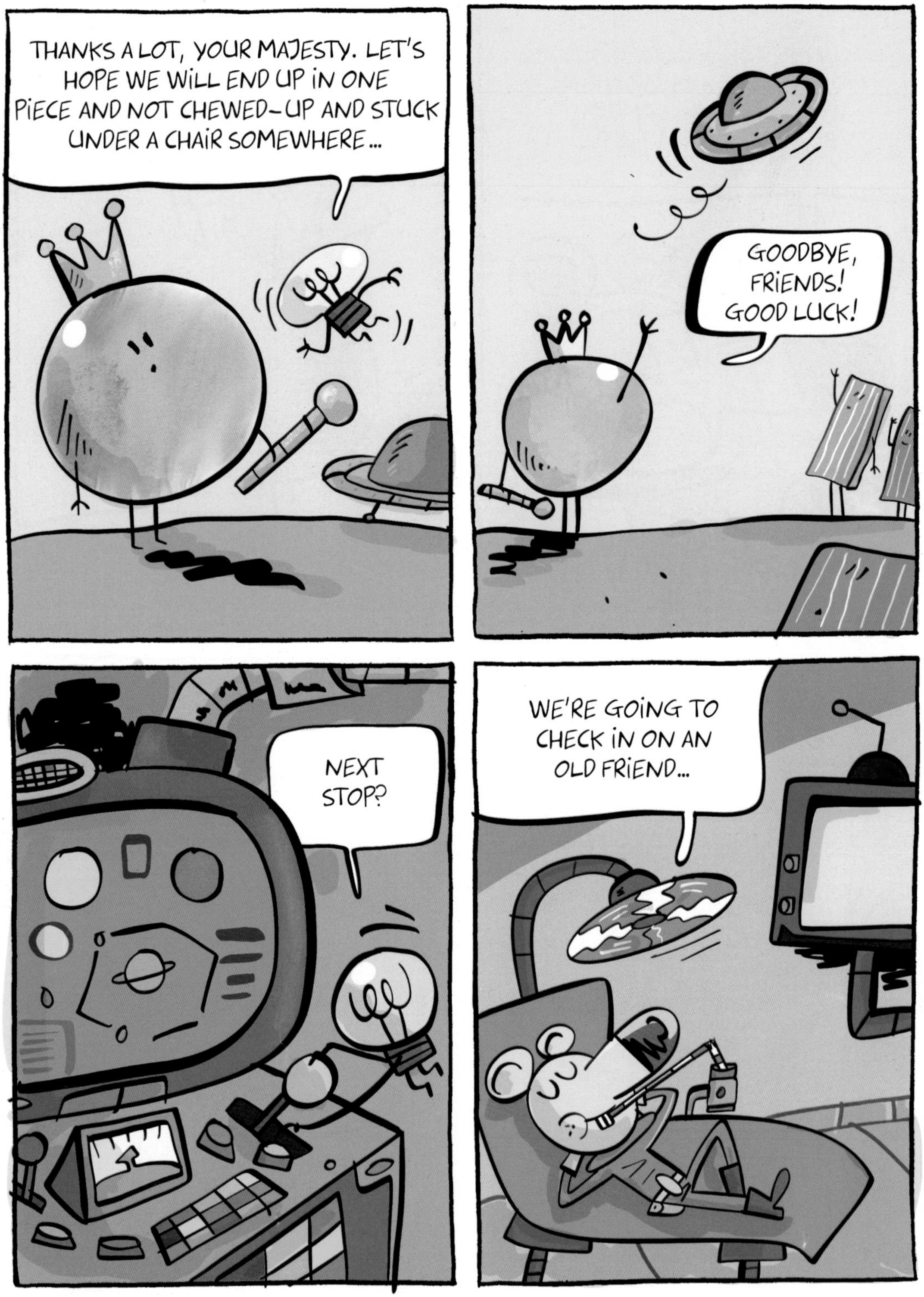
THANKS A LOT, YOUR MAJESTY. LET'S HOPE WE WILL END UP IN ONE PIECE AND NOT CHEWED-UP AND STUCK UNDER A CHAIR SOMEWHERE...
GOODBYE, FRIENDS! GOOD LUCK!
NEXT STOP?
WE'RE GOING TO CHECK IN ON AN OLD FRIEND...

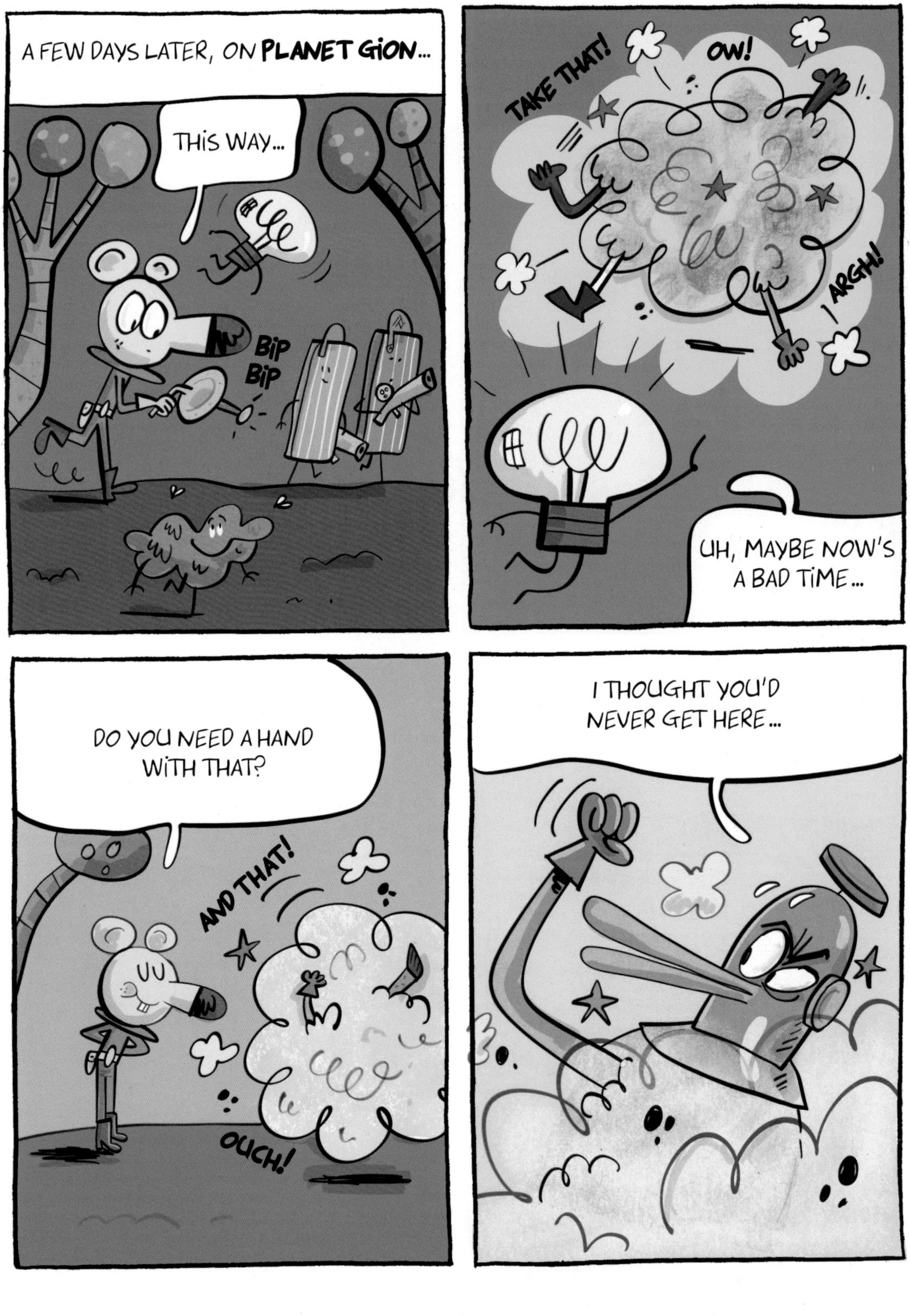
A FEW DAYS LATER, ON PLANET GiON...
THiS WAY...
BiP BiP
TAKE THAT!
OW!
ARGH!
UH, MAYBE NOW'S A BAD TiME...
DO YOU NEED A HAND WiTH THAT?
AND THAT!
OUCH!
I THOUGHT YOU'D NEVER GET HERE...

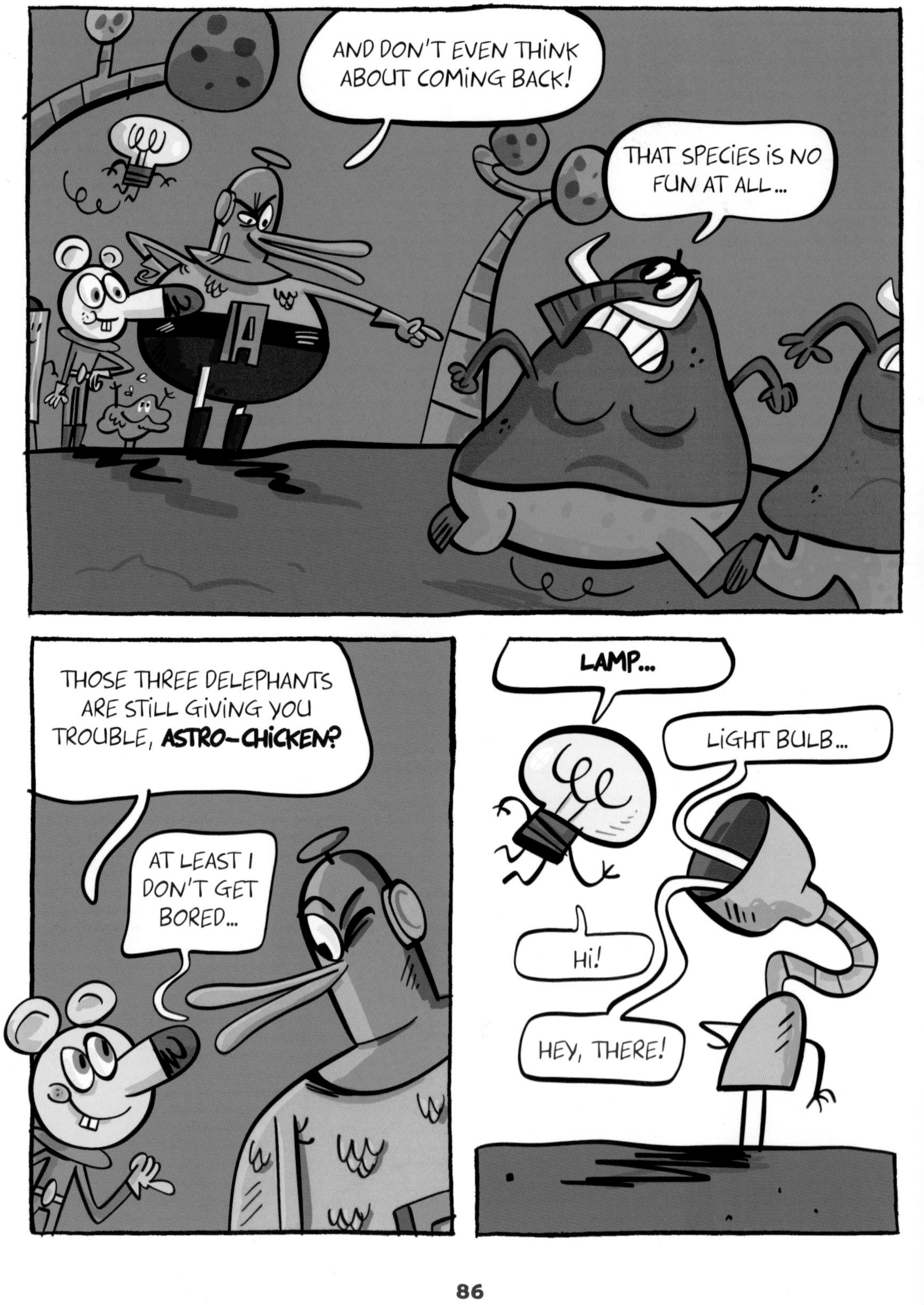
AND DON'T EVEN THINK ABOUT COMING BACK!
THAT SPECIES IS NO FUN AT ALL...
THOSE THREE DELEPHANTS ARE STILL GIVING YOU TROUBLE, **ASTRO-CHICKEN?**
AT LEAST I DON'T GET BORED...
LAMP...
LIGHT BULB...
HI!
HEY, THERE!

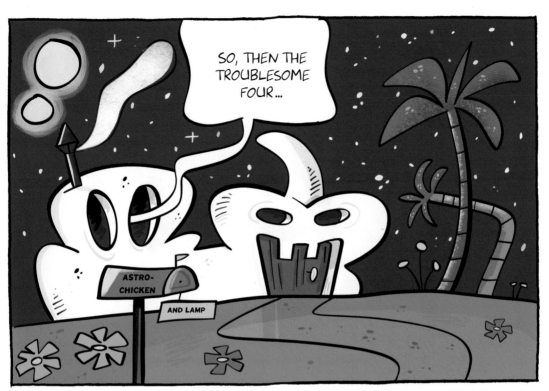

SO, THEN THE TROUBLESOME FOUR...

ASTRO-CHICKEN

AND LAMP

AS YOU KNOW, I AM VERY MUCH AGAINST TYRANNY AND OPRESSION.

YOU CAN COUNT ON US! I NEED A LITTLE BIT OF ACTION BACK IN MY LIFE...

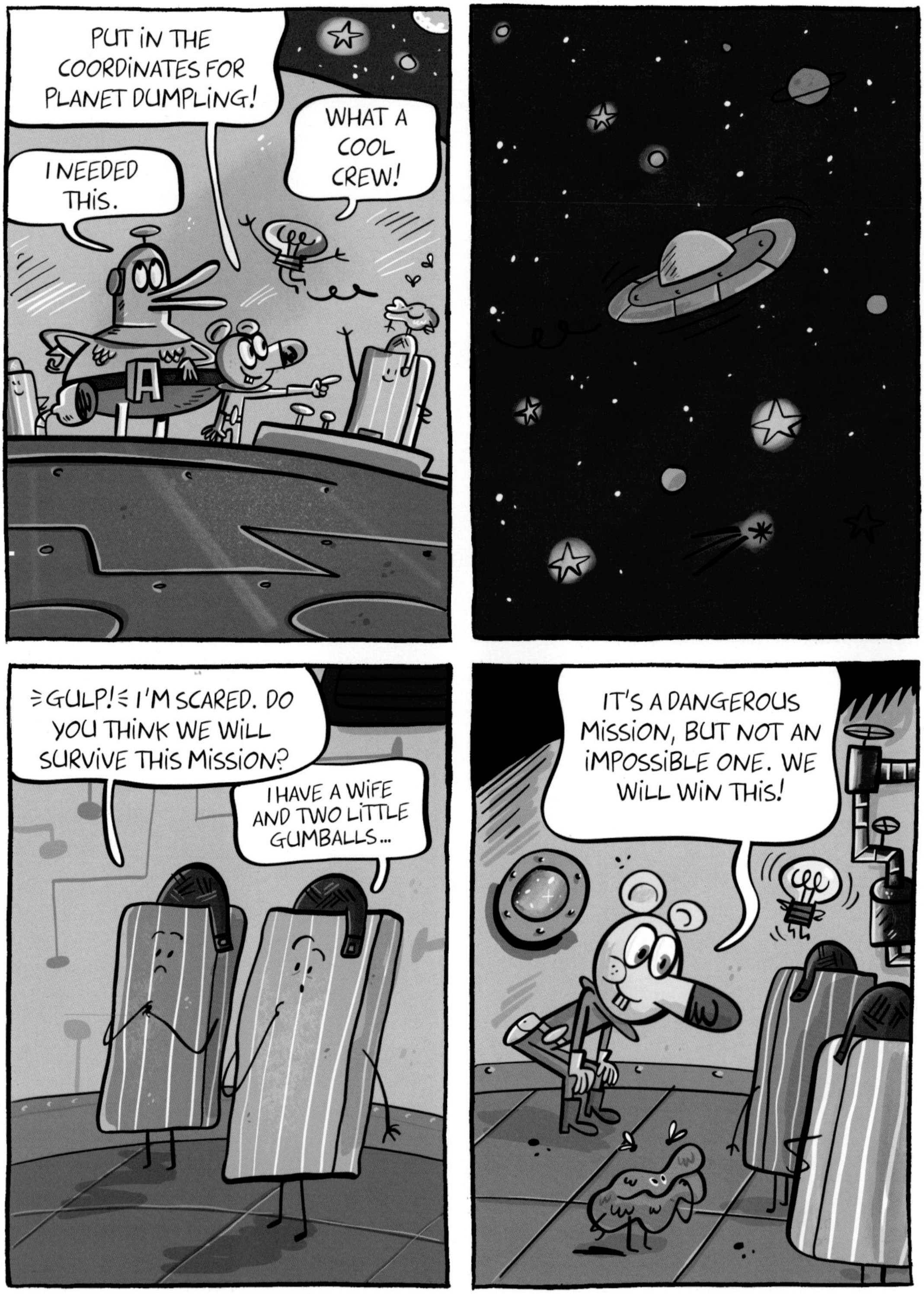
PUT IN THE COORDINATES FOR PLANET DUMPLING!
I NEEDED THIS.
WHAT A COOL CREW!
≥GULP!≤ I'M SCARED. DO YOU THINK WE WILL SURVIVE THIS MISSION?
I HAVE A WIFE AND TWO LITTLE GUMBALLS...
IT'S A DANGEROUS MISSION, BUT NOT AN IMPOSSIBLE ONE. WE WILL WIN THIS!

KEEP IN MIND, IT'S NOW SEVEN OF US AGAINST JUST FOUR OF THEM...
BUT THEY HAVE SUPERPOWERS AND WE DON'T HAVE ANYTHING...
DO WE EVEN HAVE A PLAN?
FROM WHAT YOU'VE TOLD ME, IN JUST A FEW DAYS THOSE DASTARDLY ROGUES WILL RETURN TO SHAKE DOWN THE DUMPLINGS...
WE CAN PLAN A GOOD DEFENSE. LEAVE THAT JOB TO ME. I WAS THE FIVE-TIME CHAMPION AT "SINK THE FLOAT."
THAT'S SOME **GO-OD** CHICKEN!

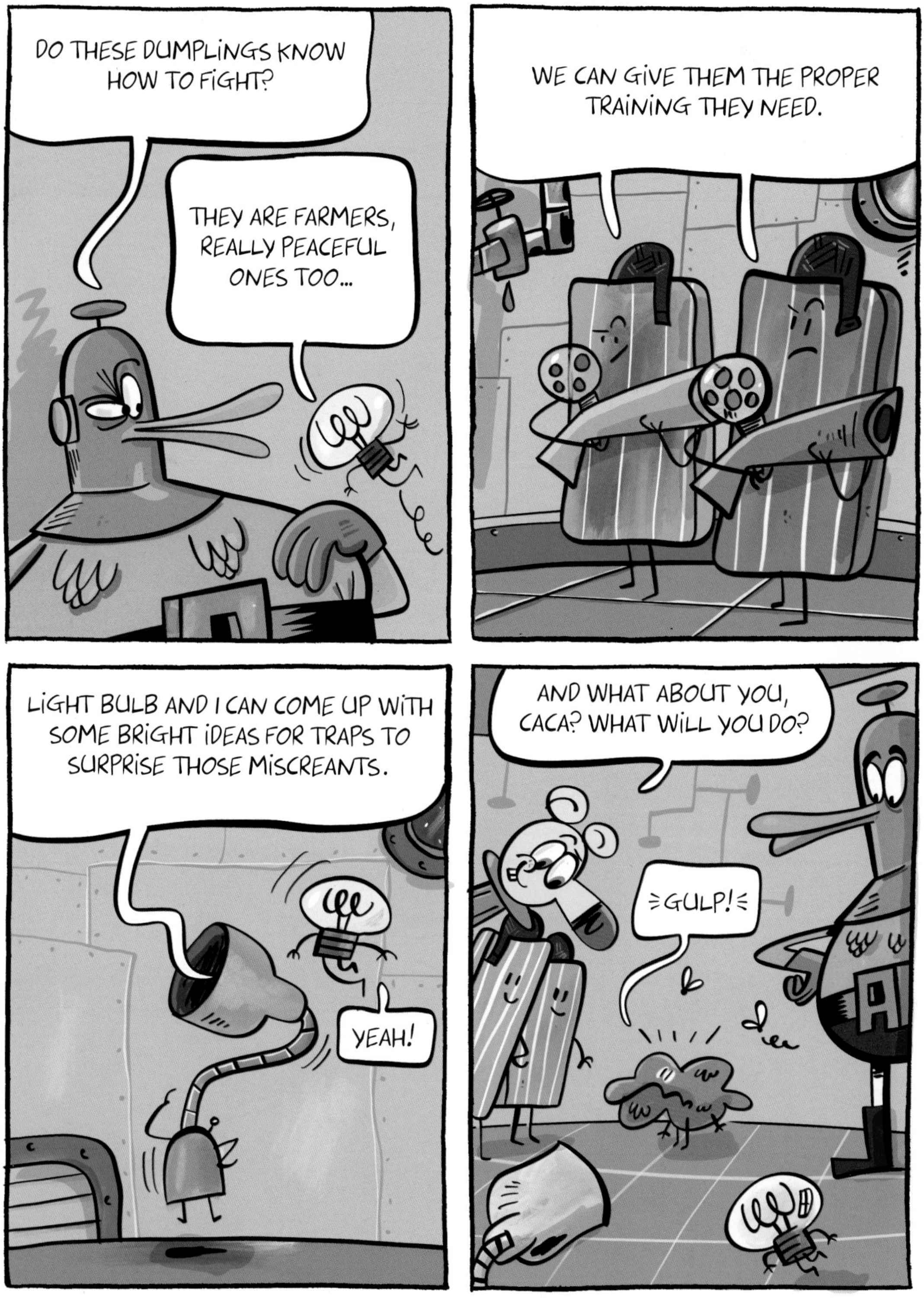
DO THESE DUMPLINGS KNOW HOW TO FIGHT?
THEY ARE FARMERS, REALLY PEACEFUL ONES TOO...
WE CAN GIVE THEM THE PROPER TRAINING THEY NEED.
LIGHT BULB AND I CAN COME UP WITH SOME BRIGHT IDEAS FOR TRAPS TO SURPRISE THOSE MISCREANTS.
YEAH!
AND WHAT ABOUT YOU, CACA? WHAT WILL YOU DO?
GULP!

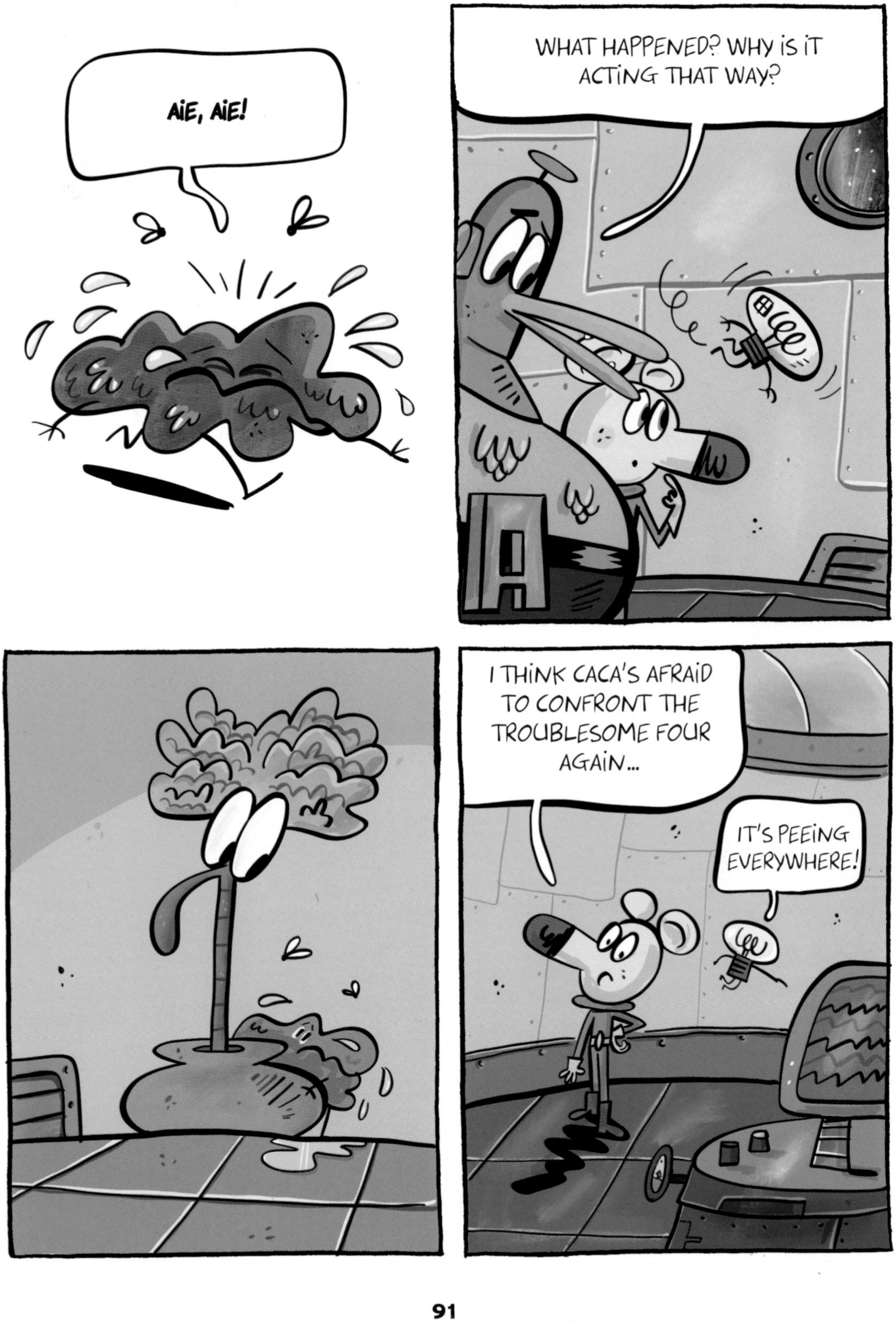
AiE, AiE!
WHAT HAPPENED? WHY IS IT ACTING THAT WAY?
I THINK CACA'S AFRAID TO CONFRONT THE TROUBLESOME FOUR AGAIN...
IT'S PEEING EVERYWHERE!

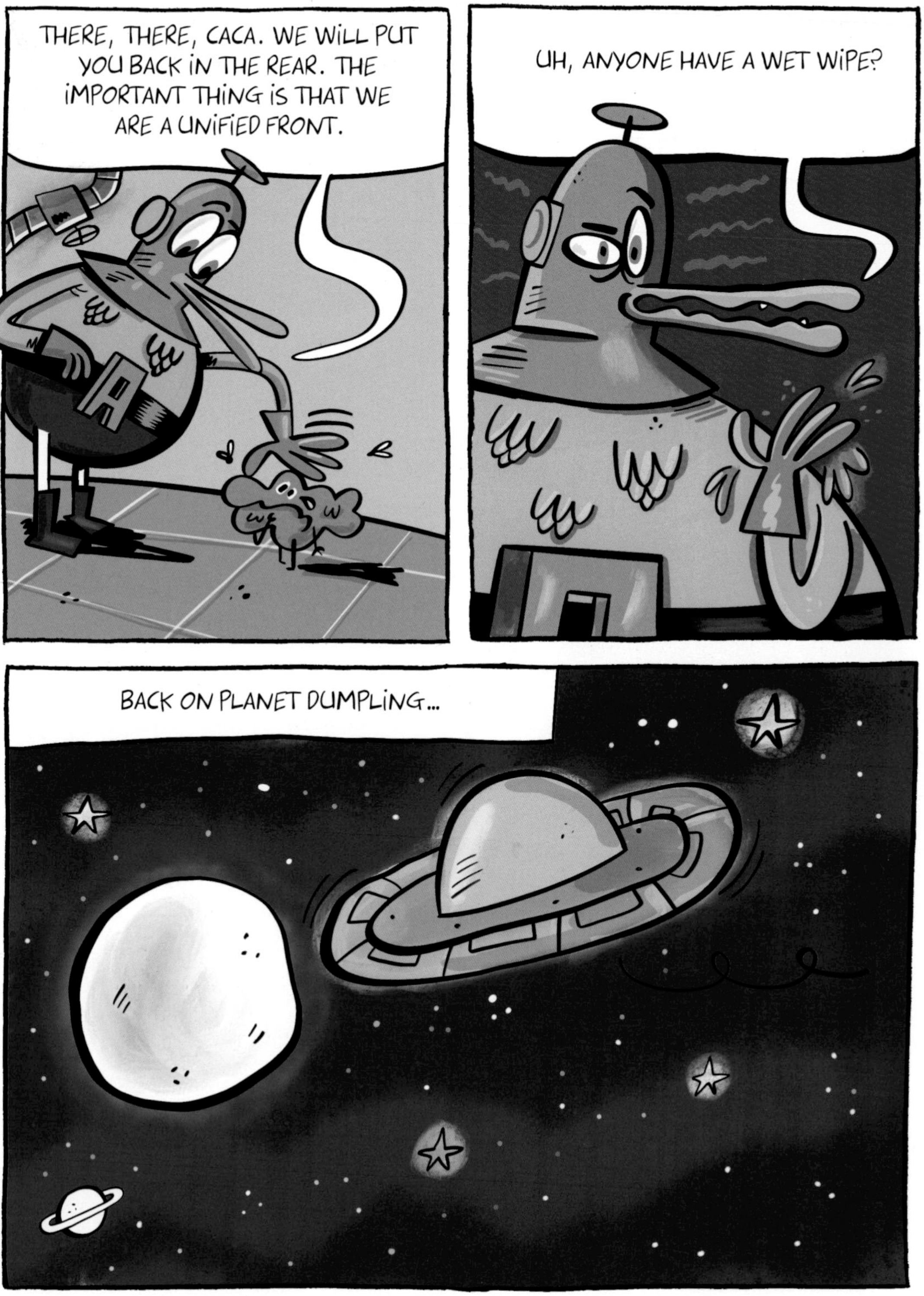
THERE, THERE, CACA. WE WILL PUT YOU BACK IN THE REAR. THE IMPORTANT THING IS THAT WE ARE A UNIFIED FRONT.
UH, ANYONE HAVE A WET WIPE?
BACK ON PLANET DUMPLING...

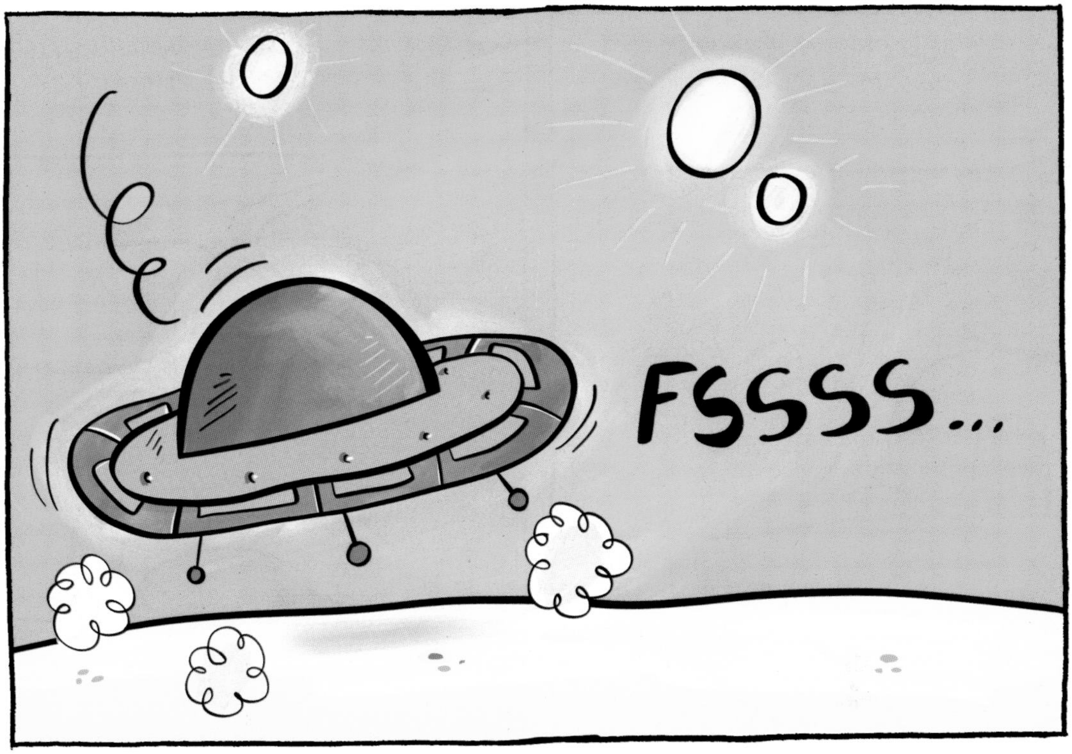
FSSSS...

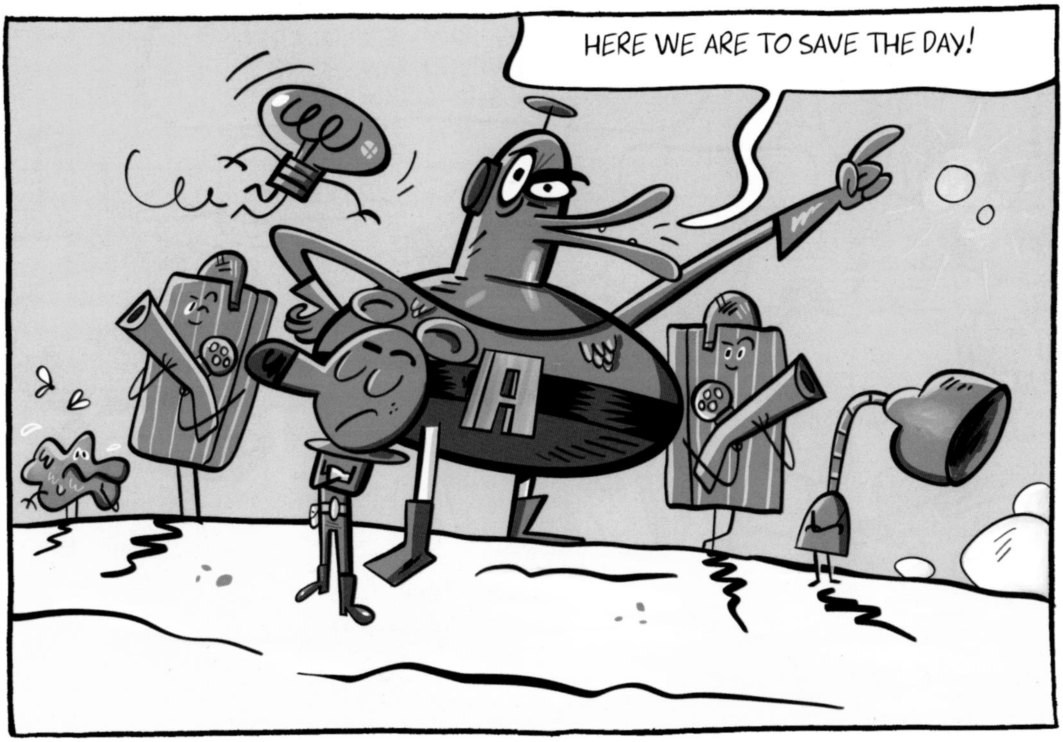
HERE WE ARE TO SAVE THE DAY!

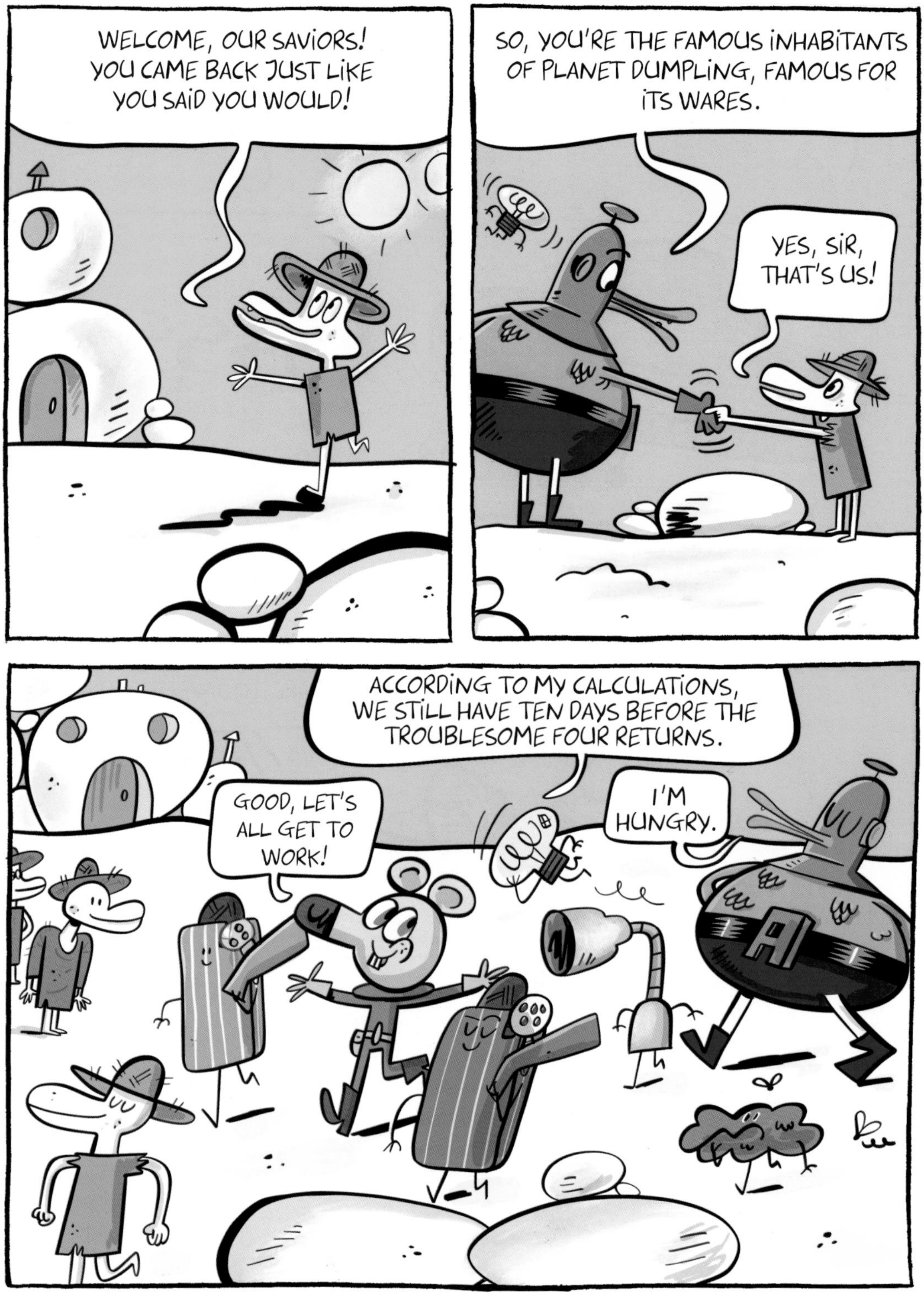
WELCOME, OUR SAVIORS! YOU CAME BACK JUST LIKE YOU SAID YOU WOULD!
SO, YOU'RE THE FAMOUS INHABITANTS OF PLANET DUMPLING, FAMOUS FOR ITS WARES.
YES, SIR, THAT'S US!
ACCORDING TO MY CALCULATIONS, WE STILL HAVE TEN DAYS BEFORE THE TROUBLESOME FOUR RETURNS.
GOOD, LET'S ALL GET TO WORK!
I'M HUNGRY.

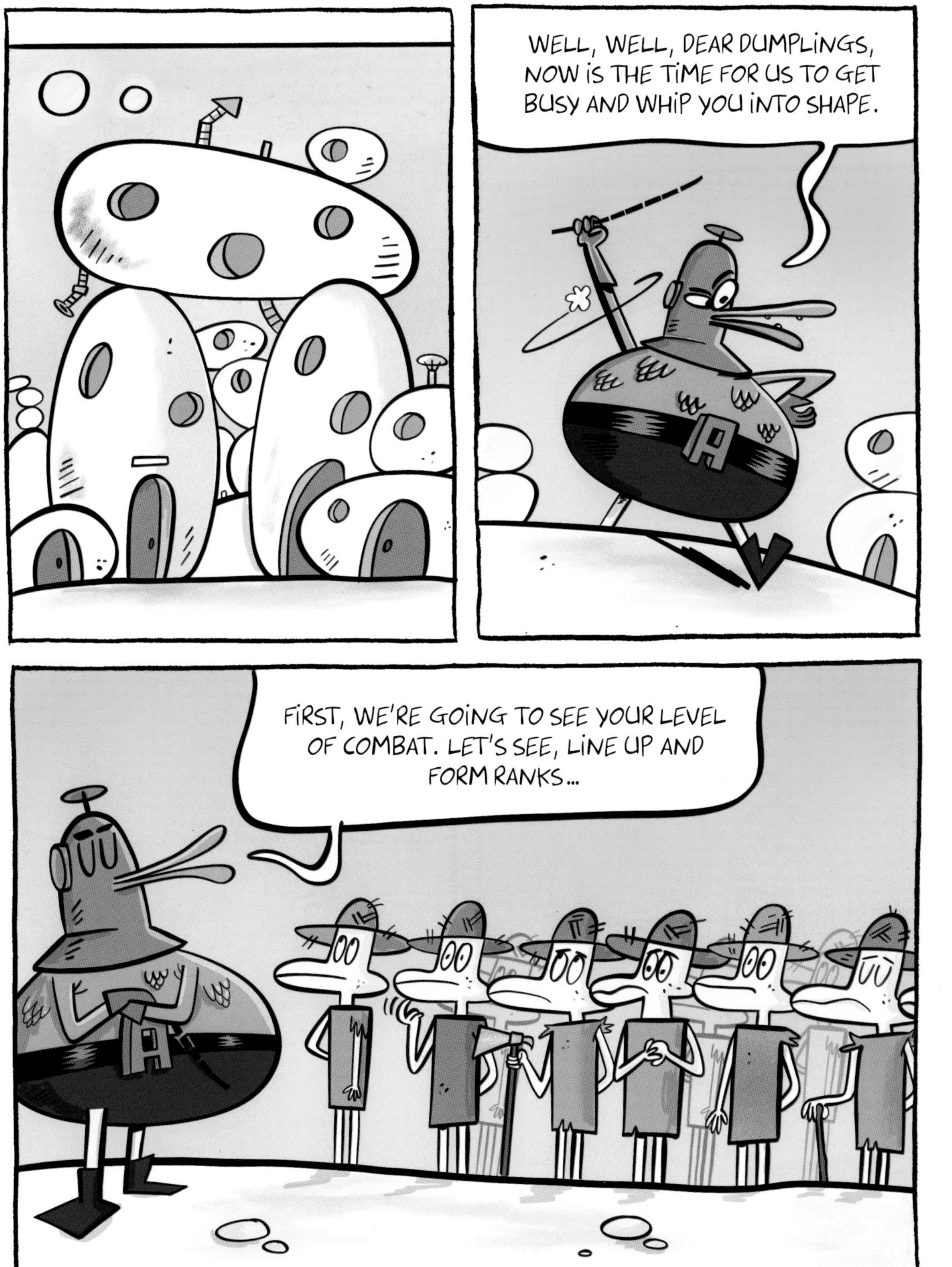
WELL, WELL, DEAR DUMPLINGS, NOW IS THE TIME FOR US TO GET BUSY AND WHIP YOU INTO SHAPE.
FIRST, WE'RE GOING TO SEE YOUR LEVEL OF COMBAT. LET'S SEE, LINE UP AND FORM RANKS...

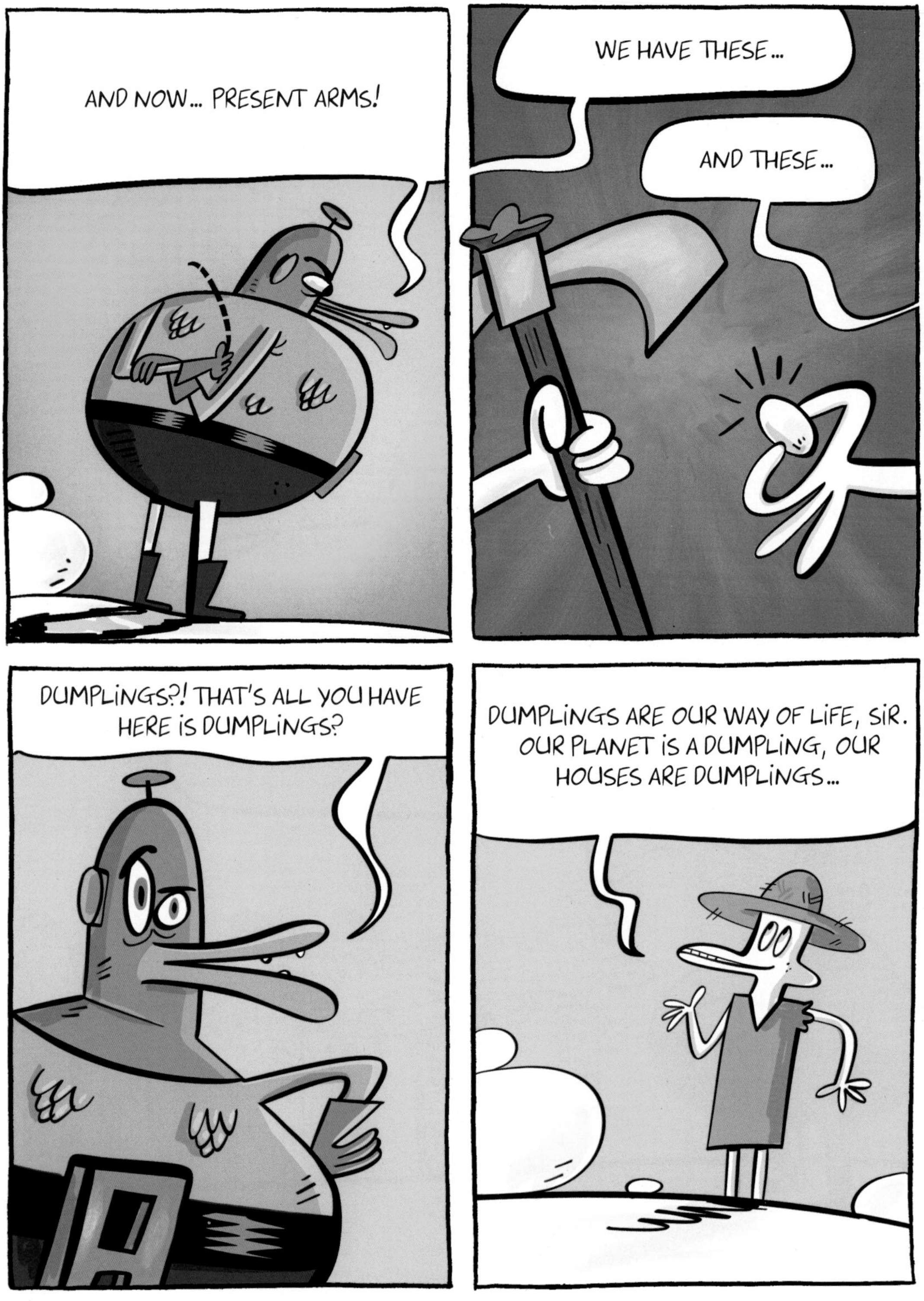
AND NOW... PRESENT ARMS!
WE HAVE THESE...
AND THESE...
DUMPLINGS?! THAT'S ALL YOU HAVE HERE IS DUMPLINGS?
DUMPLINGS ARE OUR WAY OF LIFE, SIR. OUR PLANET IS A DUMPLING, OUR HOUSES ARE DUMPLINGS...

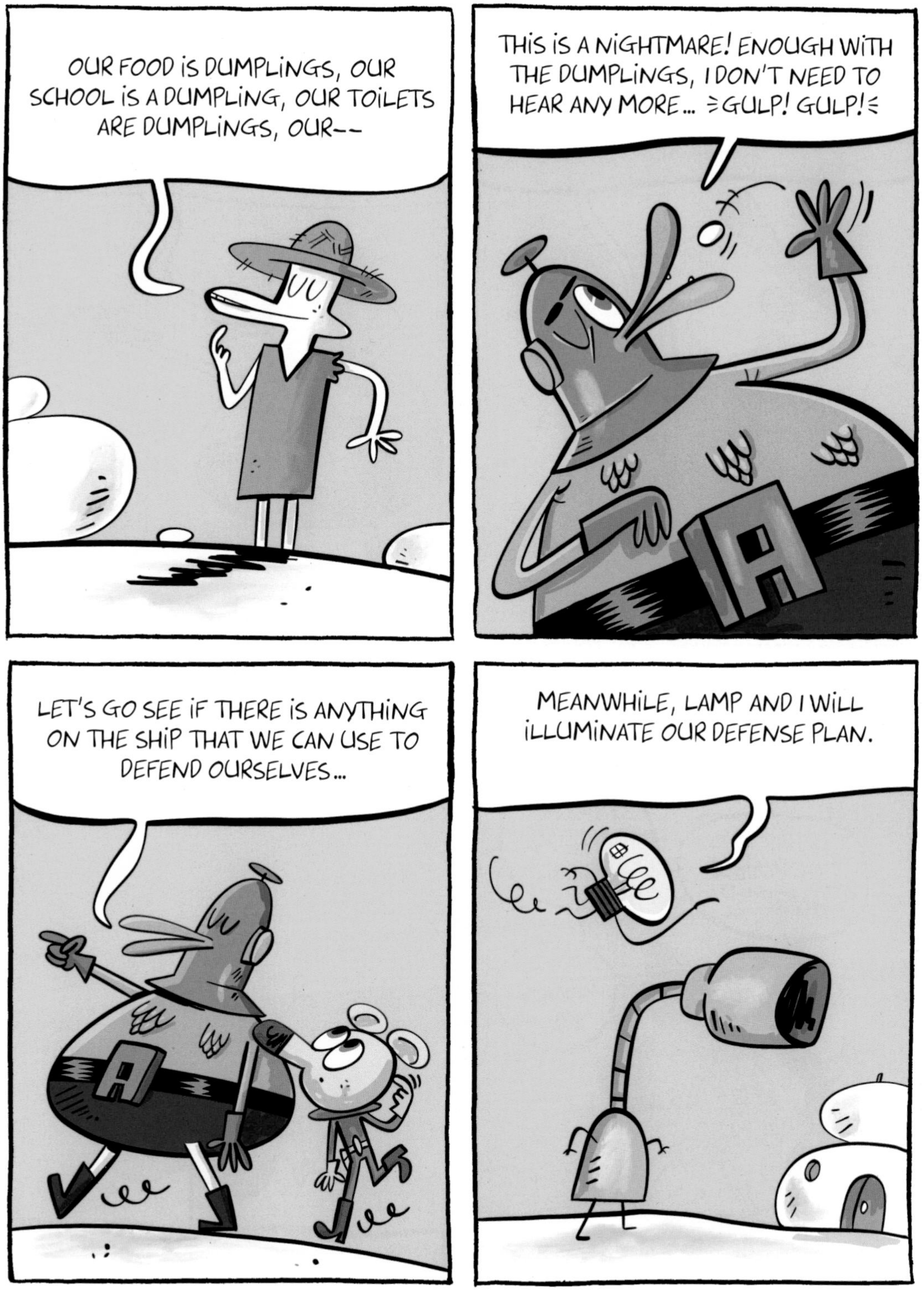
OUR FOOD IS DUMPLINGS, OUR SCHOOL IS A DUMPLING, OUR TOILETS ARE DUMPLINGS, OUR--
THIS IS A NIGHTMARE! ENOUGH WITH THE DUMPLINGS, I DON'T NEED TO HEAR ANY MORE... ⪢GULP! GULP!⪡
LET'S GO SEE IF THERE IS ANYTHING ON THE SHIP THAT WE CAN USE TO DEFEND OURSELVES...
MEANWHILE, LAMP AND I WILL ILLUMINATE OUR DEFENSE PLAN.

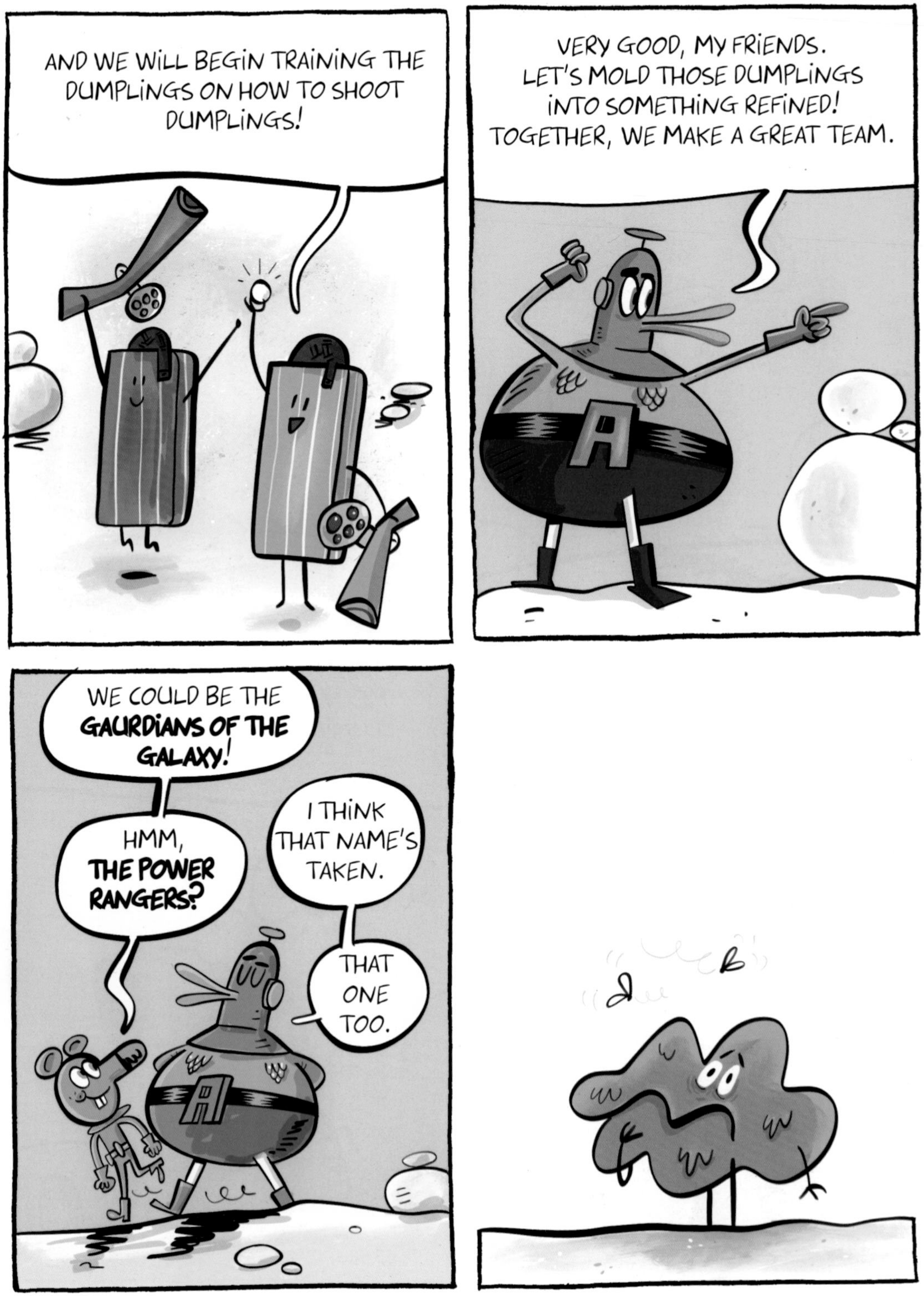
AND WE WILL BEGIN TRAINING THE DUMPLINGS ON HOW TO SHOOT DUMPLINGS!
VERY GOOD, MY FRIENDS. LET'S MOLD THOSE DUMPLINGS INTO SOMETHING REFINED! TOGETHER, WE MAKE A GREAT TEAM.
WE COULD BE THE GAURDIANS OF THE GALAXY!
I THINK THAT NAME'S TAKEN.
HMM, THE POWER RANGERS?
THAT ONE TOO.

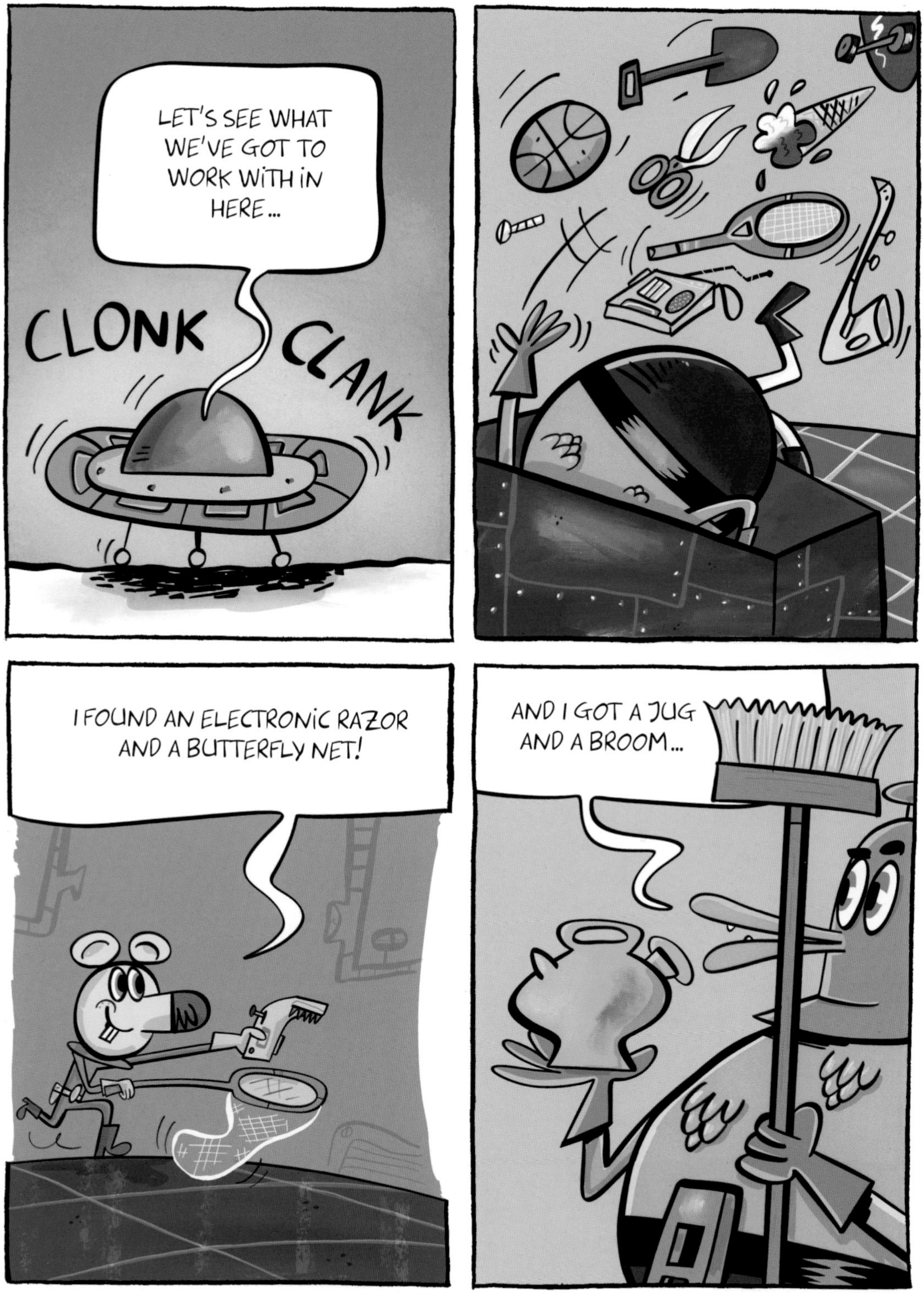
LET'S SEE WHAT WE'VE GOT TO WORK WITH IN HERE...
CLONK
CLANK
I FOUND AN ELECTRONIC RAZOR AND A BUTTERFLY NET!
AND I GOT A JUG AND A BROOM...

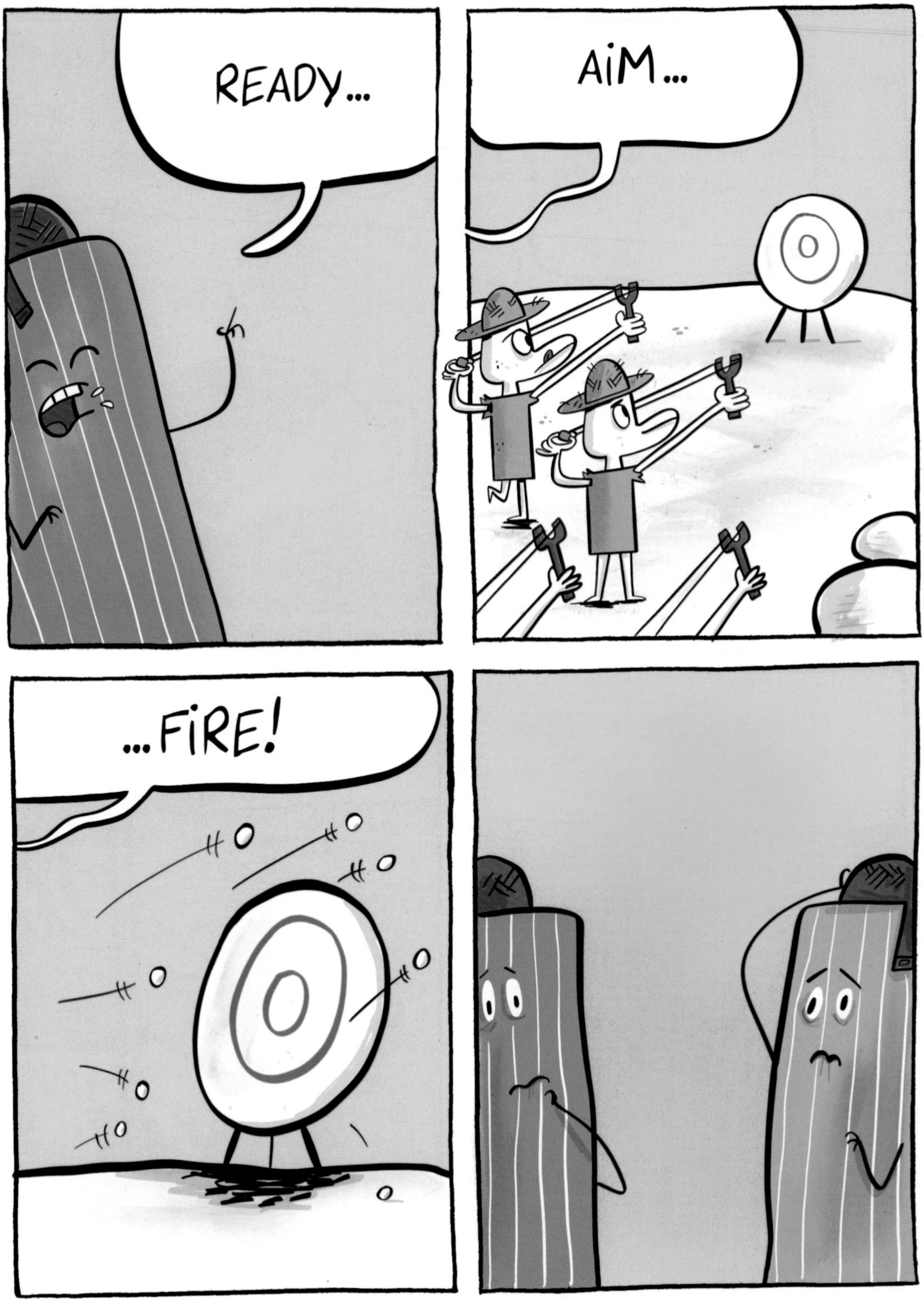
READY...
AiM...
...FiRE!

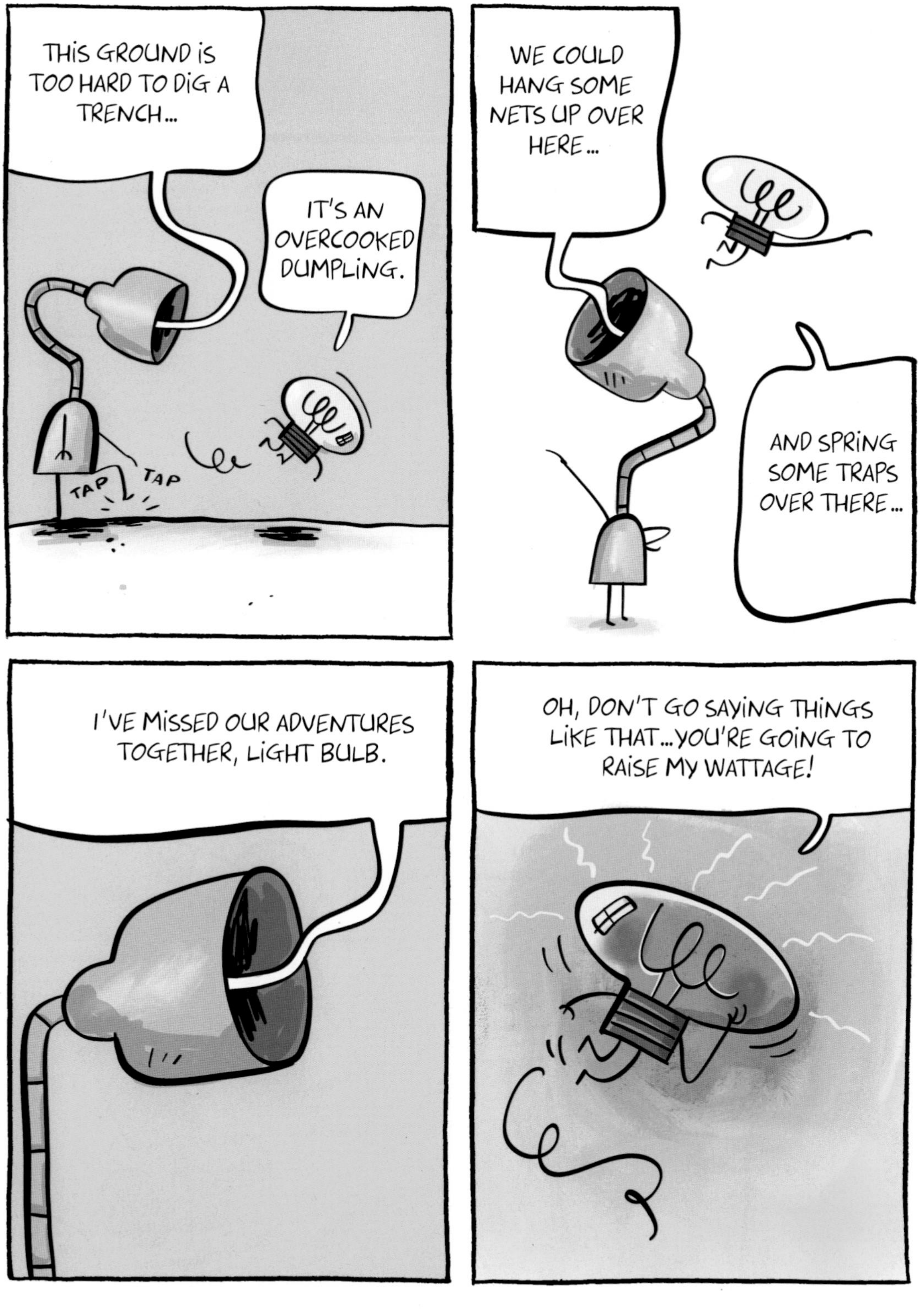
THIS GROUND IS TOO HARD TO DIG A TRENCH...
IT'S AN OVERCOOKED DUMPLING.
TAP
TAP
WE COULD HANG SOME NETS UP OVER HERE...
AND SPRING SOME TRAPS OVER THERE...
I'VE MISSED OUR ADVENTURES TOGETHER, LIGHT BULB.
OH, DON'T GO SAYING THINGS LIKE THAT...YOU'RE GOING TO RAISE MY WATTAGE!

THE DAYS GO BY AND THE FEARFUL MOMENT OF THE TROUBLESOME FOUR'S RETURN GROWS NEAR...

THE TRAPS ARE SET AND READY TO DO THEIR JOBS...

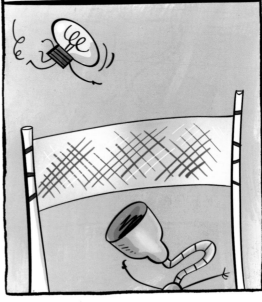

THE DUMPLINGS HAVE IMPROVED THEIR AIM...

AND ASTRO MOUSE AND CACA GATHERED ENOUGH WATER SUPPLIES FOR A GOOD WHILE.

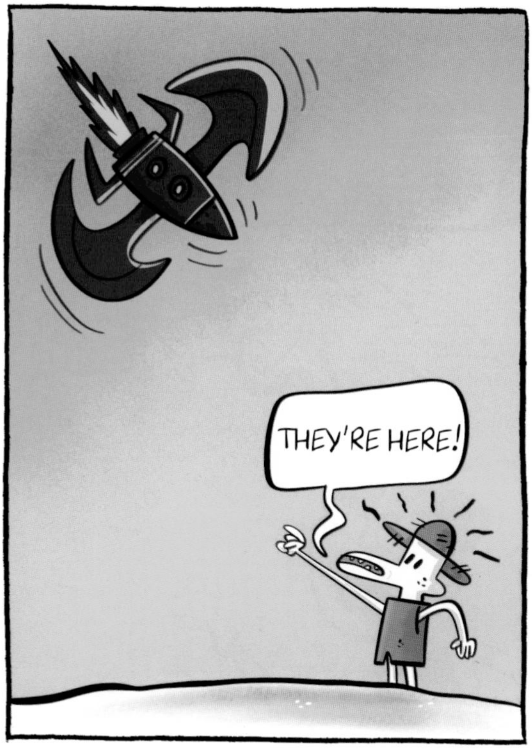
THEY'RE HERE!

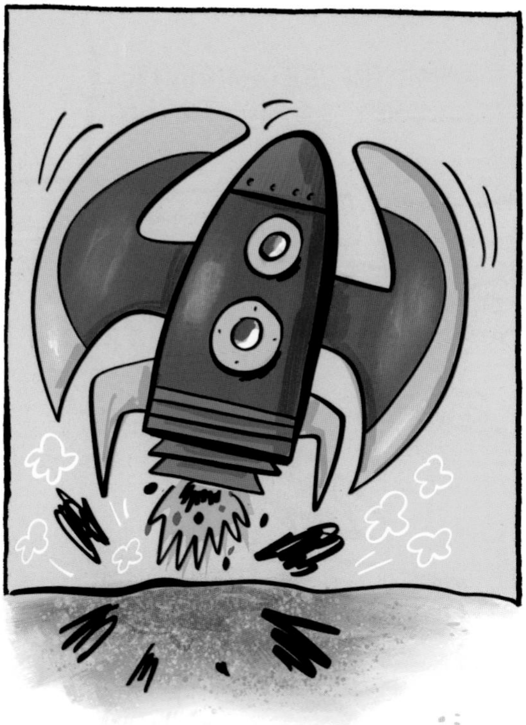

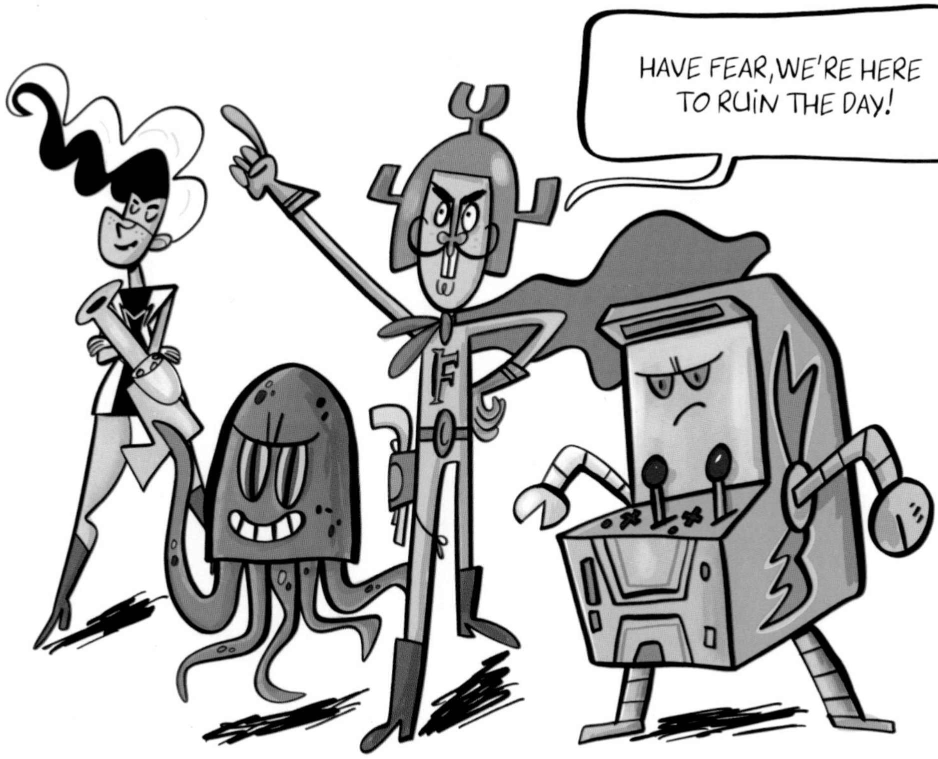
HAVE FEAR, WE'RE HERE TO RUIN THE DAY!

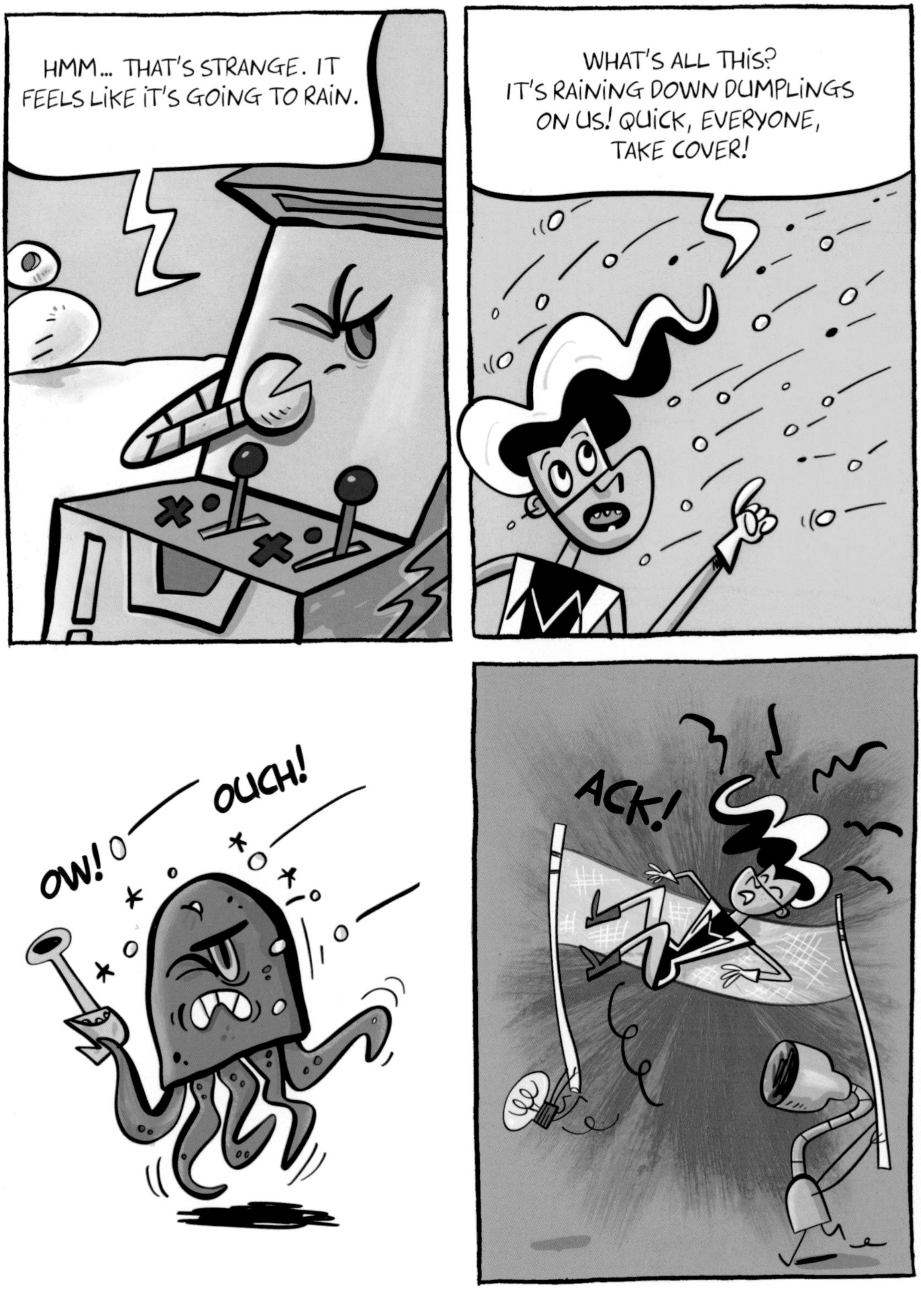
HMM... THAT'S STRANGE. IT FEELS LIKE IT'S GOING TO RAIN.
WHAT'S ALL THIS? IT'S RAINING DOWN DUMPLINGS ON US! QUICK, EVERYONE, TAKE COVER!
OW!
OUCH!
ACK!

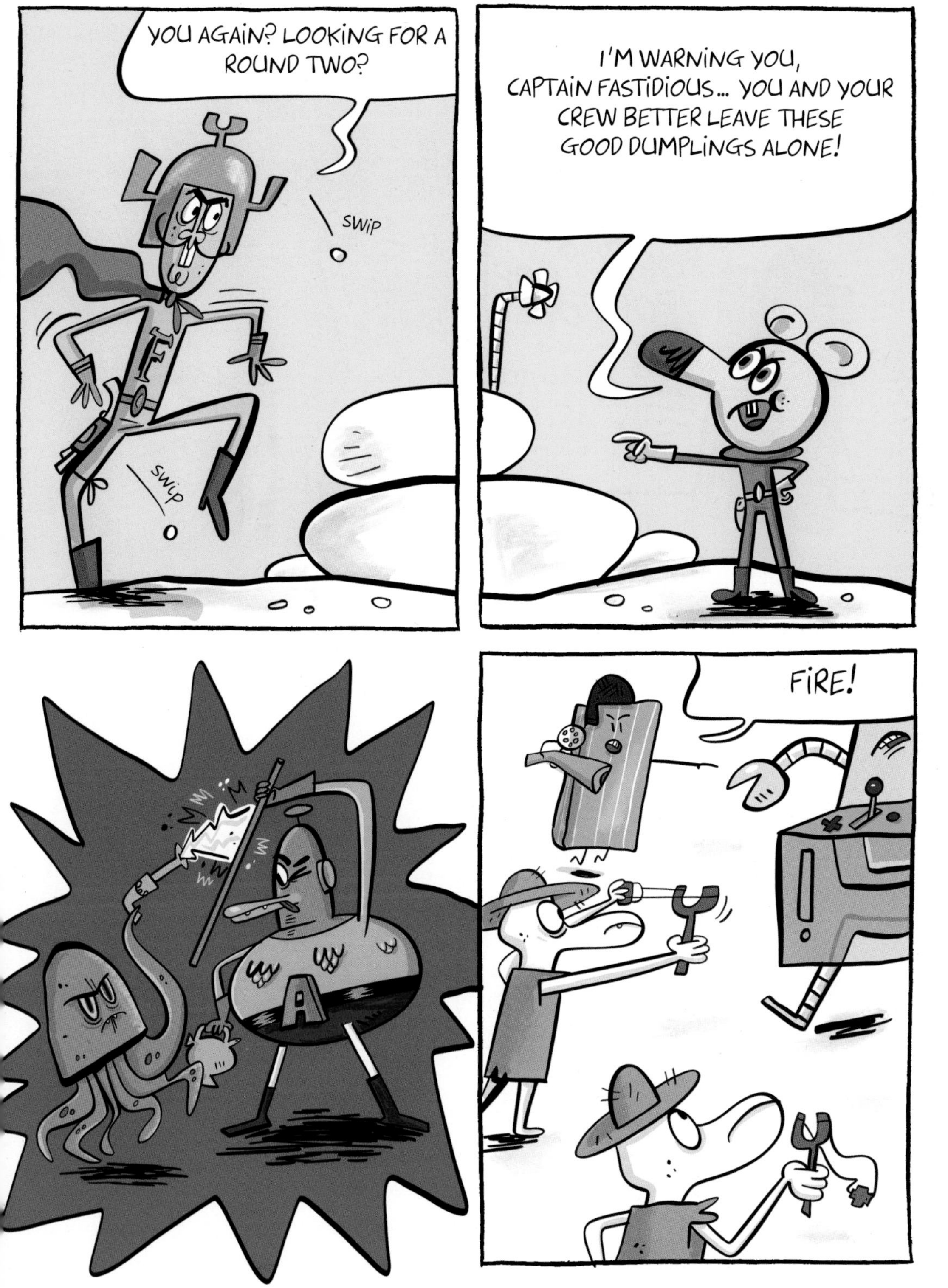
YOU AGAIN? LOOKING FOR A ROUND TWO?
SWIP
SWIP
I'M WARNING YOU, CAPTAIN FASTIDIOUS... YOU AND YOUR CREW BETTER LEAVE THESE GOOD DUMPLINGS ALONE!
FIRE!

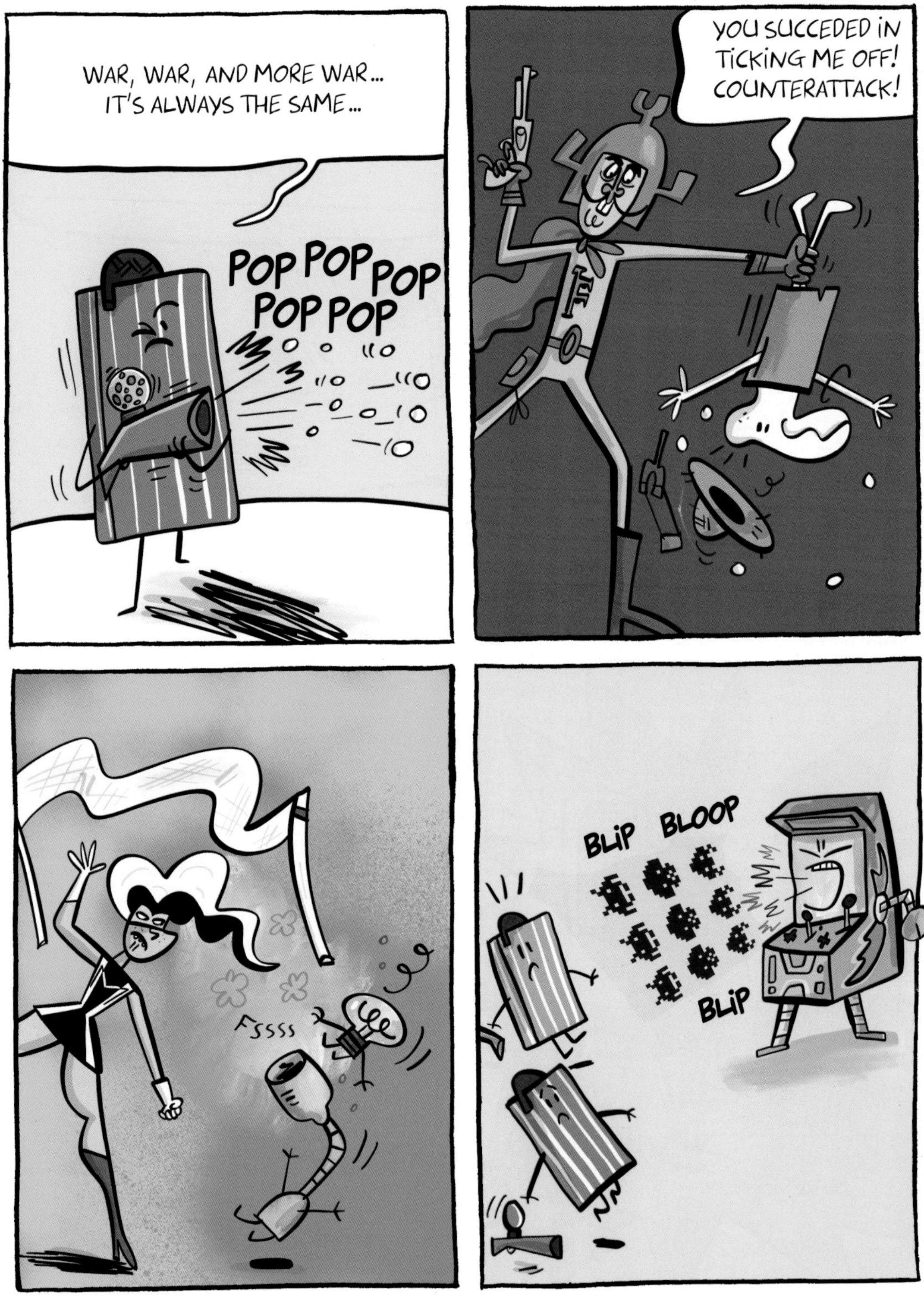
WAR, WAR, AND MORE WAR...
IT'S ALWAYS THE SAME...
POP POP POP
POP POP
YOU SUCCEDED IN
TICKING ME OFF!
COUNTERATTACK!
FSSSS
BLIP BLOOP
BLIP

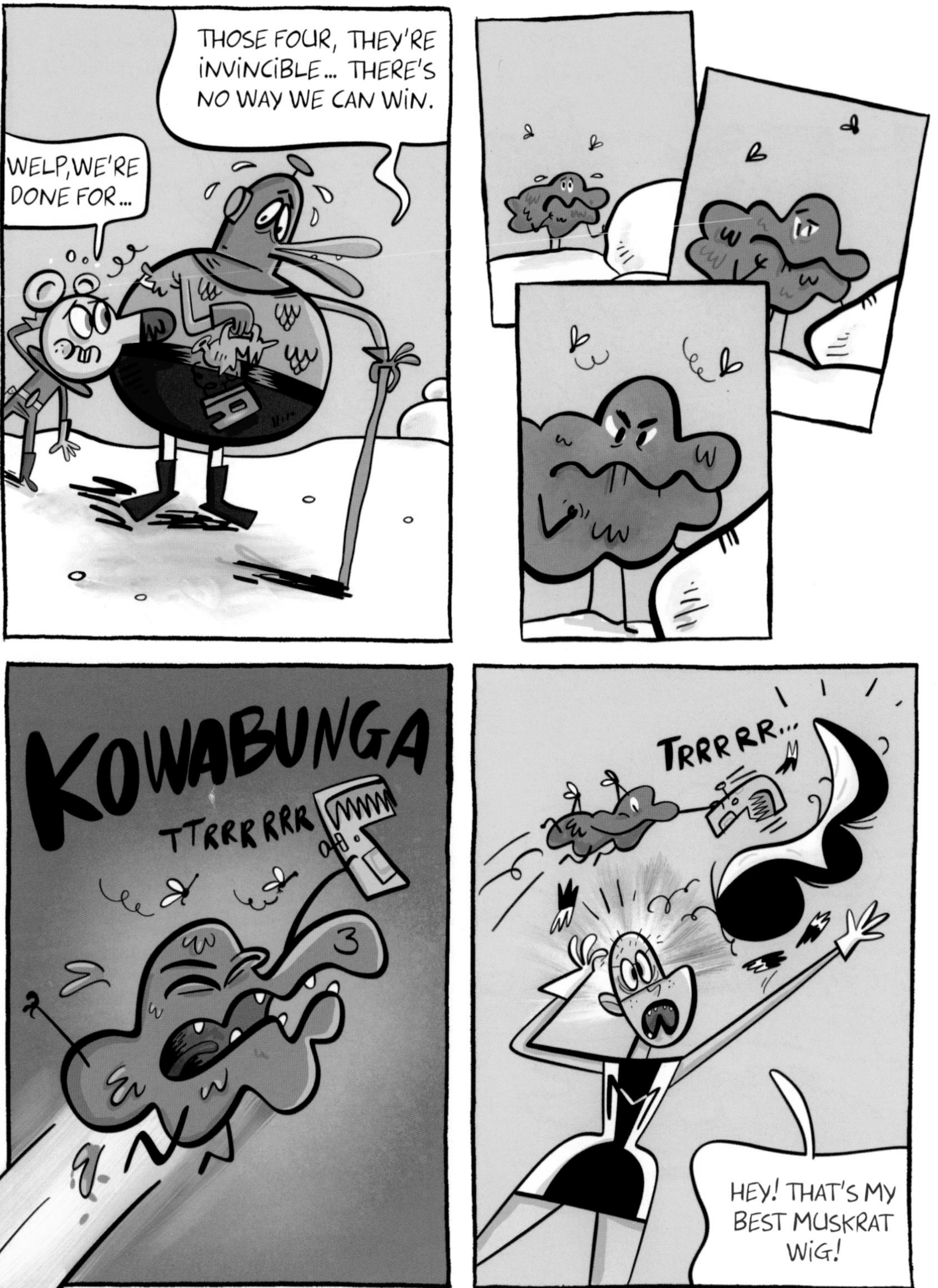
THOSE FOUR, THEY'RE INVINCIBLE... THERE'S NO WAY WE CAN WIN.
WELP, WE'RE DONE FOR...
KOWABUNGA
TTRRRRRR
TRRRRR...
HEY! THAT'S MY BEST MUSKRAT WIG!

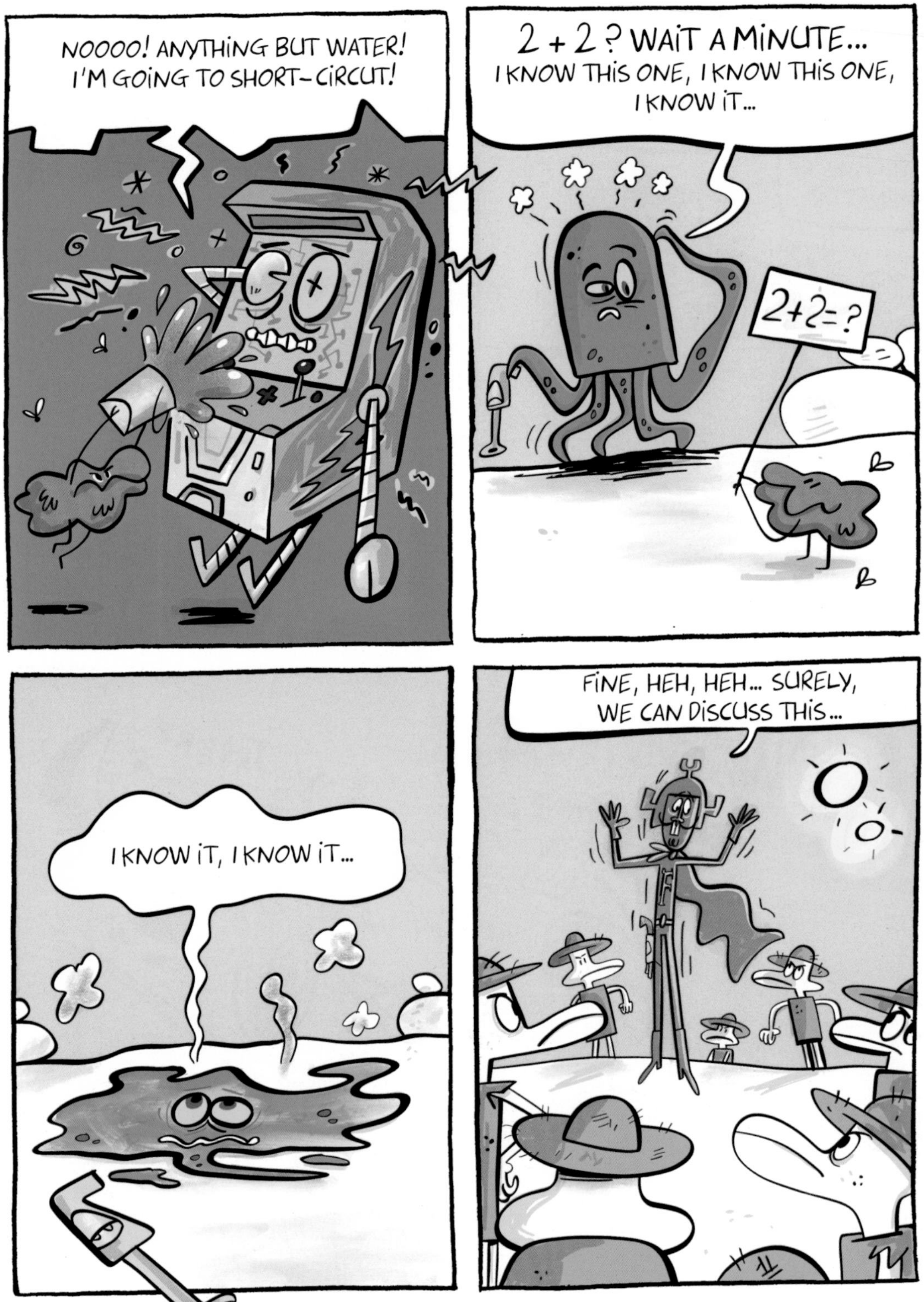
NOOOO! ANYTHING BUT WATER! I'M GOING TO SHORT-CIRCUT!
2 + 2 ? WAIT A MINUTE... I KNOW THIS ONE, I KNOW THIS ONE, I KNOW IT...
2+2=?
I KNOW IT, I KNOW IT...
FINE, HEH, HEH... SURELY, WE CAN DISCUSS THIS...

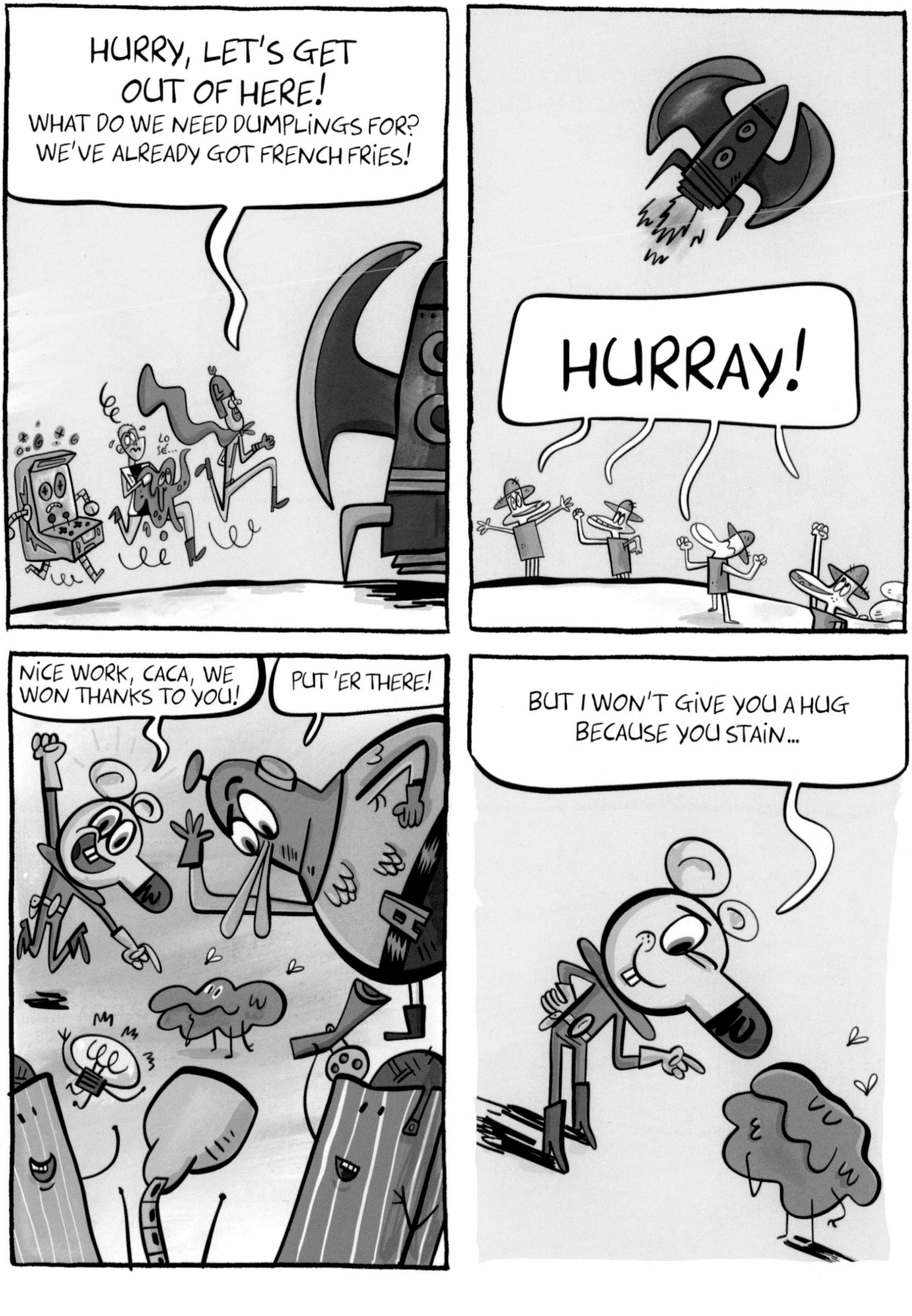
HURRY, LET'S GET OUT OF HERE!
WHAT DO WE NEED DUMPLINGS FOR? WE'VE ALREADY GOT FRENCH FRIES!
HURRAY!
NICE WORK, CACA, WE WON THANKS TO YOU!
PUT 'ER THERE!
BUT I WON'T GIVE YOU A HUG BECAUSE YOU STAIN...

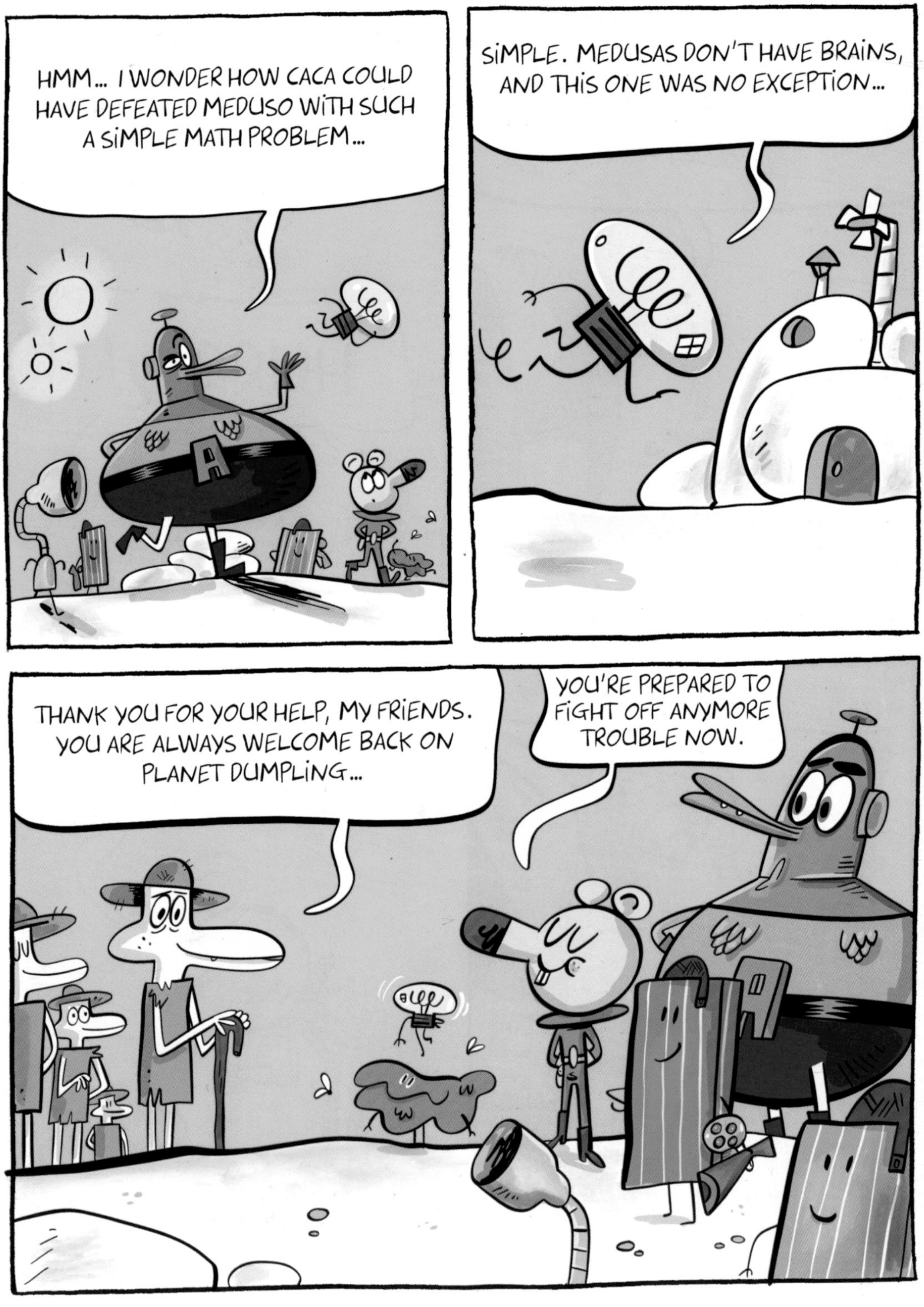
HMM... I WONDER HOW CACA COULD HAVE DEFEATED MEDUSO WITH SUCH A SIMPLE MATH PROBLEM...
SIMPLE. MEDUSAS DON'T HAVE BRAINS, AND THIS ONE WAS NO EXCEPTION...
THANK YOU FOR YOUR HELP, MY FRIENDS. YOU ARE ALWAYS WELCOME BACK ON PLANET DUMPLING...
YOU'RE PREPARED TO FIGHT OFF ANYMORE TROUBLE NOW.

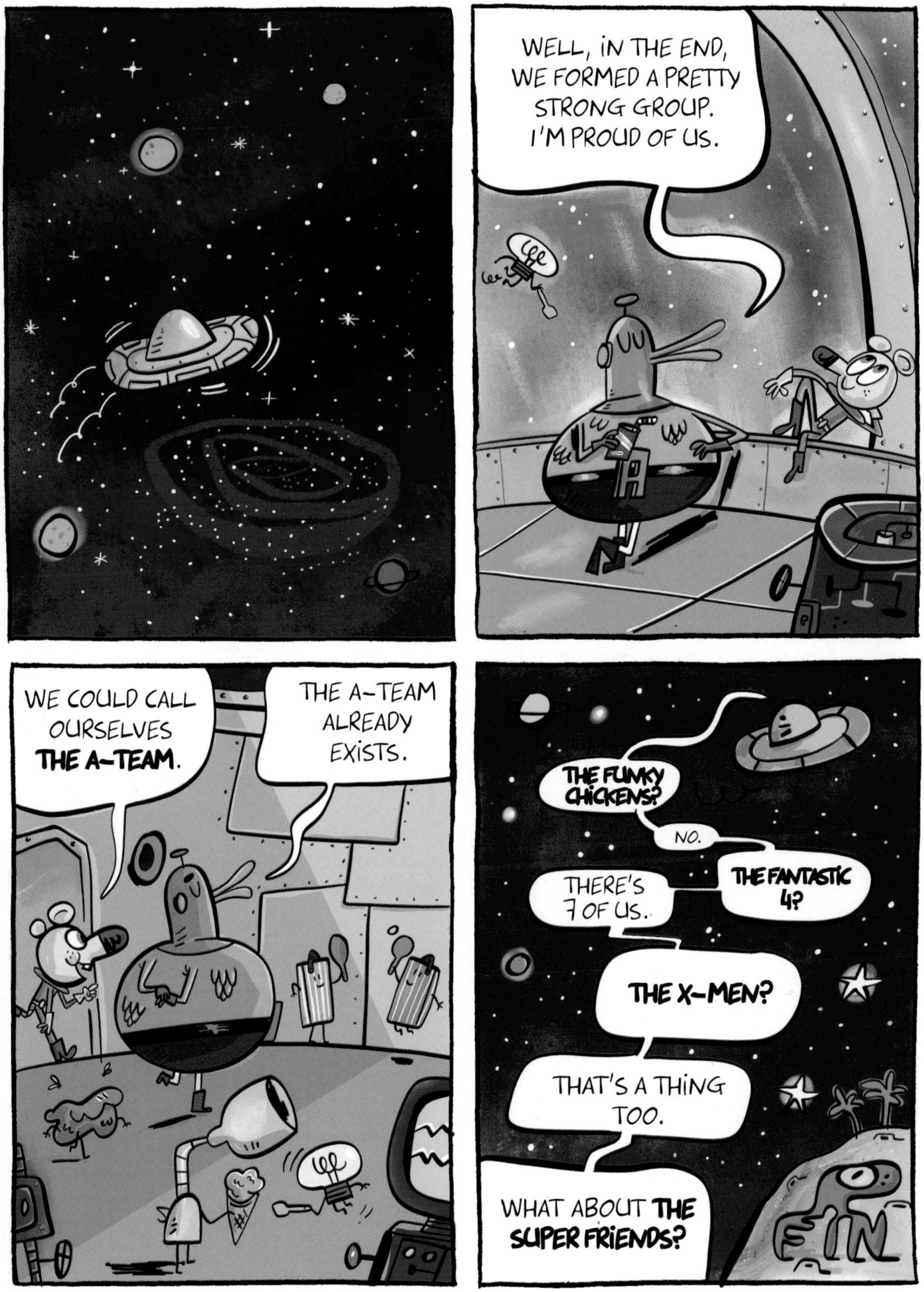
WELL, IN THE END, WE FORMED A PRETTY STRONG GROUP. I'M PROUD OF US.
WE COULD CALL OURSELVES **THE A-TEAM**.
THE A-TEAM ALREADY EXISTS.
THE FUNKY CHICKENS?
NO.
THE FANTASTIC 4?
THERE'S 7 OF US.
THE X-MEN?
THAT'S A THING TOO.
WHAT ABOUT **THE SUPER FRIENDS?**
FIN

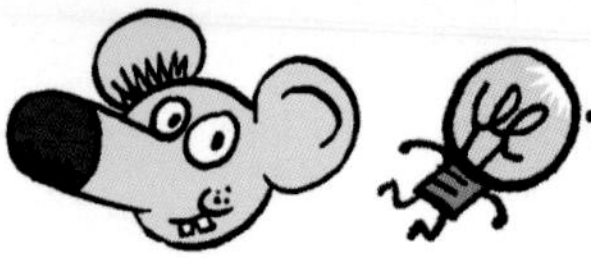

WATCH OUT FOR PAPERCUTZ

Welcome to the space-travelling, second ASTRO MOUSE AND LIGHT BULB graphic novel by Fermín Solís from Papercutz, those humanoid creatures dedicated to publishing great graphic novels for all ages. I'm Jim Salicrup, the Editor-in-Chief and Space Academy dropout, here to talk about a few other Papercutz graphic novels you may enjoy as much as ASTRO MOUSE AND LIGHT BULB. Let's consider this a special public service announcement that's designed just for you.

The first thing we have to recognize is that the humor in ASTRO MOUSE AND LIGHT BULB may not be for everyone. Only folks with an appreciation for the most sophisticated humor can truly enjoy ASTRO MOUSE AND LIGHT BULB. Therefore, since Papercutz also publishes a few other graphic novel series with a similar comedic sensibility, it is with a high degree of confidence that we suggest that these titles may also be to your liking.

Within the pages of ASTRO MOUSE AND LIGHT BULB is a character called Caca. If you look closely you'll see that Caca usually has two flies constantly hovering over it. Imagine if there was an entire graphic novel devoted to a fly. Imagine the fly had fantastic adventures. Well, world-famous, award-winning cartoonist Lewis Trondheim has imagined just that in a graphic novel entitled THE FLY. This graphic novel is also published entirely in black and white (and grey) and features a 100-page comics story without a single word of dialogue or any captions or even sound effects, yet we guarantee that you'll have no trouble following the story and enjoying every bit of it! The humor is just as funny and absurd as ASTRO MOUSE AND LIGHT BULB.

World-famous, award-winning cartoonist Art Baltazar has also created something that's just as wacky as ASTRO MOUSE AND LIGHT BULB. It's a Papercutz graphic novel series called GILLBERT about a green little merman. While the series is set under the sea, that doesn't mean there aren't aliens from outer space included in this series too. GILLBERT has a similar sophisticated style of humor found in ASTRO MOUSE AND LIGHT BULB yet a style all its own.

Best-selling cartoonist Jim Benton has created a graphic novel that may be unlike anything you ever seen before called THE ATTACK OF THE STUFF. Trying to describe it is almost impossible, but we'll give it a shot. It's all about Bill Waddler, a sort of duck/man who lives in a world of various human/animal hybrids, and he can hear inanimate objects, such as normal everyday appliances and even toilets, talk to him. And, unfortunately, they're usually complaining about something. Just as Astro Mouse and Light Bulb, the Fly, and Gillbert have all had awesome adventures, Bill Waddler also goes on a great adventure and along the way you'll experience that surreal, sophisticated humor in which these titles specialize.

But if you're really looking just for stories about space-faring mice partnered with sentient sources of light and even somewhat intelligent poop, never fear—Papercutz has got you covered. In the not-too-distant future, the next ASTRO MOUSE AND LIGHT BULB graphic novel is coming your way! Who else but Papercutz cares about making sure special needs are taken care of?

Thanks,

Jim

STAY IN TOUCH!

EMAIL: salicrup@papercutz.com
WEB: papercutz.com
TWITTER: @papercutzgn
INSTAGRAM: @papercutzgn
FACEBOOK: PAPERCUTZGRAPHICNOVELS
FAN MAIL: Papercutz, 160 Broadway, Suite 700, East Wing New York, NY 10038

GO TO PAPERCUTZ.COM AND SIGN UP FOR THE FREE PAPERCUTZ E-NEWSLETTER!

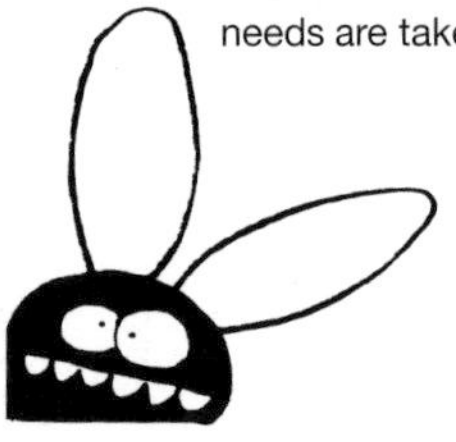

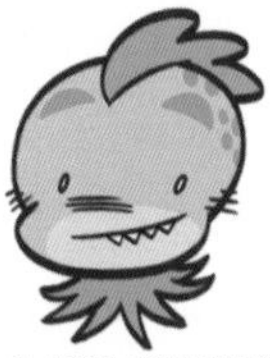

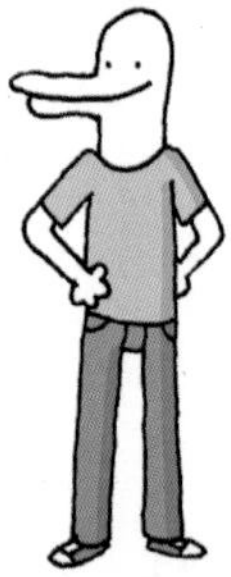

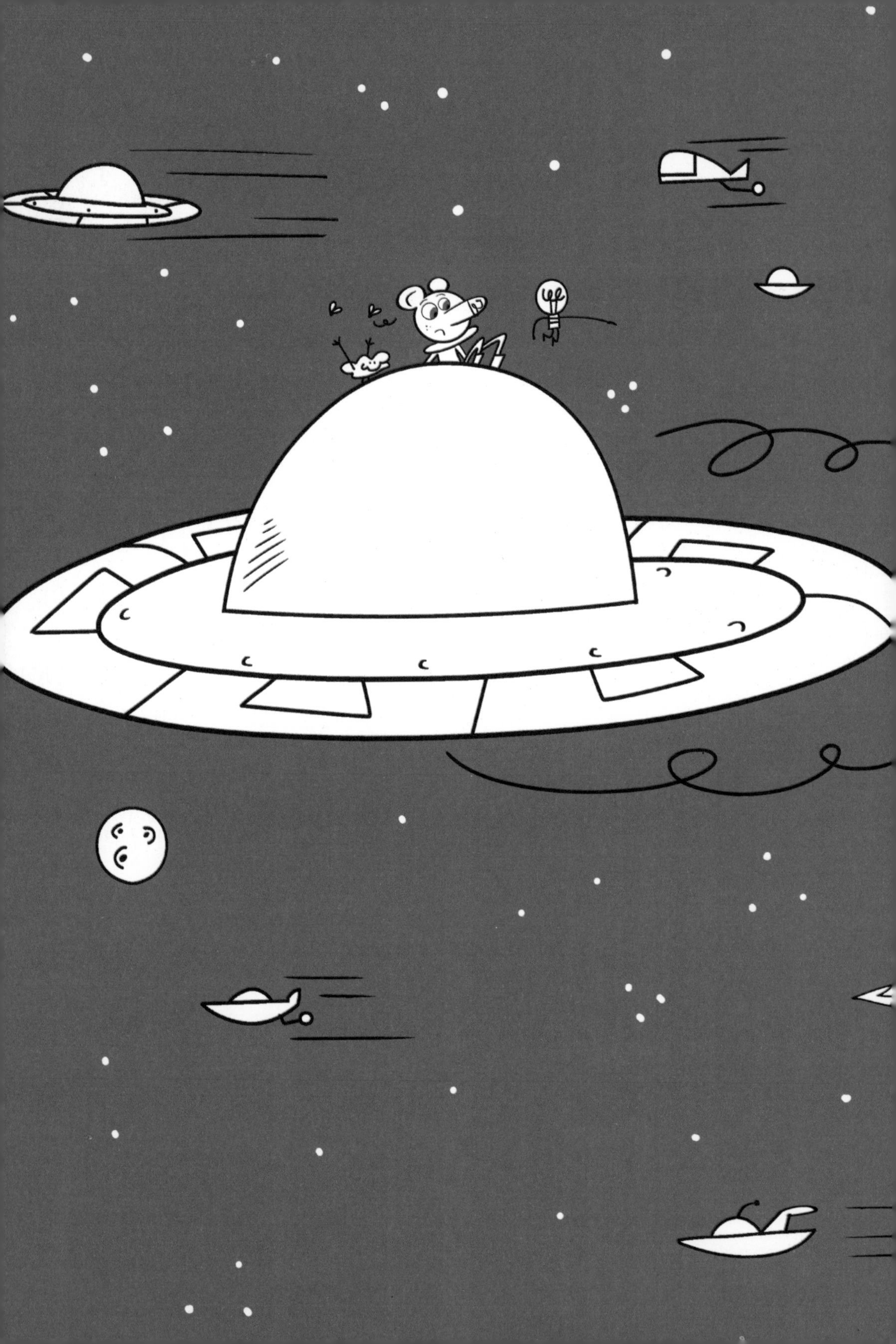